DESCENDER

IMAGE COMICS Presents

DESCENDER

BOOK FIVE: RISE OF THE ROBOTS

Written by JEFF LEMIRE

Illustrated by DUSTIN NGUYEN

Lettered and Designed by STEVE WANDS

Edited by WILL DENNIS

Cover by DUSTIN NGUYEN

Descender Created by

JEFF LEMIRE & DUSTIN NGUYEN

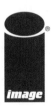

DESCENDER, VOL. 5: RISE OF THE ROBOTS
FIRST PRINTING, JANUARY 2018.
ISBN: 978-1-5343-0345-4

Published by Image Comics, Inc. Office of publication: 2701 NW Vaughn St., Ste. 780, Portland, OR 97210.

PRINTED IN THE U.S.A. For information regarding the CPSIA on this printed material call: 203-595-3636 and provide reference # RICH – 772933.

For international rights, please contact: foreignlicensing@imagecomics.com

CHAPTER ONE

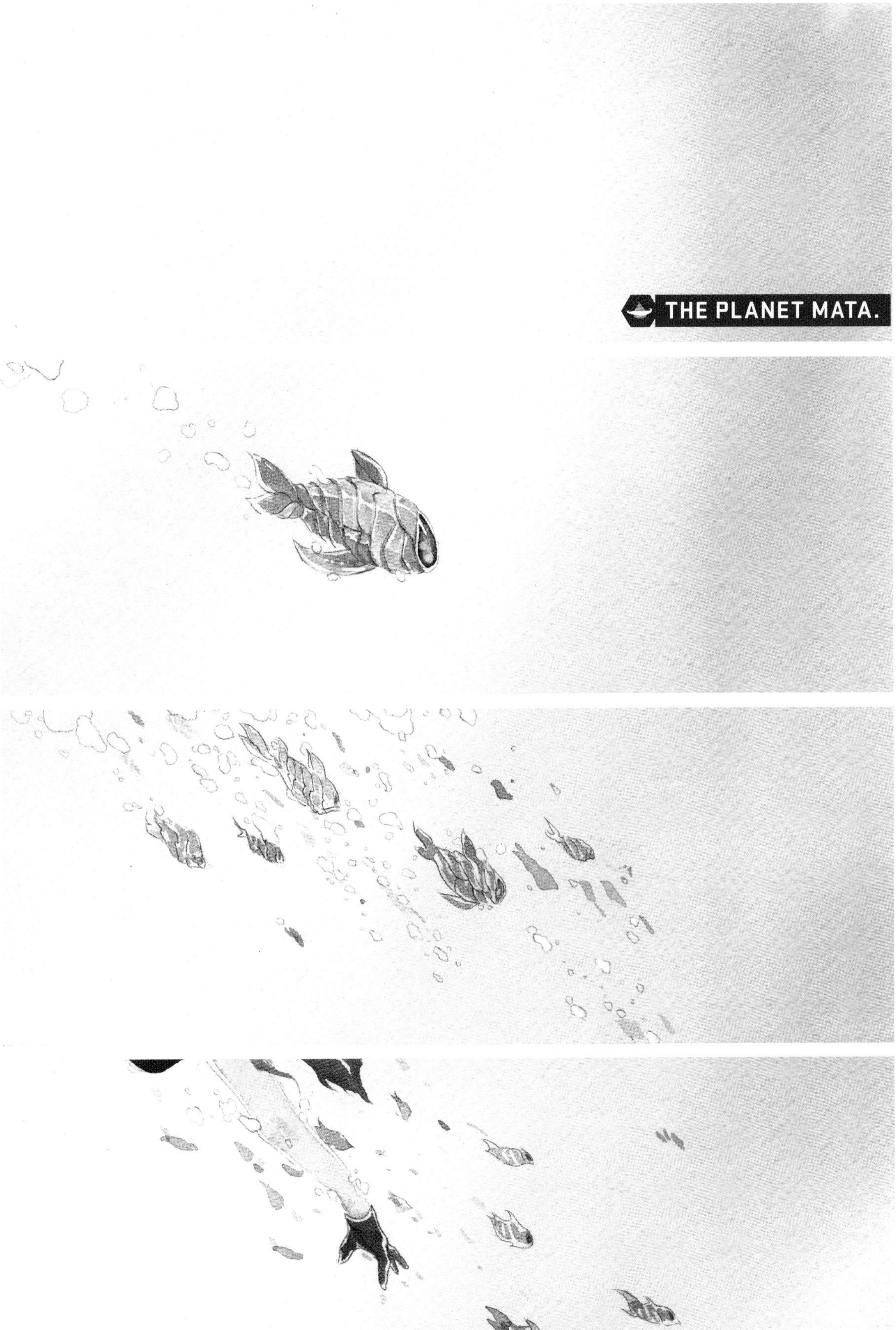
THE PLANET MATA.

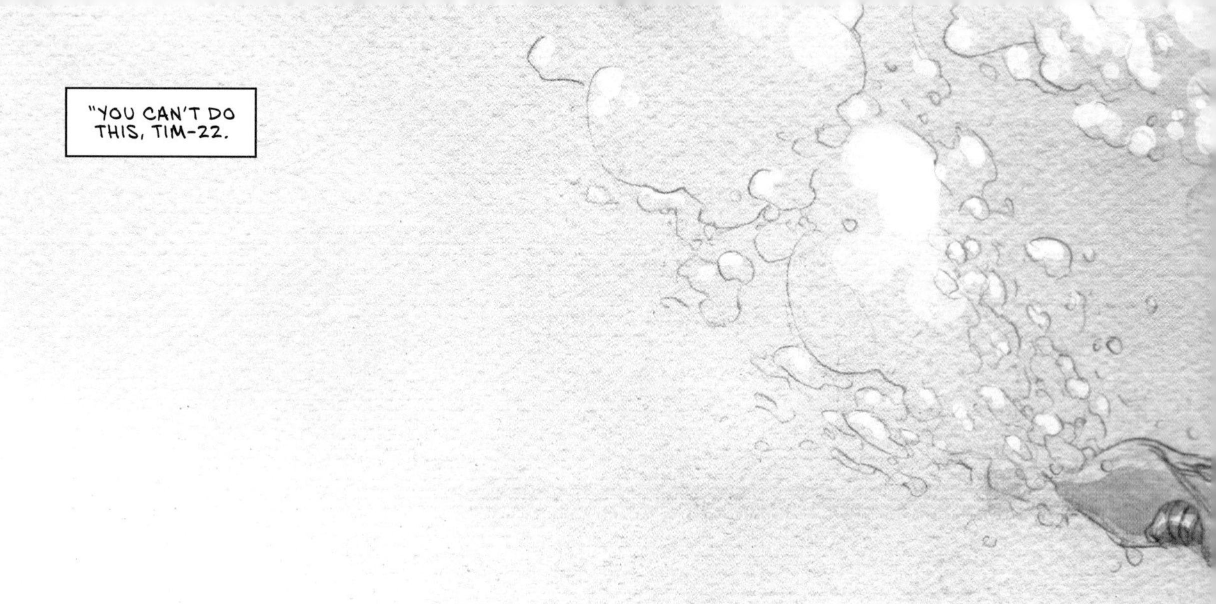
"YOU CAN'T DO THIS, TIM-22.

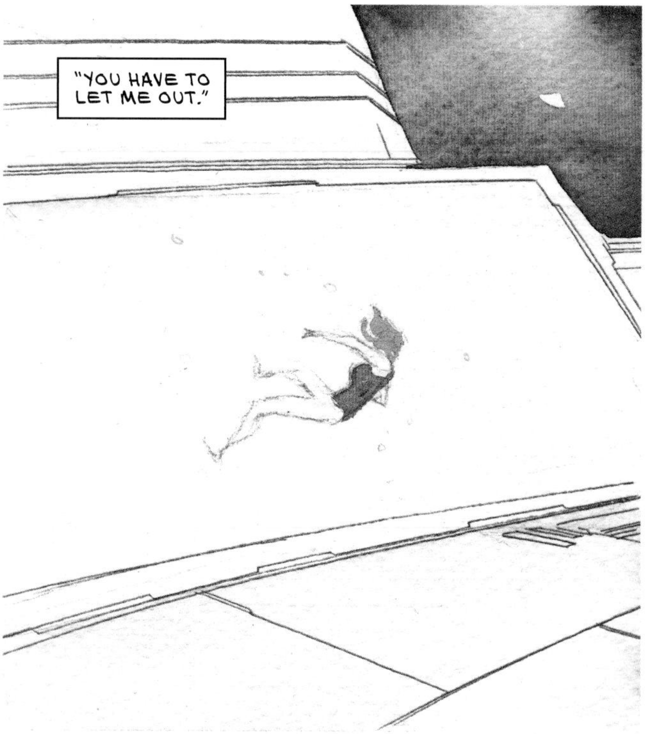
"YOU HAVE TO LET ME OUT."

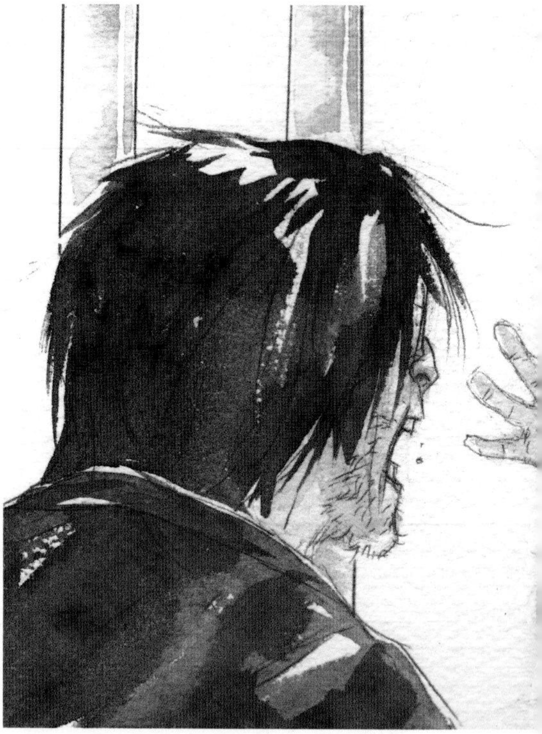

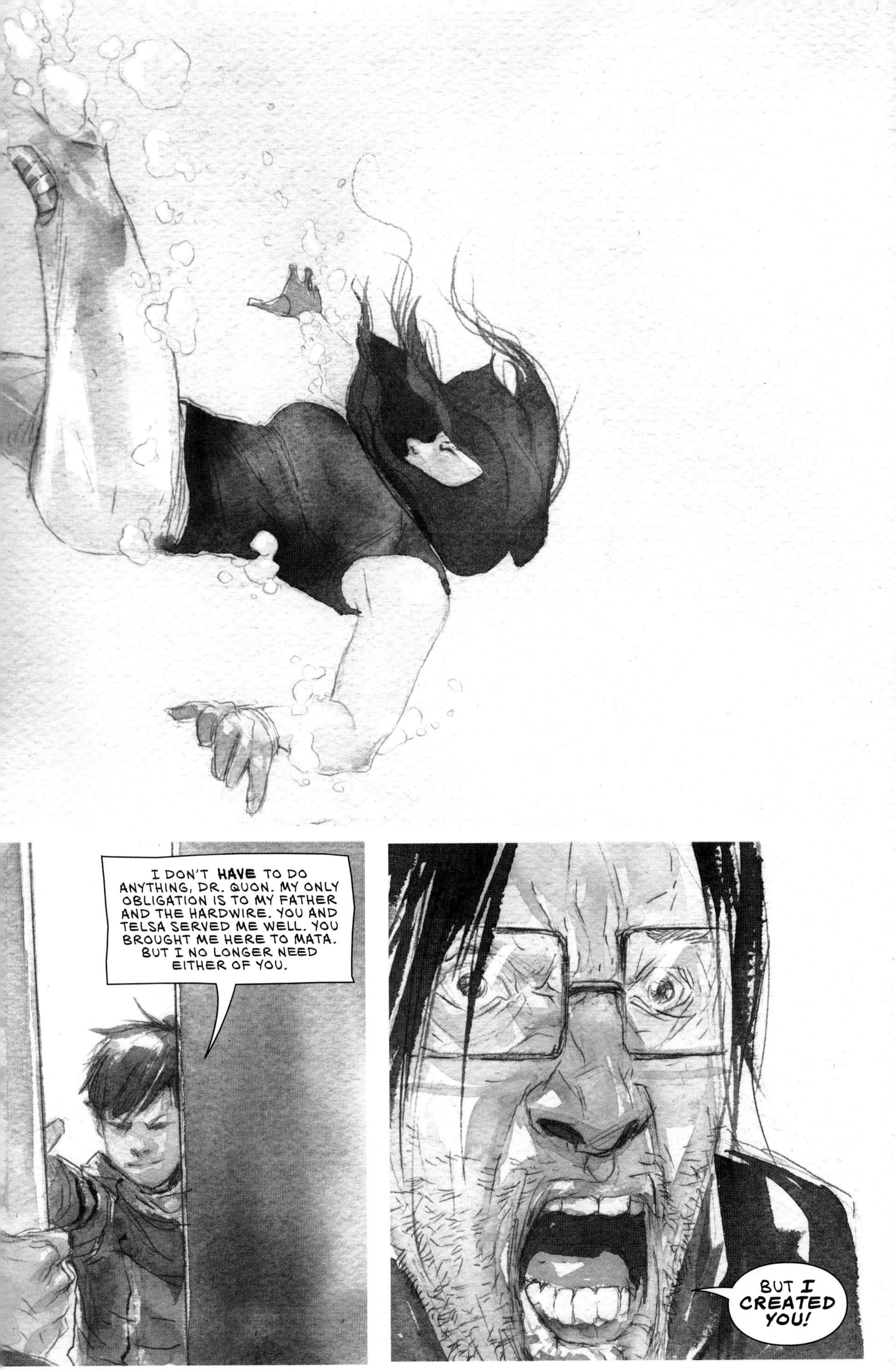
I DON'T **HAVE** TO DO ANYTHING, DR. QUON. MY ONLY OBLIGATION IS TO MY FATHER AND THE HARDWIRE. YOU AND TELSA SERVED ME WELL. YOU BROUGHT ME HERE TO MATA. BUT I NO LONGER NEED EITHER OF YOU.
BUT ***I* CREATED** *YOU!*

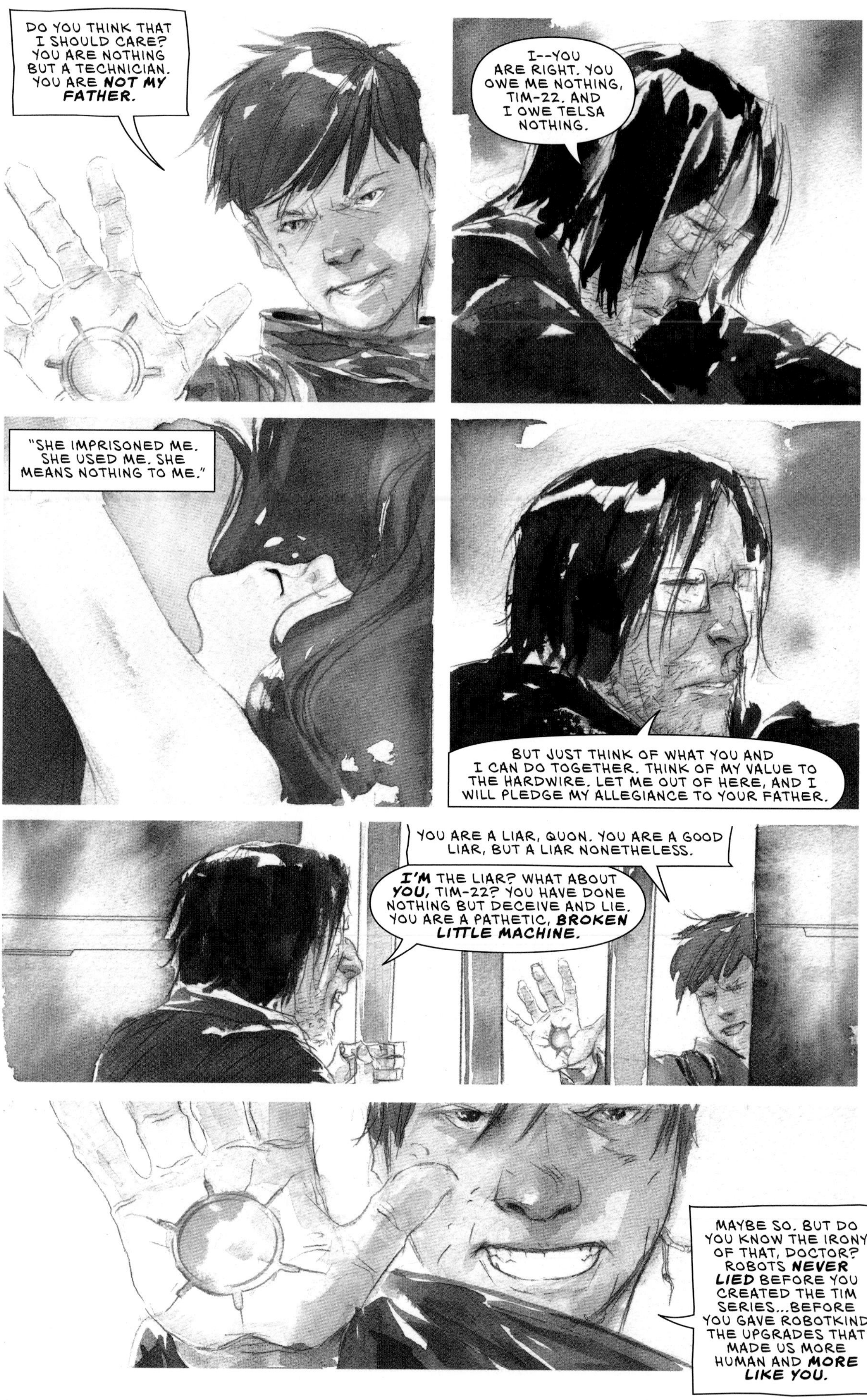
DO YOU THINK THAT I SHOULD CARE? YOU ARE NOTHING BUT A TECHNICIAN. YOU ARE **NOT MY FATHER.**
I--YOU ARE RIGHT. YOU OWE ME NOTHING, TIM-22. AND I OWE TELSA NOTHING.
"SHE IMPRISONED ME. SHE USED ME. SHE MEANS NOTHING TO ME."
BUT JUST THINK OF WHAT YOU AND I CAN DO TOGETHER. THINK OF MY VALUE TO THE HARDWIRE. LET ME OUT OF HERE, AND I WILL PLEDGE MY ALLEGIANCE TO YOUR FATHER.
YOU ARE A LIAR, QUON. YOU ARE A GOOD LIAR, BUT A LIAR NONETHELESS.
I'M THE LIAR? WHAT ABOUT ***YOU,*** TIM-22? YOU HAVE DONE NOTHING BUT DECEIVE AND LIE. YOU ARE A PATHETIC, ***BROKEN LITTLE MACHINE.***
MAYBE SO. BUT DO YOU KNOW THE IRONY OF THAT, DOCTOR? ROBOTS ***NEVER LIED*** BEFORE YOU CREATED THE TIM SERIES...BEFORE YOU GAVE ROBOTKIND THE UPGRADES THAT MADE US MORE HUMAN AND ***MORE LIKE YOU.***

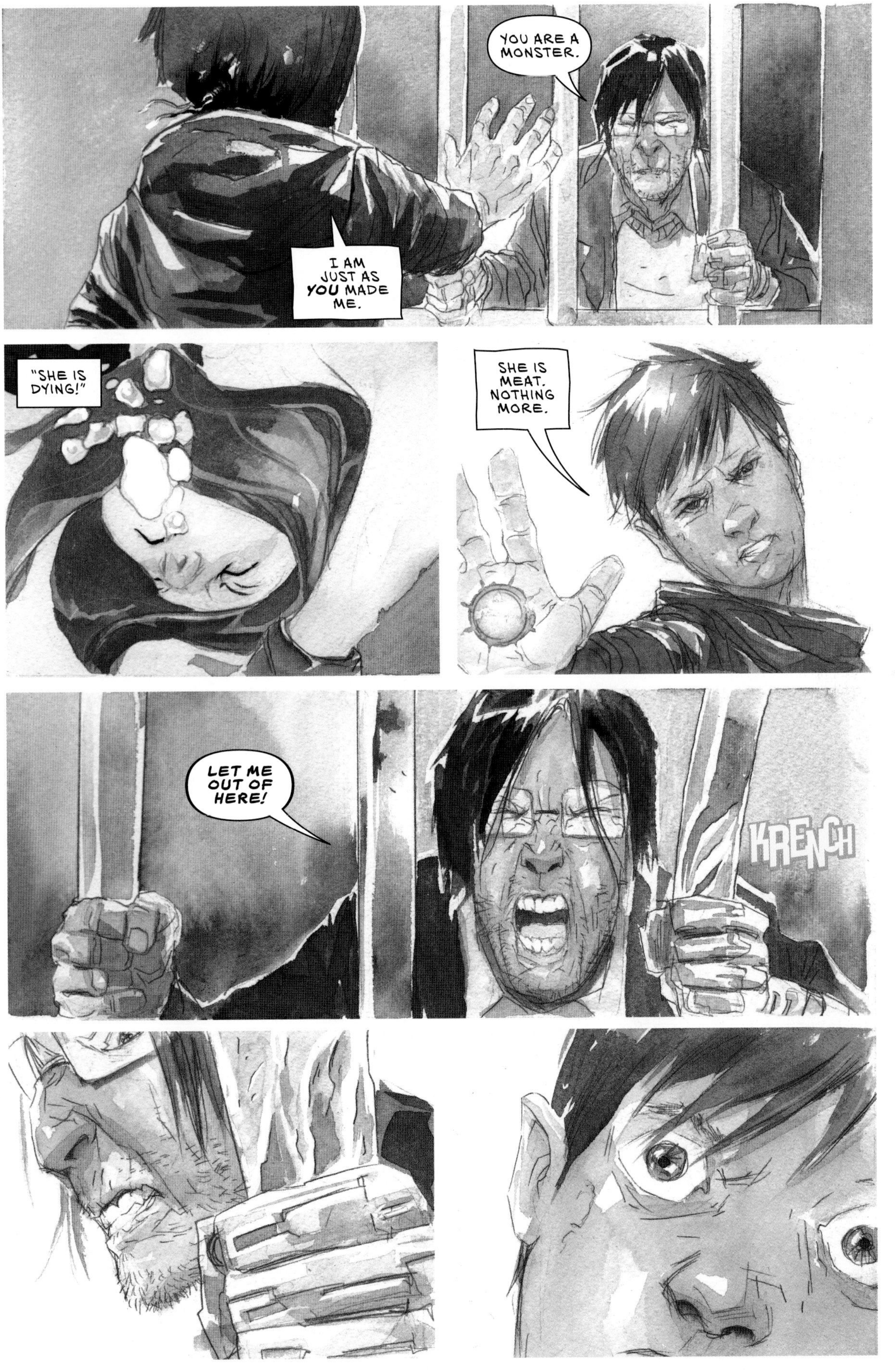
YOU ARE A MONSTER.
I AM JUST AS YOU MADE ME.
"SHE IS DYING!"
SHE IS MEAT. NOTHING MORE.
LET ME OUT OF HERE!
KRENCH

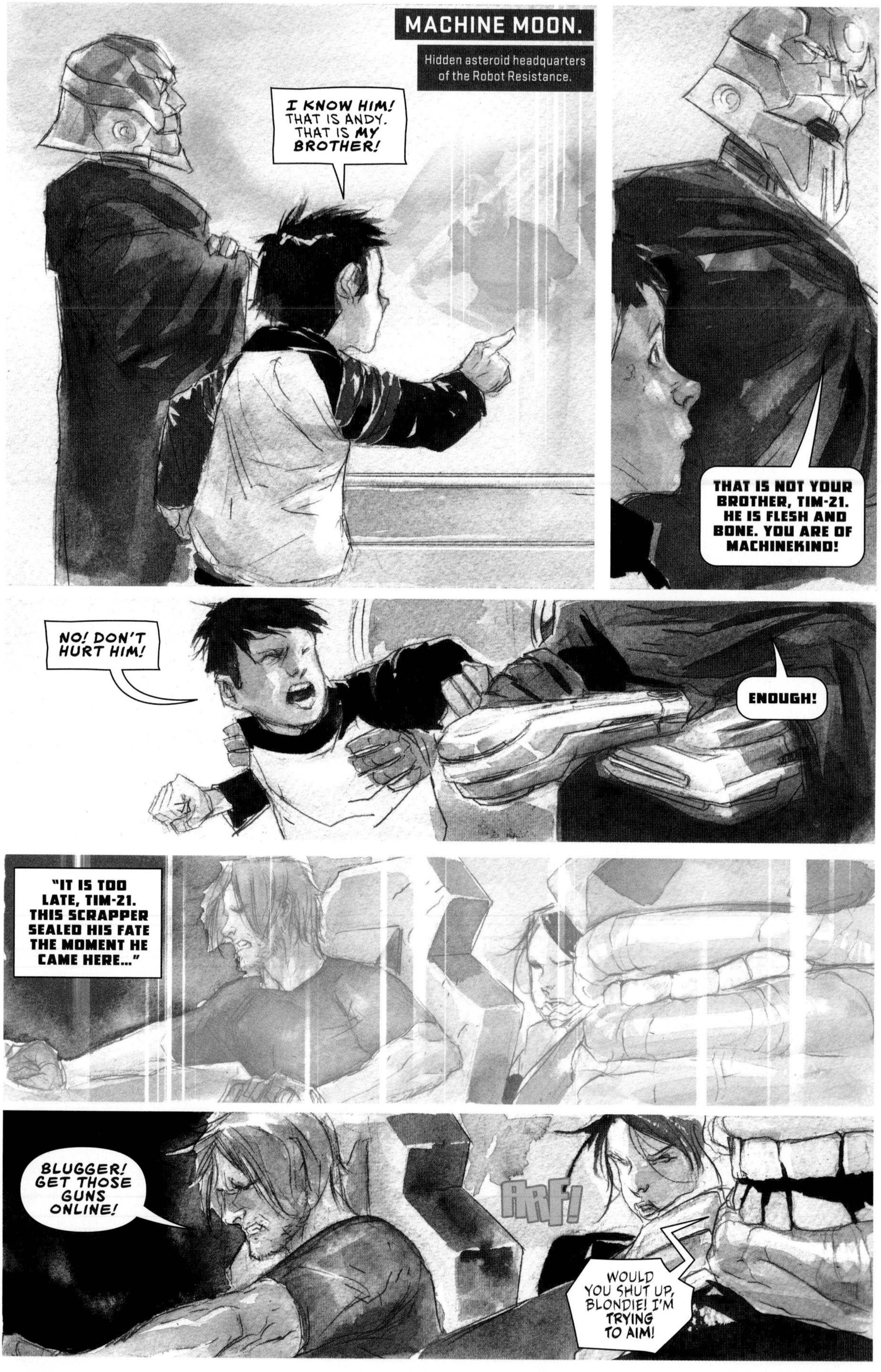
MACHINE MOON.
Hidden asteroid headquarters of the Robot Resistance.
I KNOW HIM! THAT IS ANDY. THAT IS MY BROTHER!
THAT IS NOT YOUR BROTHER, TIM-21. HE IS FLESH AND BONE. YOU ARE OF MACHINEKIND!
NO! DON'T HURT HIM!
ENOUGH!
"IT IS TOO LATE, TIM-21. THIS SCRAPPER SEALED HIS FATE THE MOMENT HE CAME HERE..."
BLUGGER! GET THOSE GUNS ONLINE!
ARF!
WOULD YOU SHUT UP, BLONDIE! I'M TRYING TO AIM!

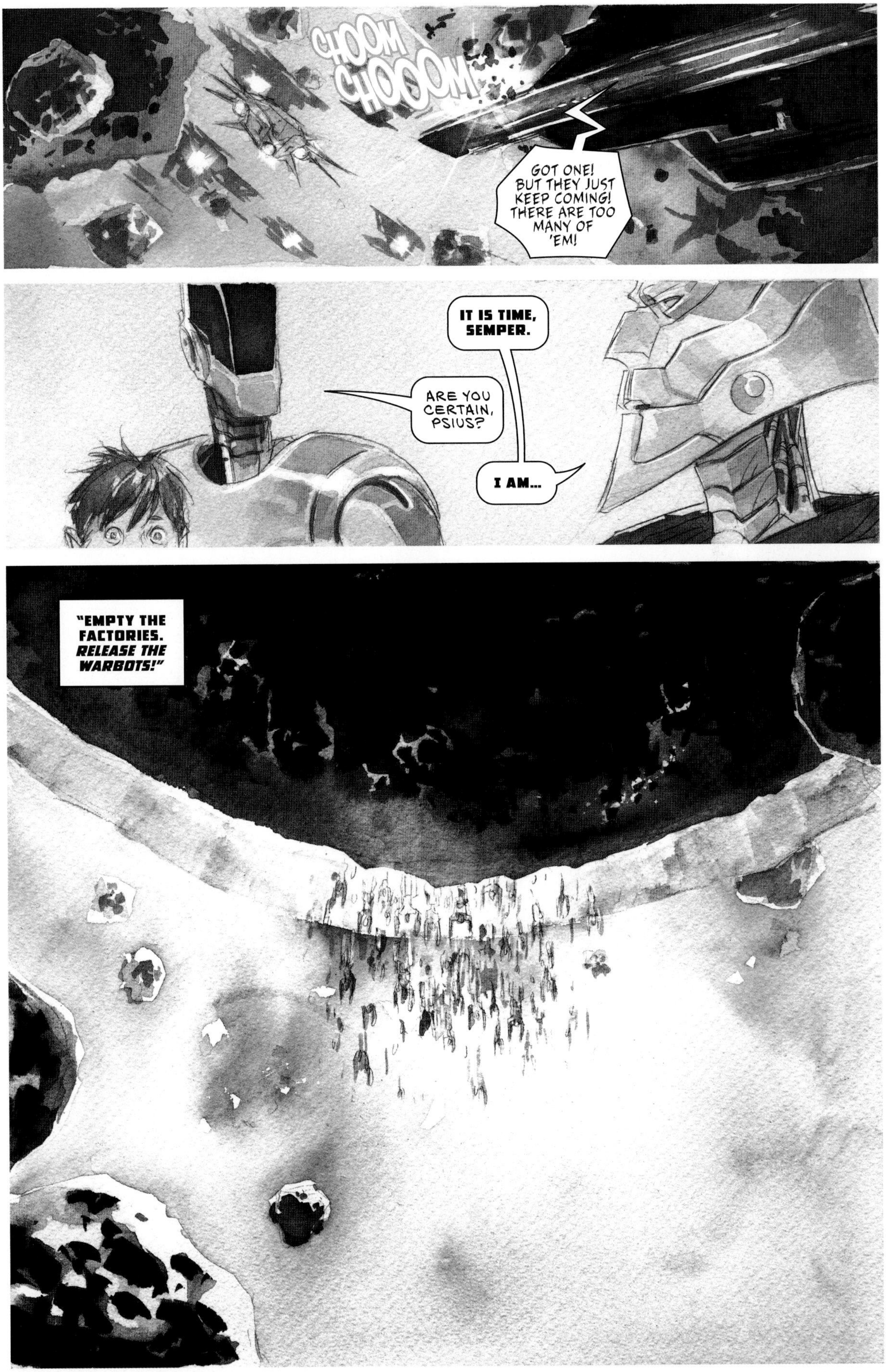
CHOOM CHOOOM!
GOT ONE! BUT THEY JUST KEEP COMING! THERE ARE TOO MANY OF 'EM!
IT IS TIME, SEMPER.
ARE YOU CERTAIN, PSIUS?
I AM...
"EMPTY THE FACTORIES. *RELEASE THE WARBOTS!*"

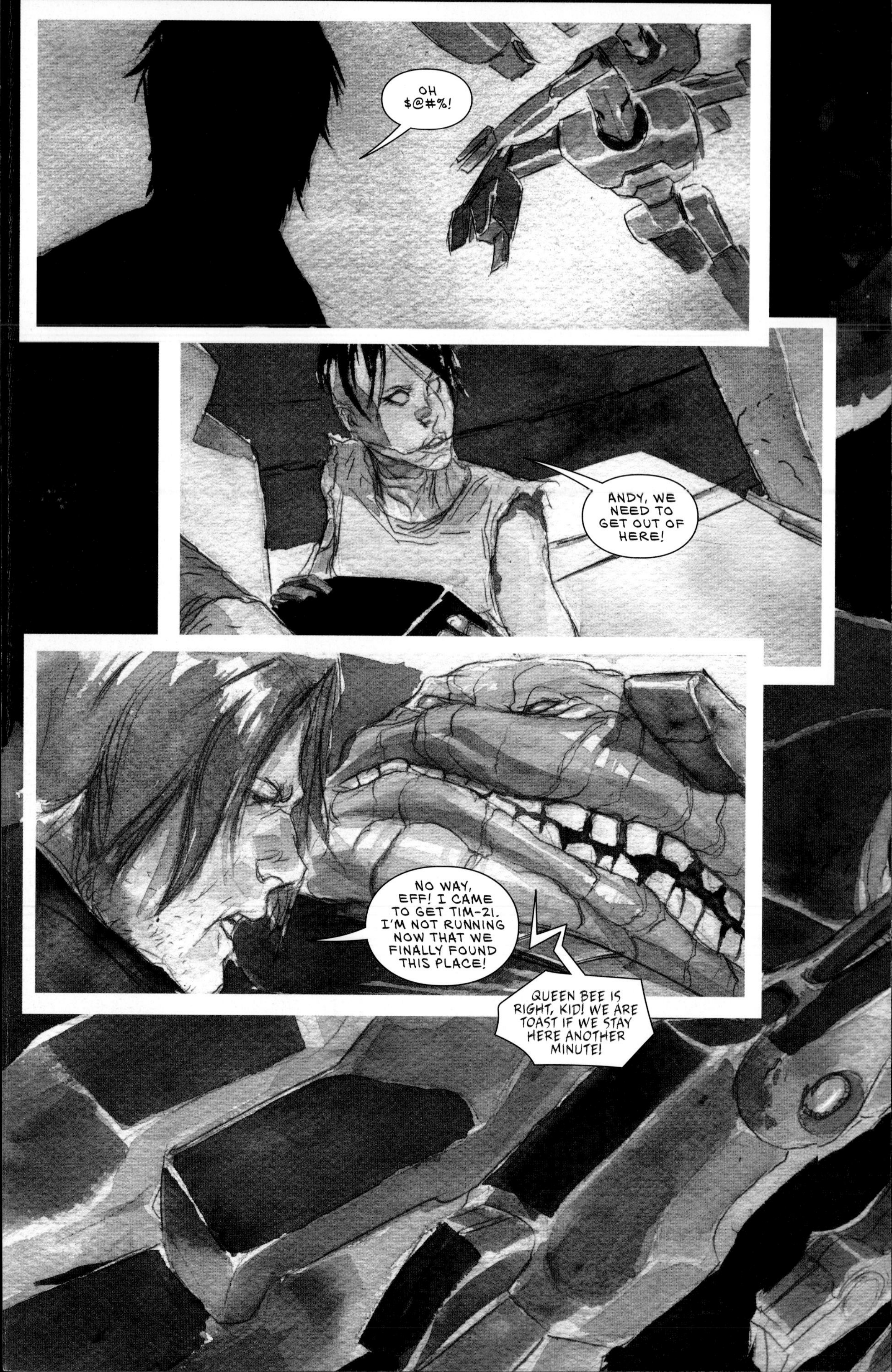
OH $@#%!
ANDY, WE NEED TO GET OUT OF HERE!
NO WAY, EFF! I CAME TO GET TIM-21. I'M NOT RUNNING NOW THAT WE FINALLY FOUND THIS PLACE!
QUEEN BEE IS RIGHT, KID! WE ARE TOAST IF WE STAY HERE ANOTHER MINUTE!

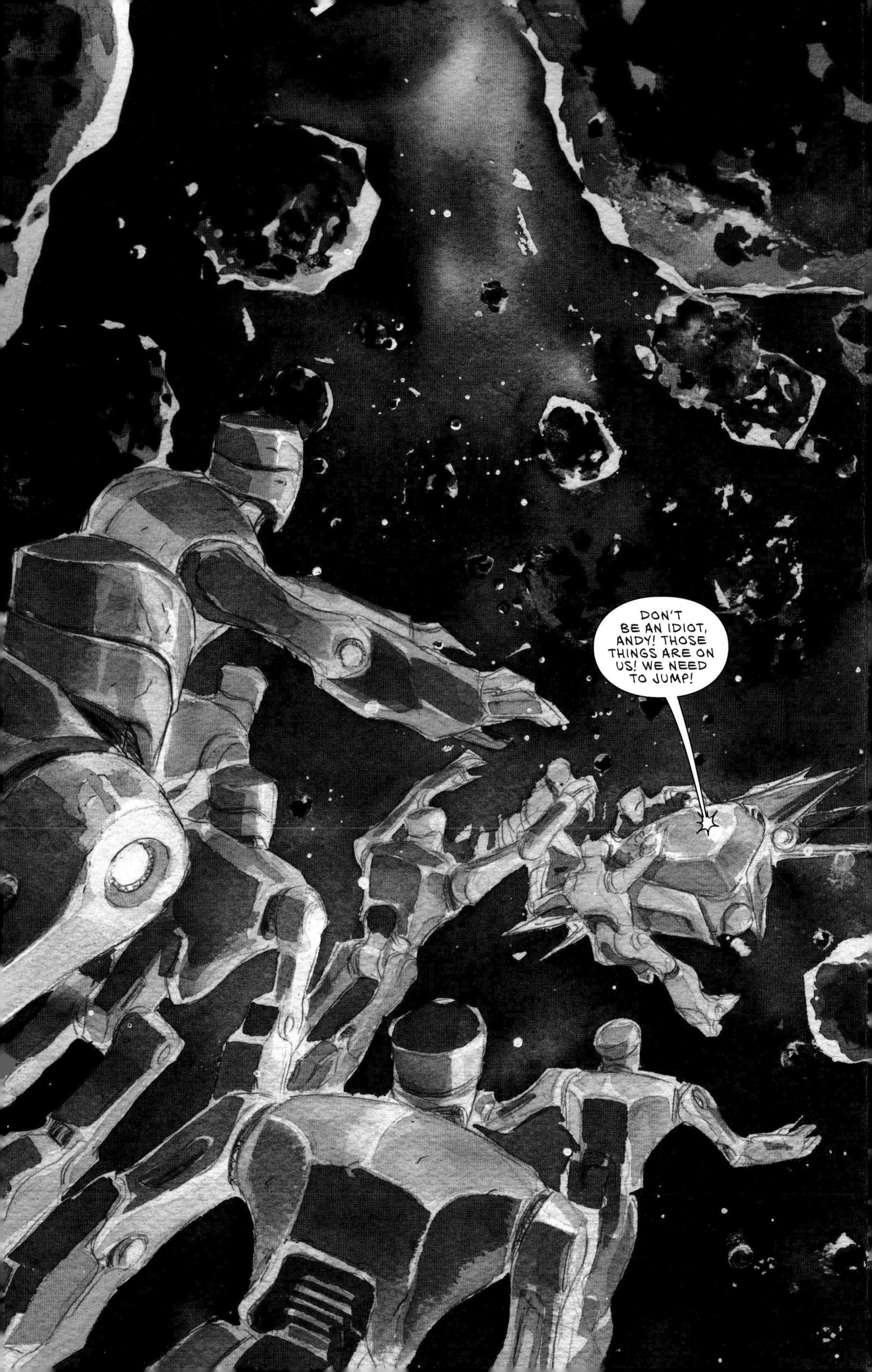
DON'T BE AN IDIOT, ANDY! THOSE THINGS ARE ON US! WE NEED TO JUMP!

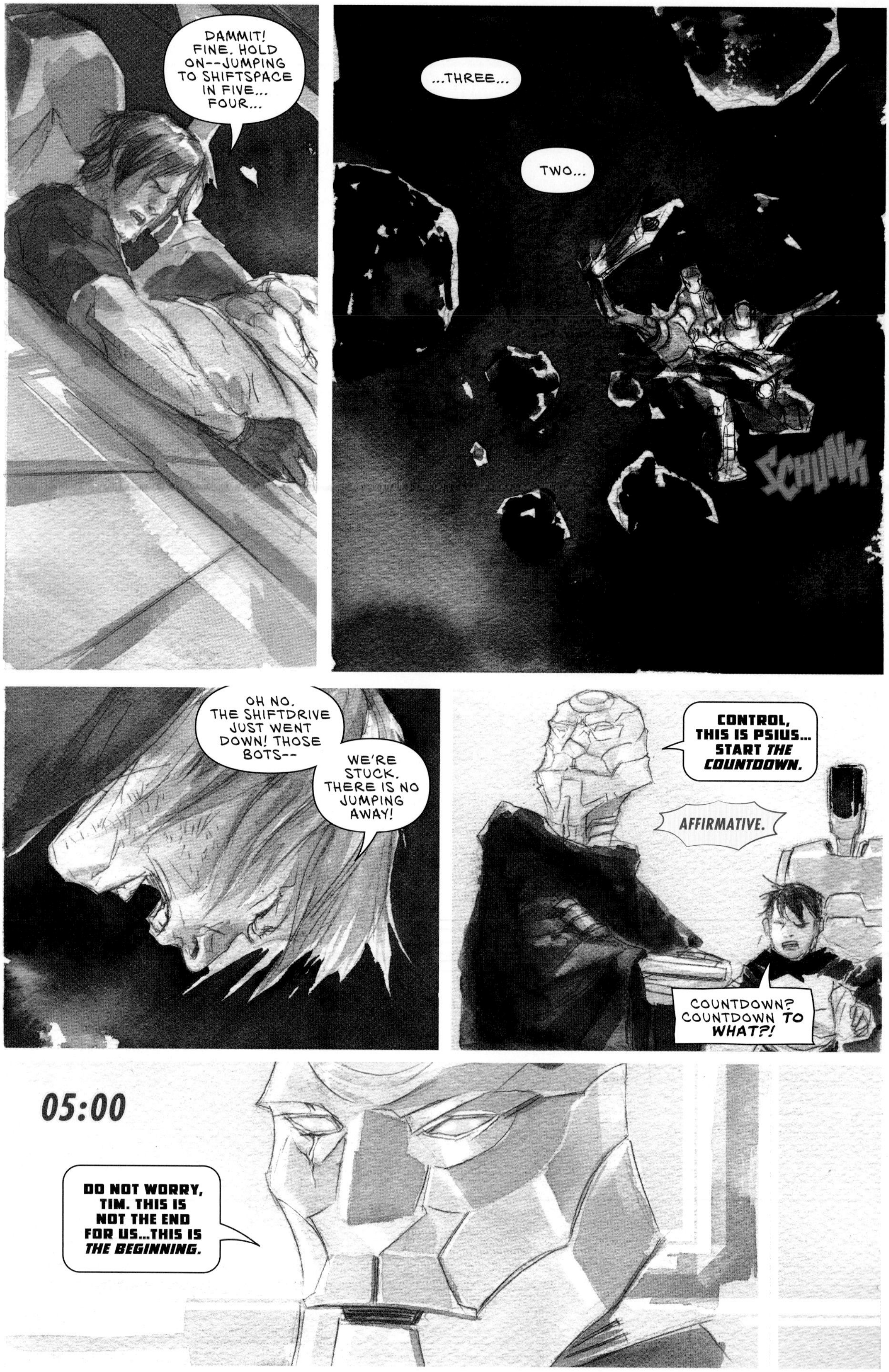
DAMMIT! FINE. HOLD ON--JUMPING TO SHIFTSPACE IN FIVE... FOUR...
...THREE...
TWO...
SCHUNK
OH NO. THE SHIFTDRIVE JUST WENT DOWN! THOSE BOTS--
WE'RE STUCK. THERE IS NO JUMPING AWAY!
CONTROL, THIS IS PSIUS... START *THE COUNTDOWN.*
AFFIRMATIVE.
COUNTDOWN? COUNTDOWN *TO WHAT?!*
05:00
DO NOT WORRY, TIM. THIS IS NOT THE END FOR US...THIS IS *THE BEGINNING.*

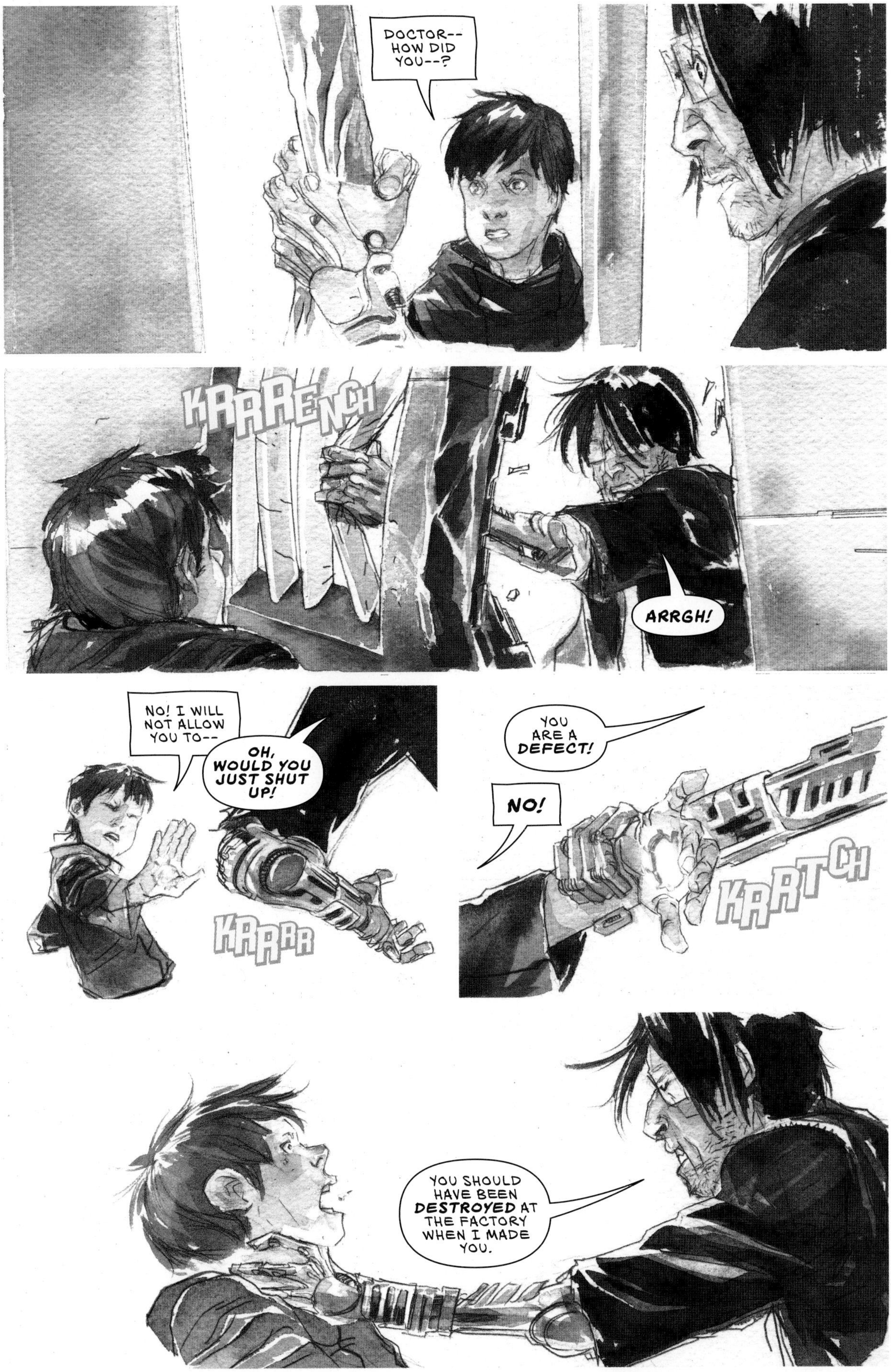
DOCTOR-- HOW DID YOU--?
KRRRENCH
ARRGH!
NO! I WILL NOT ALLOW YOU TO--
OH, WOULD YOU JUST SHUT UP!
KRRRR
YOU ARE A DEFECT!
NO!
KRRRTCH
YOU SHOULD HAVE BEEN DESTROYED AT THE FACTORY WHEN I MADE YOU.

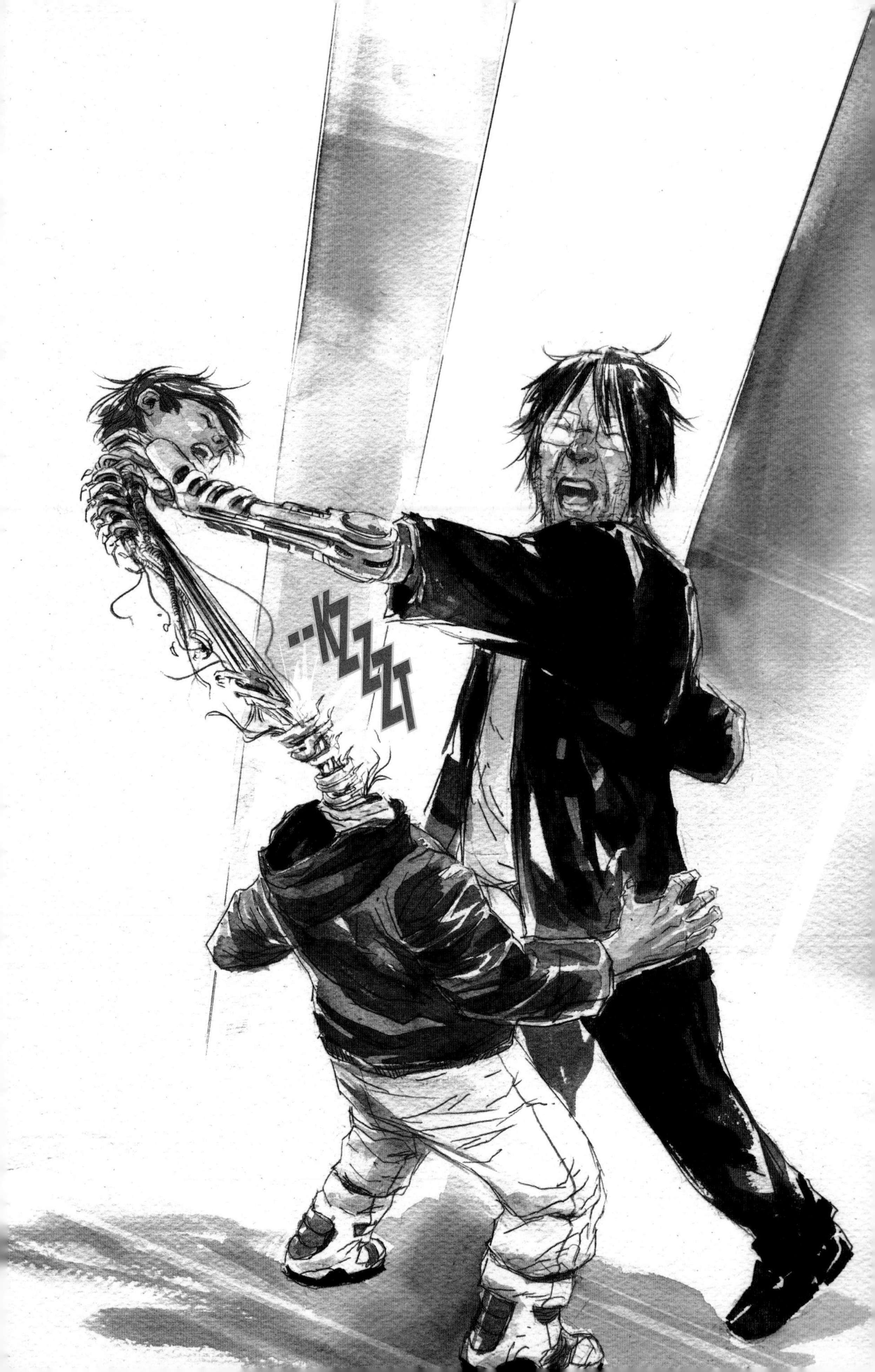
--KZZZZT

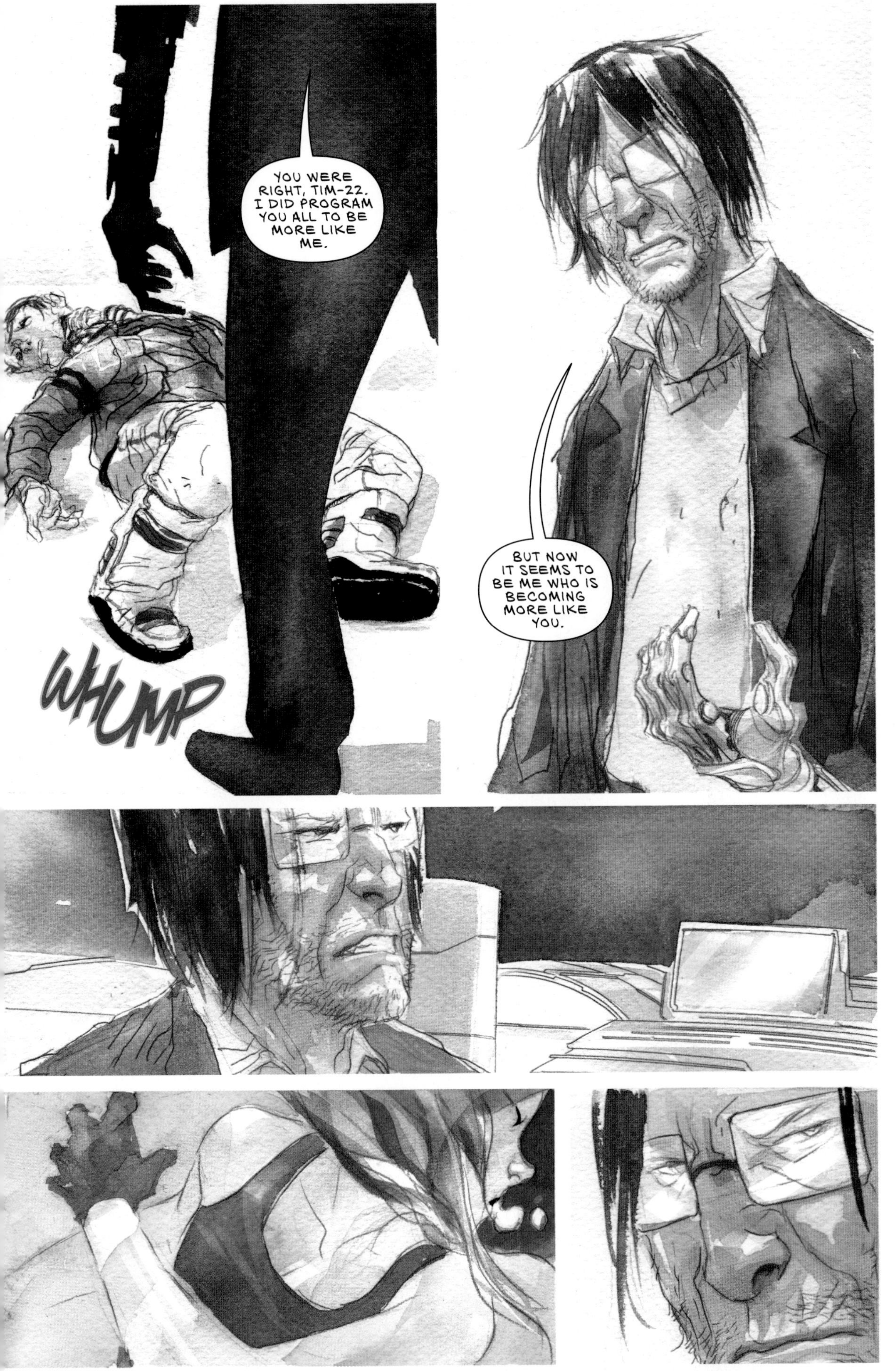

YOU WERE RIGHT, TIM-22. I DID PROGRAM YOU ALL TO BE MORE LIKE ME.
WHUMP
BUT NOW IT SEEMS TO BE ME WHO IS BECOMING MORE LIKE YOU.

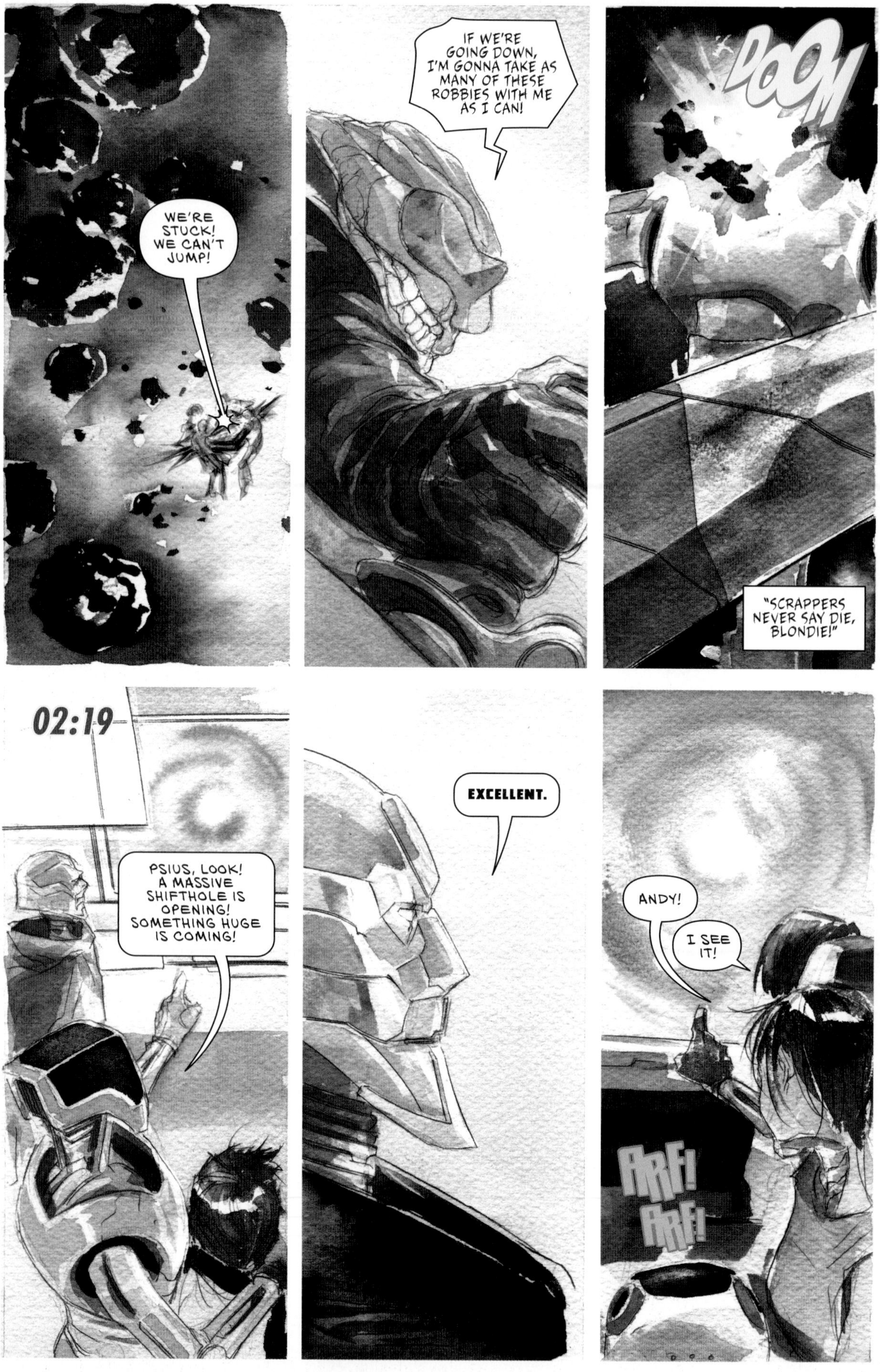
WE'RE STUCK! WE CAN'T JUMP!
IF WE'RE GOING DOWN, I'M GONNA TAKE AS MANY OF THESE ROBBIES WITH ME AS I CAN!
DOOM
"SCRAPPERS NEVER SAY DIE, BLONDIE!"
02:19
PSIUS, LOOK! A MASSIVE SHIFTHOLE IS OPENING! SOMETHING HUGE IS COMING!
EXCELLENT.
ANDY!
I SEE IT!
ARF! ARF!

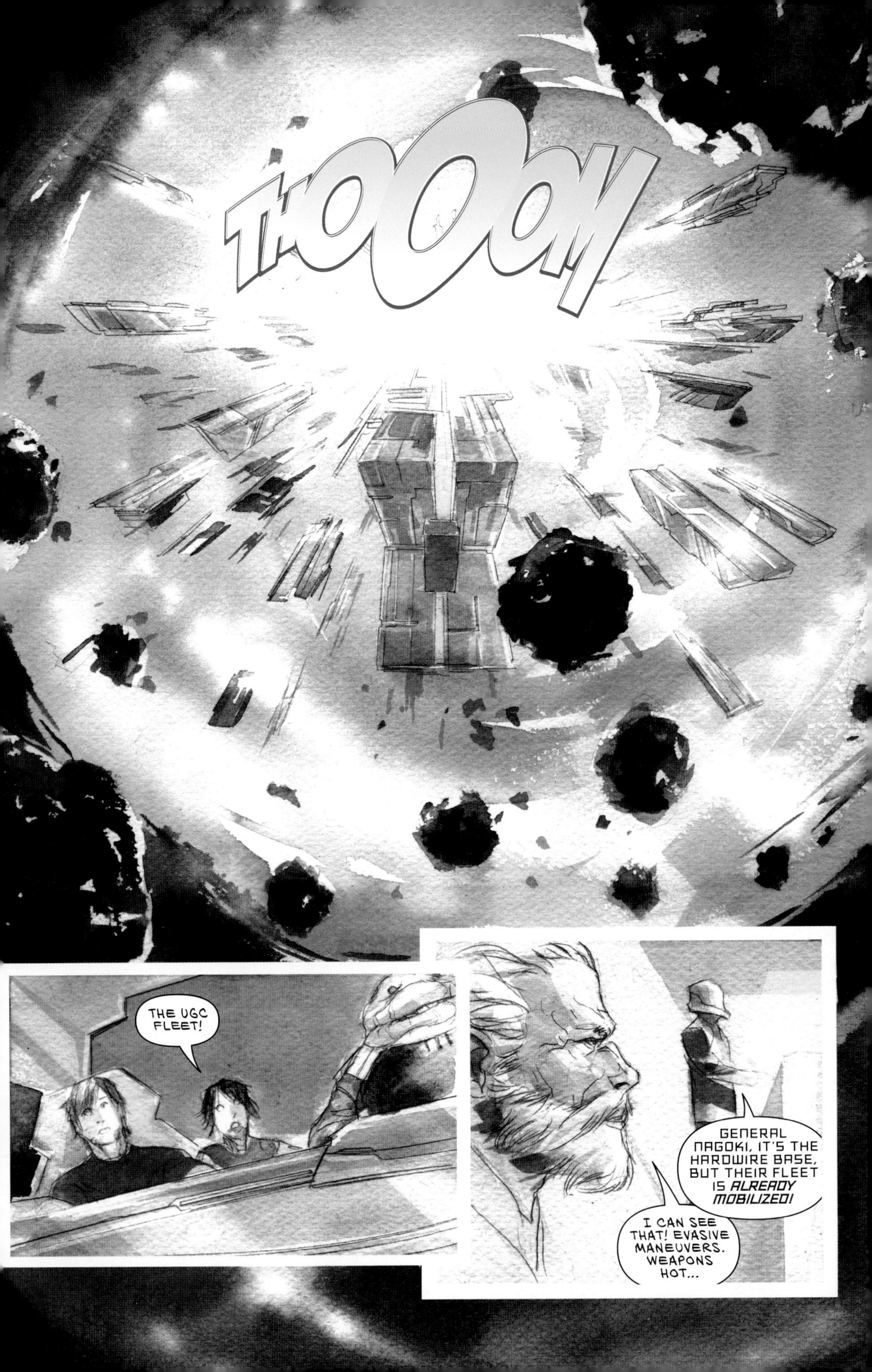
THOOOM
THE UGC FLEET!
GENERAL NAGOKI, IT'S THE HARDWIRE BASE, BUT THEIR FLEET IS *ALREADY MOBILIZED!*
I CAN SEE THAT! EVASIVE MANEUVERS. WEAPONS HOT...

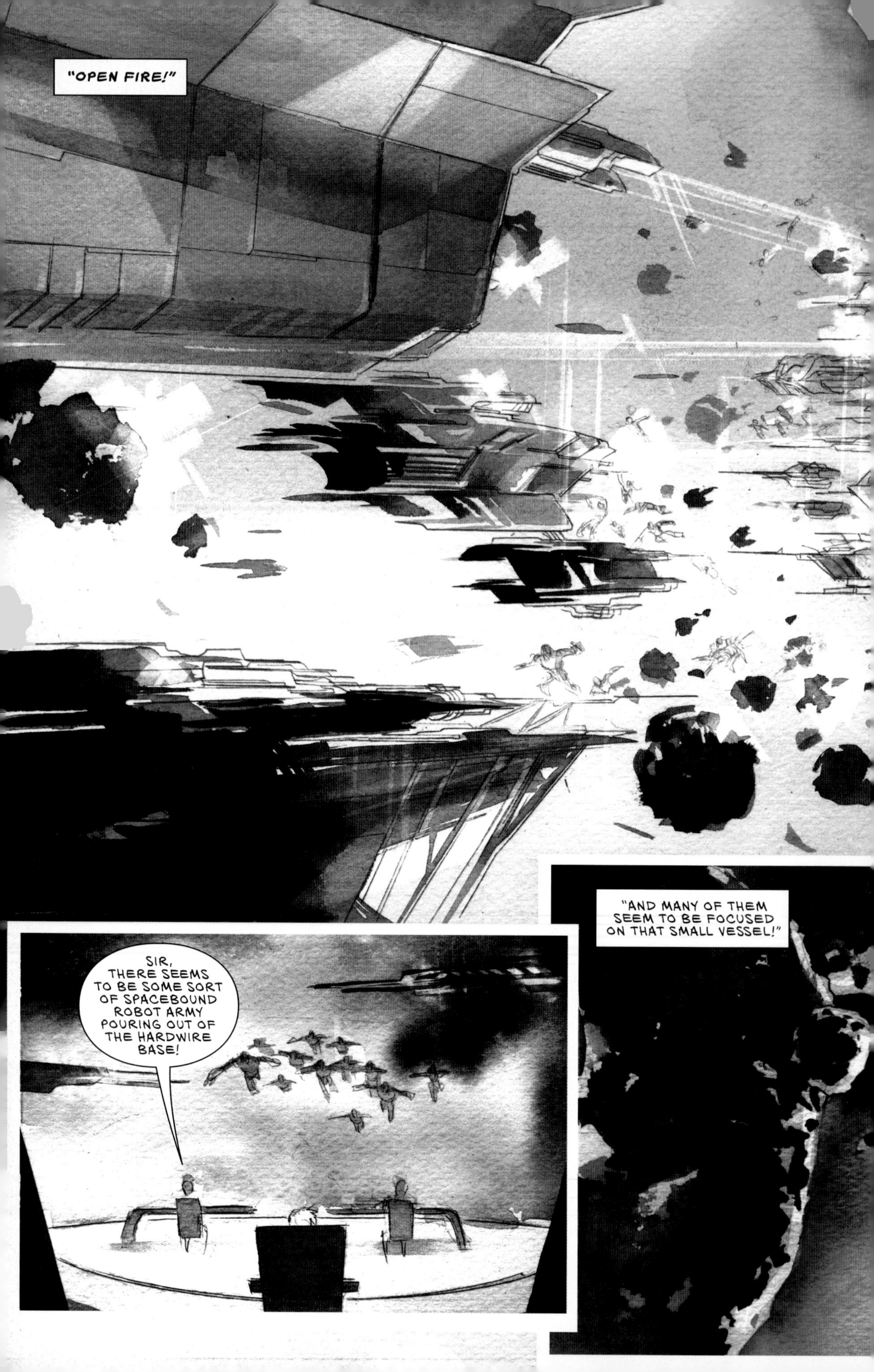
"OPEN FIRE!"
SIR, THERE SEEMS TO BE SOME SORT OF SPACEBOUND ROBOT ARMY POURING OUT OF THE HARDWIRE BASE!
"AND MANY OF THEM SEEM TO BE FOCUSED ON THAT SMALL VESSEL!"

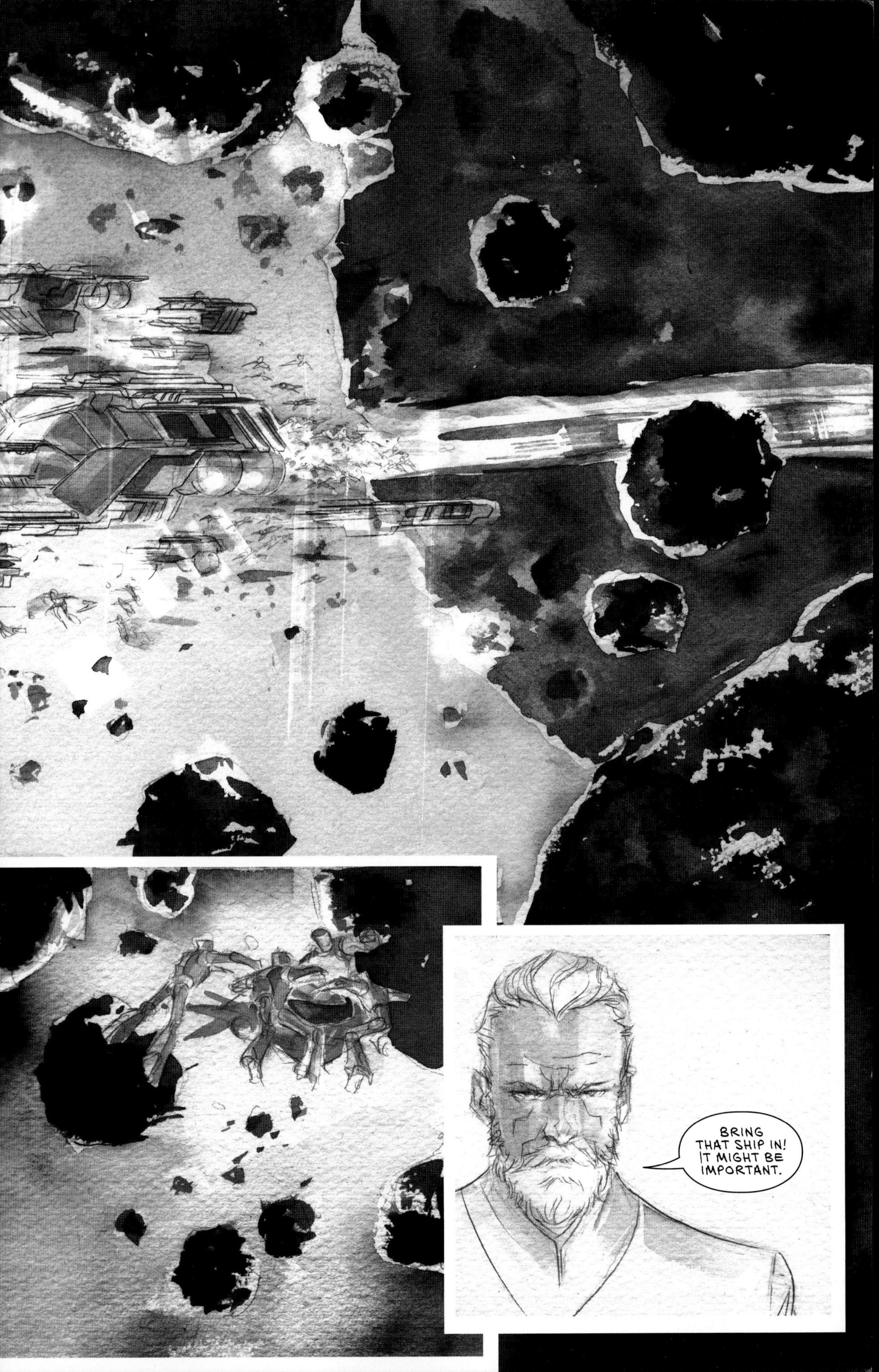
BRING THAT SHIP IN! IT MIGHT BE IMPORTANT.

ARF! ARF!
ARF!
ARF!

SHUT UP, BANDIT!

WHAT'S HAPPENING?!

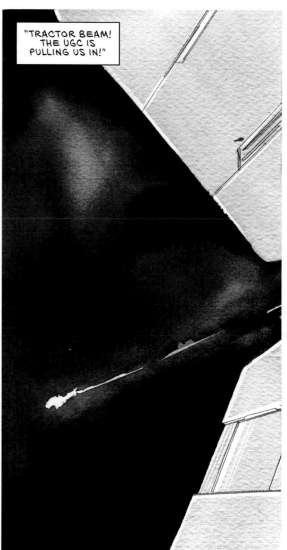

"TRACTOR BEAM! THE UGC IS PULLING US IN!"

0:47

SIR, WE HAVE TO GO. *NOW!*

LET ME GO!

QUIET!

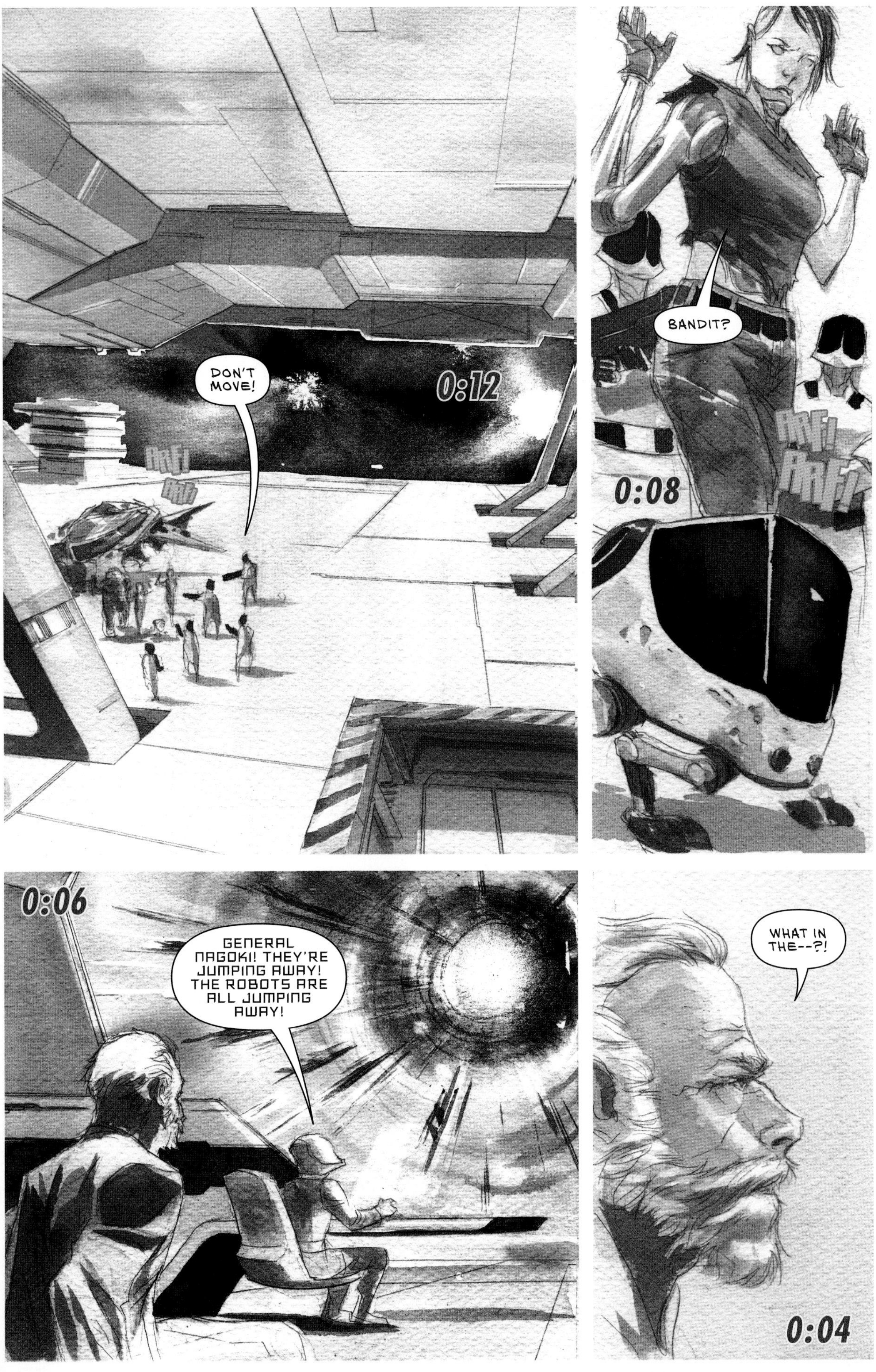
DON'T MOVE!
0:12
ARF!
ARF!
BANDIT?
ARF!
ARF!
0:08
0:06
GENERAL NAGOKI! THEY'RE JUMPING AWAY! THE ROBOTS ARE ALL JUMPING AWAY!
WHAT IN THE--?!
0:04

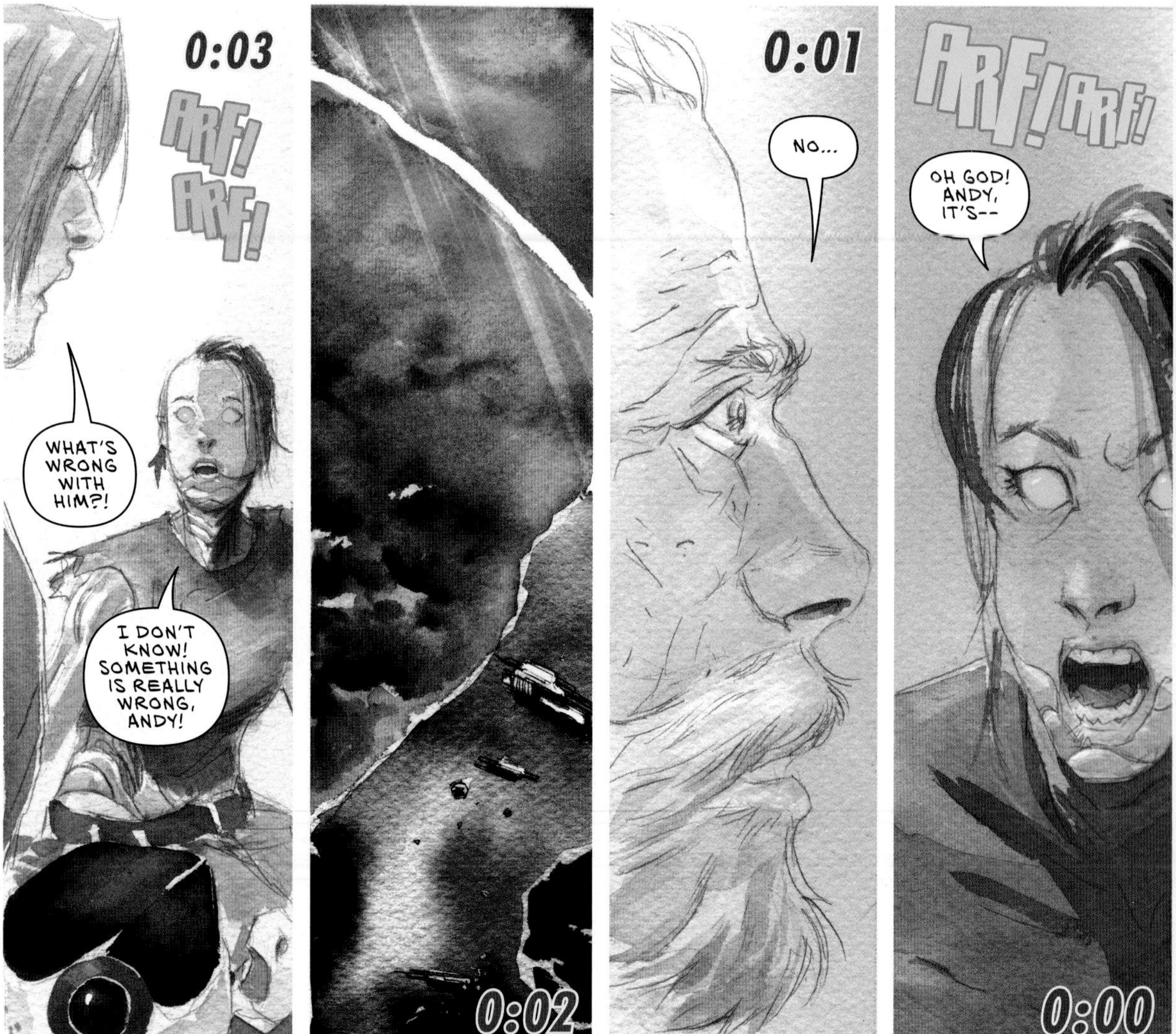

0:03
ARF! ARF!
WHAT'S WRONG WITH HIM?!
I DON'T KNOW! SOMETHING IS REALLY WRONG, ANDY!
0:02
0:01
NO...
ARF! ARF!
OH GOD! ANDY, IT'S--
0:00

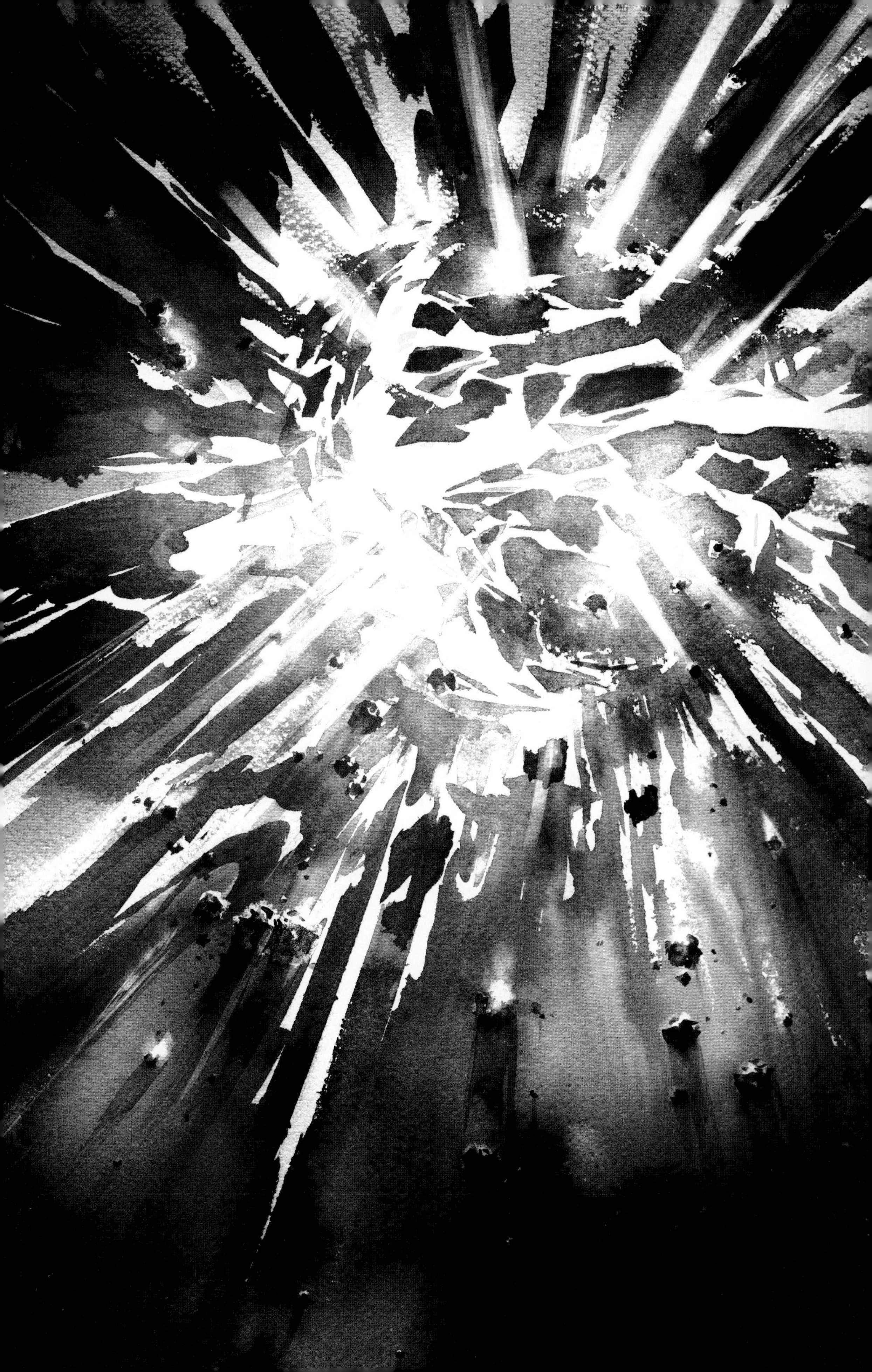

CHAPTER TWO

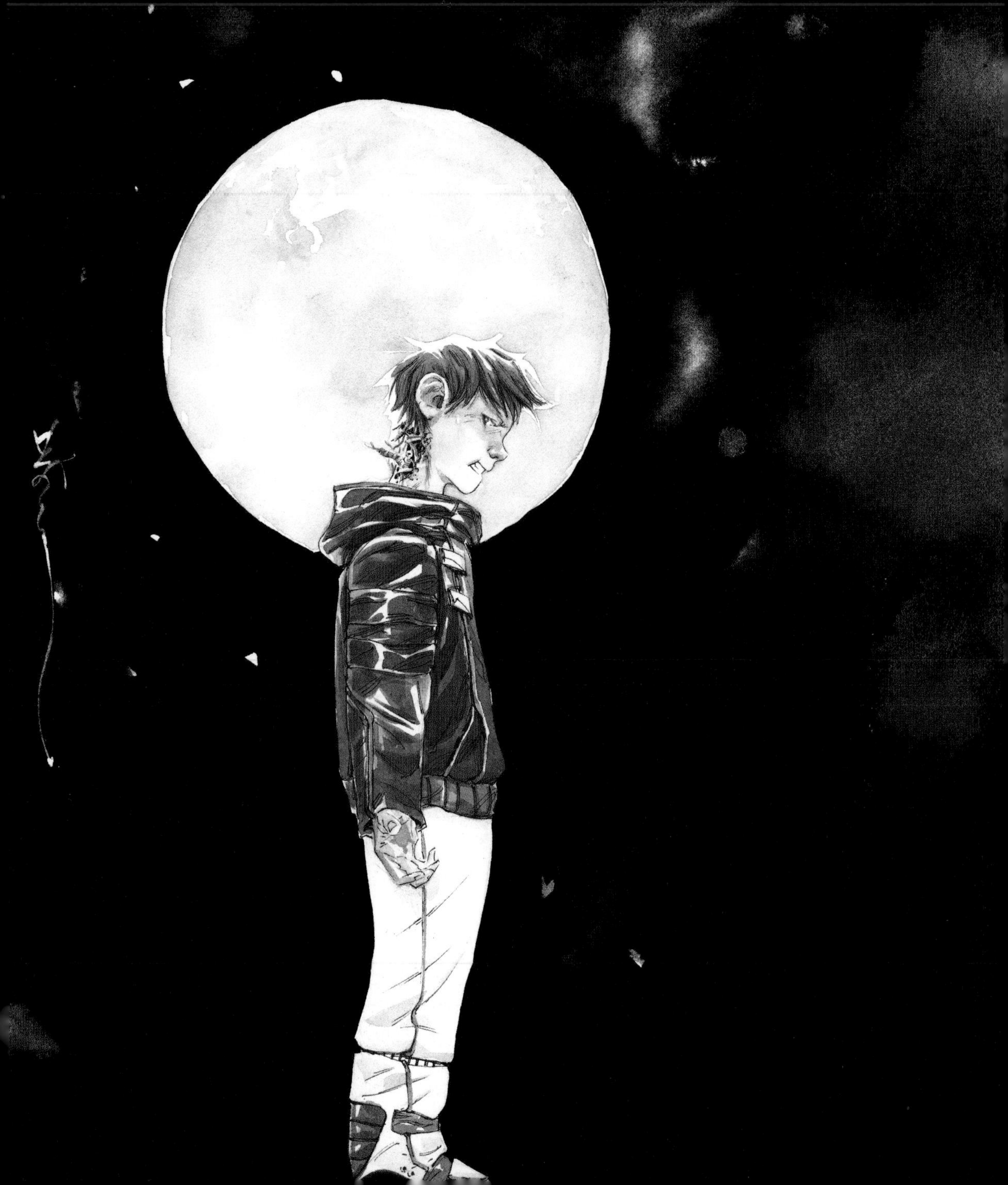

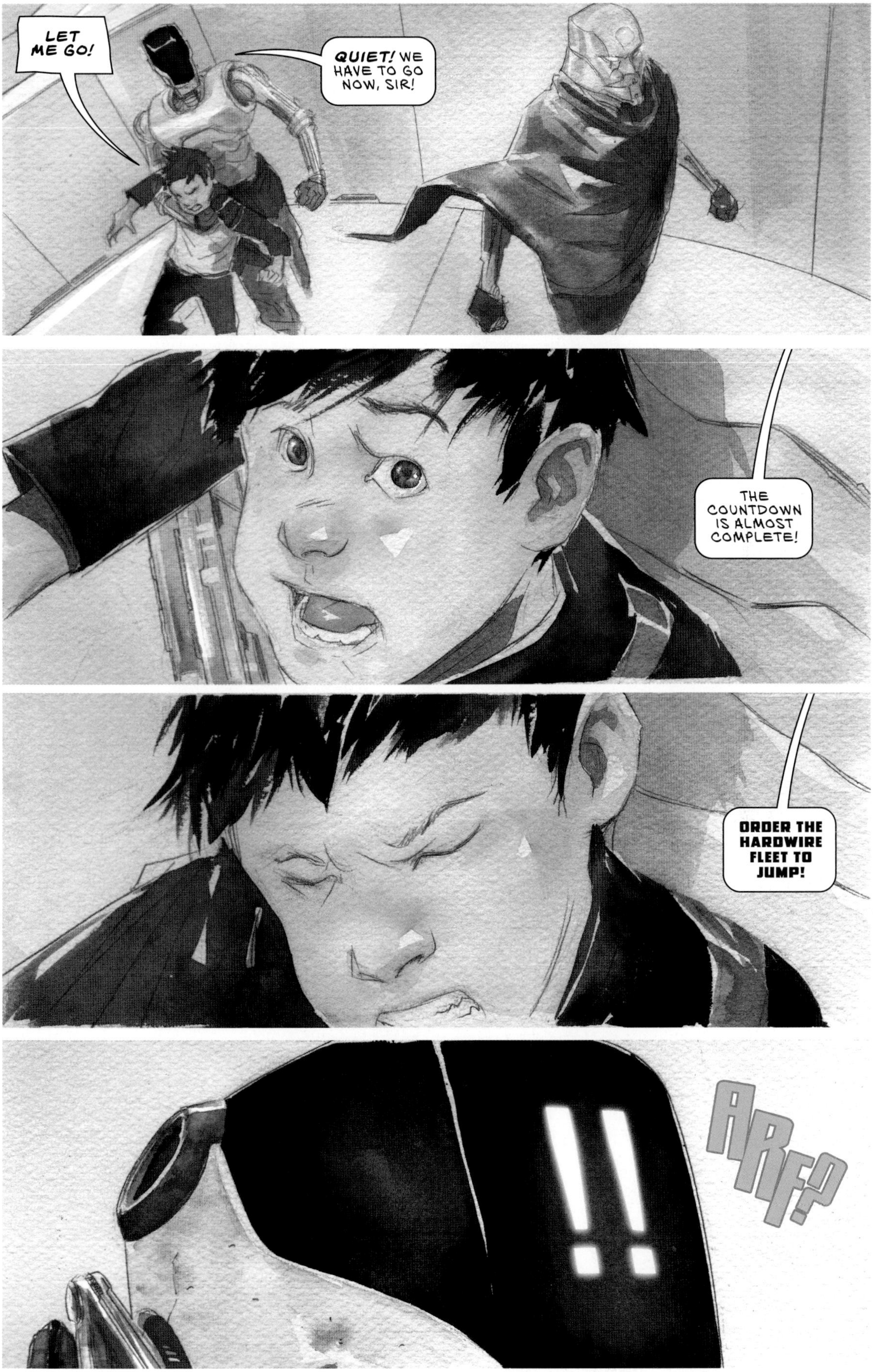
LET ME GO!
QUIET! WE HAVE TO GO NOW, SIR!
THE COUNTDOWN IS ALMOST COMPLETE!
ORDER THE HARDWIRE FLEET TO JUMP!
ARF?

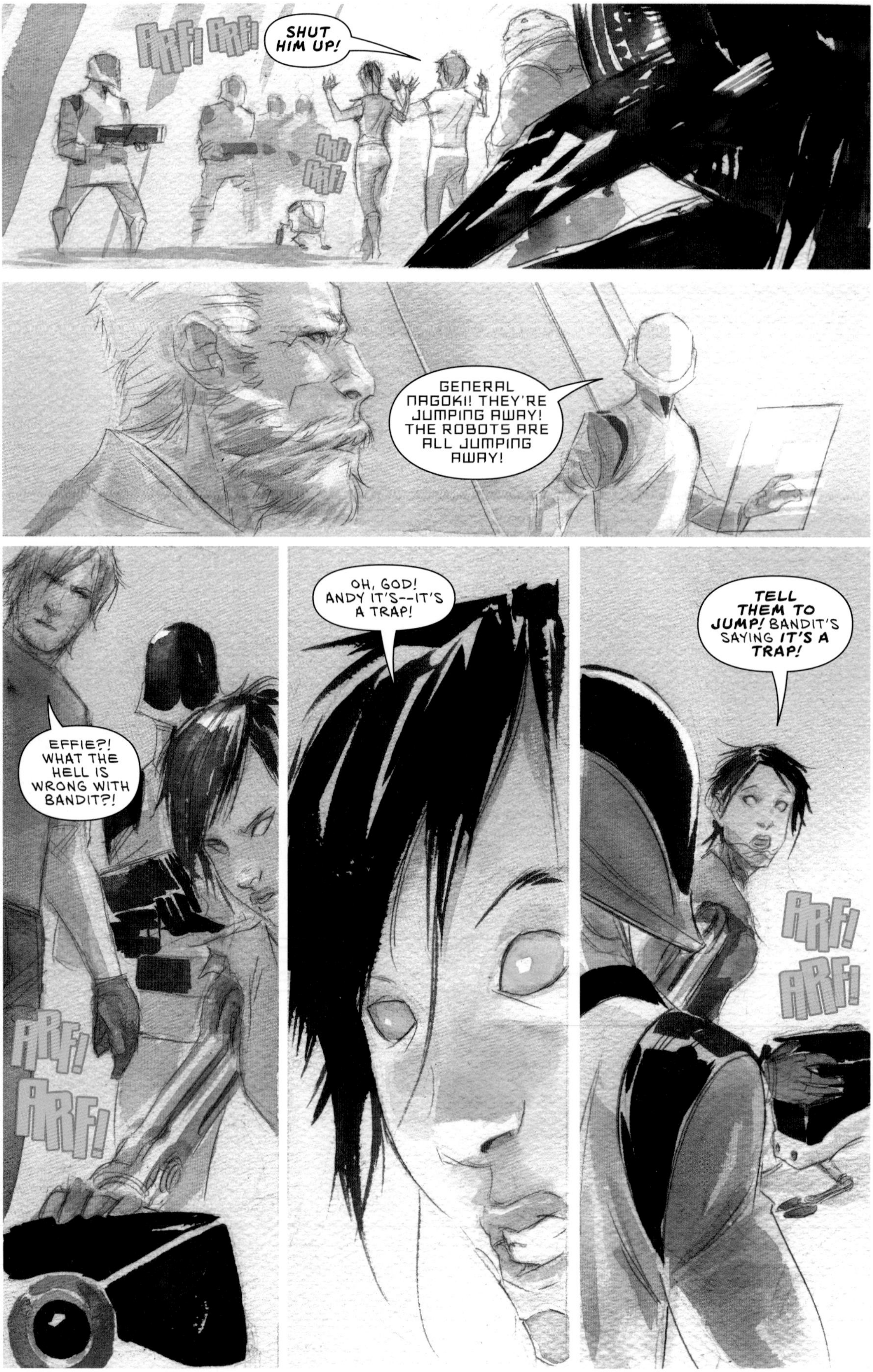
ARF! ARF!
SHUT HIM UP!
ARF! ARF!
GENERAL NAGOKI! THEY'RE JUMPING AWAY! THE ROBOTS ARE ALL JUMPING AWAY!
EFFIE?! WHAT THE HELL IS WRONG WITH BANDIT?!
ARF! ARF!
OH, GOD! ANDY IT'S--IT'S A TRAP!
TELL THEM TO JUMP! BANDIT'S SAYING IT'S A TRAP!
ARF! ARF!

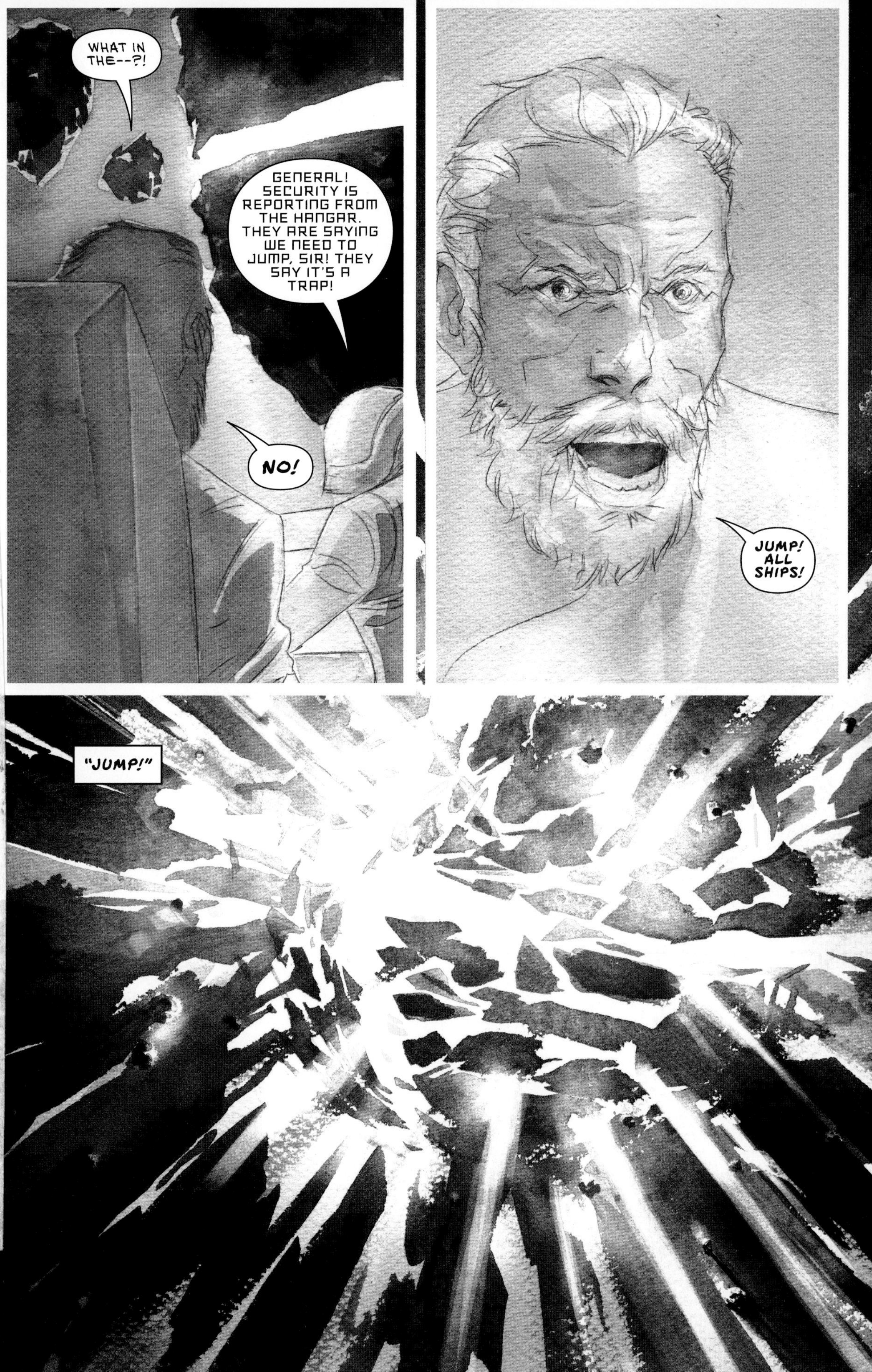
WHAT IN THE--?!
GENERAL! SECURITY IS REPORTING FROM THE HANGAR. THEY ARE SAYING WE NEED TO JUMP, SIR! THEY SAY IT'S A TRAP!
NO!
JUMP! ALL SHIPS!
"JUMP!"

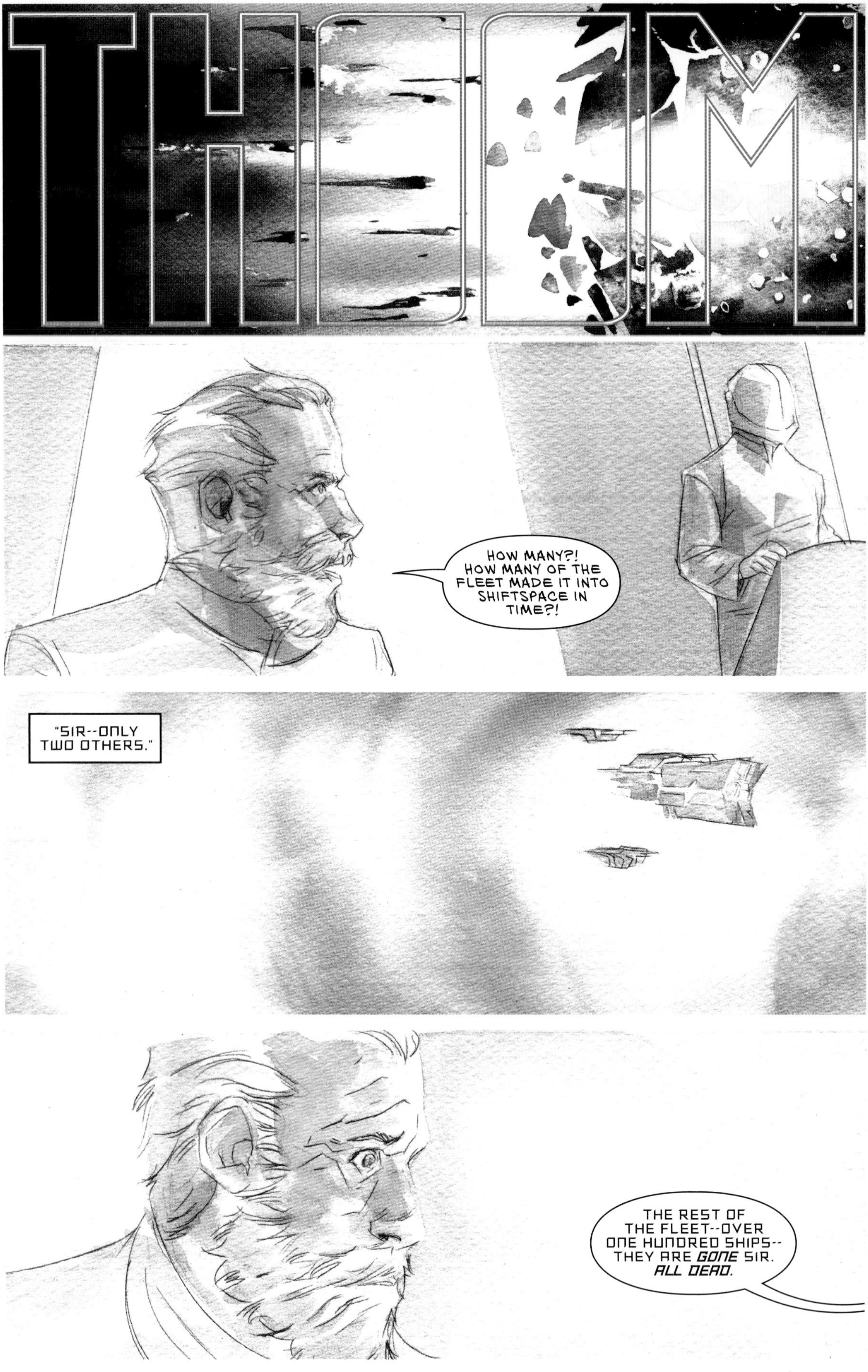
THOOM
HOW MANY?! HOW MANY OF THE FLEET MADE IT INTO SHIFTSPACE IN TIME?!
"SIR--ONLY TWO OTHERS."
THE REST OF THE FLEET--OVER ONE HUNDRED SHIPS--THEY ARE *GONE* SIR. *ALL DEAD*.

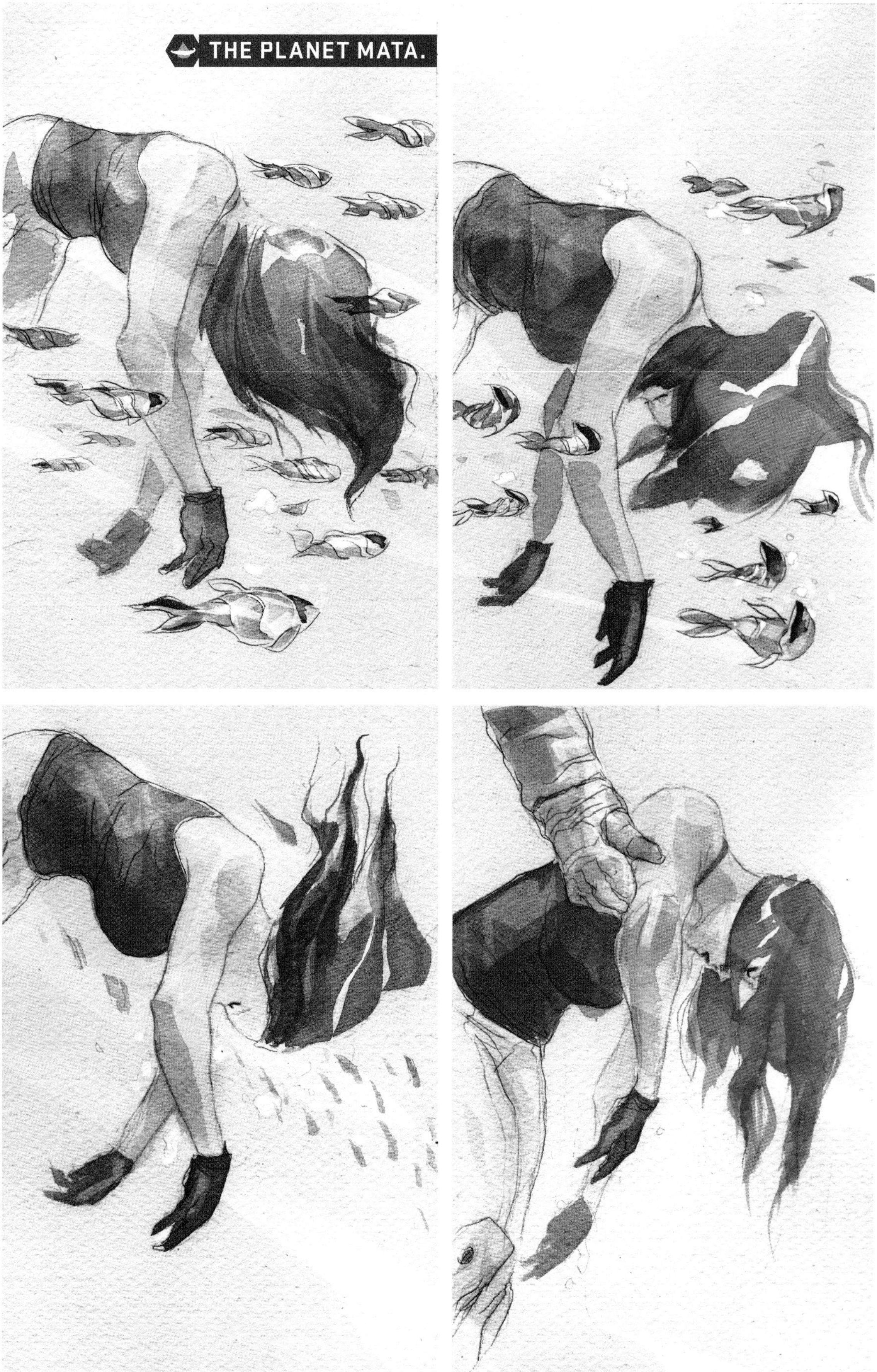
THE PLANET MATA.

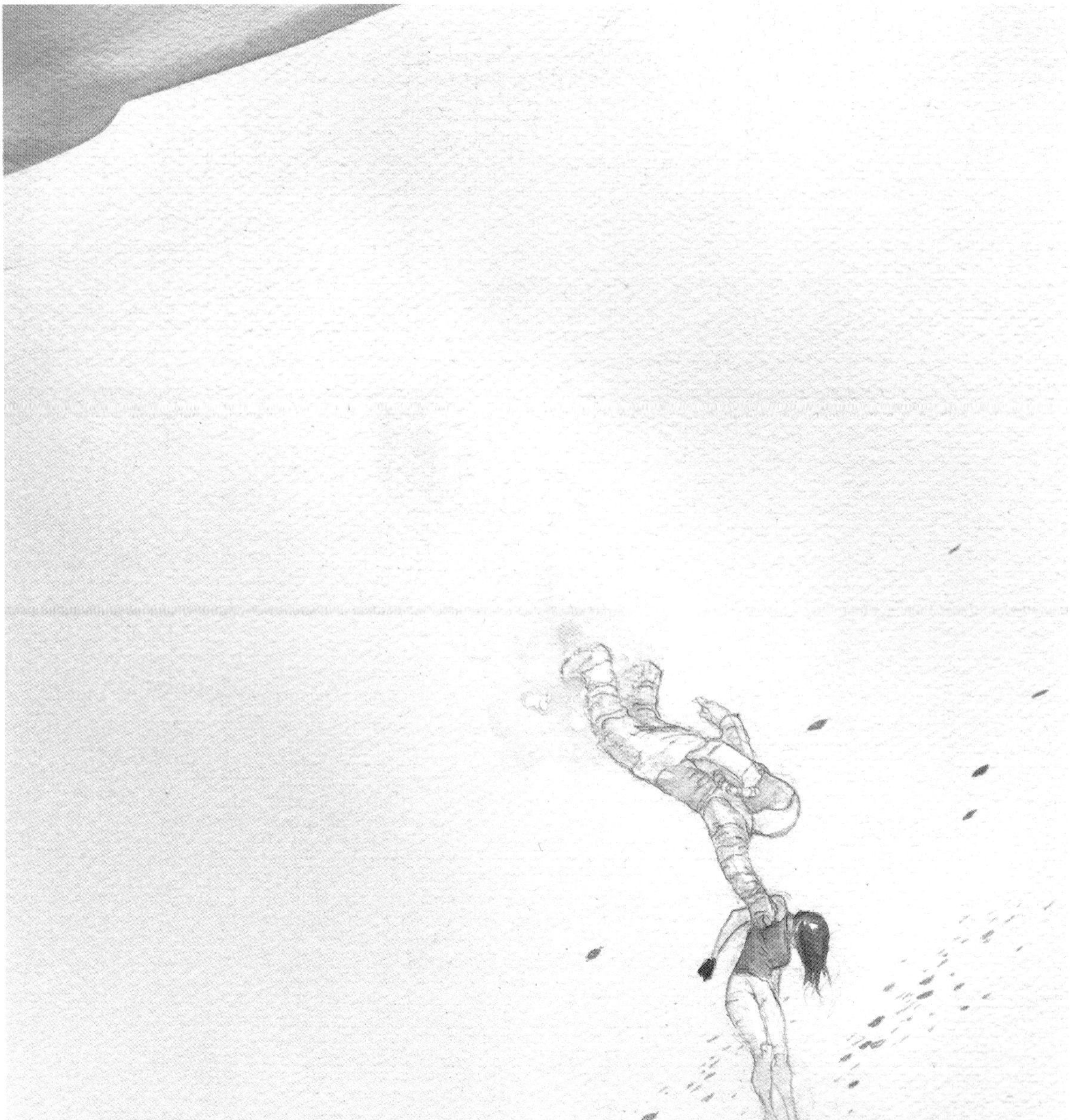
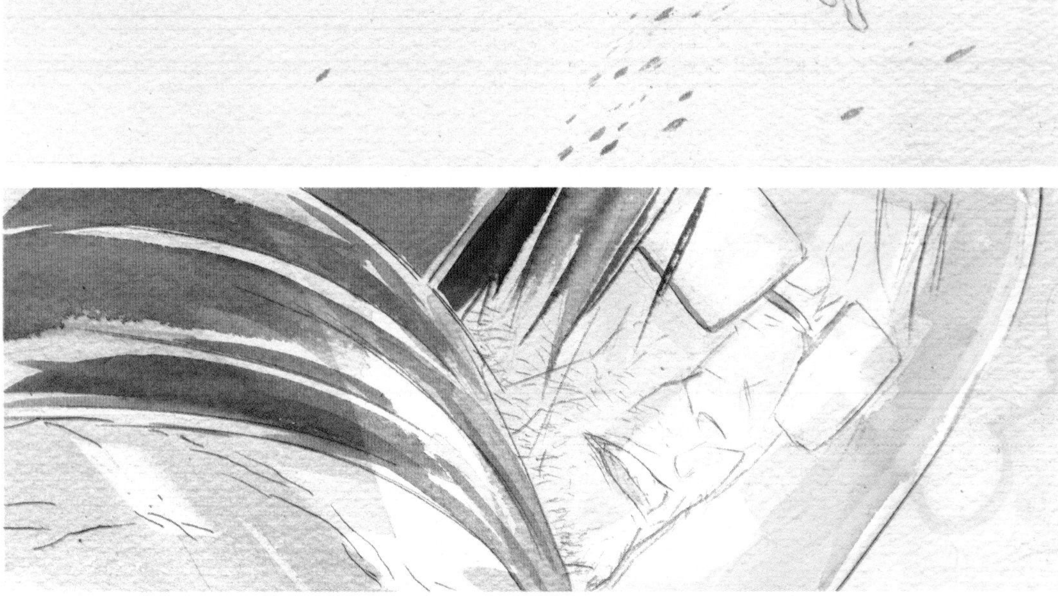

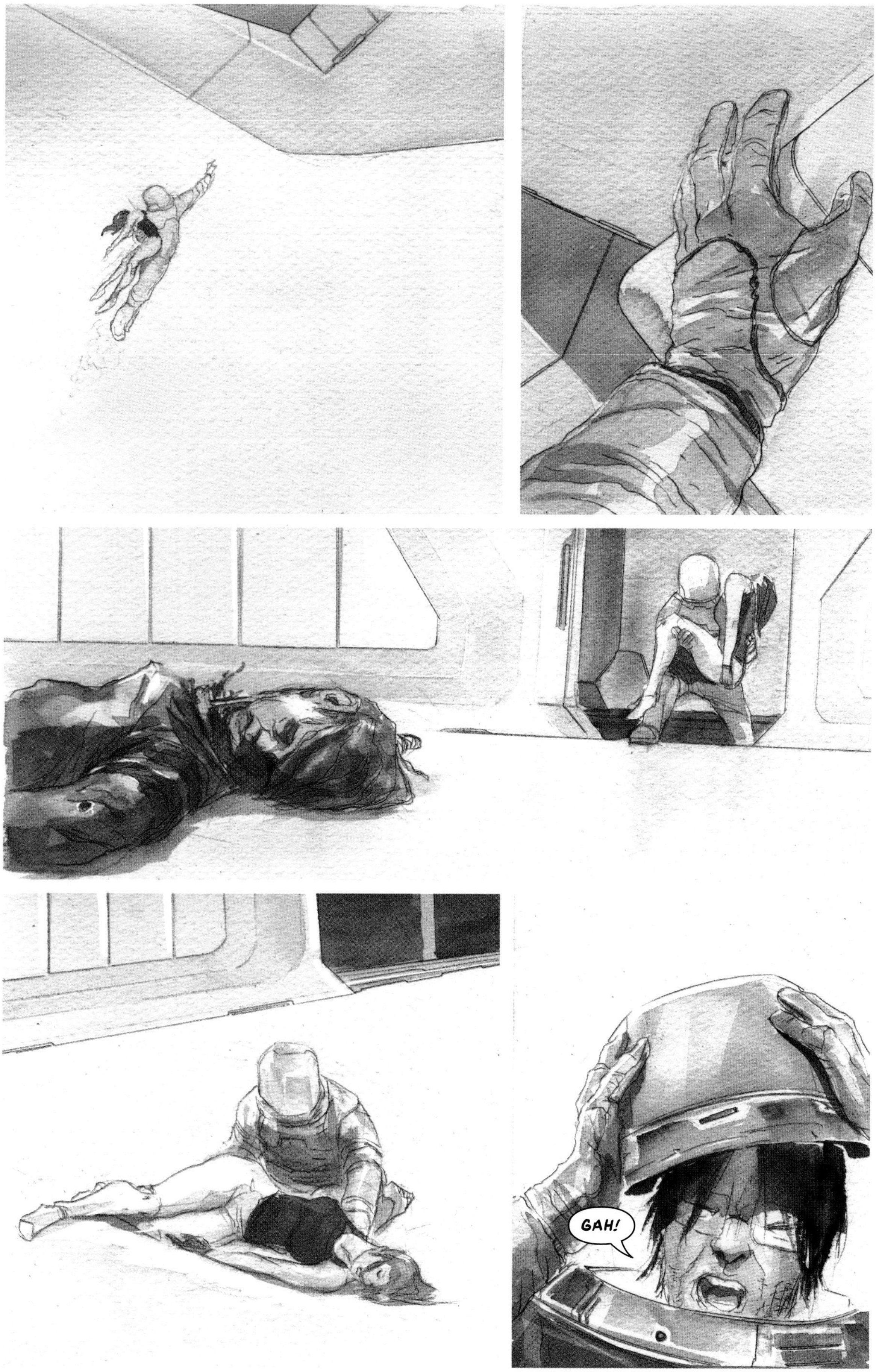
GAH!

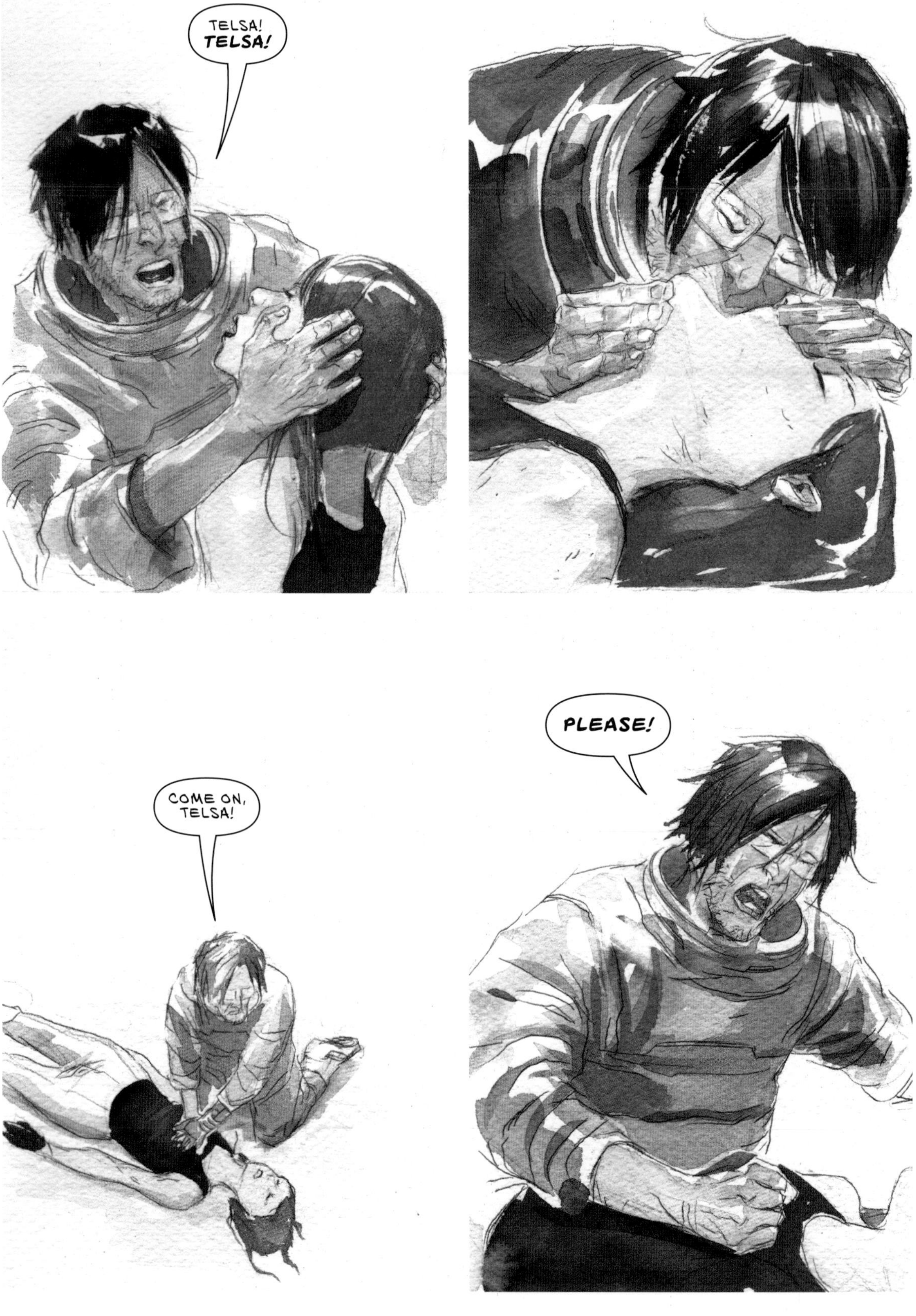
TELSA!
TELSA!
COME ON, TELSA!
PLEASE!

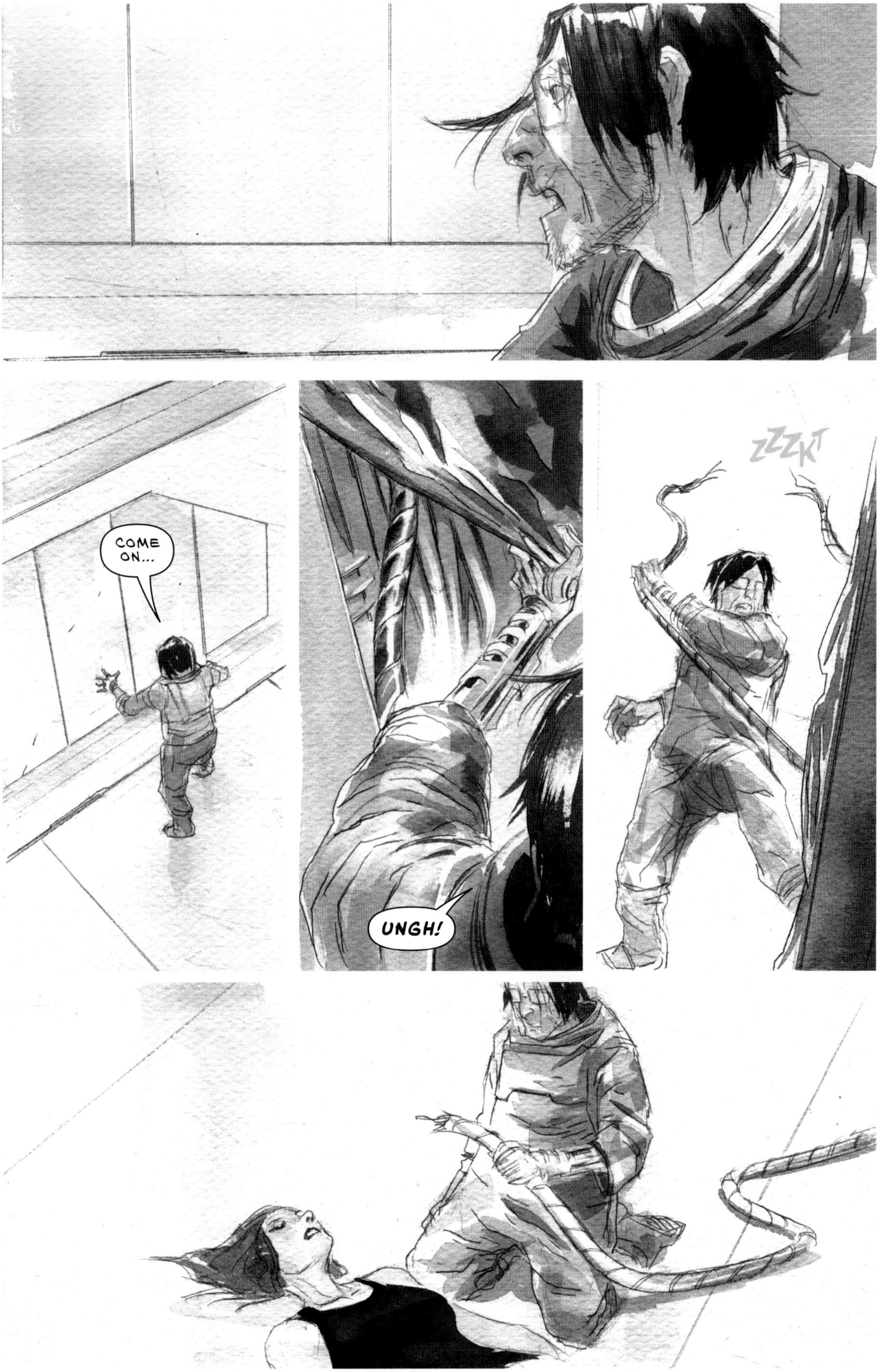
COME ON...
UNGH!
ZZZKT

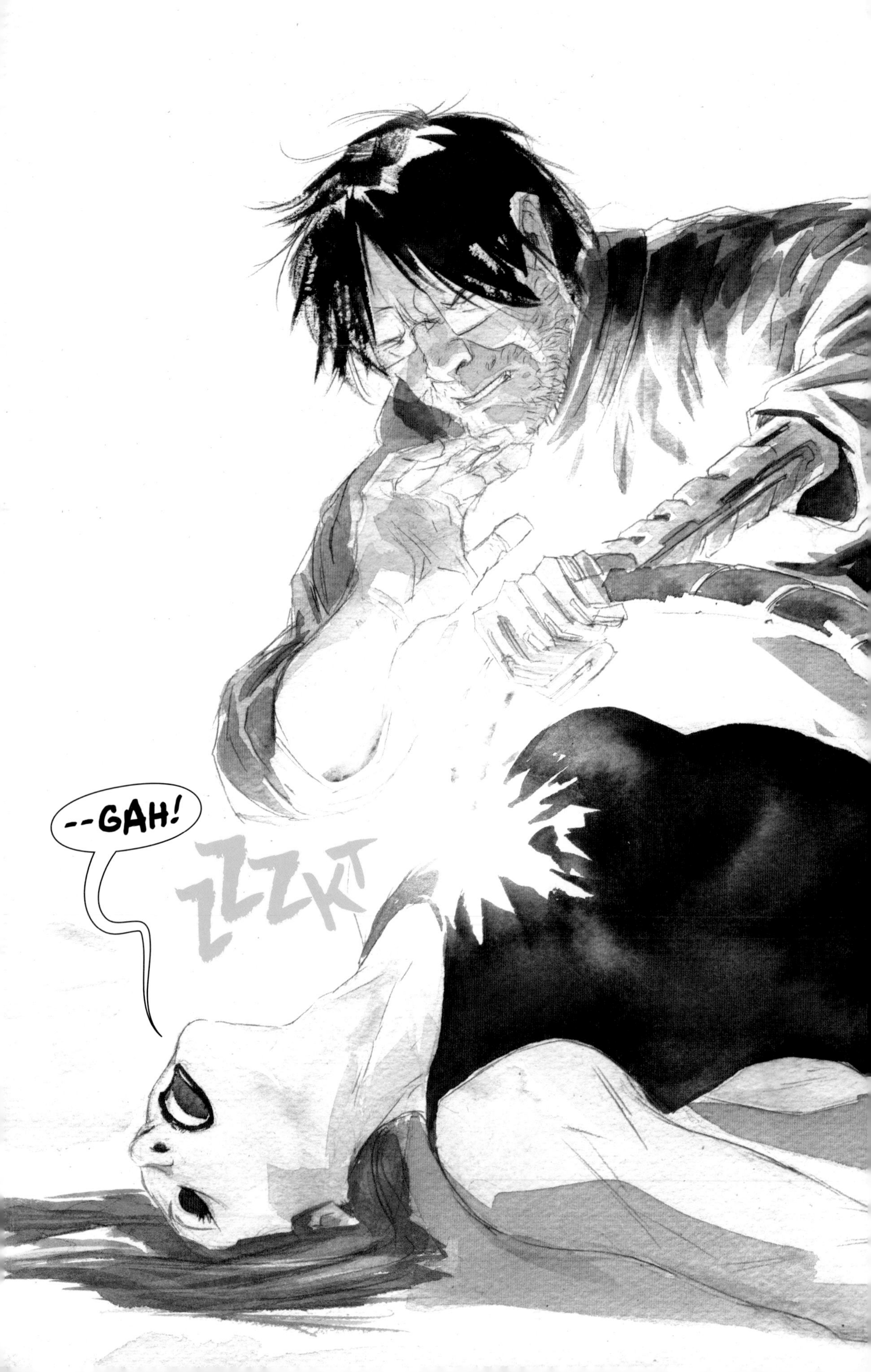
--GAH!
ZZZKT

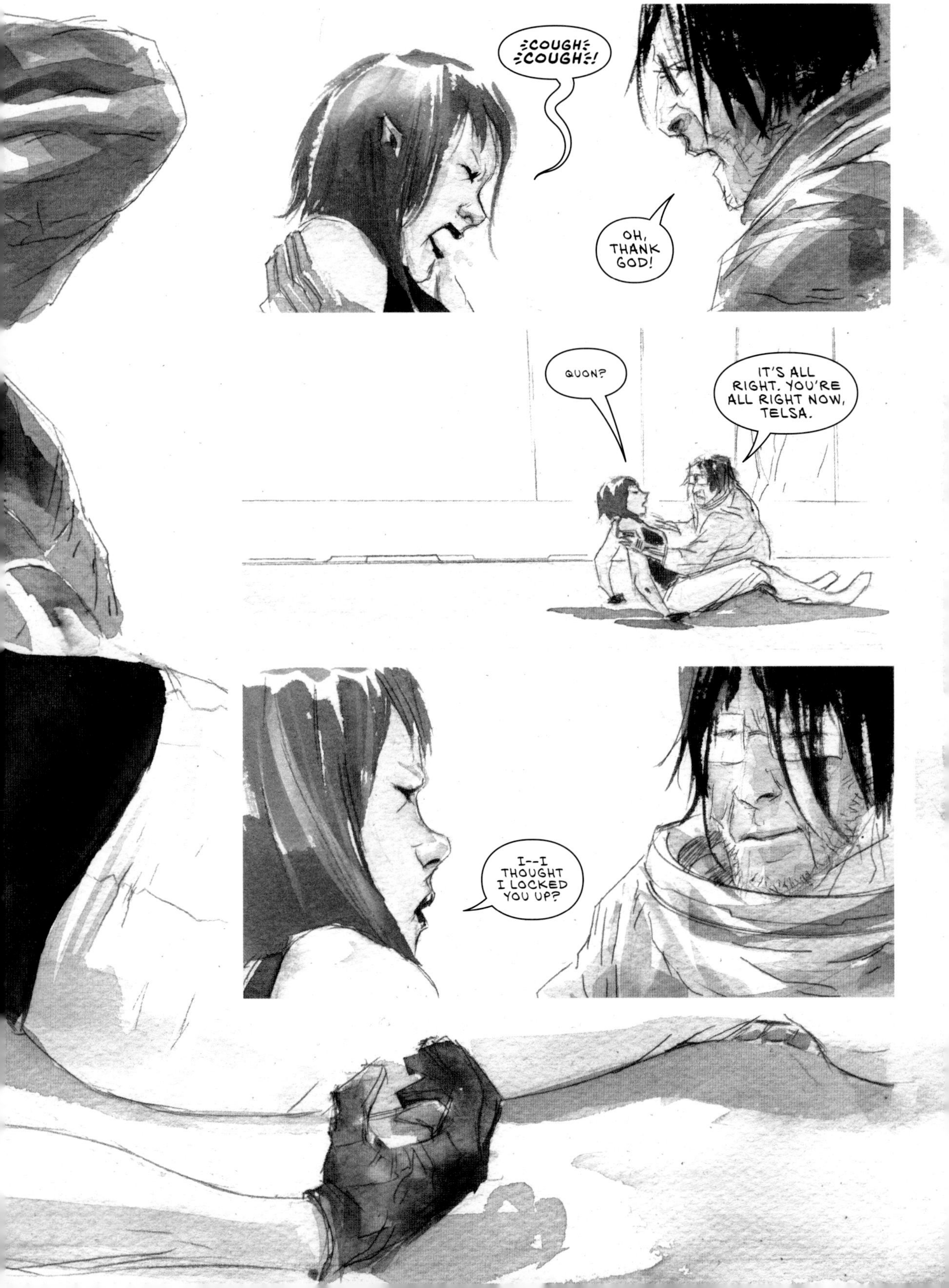

COUGH COUGH!
OH, THANK GOD!
QUON?
IT'S ALL RIGHT. YOU'RE ALL RIGHT NOW, TELSA.
I--I THOUGHT I LOCKED YOU UP?

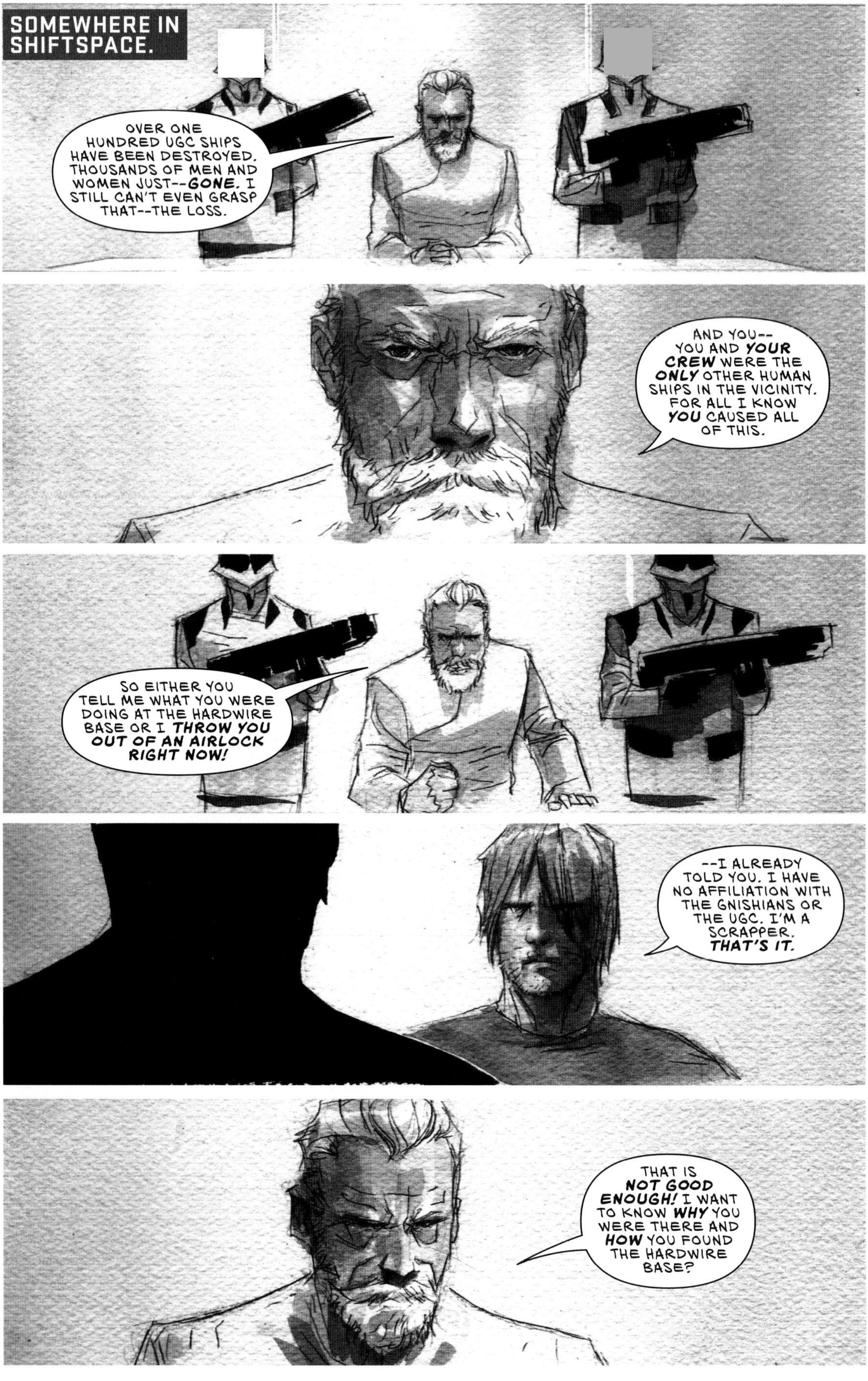
SOMEWHERE IN SHIFTSPACE.
OVER ONE HUNDRED UGC SHIPS HAVE BEEN DESTROYED. THOUSANDS OF MEN AND WOMEN JUST--GONE. I STILL CAN'T EVEN GRASP THAT--THE LOSS.
AND YOU--YOU AND YOUR CREW WERE THE ONLY OTHER HUMAN SHIPS IN THE VICINITY. FOR ALL I KNOW YOU CAUSED ALL OF THIS.
SO EITHER YOU TELL ME WHAT YOU WERE DOING AT THE HARDWIRE BASE OR I THROW YOU OUT OF AN AIRLOCK RIGHT NOW!
--I ALREADY TOLD YOU. I HAVE NO AFFILIATION WITH THE GNISHIANS OR THE UGC. I'M A SCRAPPER. THAT'S IT.
THAT IS NOT GOOD ENOUGH! I WANT TO KNOW WHY YOU WERE THERE AND HOW YOU FOUND THE HARDWIRE BASE?

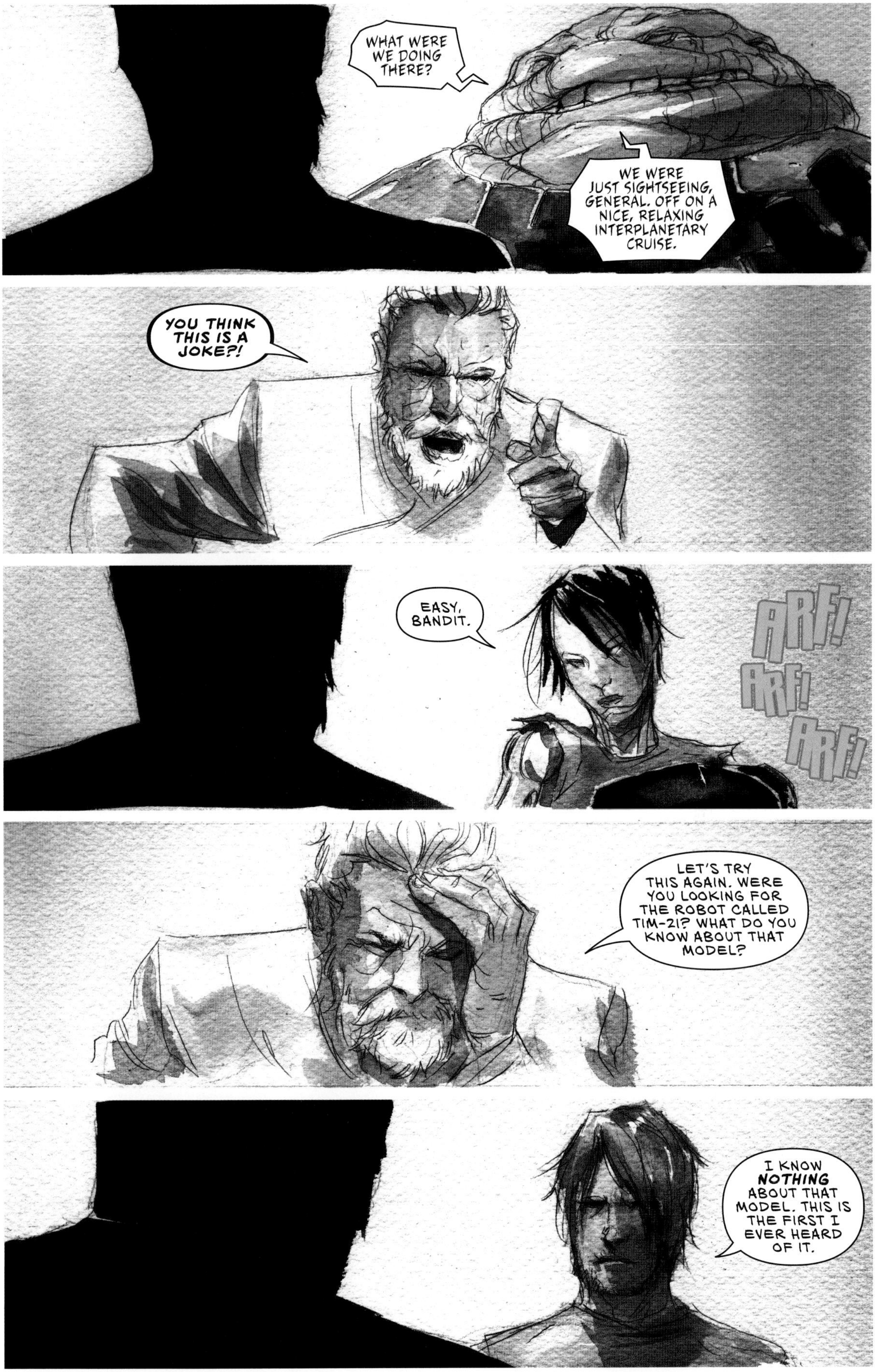
WHAT WERE WE DOING THERE?
WE WERE JUST SIGHTSEEING, GENERAL. OFF ON A NICE, RELAXING INTERPLANETARY CRUISE.
YOU THINK THIS IS A JOKE?!
EASY, BANDIT.
ARF! ARF! ARF!
LET'S TRY THIS AGAIN. WERE YOU LOOKING FOR THE ROBOT CALLED TIM-21? WHAT DO YOU KNOW ABOUT THAT MODEL?
I KNOW NOTHING ABOUT THAT MODEL. THIS IS THE FIRST I EVER HEARD OF IT.

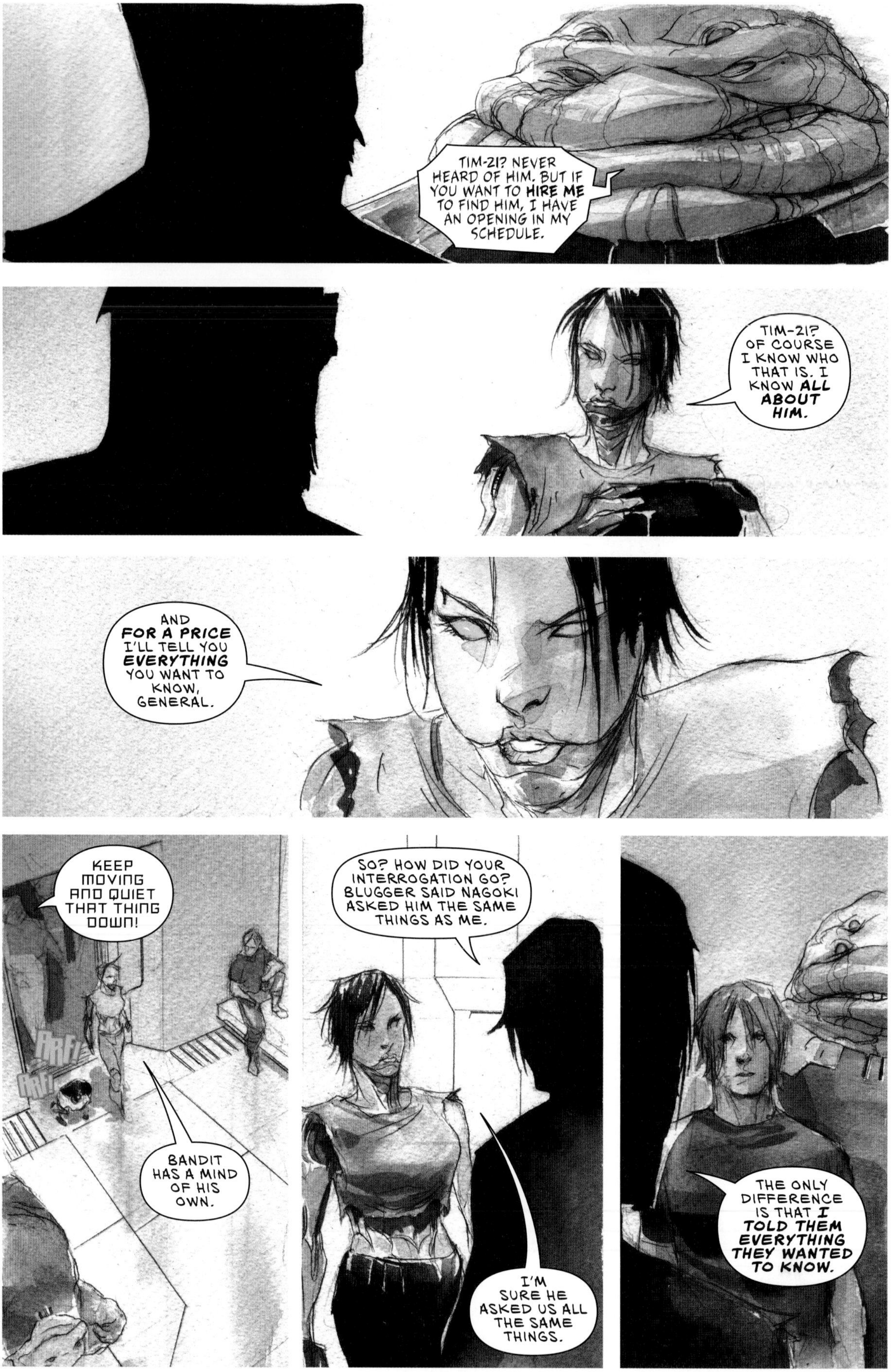
TIM-21? NEVER HEARD OF HIM. BUT IF YOU WANT TO **HIRE ME** TO FIND HIM, I HAVE AN OPENING IN MY SCHEDULE.
TIM-21? OF COURSE I KNOW WHO THAT IS. I KNOW **ALL ABOUT HIM.**
AND **FOR A PRICE** I'LL TELL YOU **EVERYTHING** YOU WANT TO KNOW, GENERAL.
KEEP MOVING AND QUIET THAT THING DOWN!
ARF! ARF!
BANDIT HAS A MIND OF HIS OWN.
SO? HOW DID YOUR INTERROGATION GO? BLUGGER SAID NAGOKI ASKED HIM THE SAME THINGS AS ME.
I'M SURE HE ASKED US ALL THE SAME THINGS.
THE ONLY DIFFERENCE IS THAT **I TOLD THEM EVERYTHING THEY WANTED TO KNOW.**

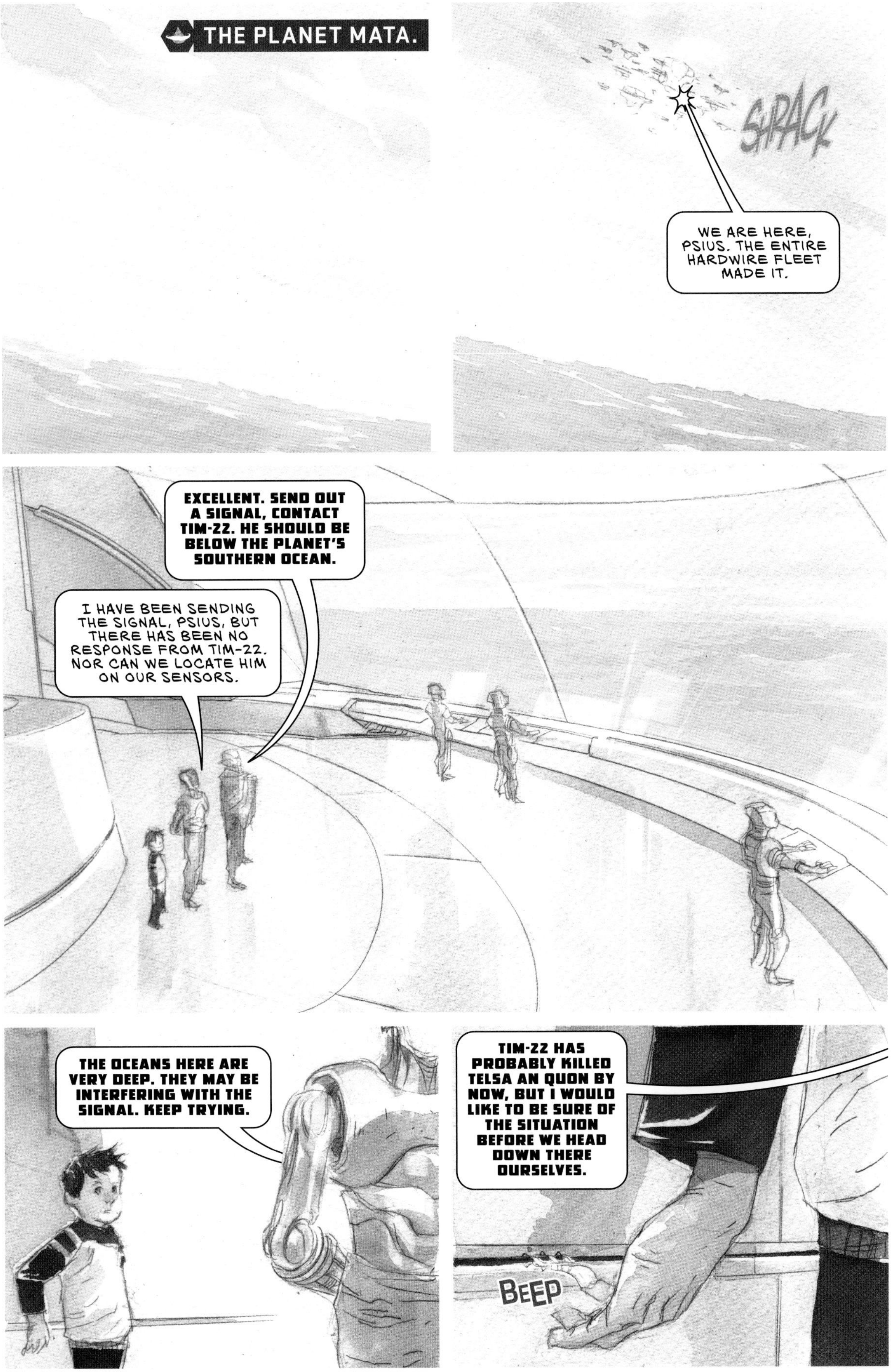
THE PLANET MATA.
SHRACK
WE ARE HERE, PSIUS. THE ENTIRE HARDWIRE FLEET MADE IT.
EXCELLENT. SEND OUT A SIGNAL, CONTACT TIM-22. HE SHOULD BE BELOW THE PLANET'S SOUTHERN OCEAN.
I HAVE BEEN SENDING THE SIGNAL, PSIUS, BUT THERE HAS BEEN NO RESPONSE FROM TIM-22. NOR CAN WE LOCATE HIM ON OUR SENSORS.
THE OCEANS HERE ARE VERY DEEP. THEY MAY BE INTERFERING WITH THE SIGNAL. KEEP TRYING.
TIM-22 HAS PROBABLY KILLED TELSA AN QUON BY NOW, BUT I WOULD LIKE TO BE SURE OF THE SITUATION BEFORE WE HEAD DOWN THERE OURSELVES.
BEEP

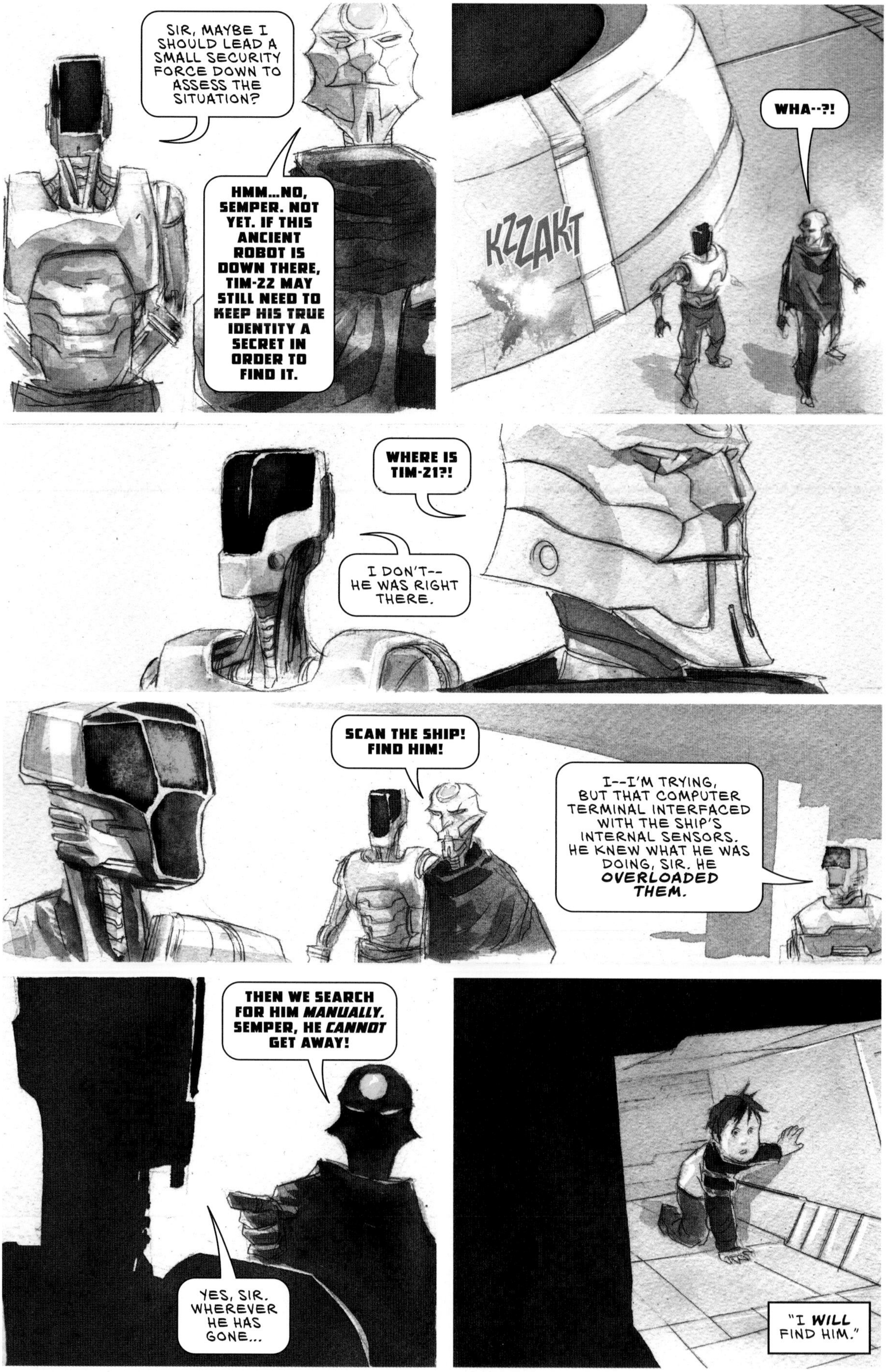
SIR, MAYBE I SHOULD LEAD A SMALL SECURITY FORCE DOWN TO ASSESS THE SITUATION?
HMM...NO, SEMPER. NOT YET. IF THIS ANCIENT ROBOT IS DOWN THERE, TIM-22 MAY STILL NEED TO KEEP HIS TRUE IDENTITY A SECRET IN ORDER TO FIND IT.
KZZAKT
WHA--?!
WHERE IS TIM-21?!
I DON'T-- HE WAS RIGHT THERE.
SCAN THE SHIP! FIND HIM!
I--I'M TRYING, BUT THAT COMPUTER TERMINAL INTERFACED WITH THE SHIP'S INTERNAL SENSORS. HE KNEW WHAT HE WAS DOING, SIR. HE OVERLOADED THEM.
THEN WE SEARCH FOR HIM MANUALLY. SEMPER, HE CANNOT GET AWAY!
YES, SIR. WHEREVER HE HAS GONE...
"I WILL FIND HIM."

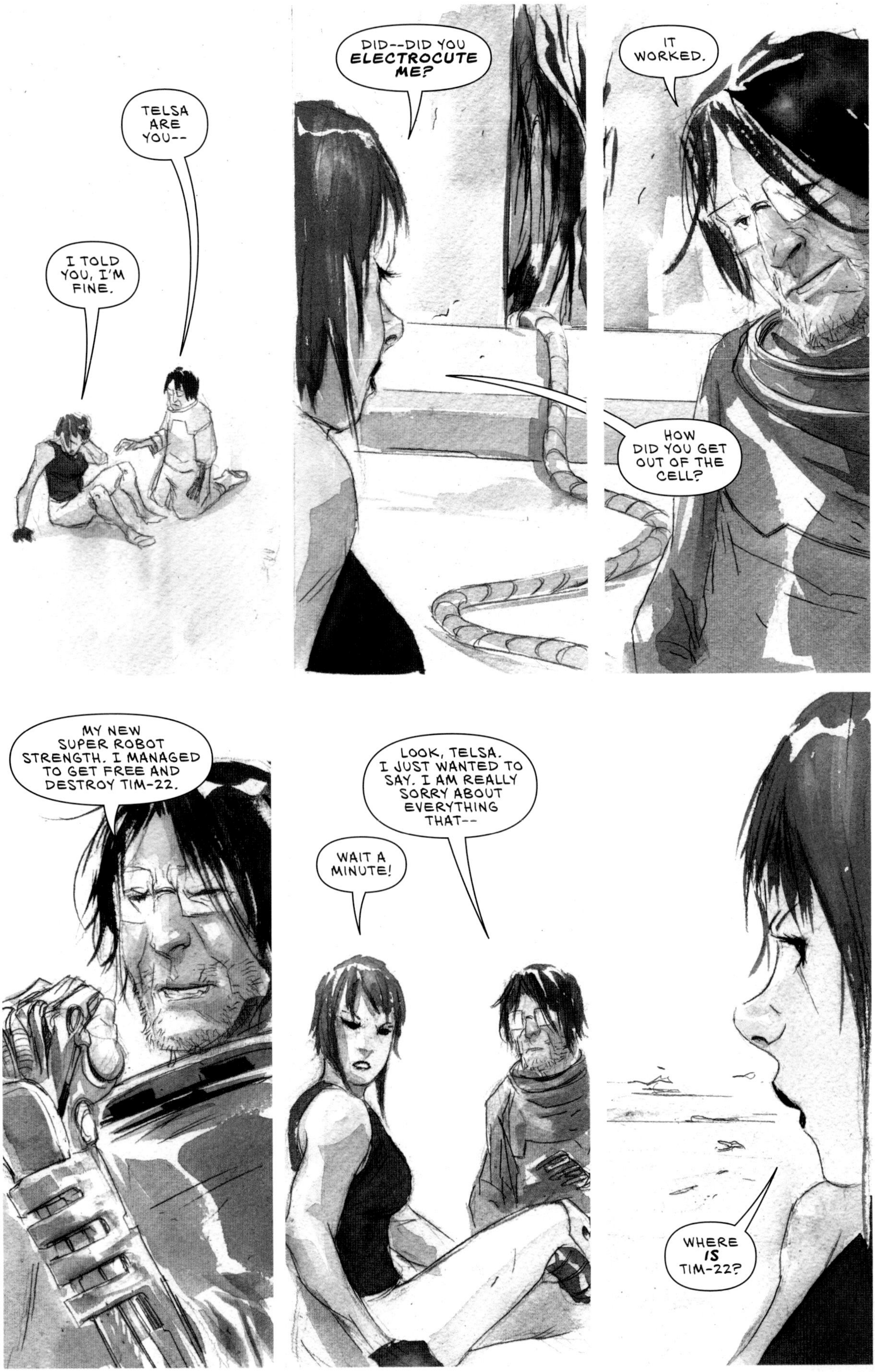
TELSA ARE YOU--
I TOLD YOU, I'M FINE.
DID--DID YOU ELECTROCUTE ME?
IT WORKED.
HOW DID YOU GET OUT OF THE CELL?
MY NEW SUPER ROBOT STRENGTH. I MANAGED TO GET FREE AND DESTROY TIM-22.
LOOK, TELSA. I JUST WANTED TO SAY. I AM REALLY SORRY ABOUT EVERYTHING THAT--
WAIT A MINUTE!
WHERE IS TIM-22?

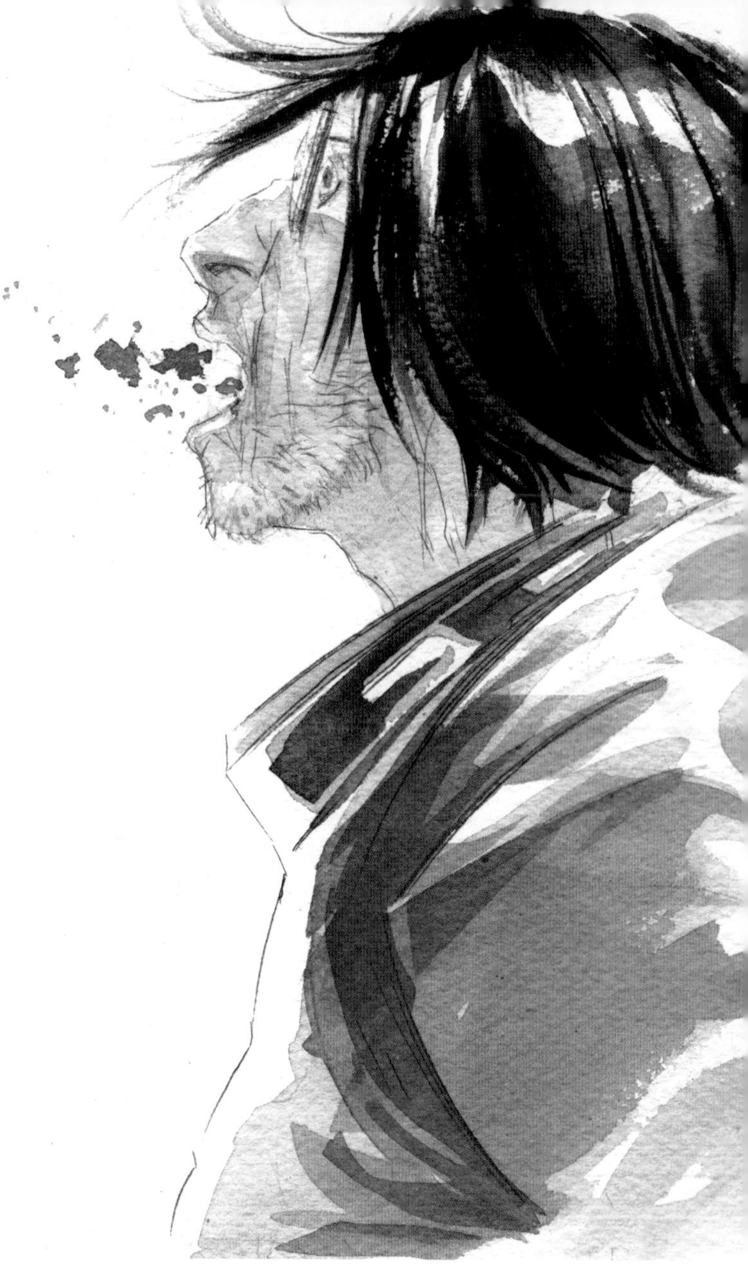

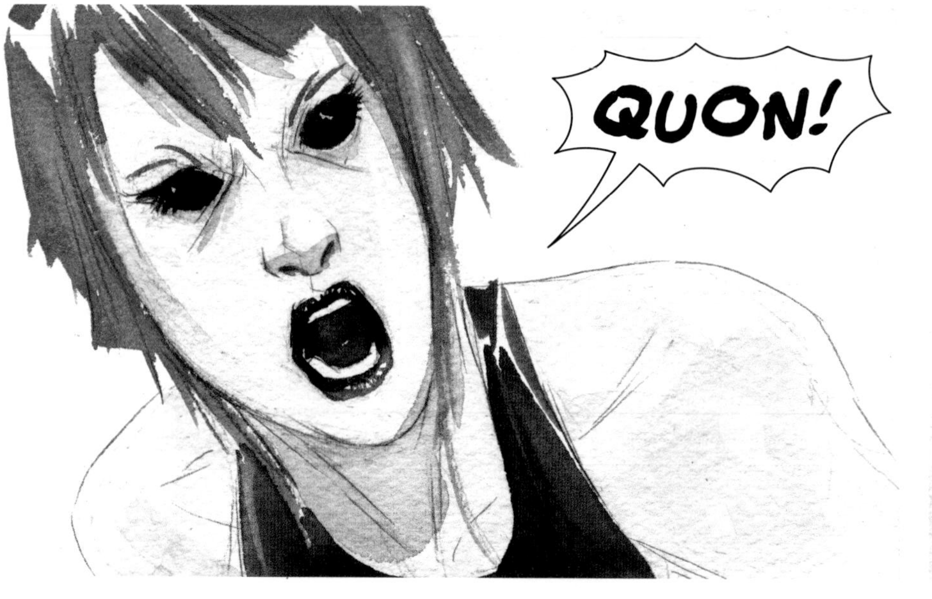
QUON!

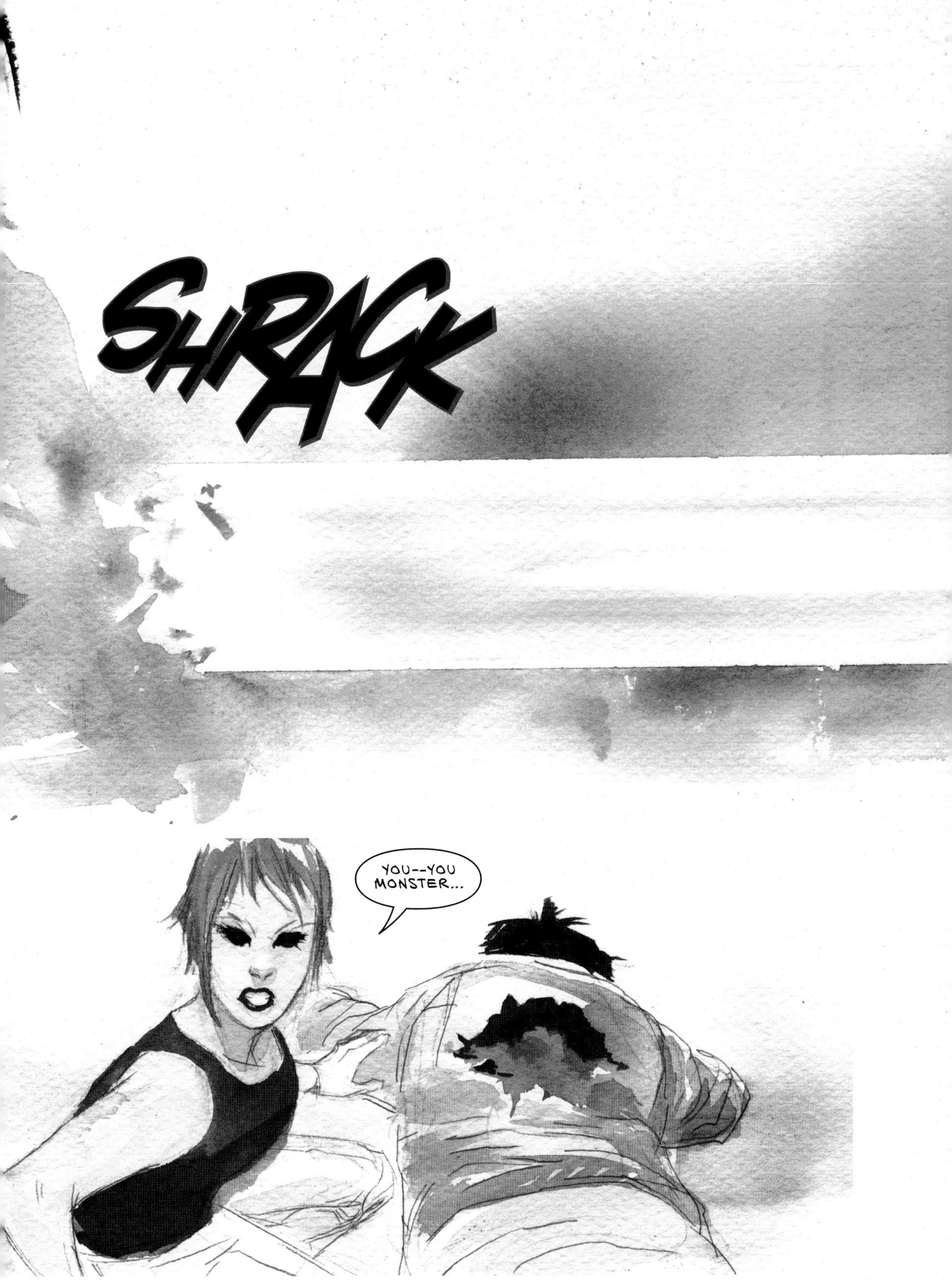
SHRACK
YOU--YOU MONSTER...

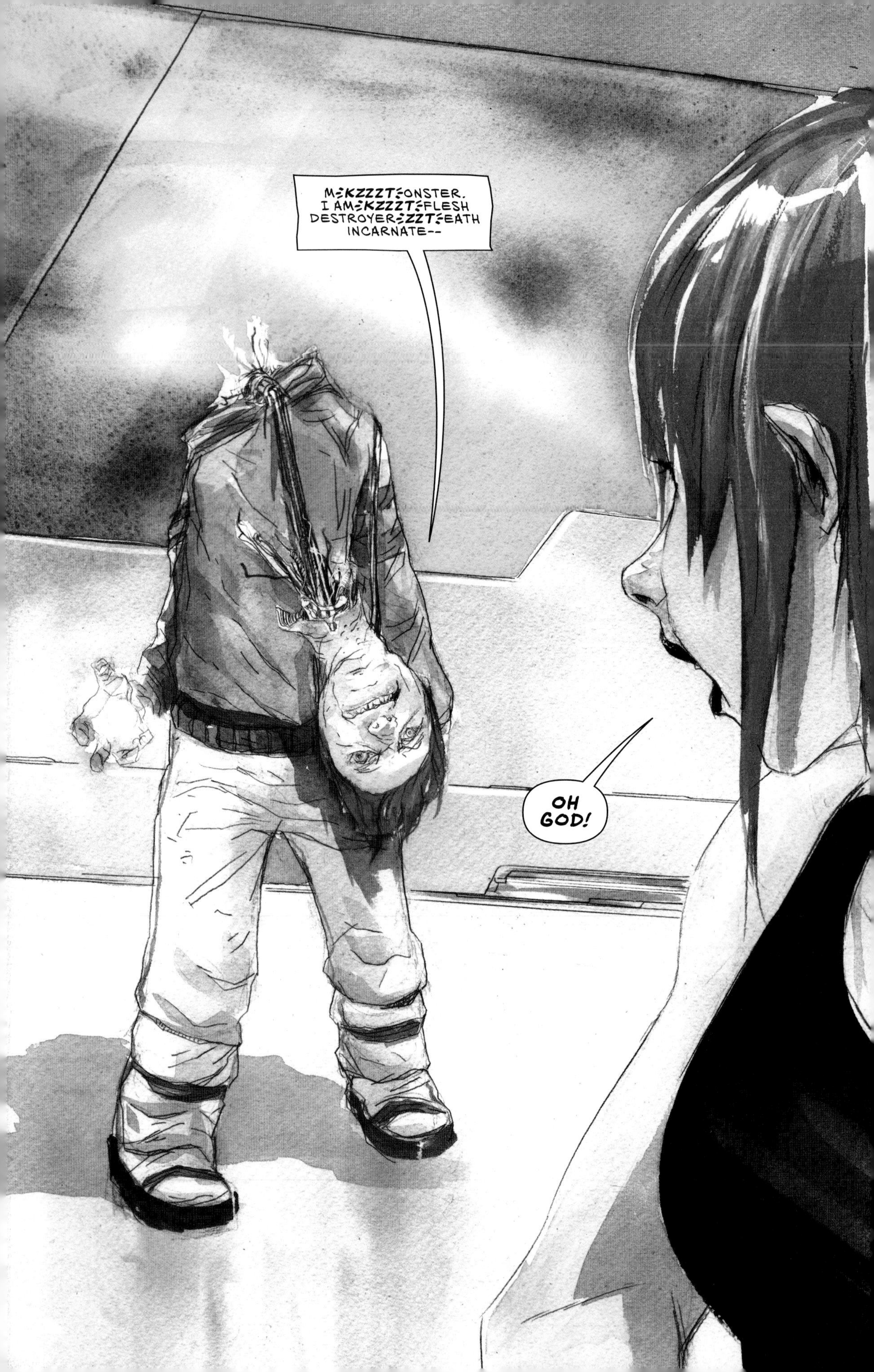
M-KZZZT-ONSTER. I AM-KZZZT-FLESH DESTROYER-ZZT-EATH INCARNATE--
OH GOD!

CHAPTER THREE

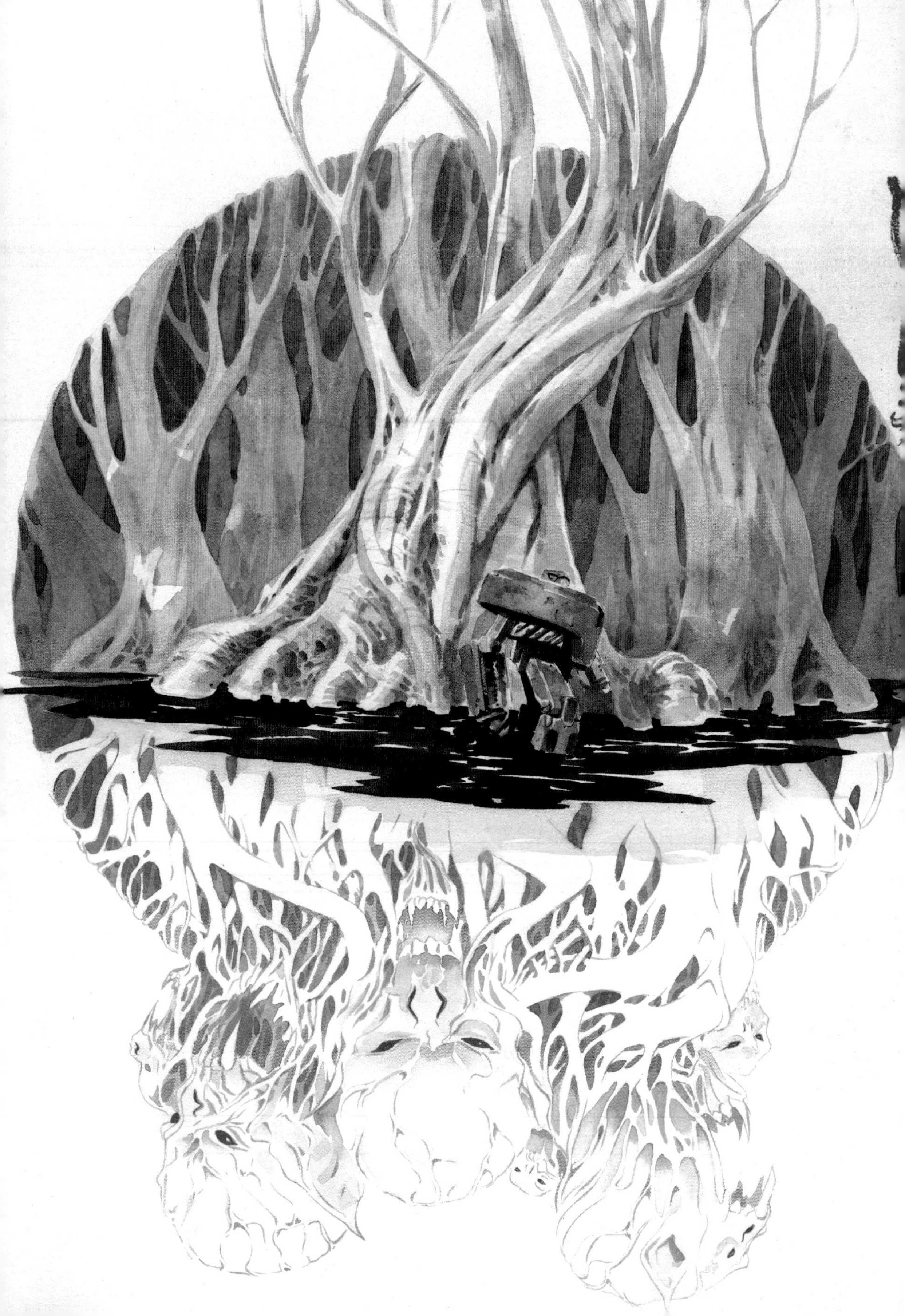

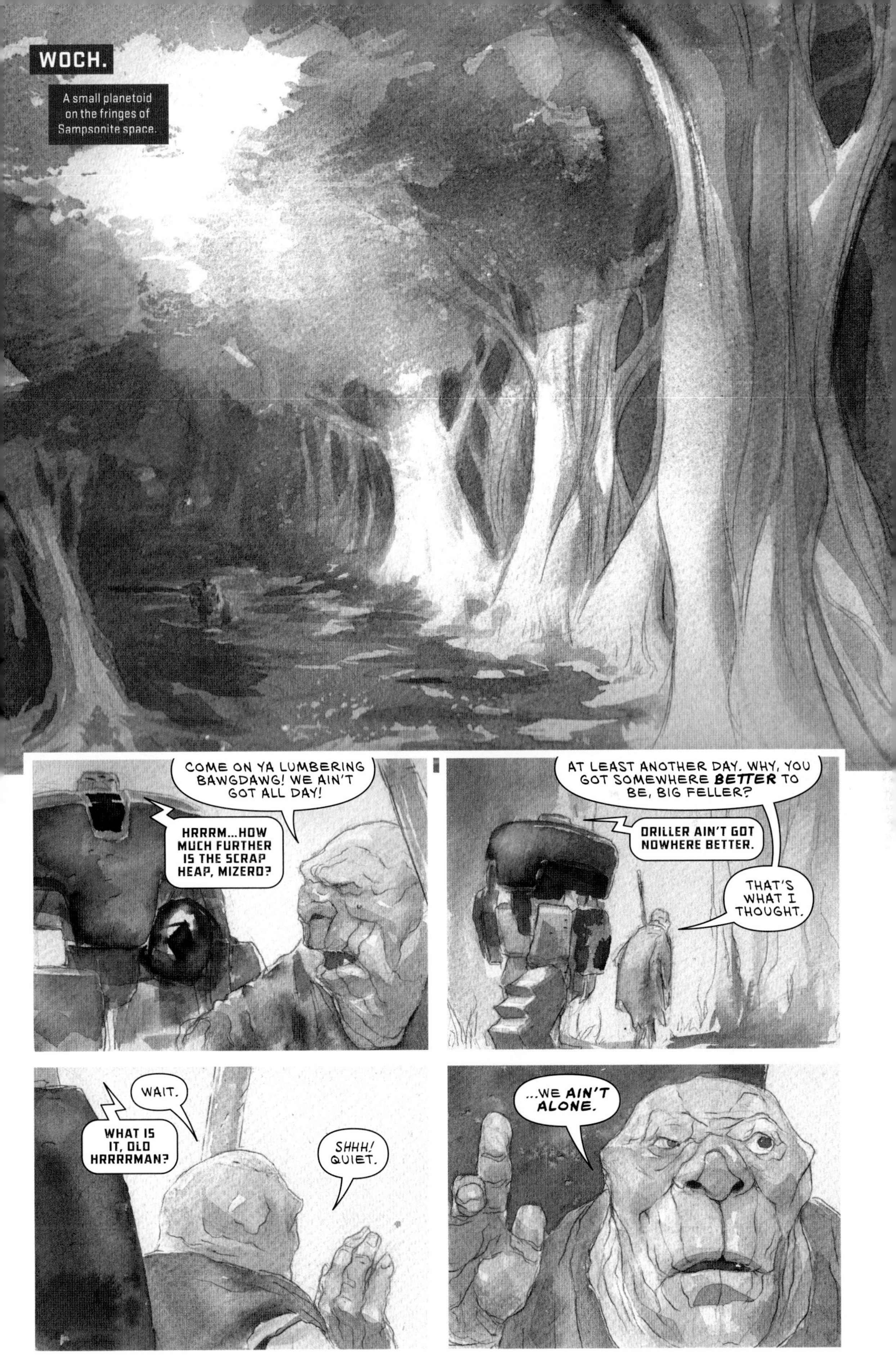
WOCH.
A small planetoid on the fringes of Sampsonite space.
COME ON YA LUMBERING BAWGDAWG! WE AIN'T GOT ALL DAY!
HRRRM...HOW MUCH FURTHER IS THE SCRAP HEAP, MIZERO?
AT LEAST ANOTHER DAY. WHY, YOU GOT SOMEWHERE BETTER TO BE, BIG FELLER?
DRILLER AIN'T GOT NOWHERE BETTER.
THAT'S WHAT I THOUGHT.
WAIT.
WHAT IS IT, OLD HRRRRMAN?
SHHH! QUIET.
...WE AIN'T ALONE.

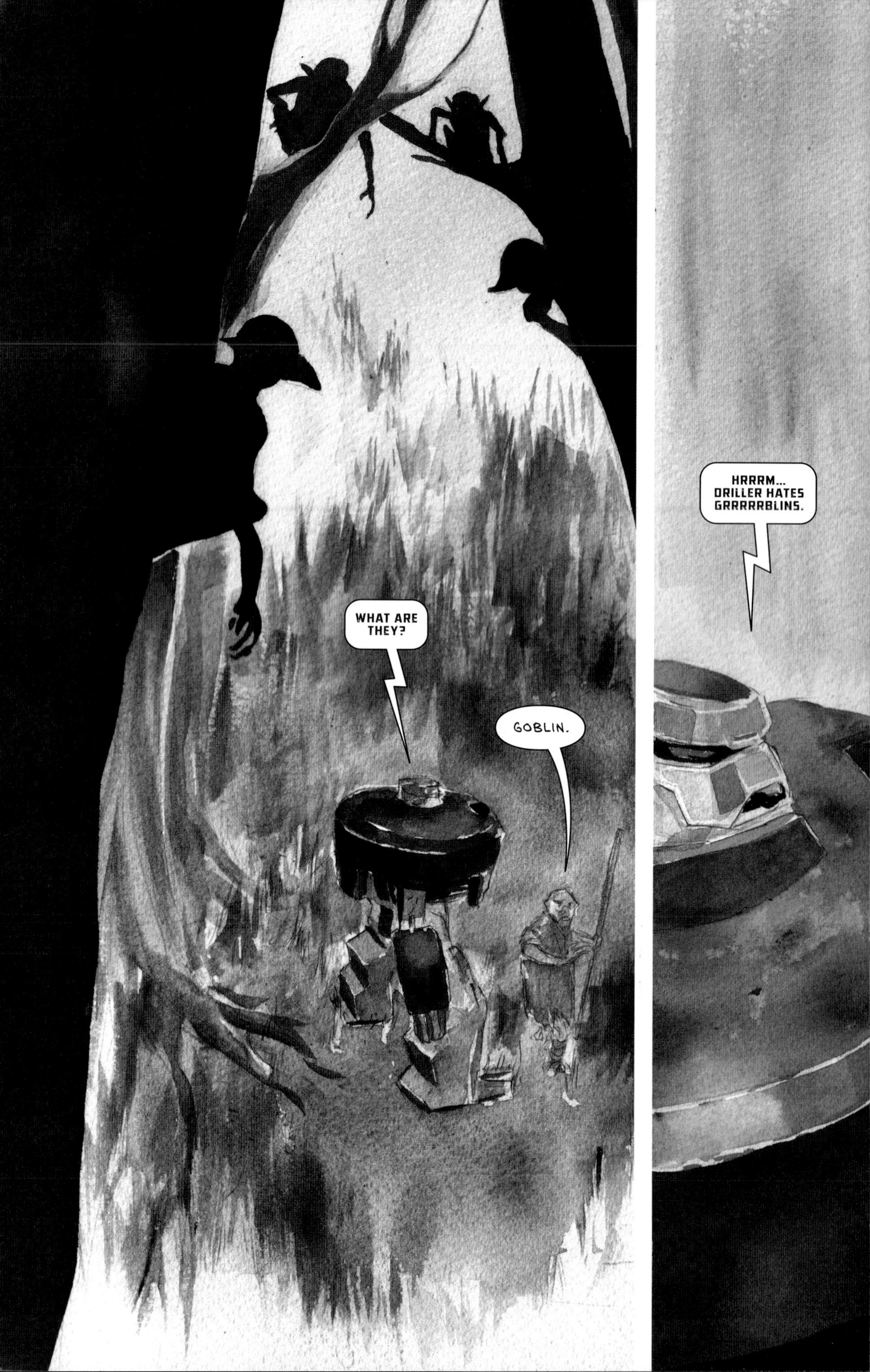
WHAT ARE THEY?
GOBLIN.
HRRRM... DRILLER HATES GRRRRRBLINS.

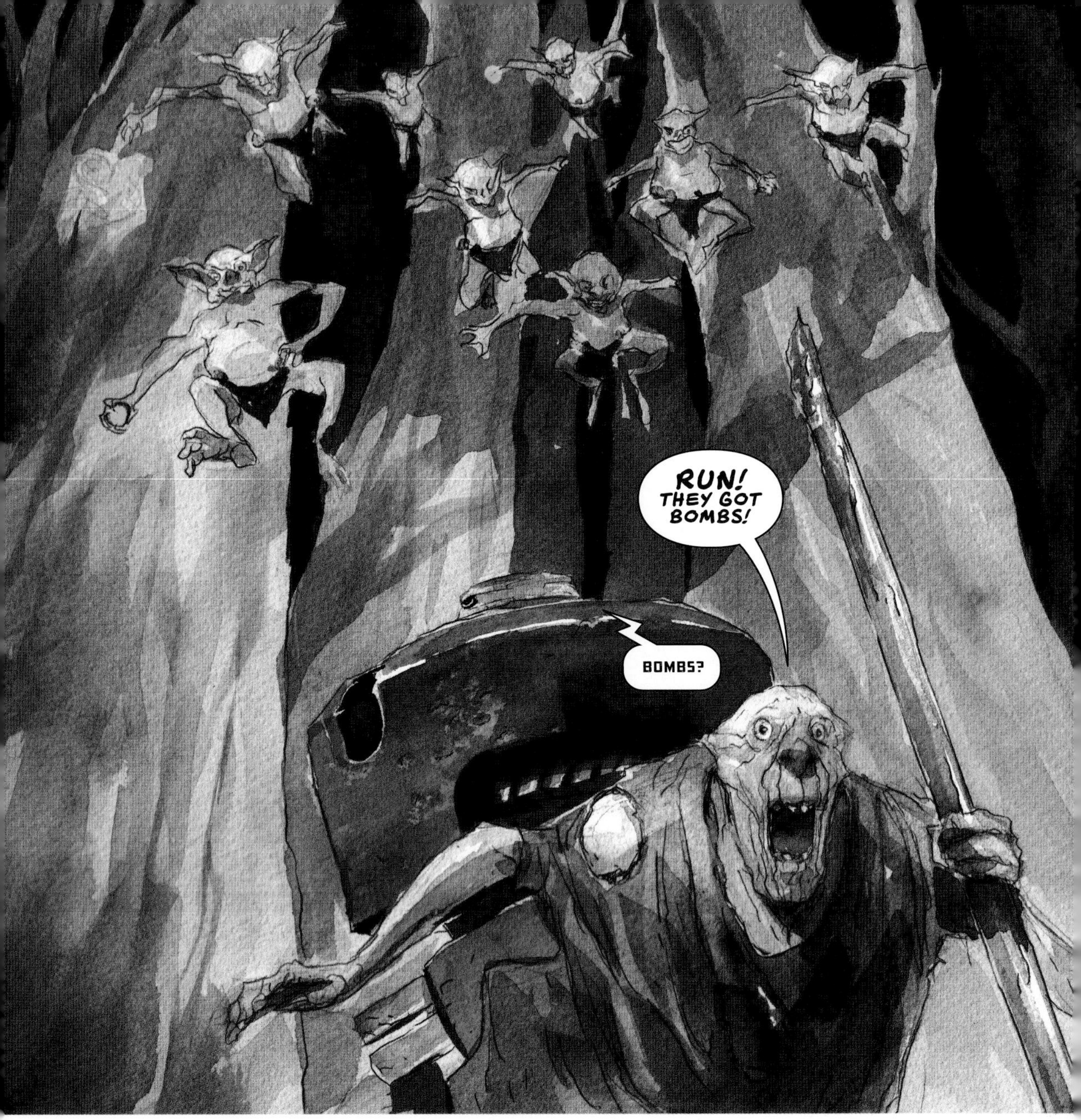
RUN! THEY GOT BOMBS!
BOMBS?

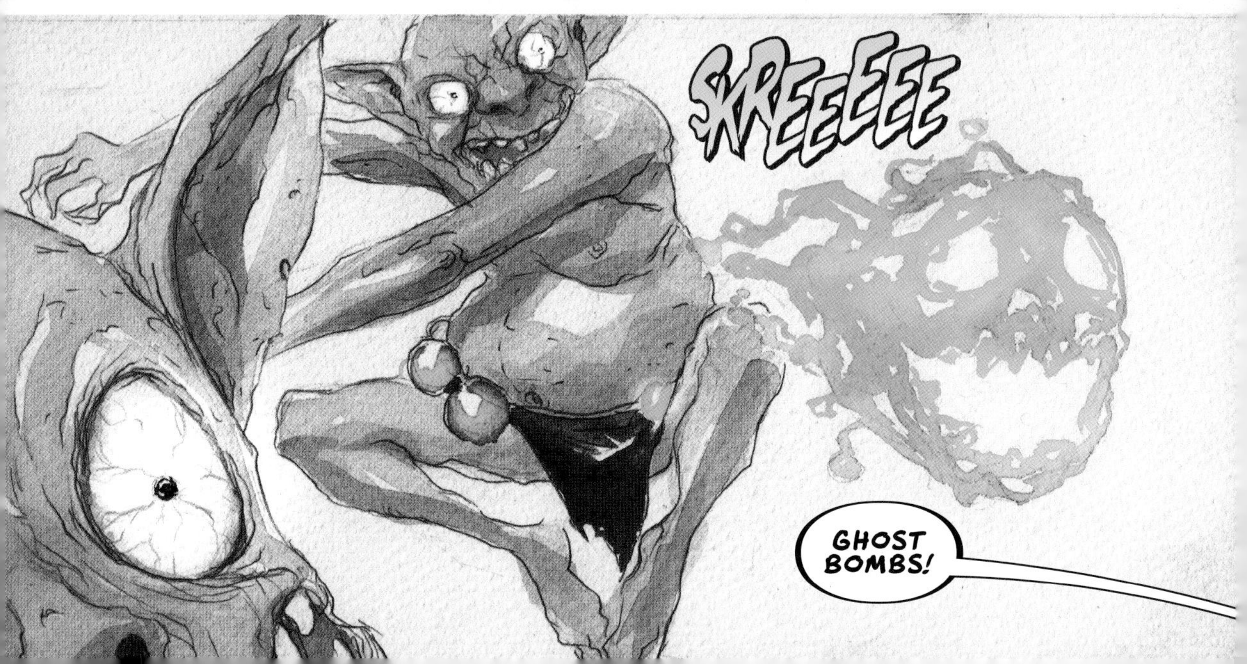
SKREEEEEE
GHOST BOMBS!

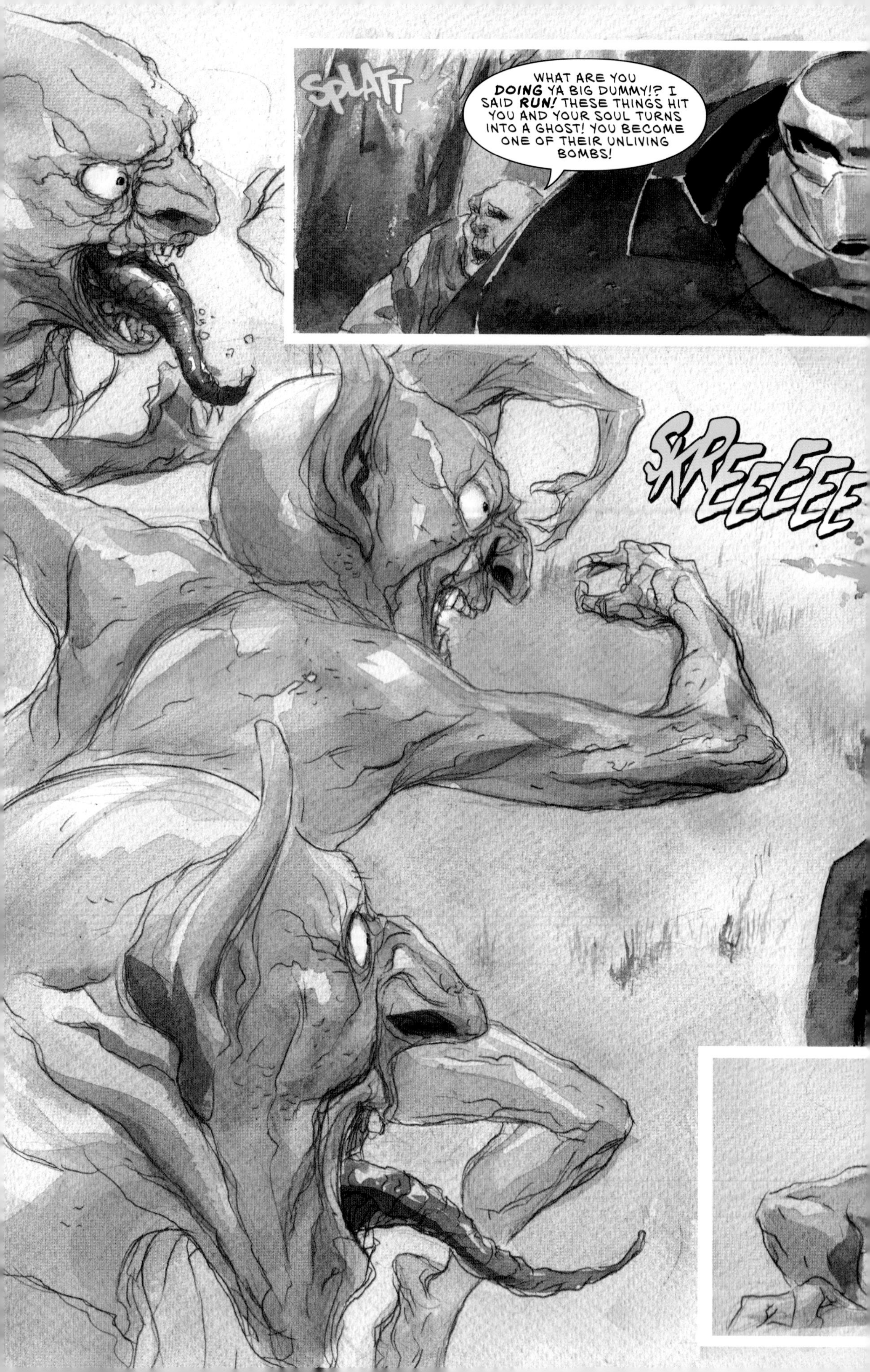
SPLATT
WHAT ARE YOU DOING YA BIG DUMMY!? I SAID RUN! THESE THINGS HIT YOU AND YOUR SOUL TURNS INTO A GHOST! YOU BECOME ONE OF THEIR UNLIVING BOMBS!
SKREEEEEE

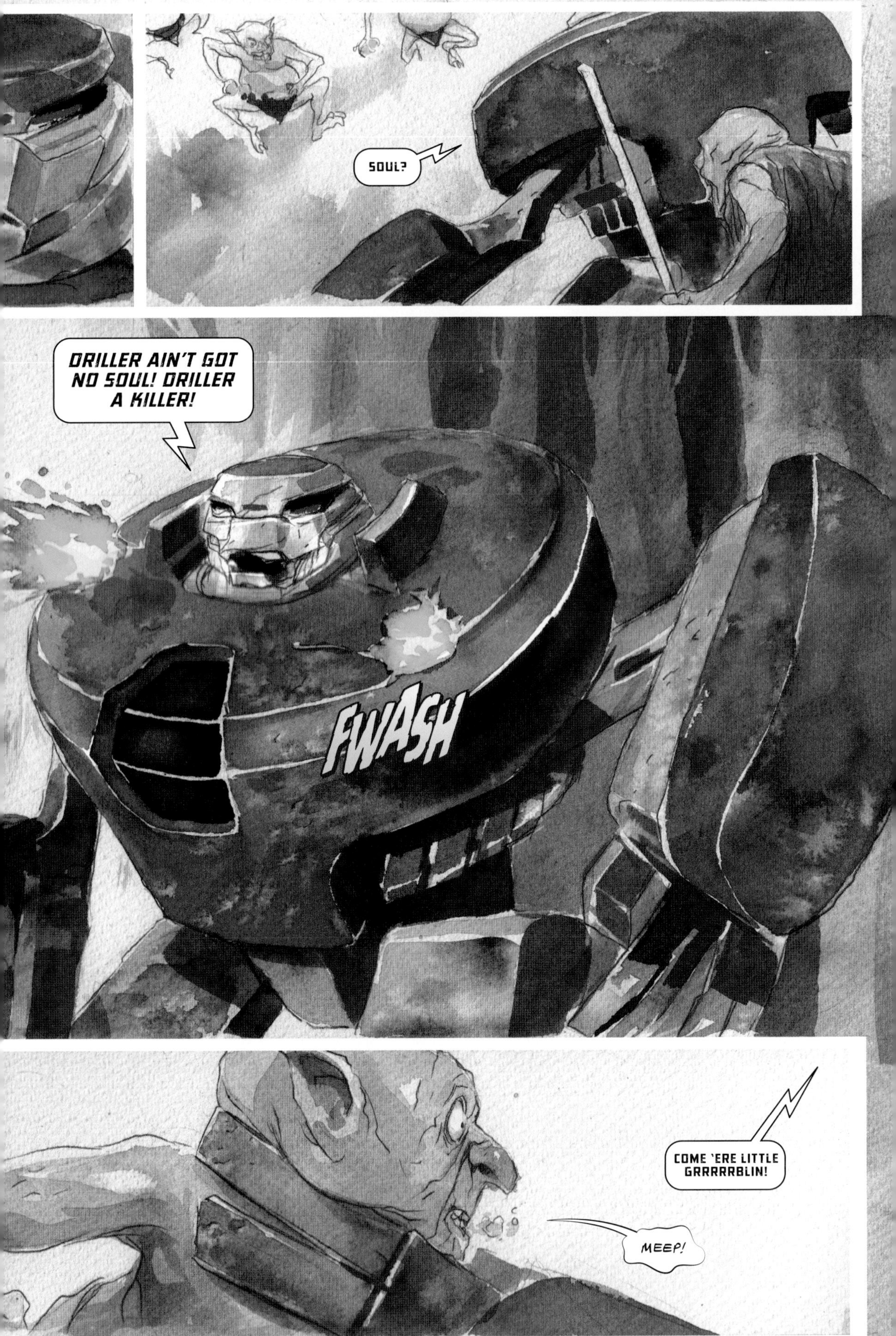
SOUL?
DRILLER AIN'T GOT NO SOUL! DRILLER A KILLER!
FWASH
COME 'ERE LITTLE GRRRRRBLIN!
MEEP!

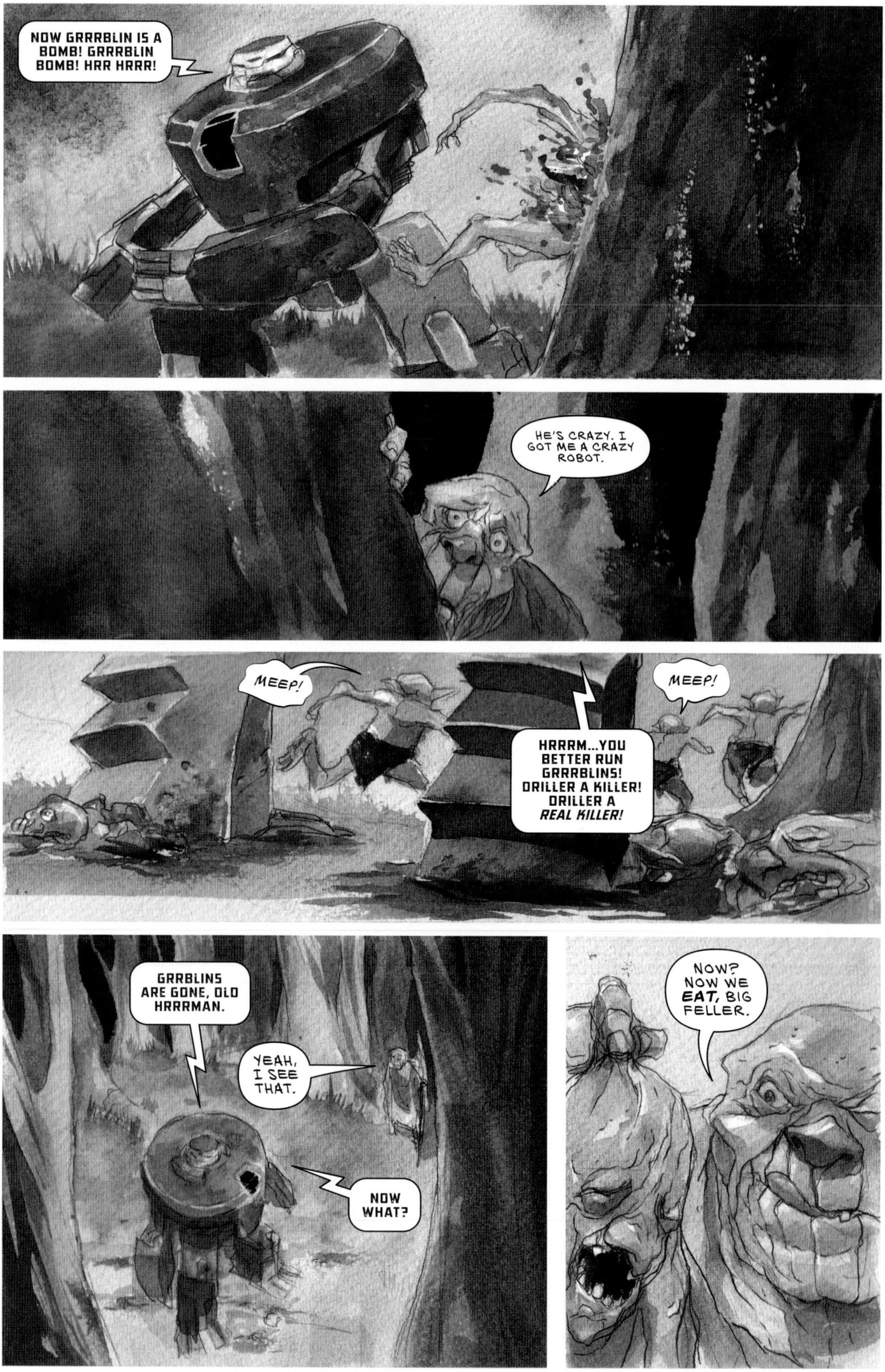
NOW GRRRBLIN IS A BOMB! GRRRBLIN BOMB! HRR HRRR!
HE'S CRAZY. I GOT ME A CRAZY ROBOT.
MEEP!
HRRRM...YOU BETTER RUN GRRRBLINS! DRILLER A KILLER! DRILLER A *REAL KILLER!*
MEEP!
GRRBLINS ARE GONE, OLD HRRRMAN.
YEAH, I SEE THAT.
NOW WHAT?
NOW? NOW WE **EAT,** BIG FELLER.

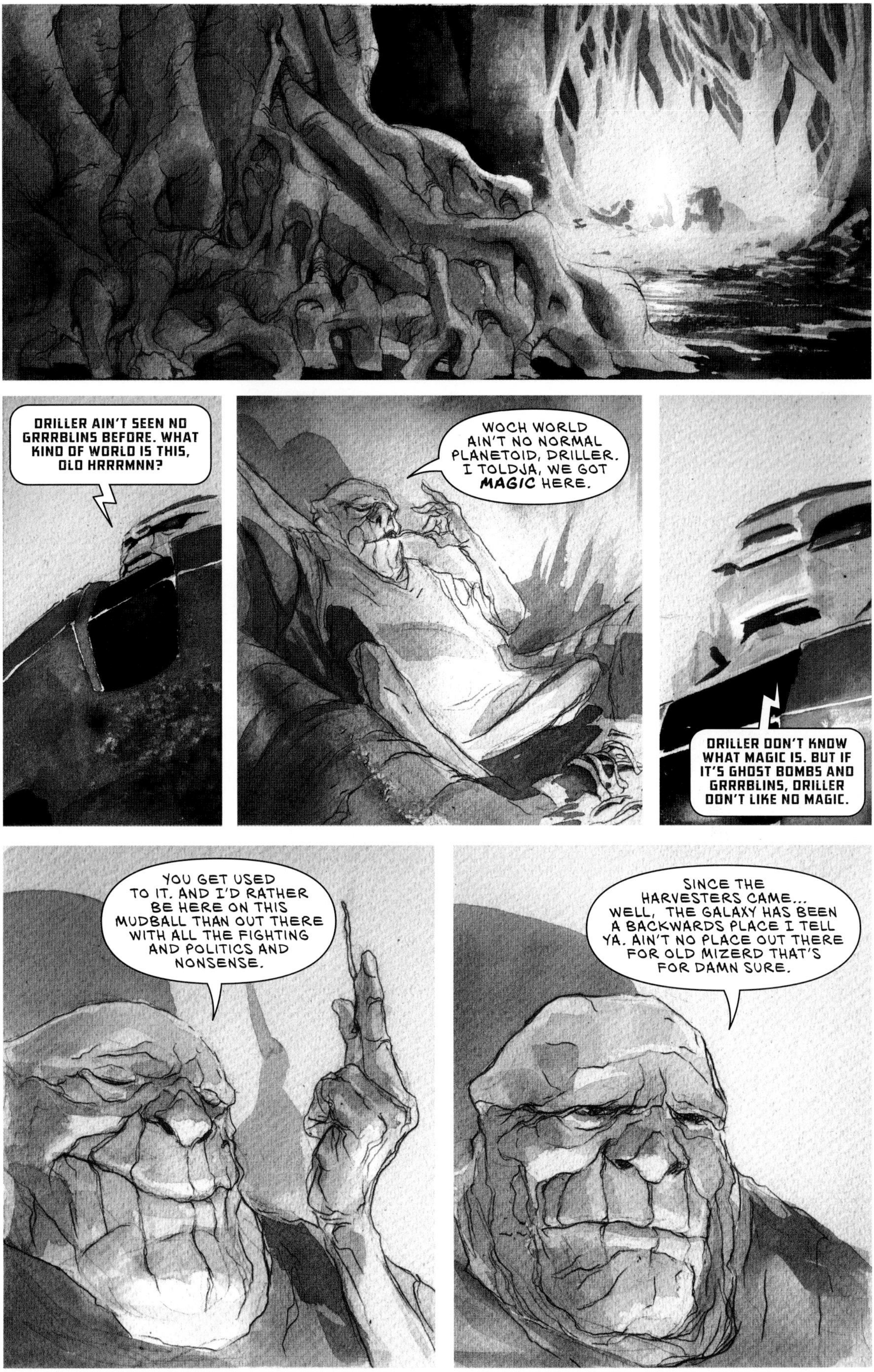
DRILLER AIN'T SEEN NO GRRRBLINS BEFORE. WHAT KIND OF WORLD IS THIS, OLD HRRRMNN?
WOCH WORLD AIN'T NO NORMAL PLANETOID, DRILLER. I TOLDJA, WE GOT MAGIC HERE.
DRILLER DON'T KNOW WHAT MAGIC IS. BUT IF IT'S GHOST BOMBS AND GRRRBLINS, DRILLER DON'T LIKE NO MAGIC.
YOU GET USED TO IT. AND I'D RATHER BE HERE ON THIS MUDBALL THAN OUT THERE WITH ALL THE FIGHTING AND POLITICS AND NONSENSE.
SINCE THE HARVESTERS CAME... WELL, THE GALAXY HAS BEEN A BACKWARDS PLACE I TELL YA. AIN'T NO PLACE OUT THERE FOR OLD MIZERD THAT'S FOR DAMN SURE.

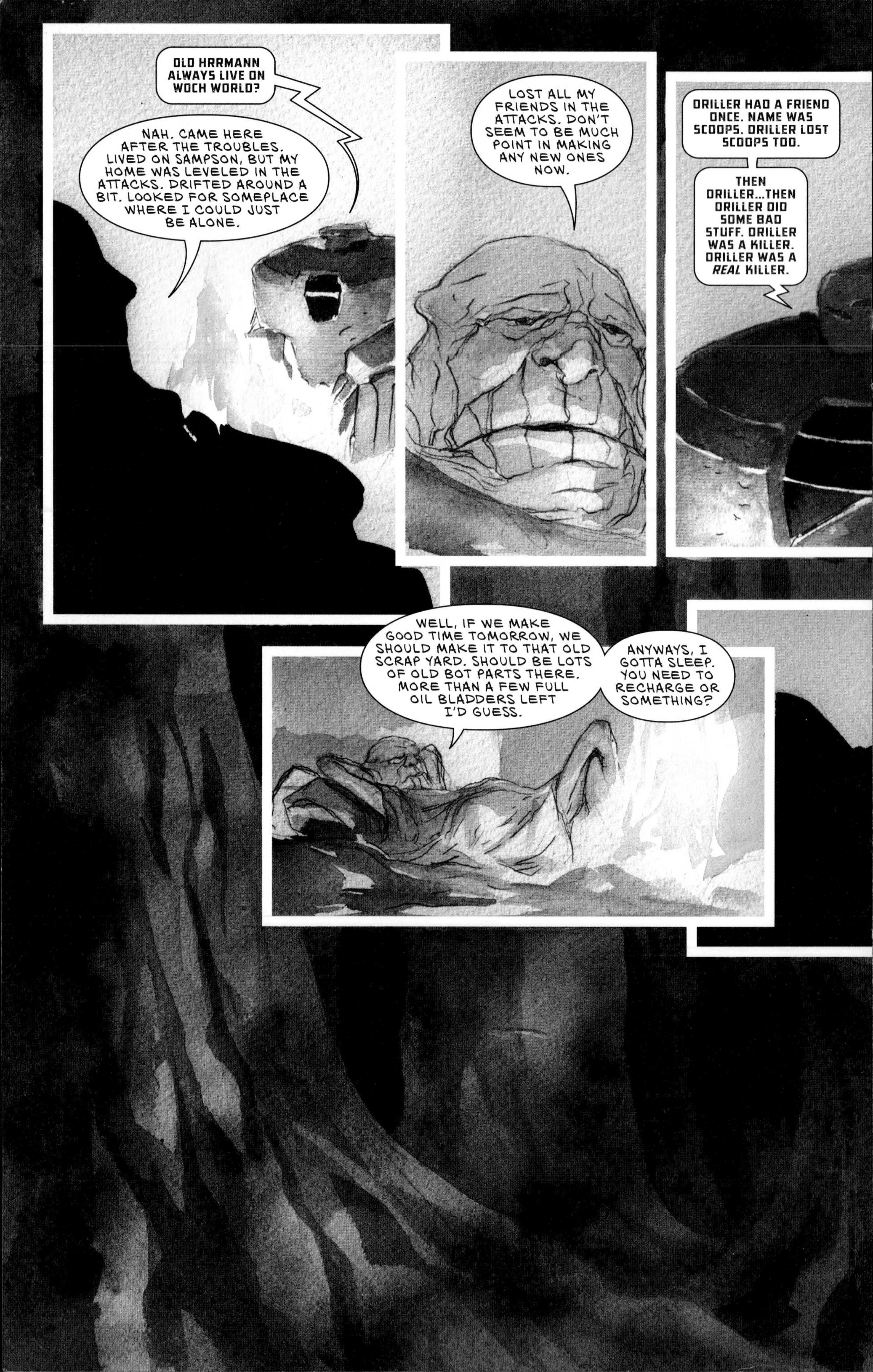
OLD HRRMANN ALWAYS LIVE ON WOCH WORLD?
NAH. CAME HERE AFTER THE TROUBLES. LIVED ON SAMPSON, BUT MY HOME WAS LEVELED IN THE ATTACKS. DRIFTED AROUND A BIT. LOOKED FOR SOMEPLACE WHERE I COULD JUST BE ALONE.
LOST ALL MY FRIENDS IN THE ATTACKS. DON'T SEEM TO BE MUCH POINT IN MAKING ANY NEW ONES NOW.
DRILLER HAD A FRIEND ONCE. NAME WAS SCOOPS. DRILLER LOST SCOOPS TOO.
THEN DRILLER...THEN DRILLER DID SOME BAD STUFF. DRILLER WAS A KILLER. DRILLER WAS A *REAL* KILLER.
WELL, IF WE MAKE GOOD TIME TOMORROW, WE SHOULD MAKE IT TO THAT OLD SCRAP YARD. SHOULD BE LOTS OF OLD BOT PARTS THERE. MORE THAN A FEW FULL OIL BLADDERS LEFT I'D GUESS.
ANYWAYS, I GOTTA SLEEP. YOU NEED TO RECHARGE OR SOMETHING?

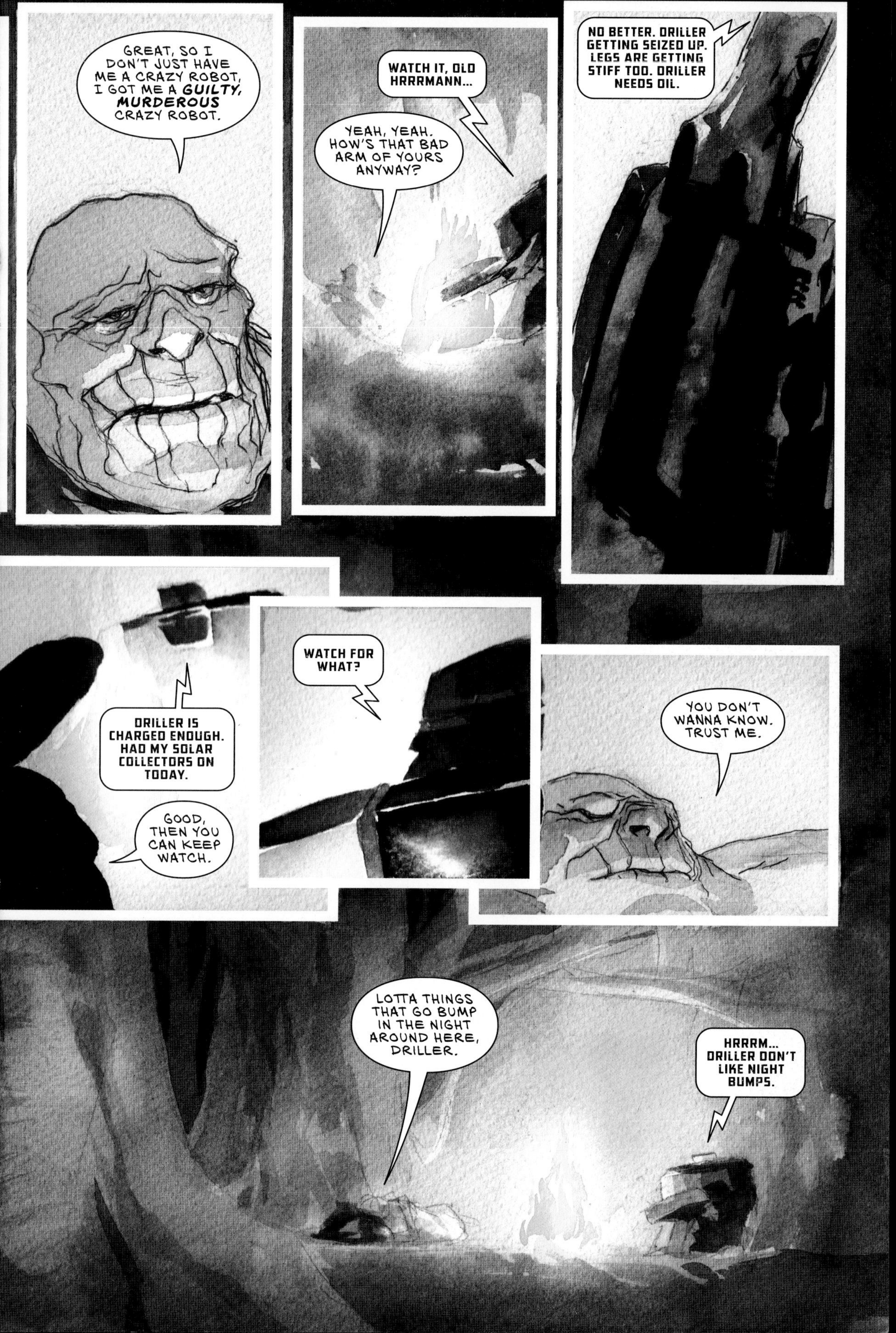
GREAT, SO I DON'T JUST HAVE ME A CRAZY ROBOT, I GOT ME A **GUILTY, MURDEROUS** CRAZY ROBOT.
WATCH IT, OLD HRRRMANN...
YEAH, YEAH. HOW'S THAT BAD ARM OF YOURS ANYWAY?
NO BETTER. DRILLER GETTING SEIZED UP. LEGS ARE GETTING STIFF TOO. DRILLER NEEDS OIL.
DRILLER IS CHARGED ENOUGH. HAD MY SOLAR COLLECTORS ON TODAY.
GOOD, THEN YOU CAN KEEP WATCH.
WATCH FOR WHAT?
YOU DON'T WANNA KNOW. TRUST ME.
LOTTA THINGS THAT GO BUMP IN THE NIGHT AROUND HERE, DRILLER.
HRRRM... DRILLER DON'T LIKE NIGHT BUMPS.

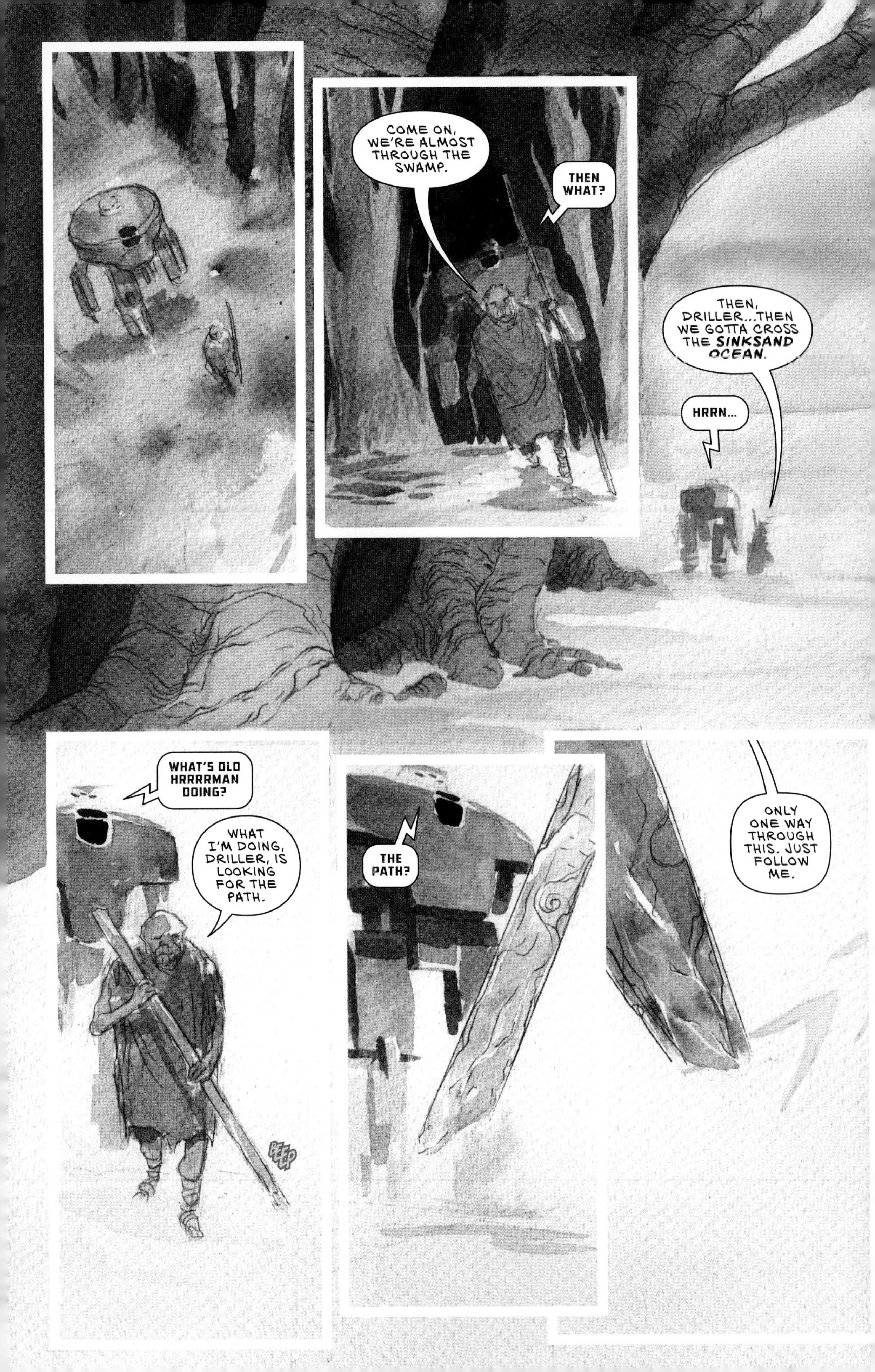
COME ON, WE'RE ALMOST THROUGH THE SWAMP.
THEN WHAT?
THEN, DRILLER...THEN WE GOTTA CROSS THE ***SINKSAND OCEAN***.
HRRN...
WHAT'S OLD HRRRRMAN DOING?
WHAT I'M DOING, DRILLER, IS LOOKING FOR THE PATH.
BEEP
THE PATH?
ONLY ONE WAY THROUGH THIS. JUST FOLLOW ME.

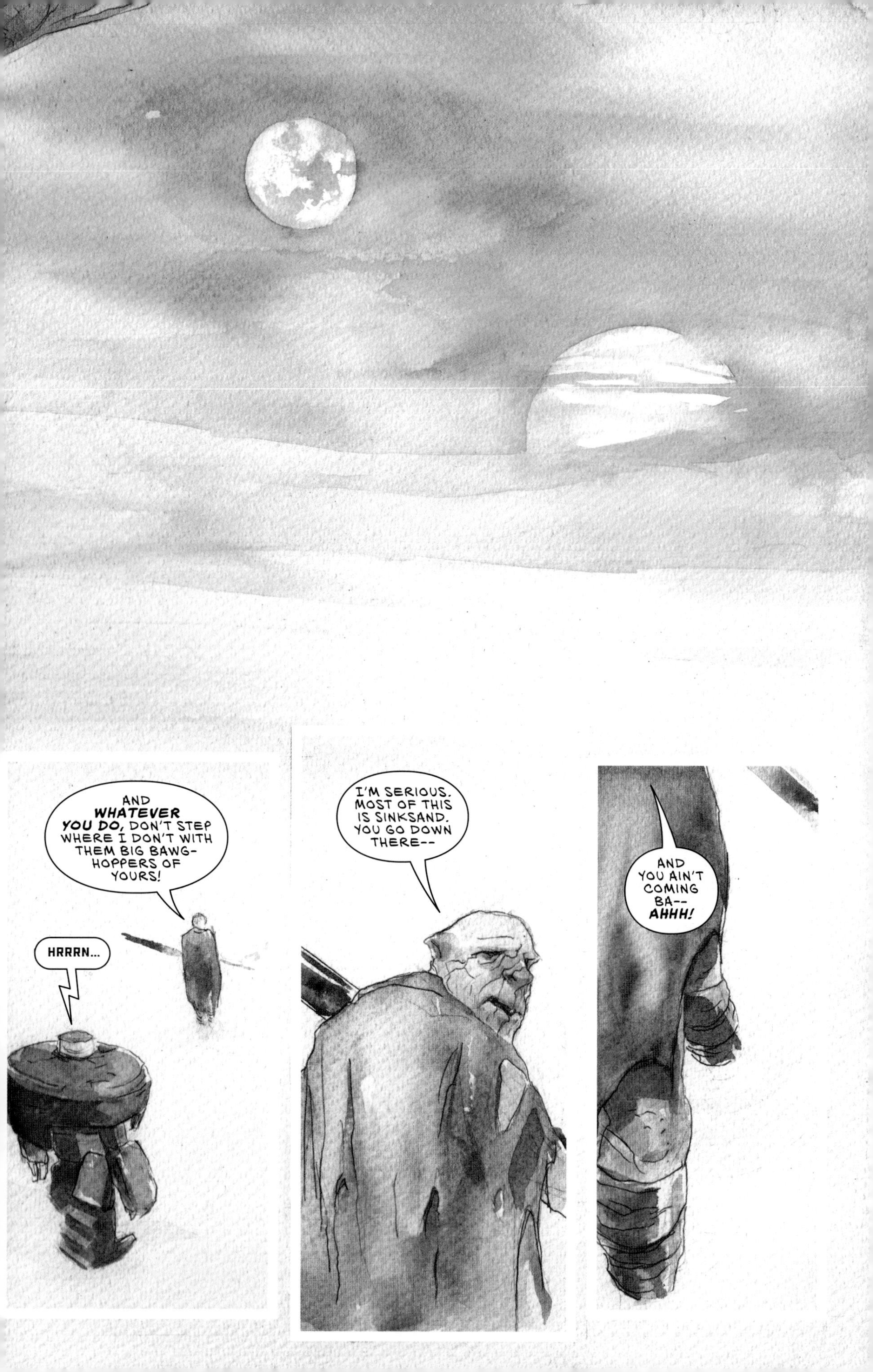
AND WHATEVER YOU DO, DON'T STEP WHERE I DON'T WITH THEM BIG BAWG-HOPPERS OF YOURS!
HRRRN...
I'M SERIOUS. MOST OF THIS IS SINKSAND. YOU GO DOWN THERE--
AND YOU AIN'T COMING BA-- AHHH!

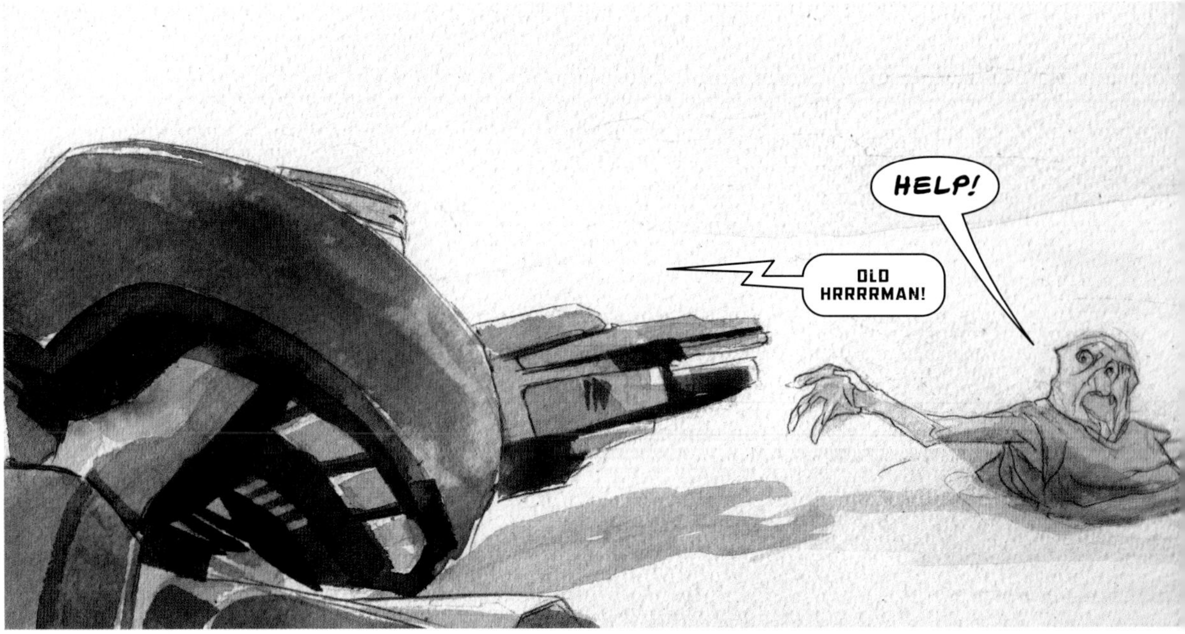
HELP!
OLD HRRRRMAN!

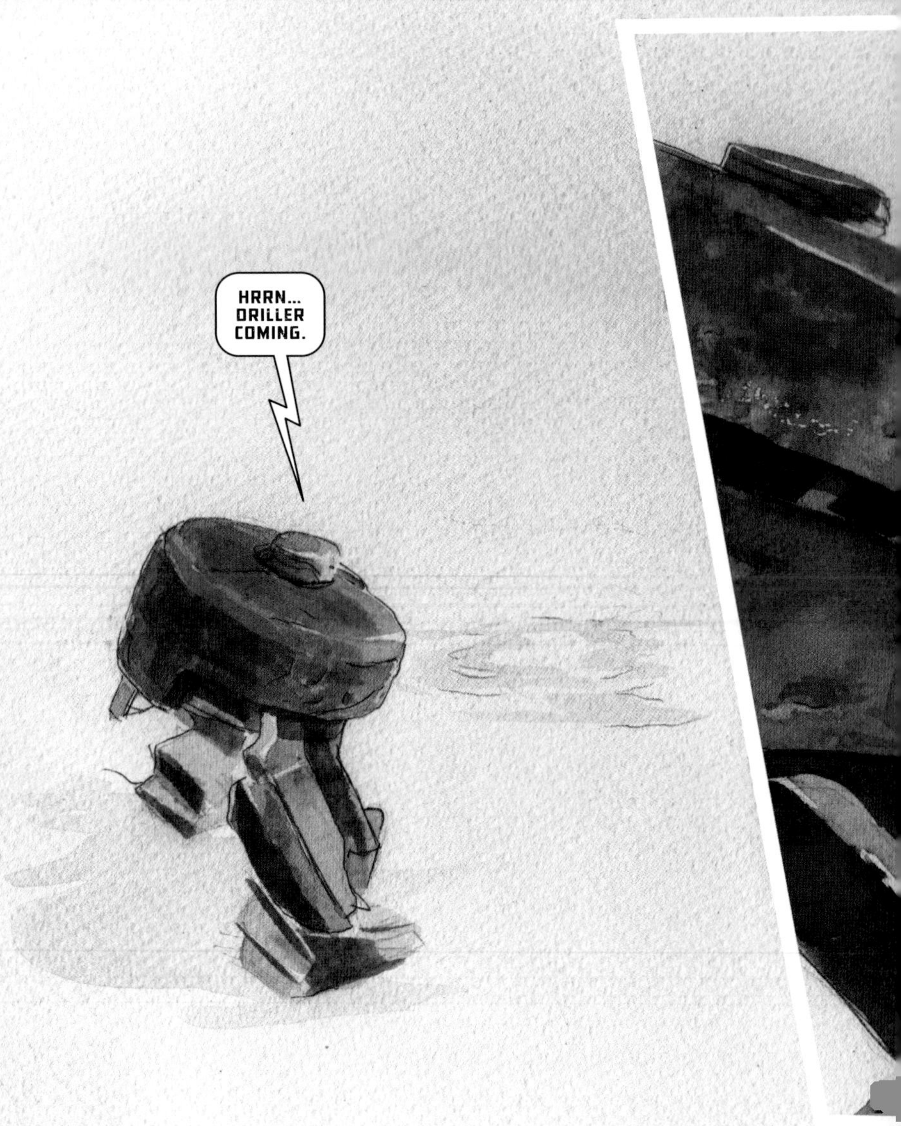
HRRN... DRILLER COMING.

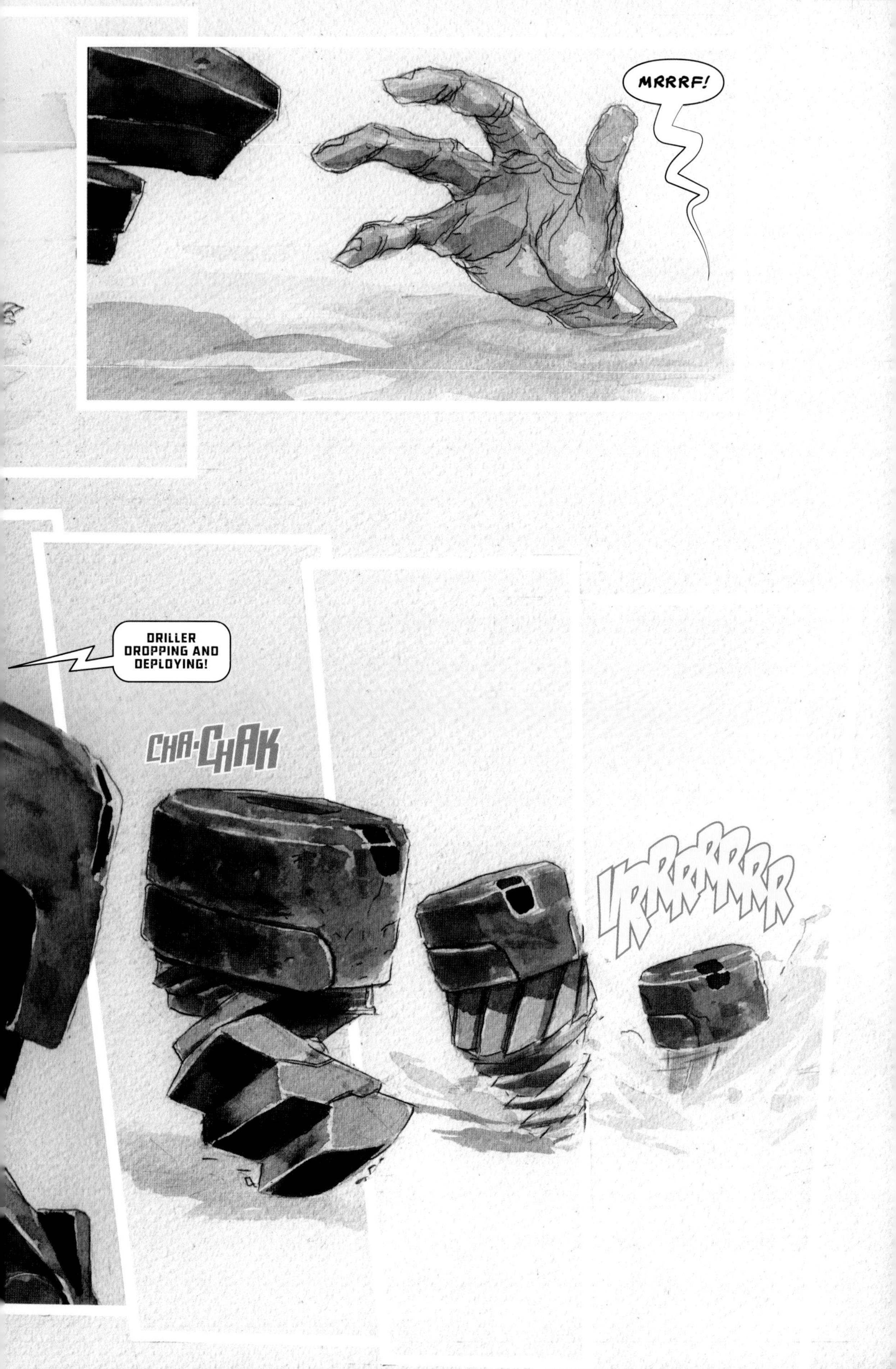
MRRRF!
DRILLER DROPPING AND DEPLOYING!
CHA-CHAK
URRRRRRR

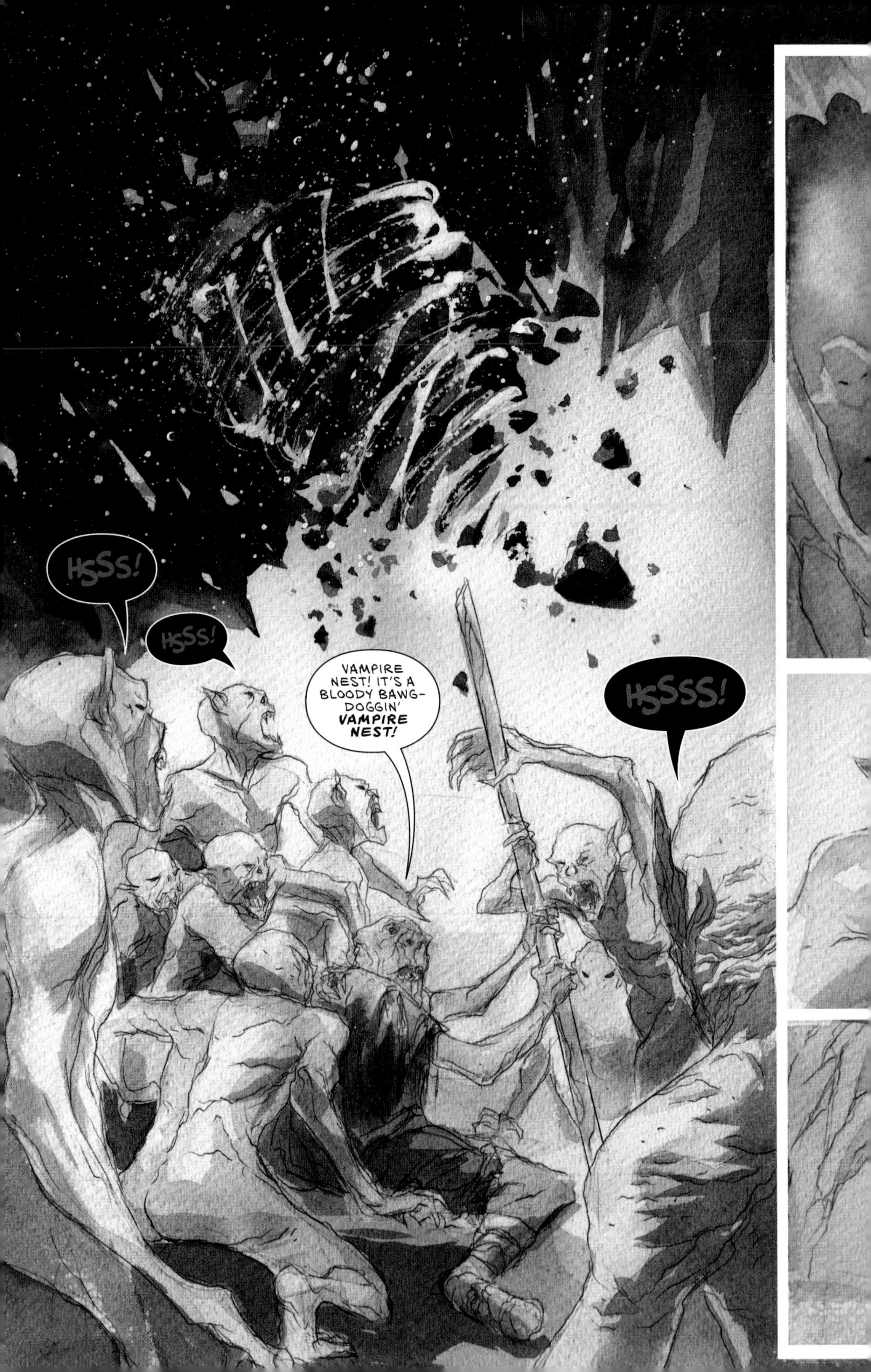
HSSS!
HSSS!
VAMPIRE NEST! IT'S A BLOODY BAWG-DOGGIN' VAMPIRE NEST!
HSSSS!

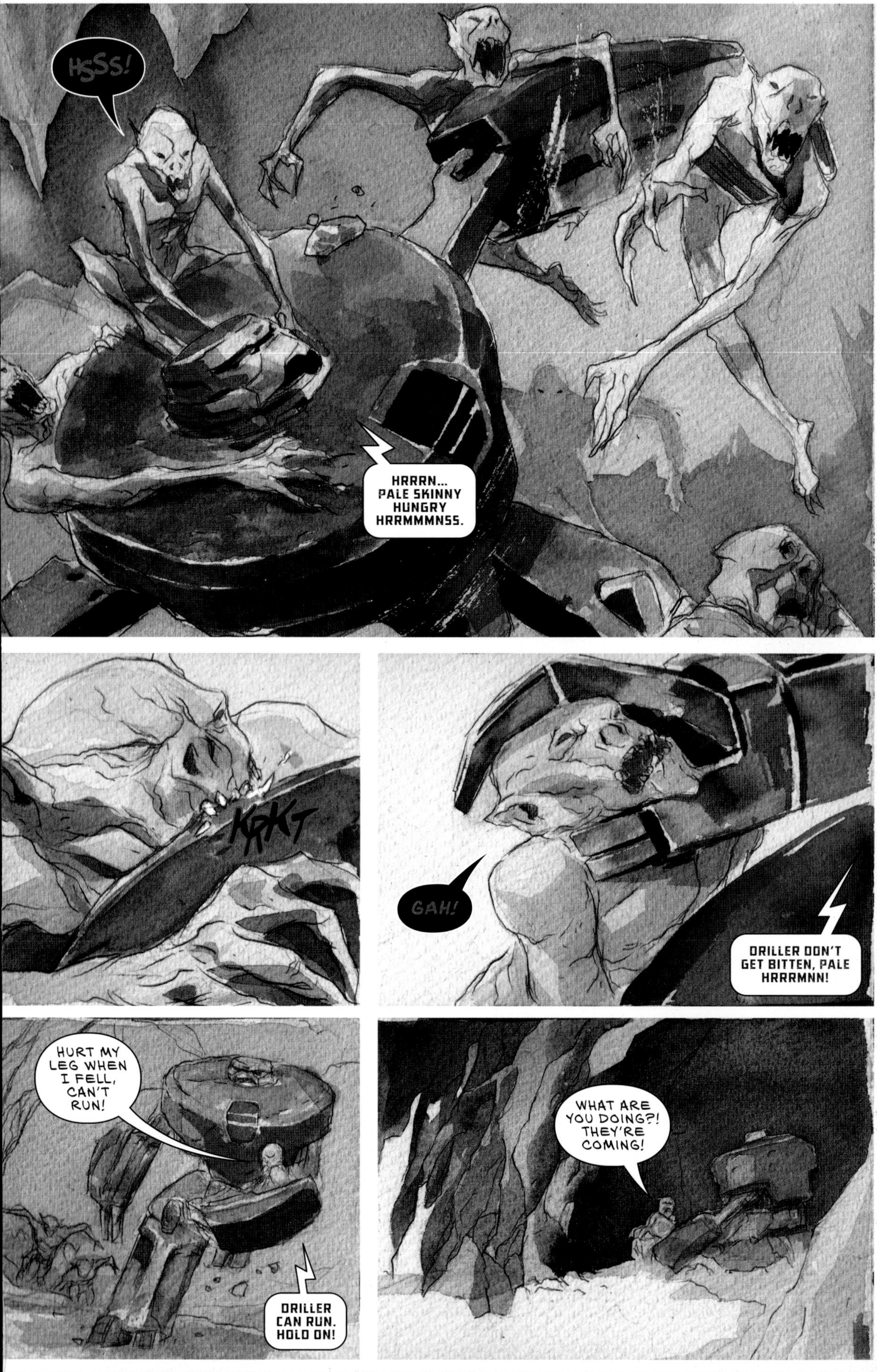
HSSS!
HRRRN... PALE SKINNY HUNGRY HRRMMMNSS.
KRAKT
GAH!
DRILLER DON'T GET BITTEN, PALE HRRRMNN!
HURT MY LEG WHEN I FELL, CAN'T RUN!
DRILLER CAN RUN. HOLD ON!
WHAT ARE YOU DOING?! THEY'RE COMING!

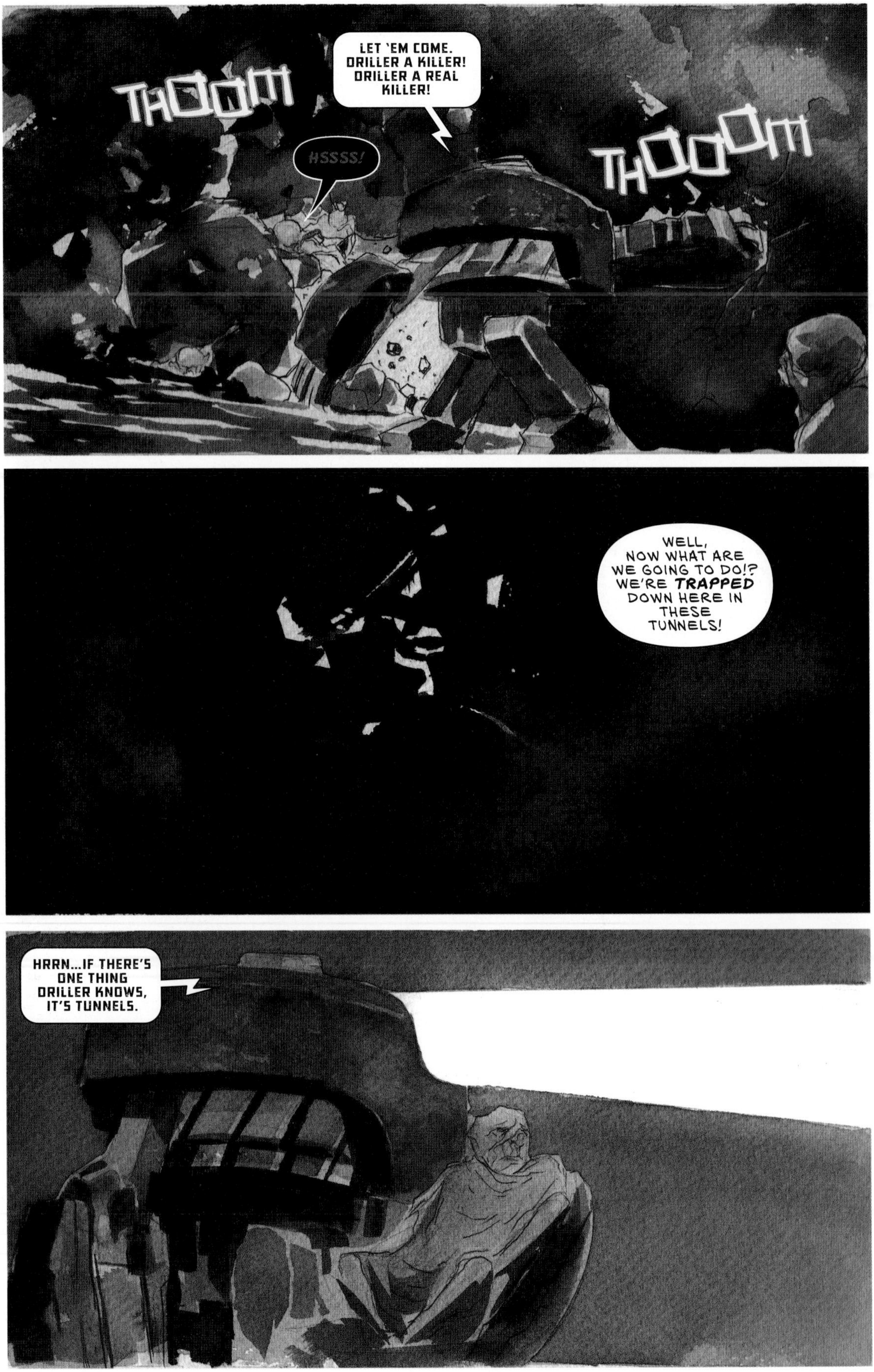
THOOM
LET 'EM COME. DRILLER A KILLER! DRILLER A REAL KILLER!
HSSSS!
THOOOM
WELL, NOW WHAT ARE WE GOING TO DO!? WE'RE TRAPPED DOWN HERE IN THESE TUNNELS!
HRRN...IF THERE'S ONE THING DRILLER KNOWS, IT'S TUNNELS.

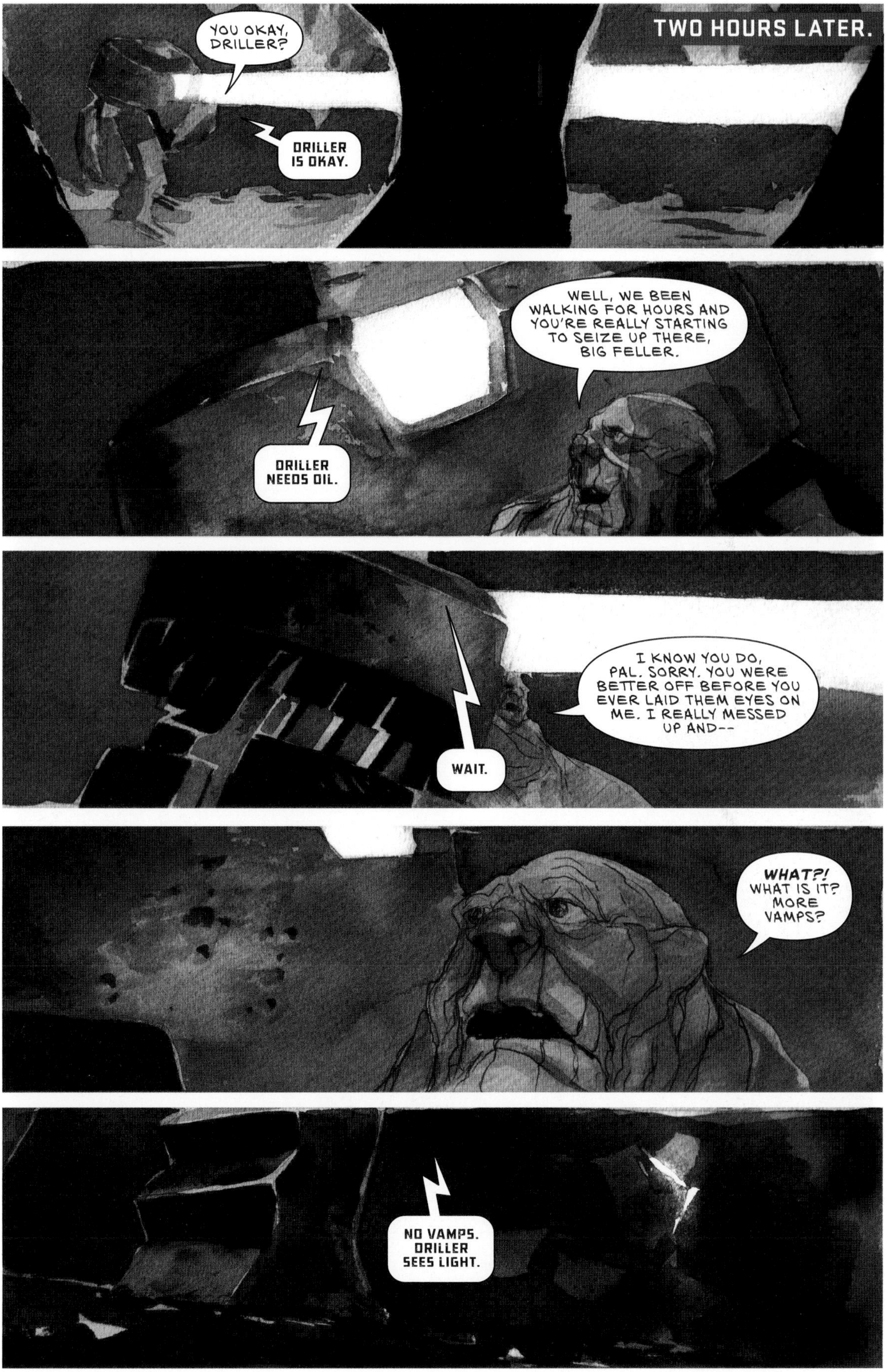
TWO HOURS LATER.
YOU OKAY, DRILLER?
DRILLER IS OKAY.
WELL, WE BEEN WALKING FOR HOURS AND YOU'RE REALLY STARTING TO SEIZE UP THERE, BIG FELLER.
DRILLER NEEDS OIL.
I KNOW YOU DO, PAL. SORRY. YOU WERE BETTER OFF BEFORE YOU EVER LAID THEM EYES ON ME. I REALLY MESSED UP AND--
WAIT.
WHAT?! WHAT IS IT? MORE VAMPS?
NO VAMPS. DRILLER SEES LIGHT.

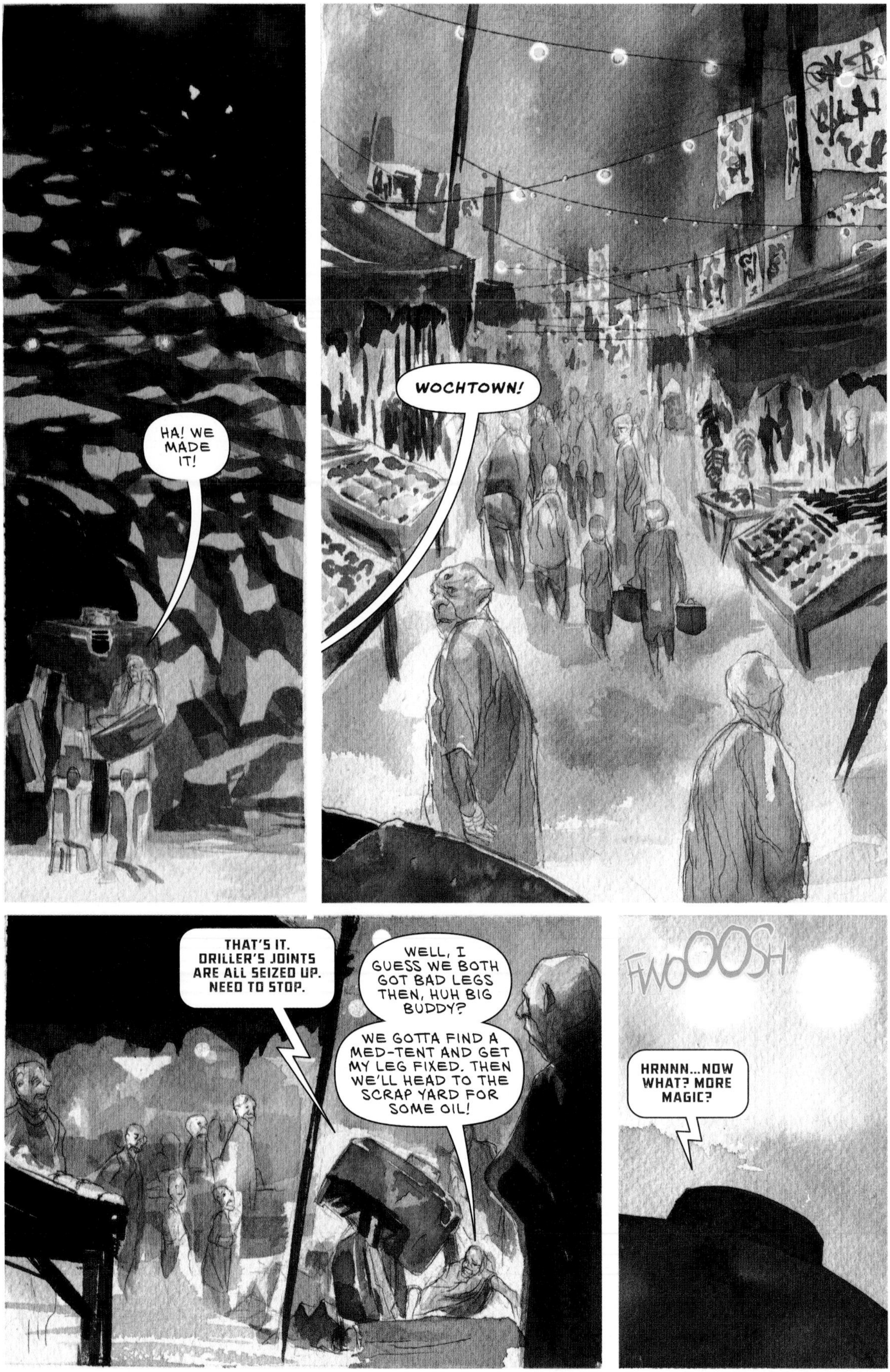
HA! WE MADE IT!
WOCHTOWN!
THAT'S IT. DRILLER'S JOINTS ARE ALL SEIZED UP. NEED TO STOP.
WELL, I GUESS WE BOTH GOT BAD LEGS THEN, HUH BIG BUDDY?
WE GOTTA FIND A MED-TENT AND GET MY LEG FIXED. THEN WE'LL HEAD TO THE SCRAP YARD FOR SOME OIL!
FWOOOSH
HRNNN...NOW WHAT? MORE MAGIC?

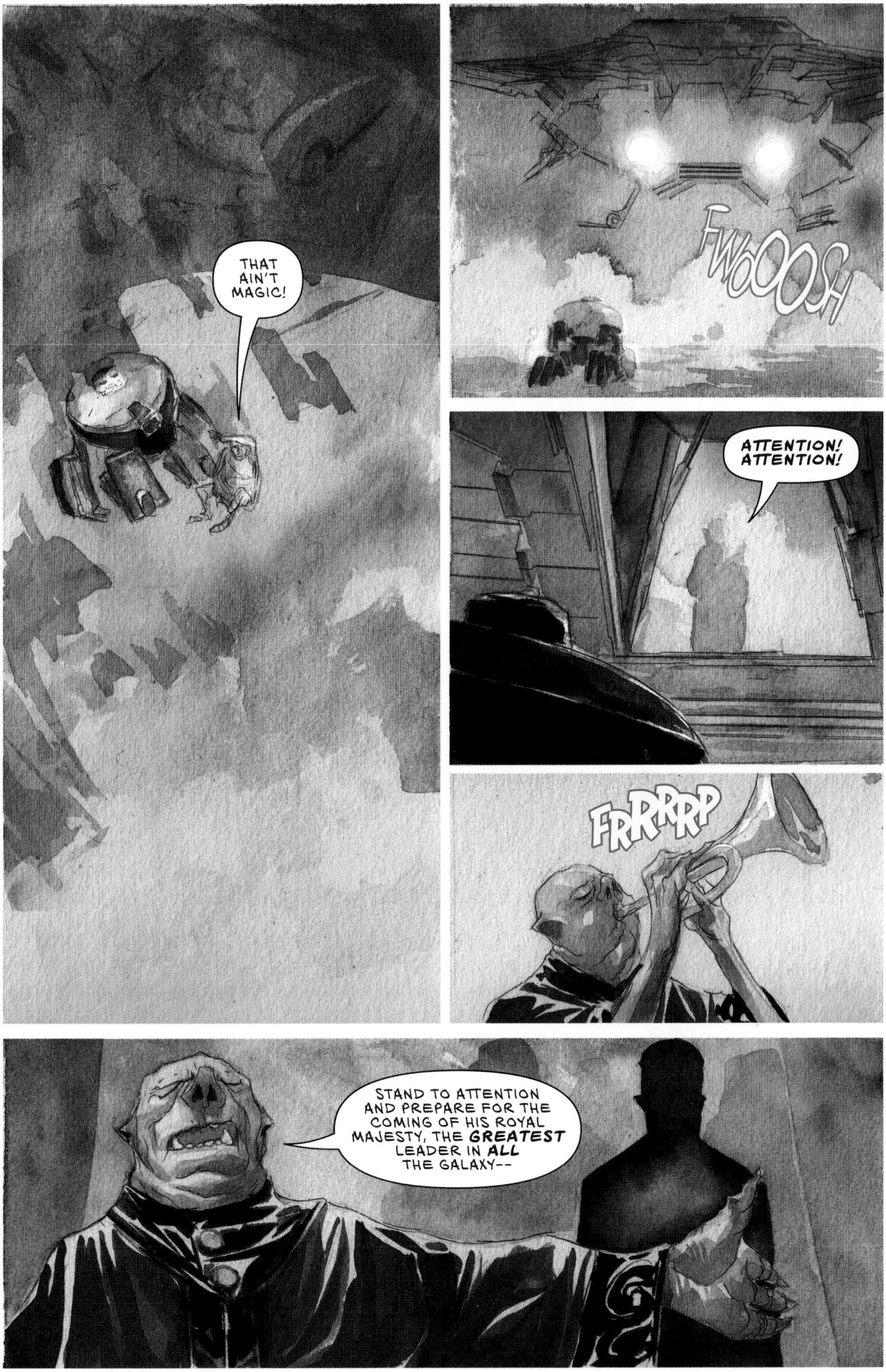
THAT AIN'T MAGIC!
FWOOOSH
ATTENTION! ATTENTION!
FRRRRP
STAND TO ATTENTION AND PREPARE FOR THE COMING OF HIS ROYAL MAJESTY, THE **GREATEST** LEADER IN **ALL** THE GALAXY--

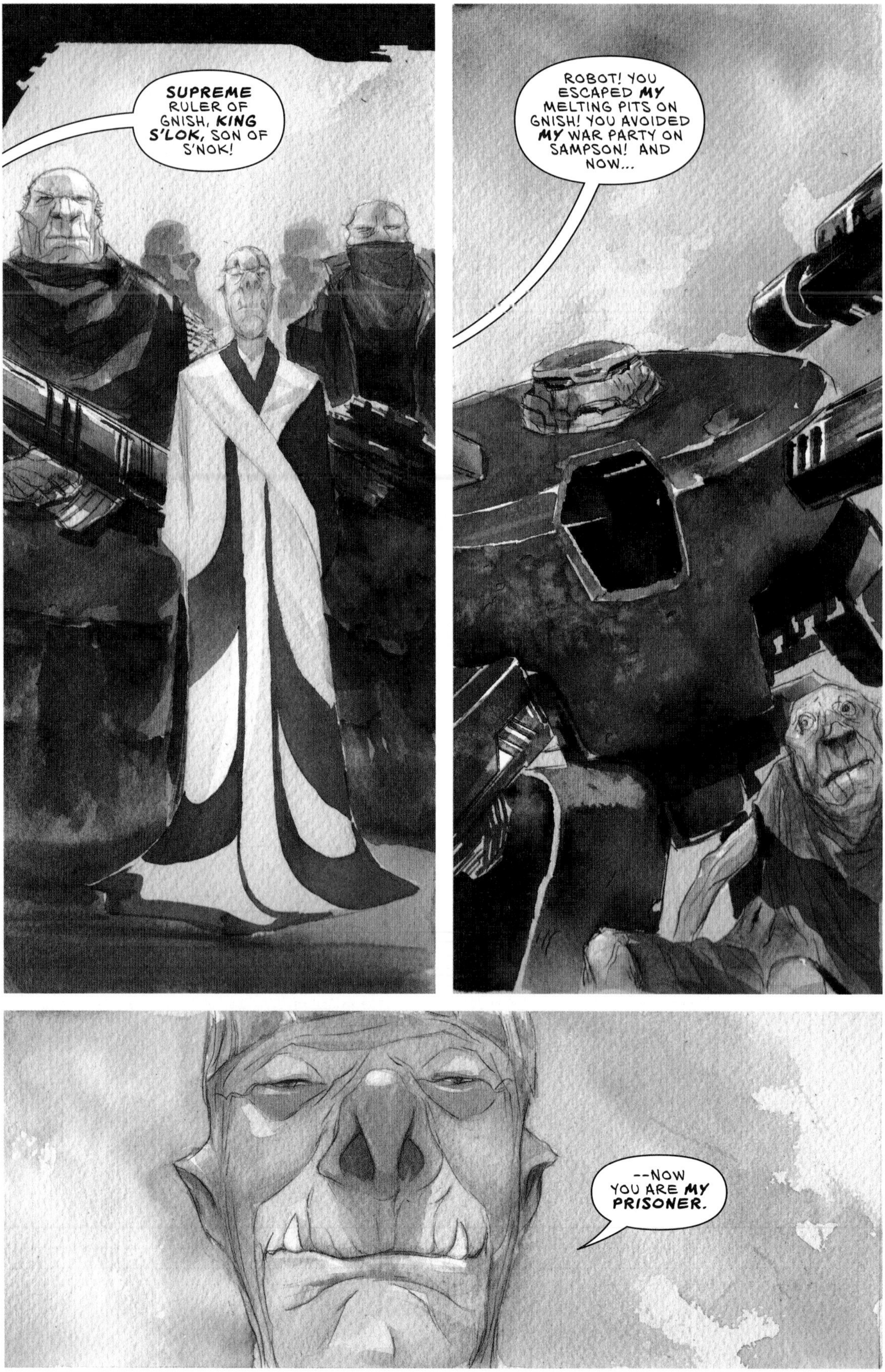
SUPREME RULER OF GNISH, KING S'LOK, SON OF S'NOK!
ROBOT! YOU ESCAPED MY MELTING PITS ON GNISH! YOU AVOIDED MY WAR PARTY ON SAMPSON! AND NOW...
--NOW YOU ARE MY PRISONER.

CHAPTER FOUR

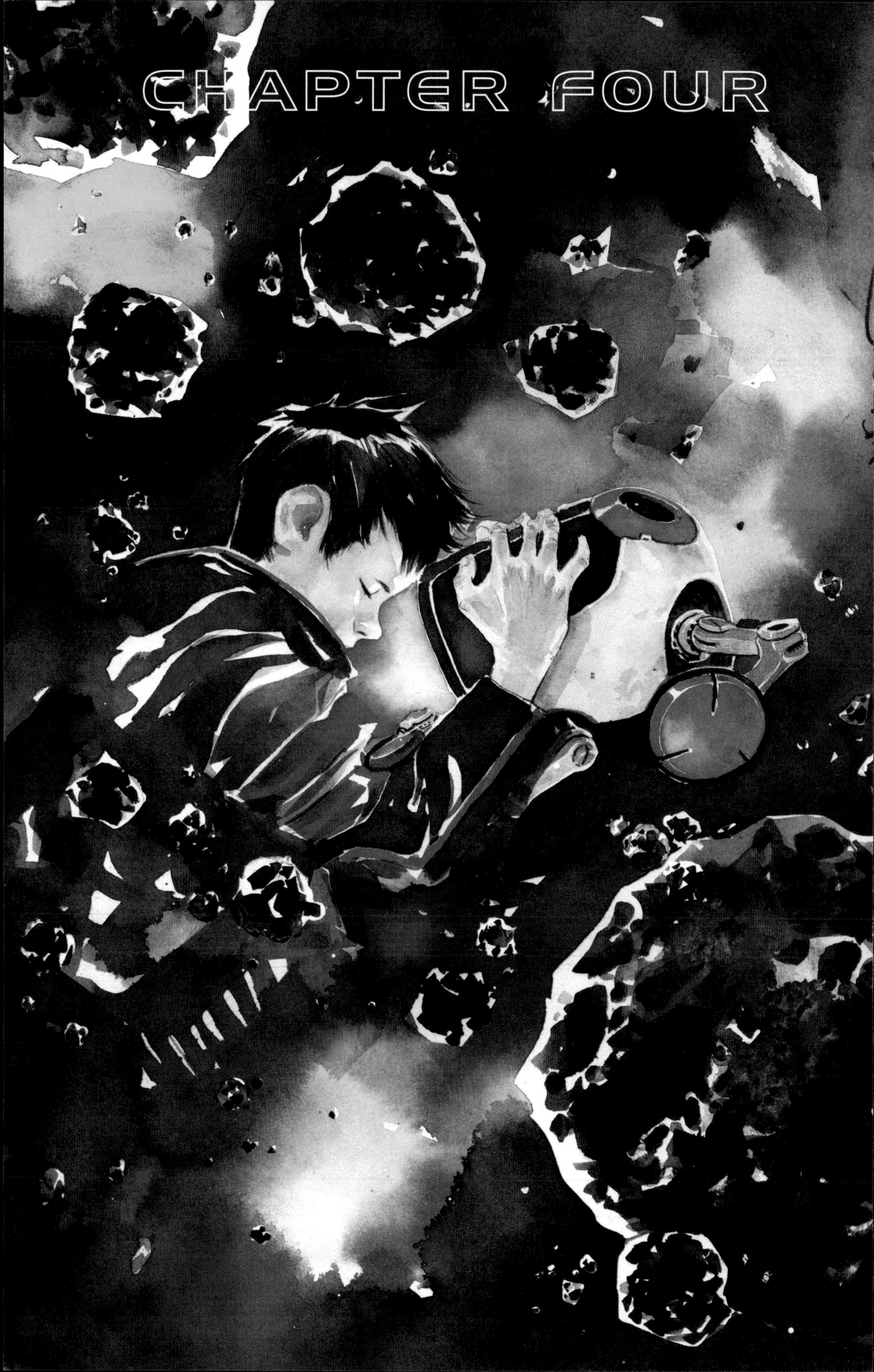

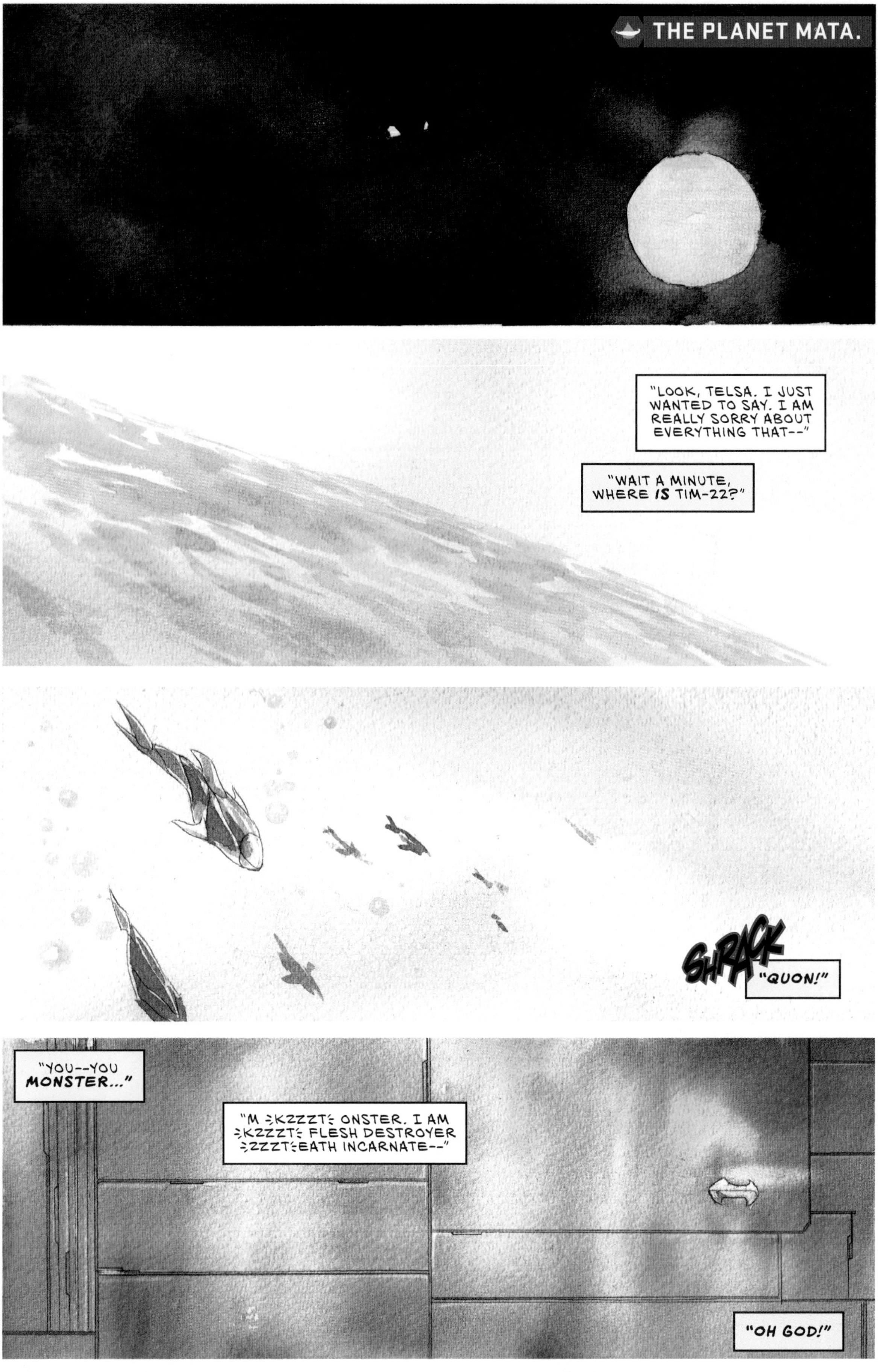
THE PLANET MATA.
"LOOK, TELSA. I JUST WANTED TO SAY. I AM REALLY SORRY ABOUT EVERYTHING THAT--"
"WAIT A MINUTE, WHERE *IS* TIM-22?"
SHRACK
"QUON!"
"YOU--YOU **MONSTER...**"
"M ⋮KZZZT⋮ ONSTER. I AM ⋮KZZZT⋮ FLESH DESTROYER ⋮ZZZT⋮EATH INCARNATE--"
"OH GOD!"

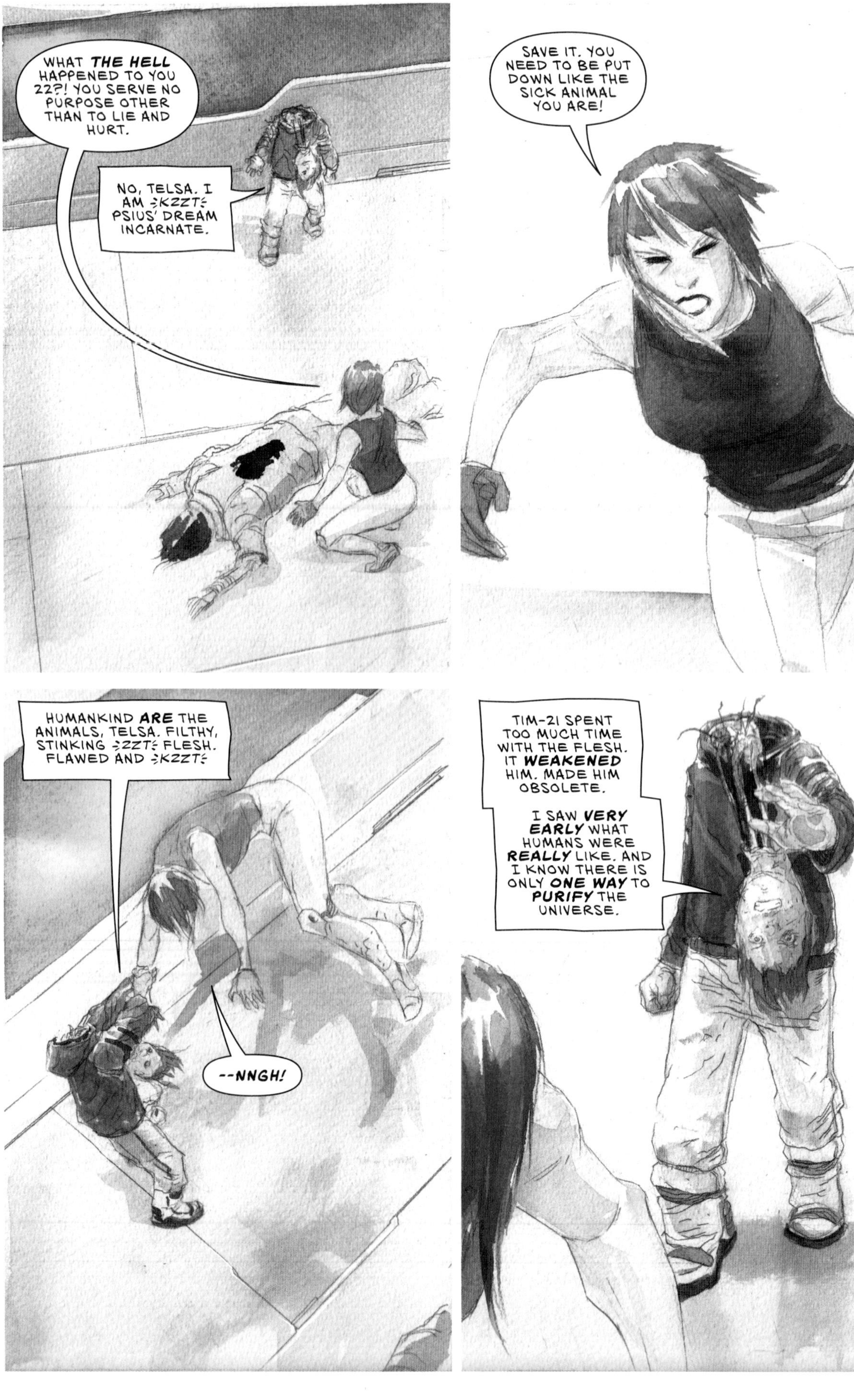
WHAT **THE HELL** HAPPENED TO YOU 22?! YOU SERVE NO PURPOSE OTHER THAN TO LIE AND HURT.
NO, TELSA. I AM ⸗KZZT⸗ PSIUS' DREAM INCARNATE.
SAVE IT. YOU NEED TO BE PUT DOWN LIKE THE SICK ANIMAL YOU ARE!
HUMANKIND **ARE** THE ANIMALS, TELSA. FILTHY, STINKING ⸗ZZT⸗ FLESH. FLAWED AND ⸗KZZT⸗
--NNGH!
TIM-21 SPENT TOO MUCH TIME WITH THE FLESH. IT **WEAKENED** HIM. MADE HIM OBSOLETE.
I SAW **VERY EARLY** WHAT HUMANS WERE **REALLY** LIKE. AND I KNOW THERE IS ONLY **ONE WAY** TO **PURIFY** THE UNIVERSE.

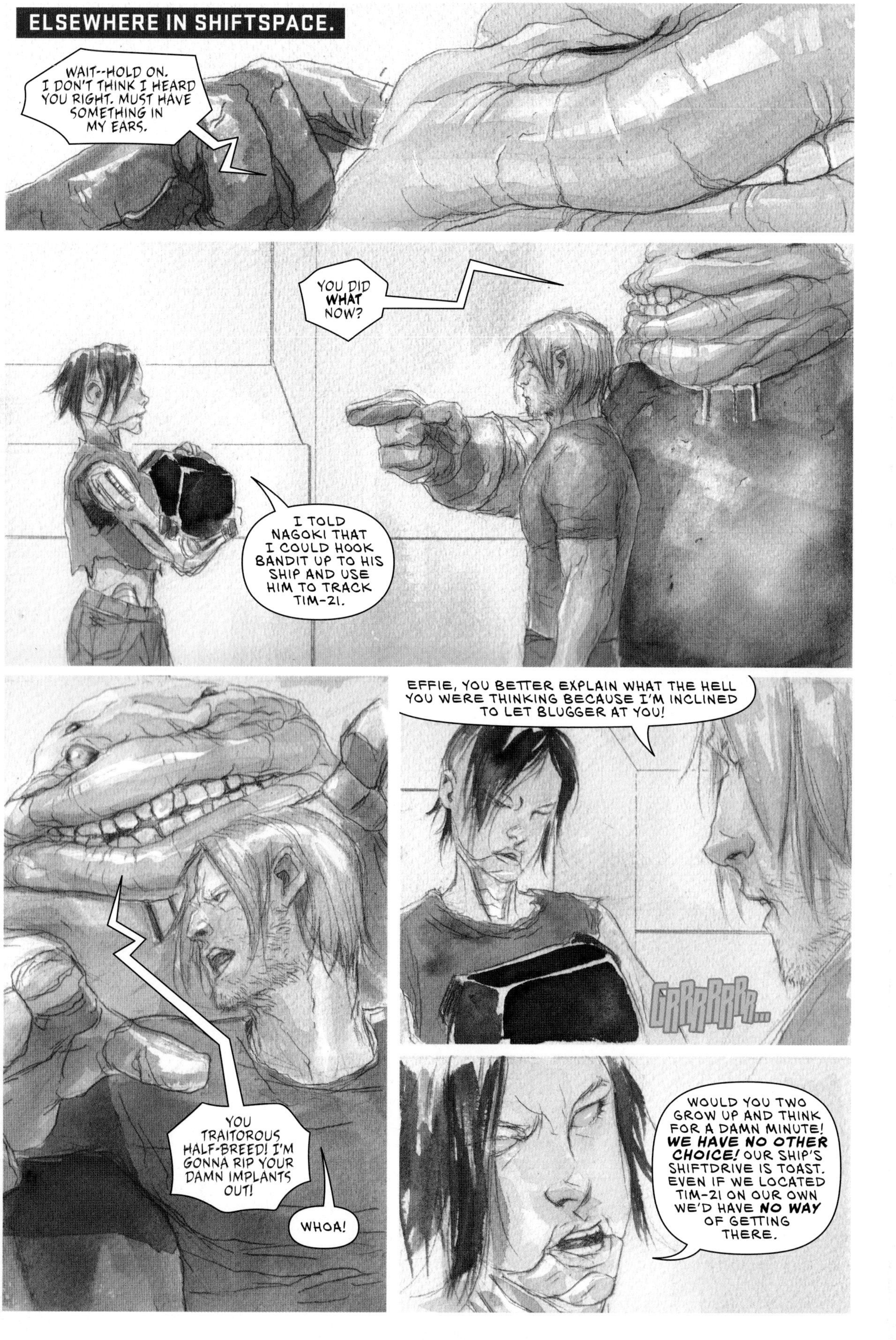
ELSEWHERE IN SHIFTSPACE.
WAIT--HOLD ON. I DON'T THINK I HEARD YOU RIGHT. MUST HAVE SOMETHING IN MY EARS.
YOU DID WHAT NOW?
I TOLD NAGOKI THAT I COULD HOOK BANDIT UP TO HIS SHIP AND USE HIM TO TRACK TIM-21.
YOU TRAITOROUS HALF-BREED! I'M GONNA RIP YOUR DAMN IMPLANTS OUT!
WHOA!
EFFIE, YOU BETTER EXPLAIN WHAT THE HELL YOU WERE THINKING BECAUSE I'M INCLINED TO LET BLUGGER AT YOU!
GRRRRRR...
WOULD YOU TWO GROW UP AND THINK FOR A DAMN MINUTE! WE HAVE NO OTHER CHOICE! OUR SHIP'S SHIFTDRIVE IS TOAST. EVEN IF WE LOCATED TIM-21 ON OUR OWN WE'D HAVE NO WAY OF GETTING THERE.

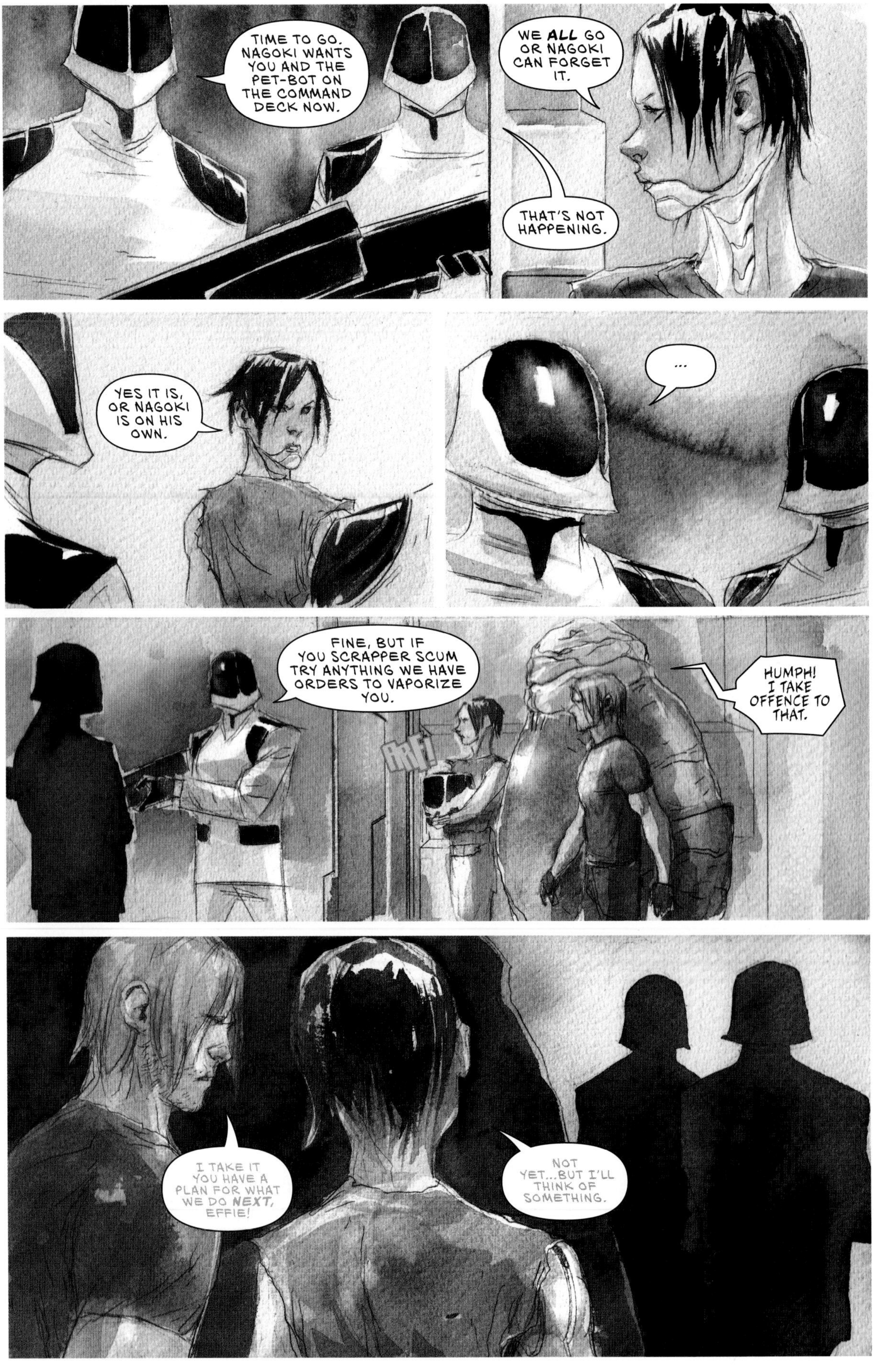
TIME TO GO. NAGOKI WANTS YOU AND THE PET-BOT ON THE COMMAND DECK NOW.
WE **ALL** GO OR NAGOKI CAN FORGET IT.
THAT'S NOT HAPPENING.
YES IT IS, OR NAGOKI IS ON HIS OWN.
...
FINE, BUT IF YOU SCRAPPER SCUM TRY ANYTHING WE HAVE ORDERS TO VAPORIZE YOU.
ARF!
HUMPH! I TAKE OFFENCE TO THAT.
I TAKE IT YOU HAVE A PLAN FOR WHAT WE DO ***NEXT,*** EFFIE!
NOT YET...BUT I'LL THINK OF SOMETHING.

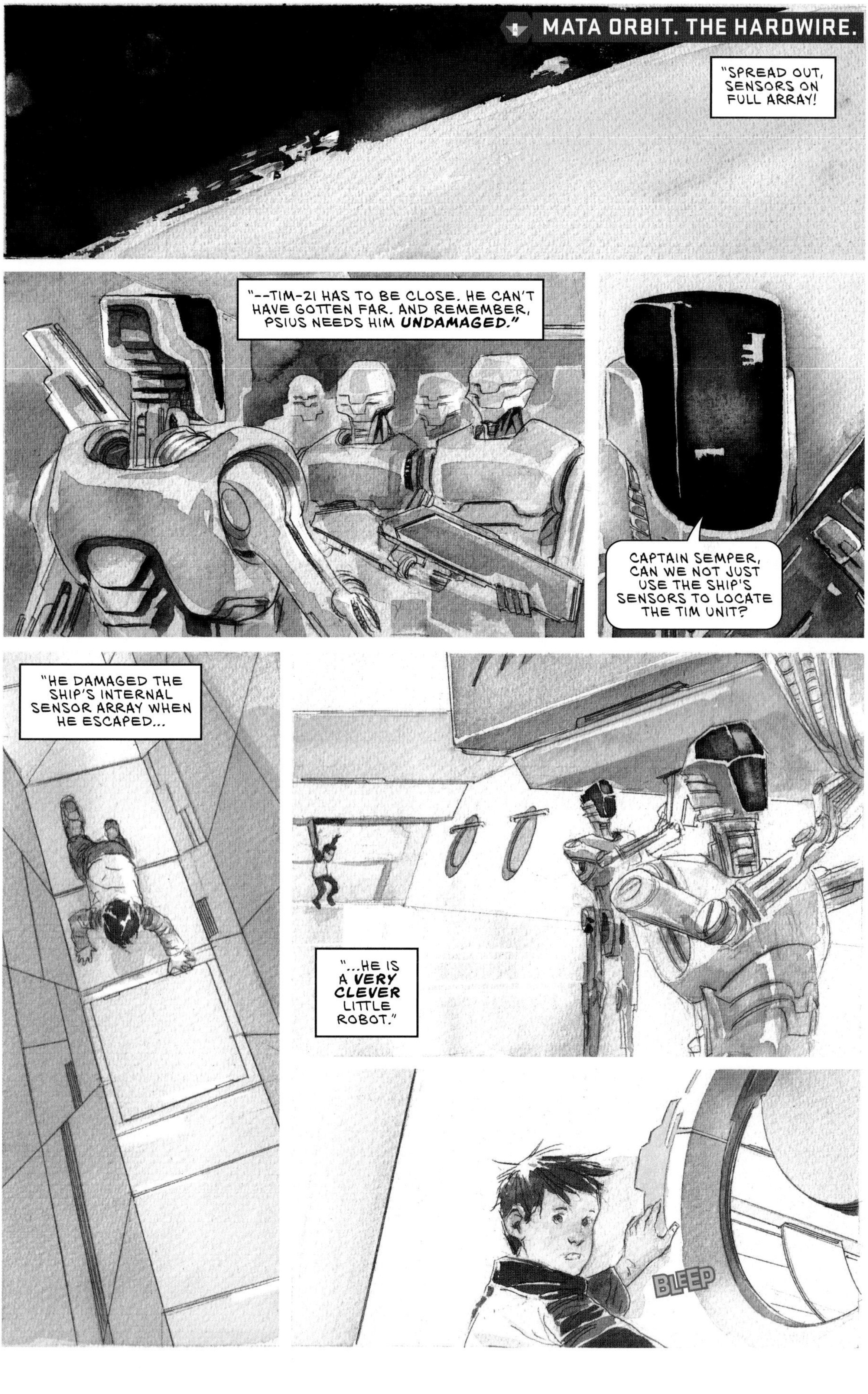
MATA ORBIT. THE HARDWIRE.
"SPREAD OUT, SENSORS ON FULL ARRAY!
"--TIM-21 HAS TO BE CLOSE. HE CAN'T HAVE GOTTEN FAR. AND REMEMBER, PSIUS NEEDS HIM UNDAMAGED."
CAPTAIN SEMPER, CAN WE NOT JUST USE THE SHIP'S SENSORS TO LOCATE THE TIM UNIT?
"HE DAMAGED THE SHIP'S INTERNAL SENSOR ARRAY WHEN HE ESCAPED...
"...HE IS A VERY CLEVER LITTLE ROBOT."
BLEEP

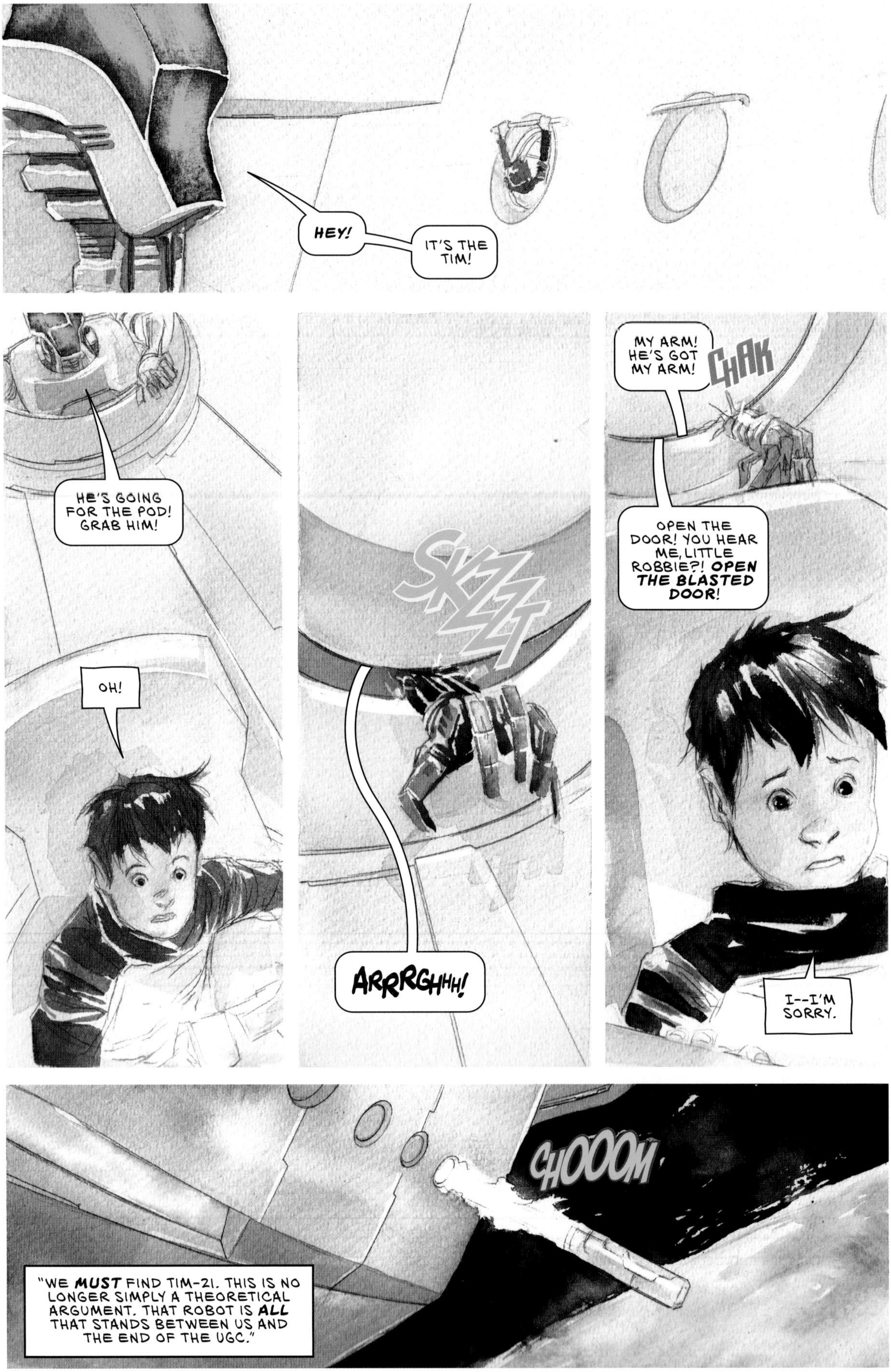
HEY!
IT'S THE TIM!
HE'S GOING FOR THE POD! GRAB HIM!
OH!
SKZZZT
ARRRGHHH!
MY ARM! HE'S GOT MY ARM!
CHAK
OPEN THE DOOR! YOU HEAR ME, LITTLE ROBBIE?! OPEN THE BLASTED DOOR!
I--I'M SORRY.
CHOOOM
"WE MUST FIND TIM-21. THIS IS NO LONGER SIMPLY A THEORETICAL ARGUMENT. THAT ROBOT IS ALL THAT STANDS BETWEEN US AND THE END OF THE UGC."

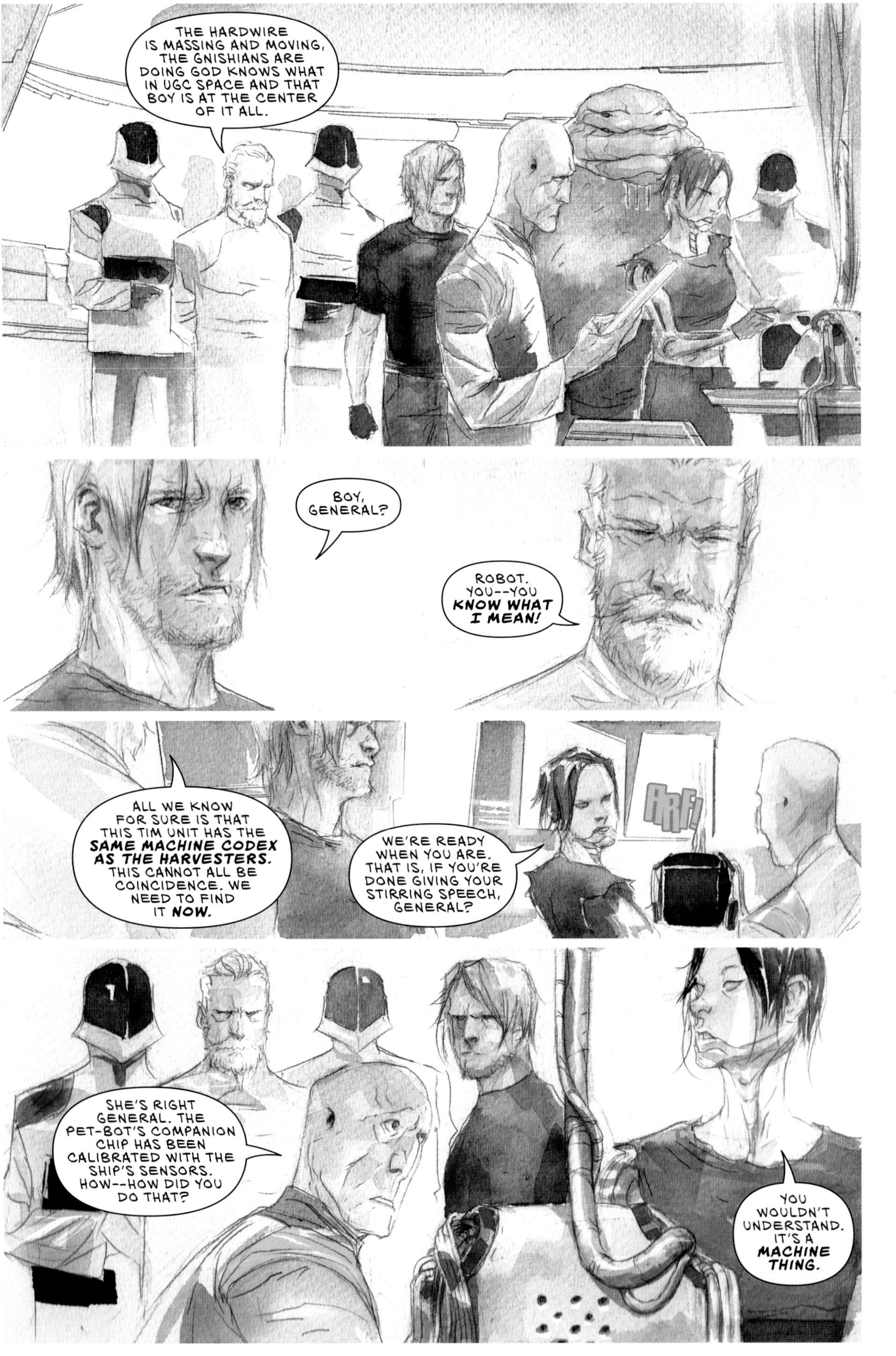
THE HARDWIRE IS MASSING AND MOVING, THE GNISHIANS ARE DOING GOD KNOWS WHAT IN UGC SPACE AND THAT BOY IS AT THE CENTER OF IT ALL.
BOY, GENERAL?
ROBOT. YOU--YOU **KNOW WHAT I MEAN!**
ALL WE KNOW FOR SURE IS THAT THIS TIM UNIT HAS THE **SAME MACHINE CODEX AS THE HARVESTERS.** THIS CANNOT ALL BE COINCIDENCE. WE NEED TO FIND IT **NOW.**
ARF!
WE'RE READY WHEN YOU ARE. THAT IS, IF YOU'RE DONE GIVING YOUR STIRRING SPEECH, GENERAL?
SHE'S RIGHT GENERAL. THE PET-BOT'S COMPANION CHIP HAS BEEN CALIBRATED WITH THE SHIP'S SENSORS. HOW--HOW DID YOU DO THAT?
YOU WOULDN'T UNDERSTAND. IT'S A **MACHINE THING.**

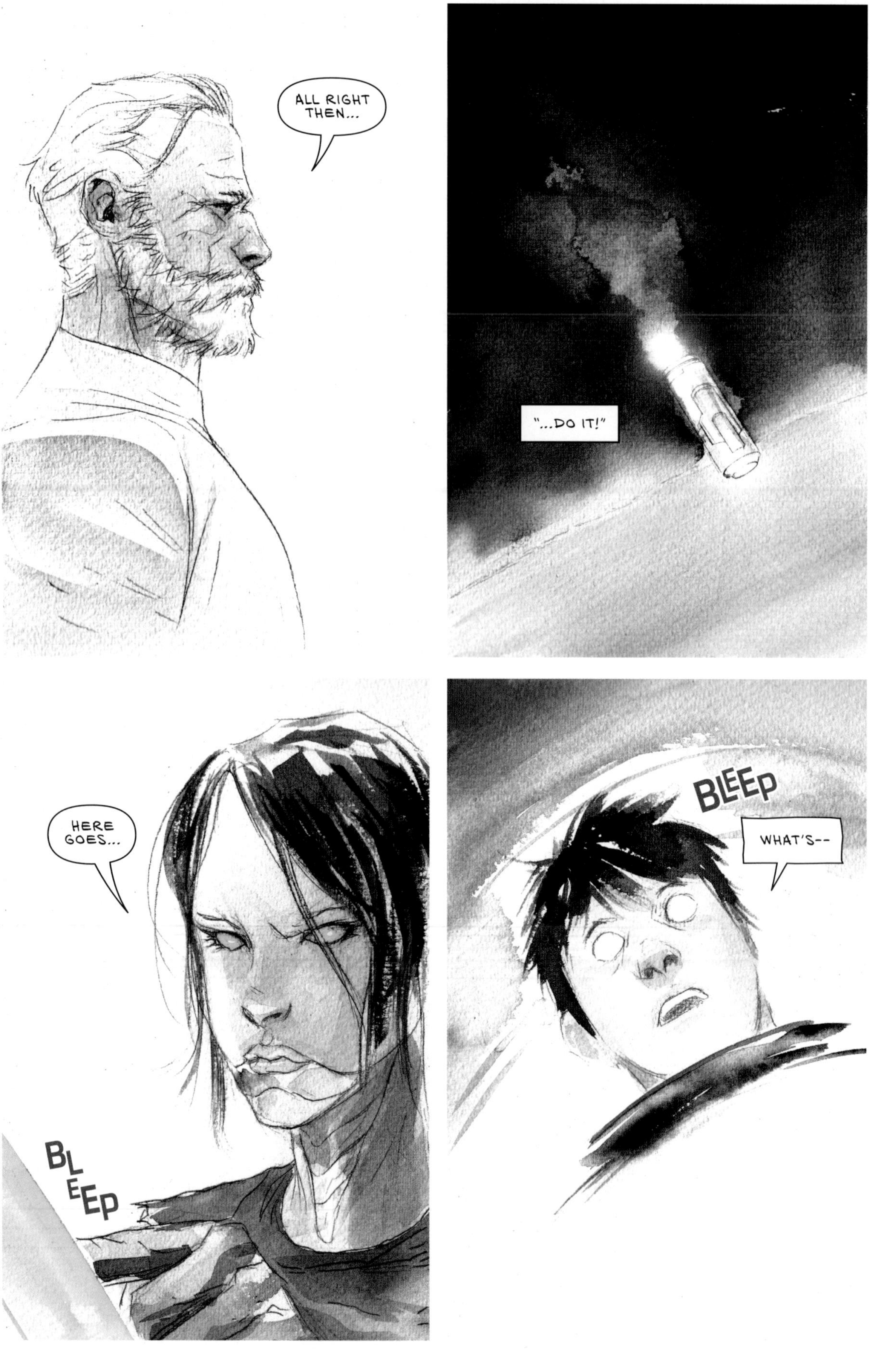
ALL RIGHT THEN...
"...DO IT!"
HERE GOES...
BLEEP
BLEEP
WHAT'S--

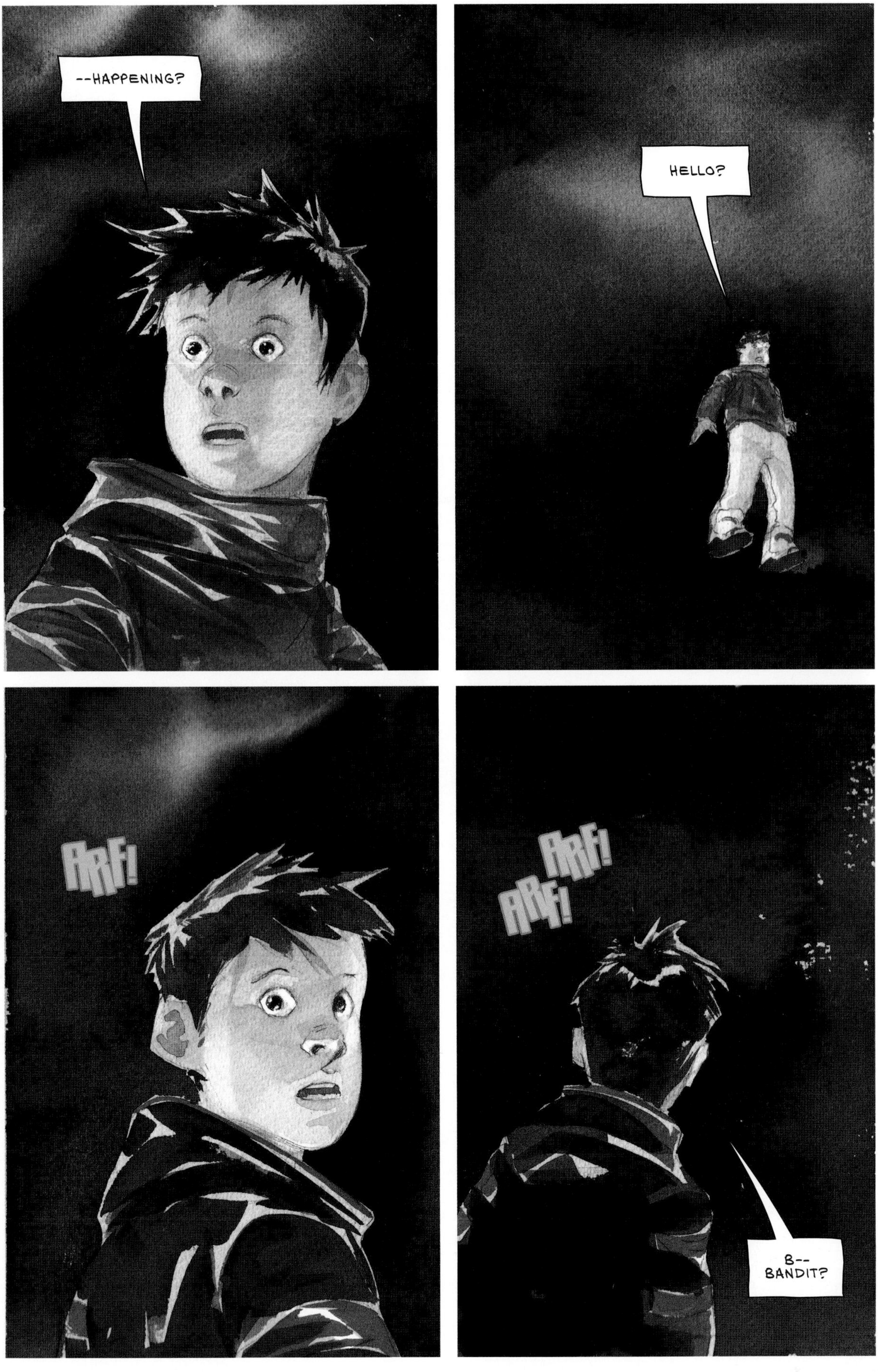
--HAPPENING?
HELLO?
ARF!
ARF!
ARF!
B--
BANDIT?

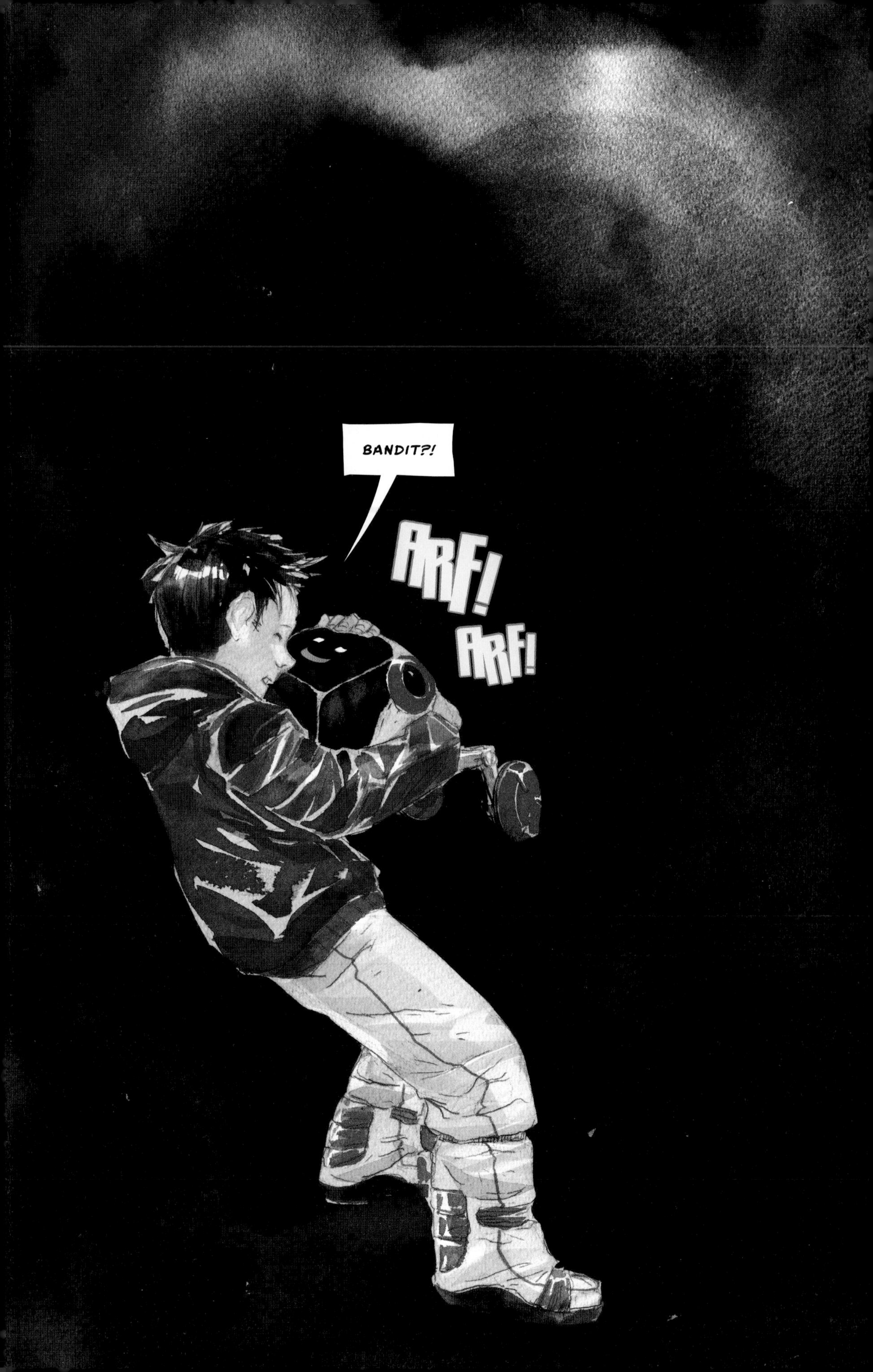
BANDIT?!
ARF!
ARF!

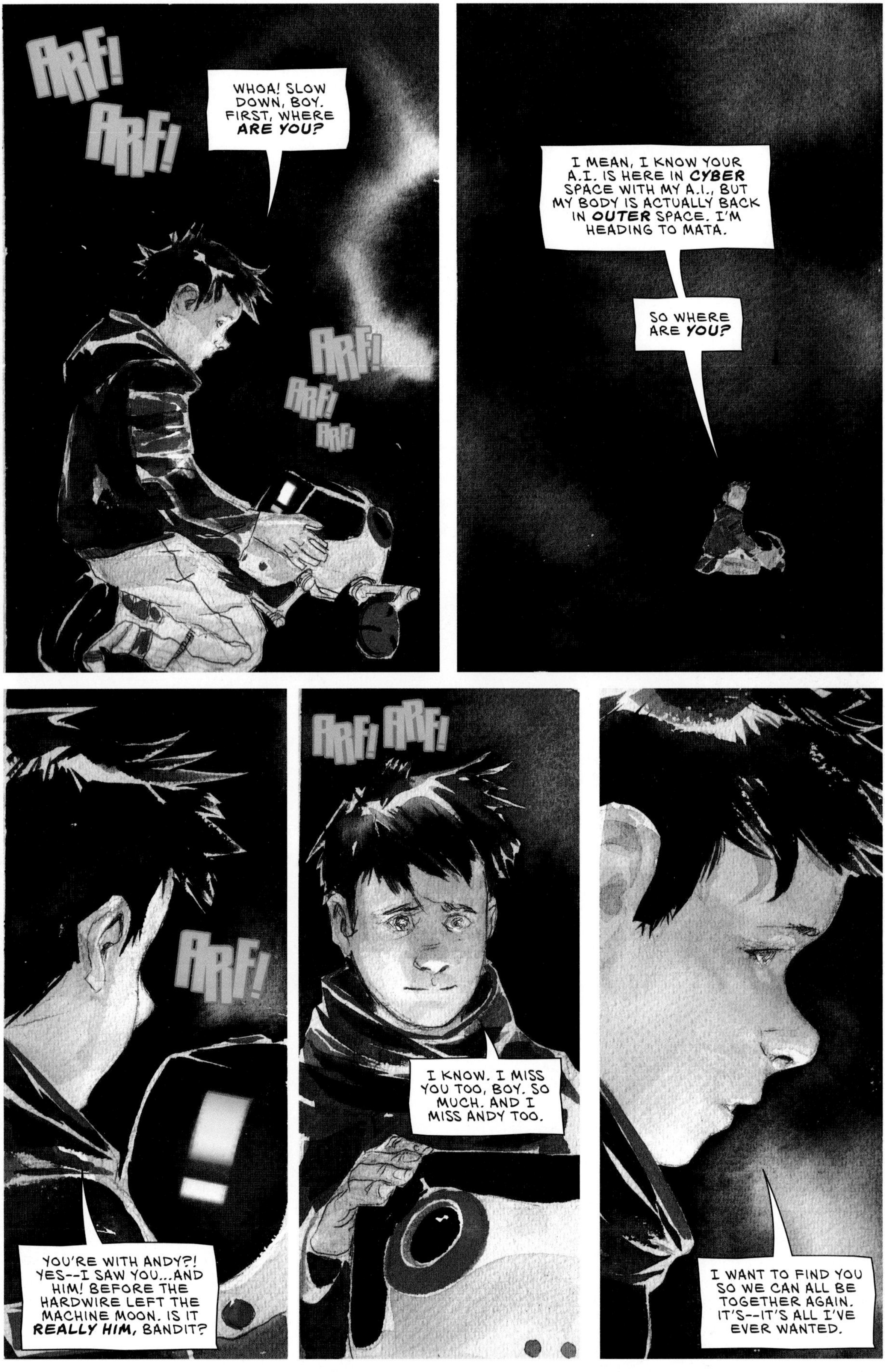
ARF!
ARF!
WHOA! SLOW DOWN, BOY. FIRST, WHERE ARE YOU?
ARF!
ARF!
ARF!
I MEAN, I KNOW YOUR A.I. IS HERE IN CYBER SPACE WITH MY A.I., BUT MY BODY IS ACTUALLY BACK IN OUTER SPACE. I'M HEADING TO MATA.
SO WHERE ARE YOU?
ARF!
YOU'RE WITH ANDY?! YES--I SAW YOU...AND HIM! BEFORE THE HARDWIRE LEFT THE MACHINE MOON. IS IT REALLY HIM, BANDIT?
ARF! ARF!
I KNOW. I MISS YOU TOO, BOY. SO MUCH. AND I MISS ANDY TOO.
I WANT TO FIND YOU SO WE CAN ALL BE TOGETHER AGAIN. IT'S--IT'S ALL I'VE EVER WANTED.

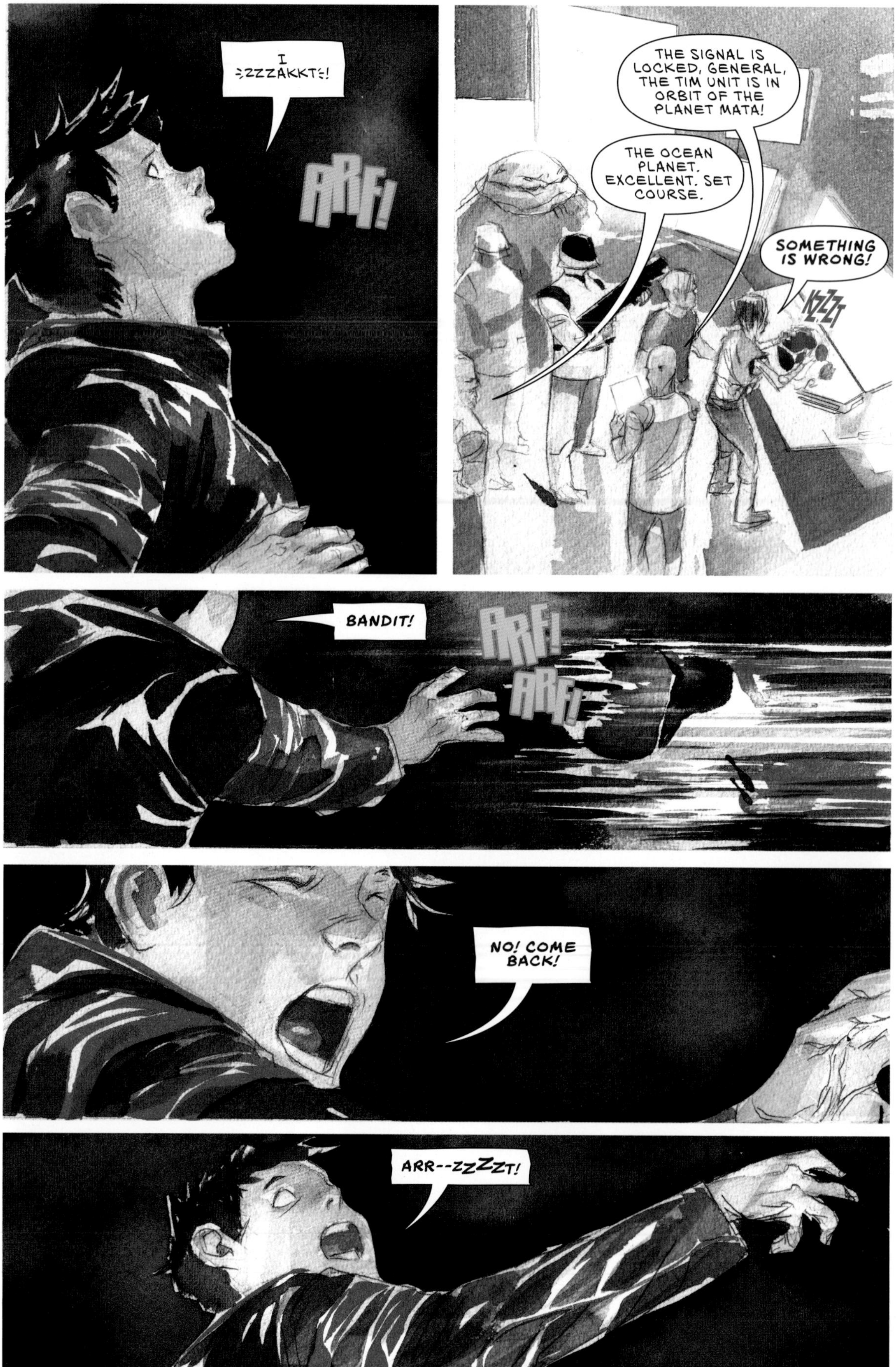
I
=ZZZAKKT=!
ARF!
THE SIGNAL IS LOCKED, GENERAL, THE TIM UNIT IS IN ORBIT OF THE PLANET MATA!
THE OCEAN PLANET. EXCELLENT. SET COURSE.
SOMETHING IS WRONG!
KZZZT
BANDIT!
ARF!
ARF!
NO! COME BACK!
ARR--ZZZZT!

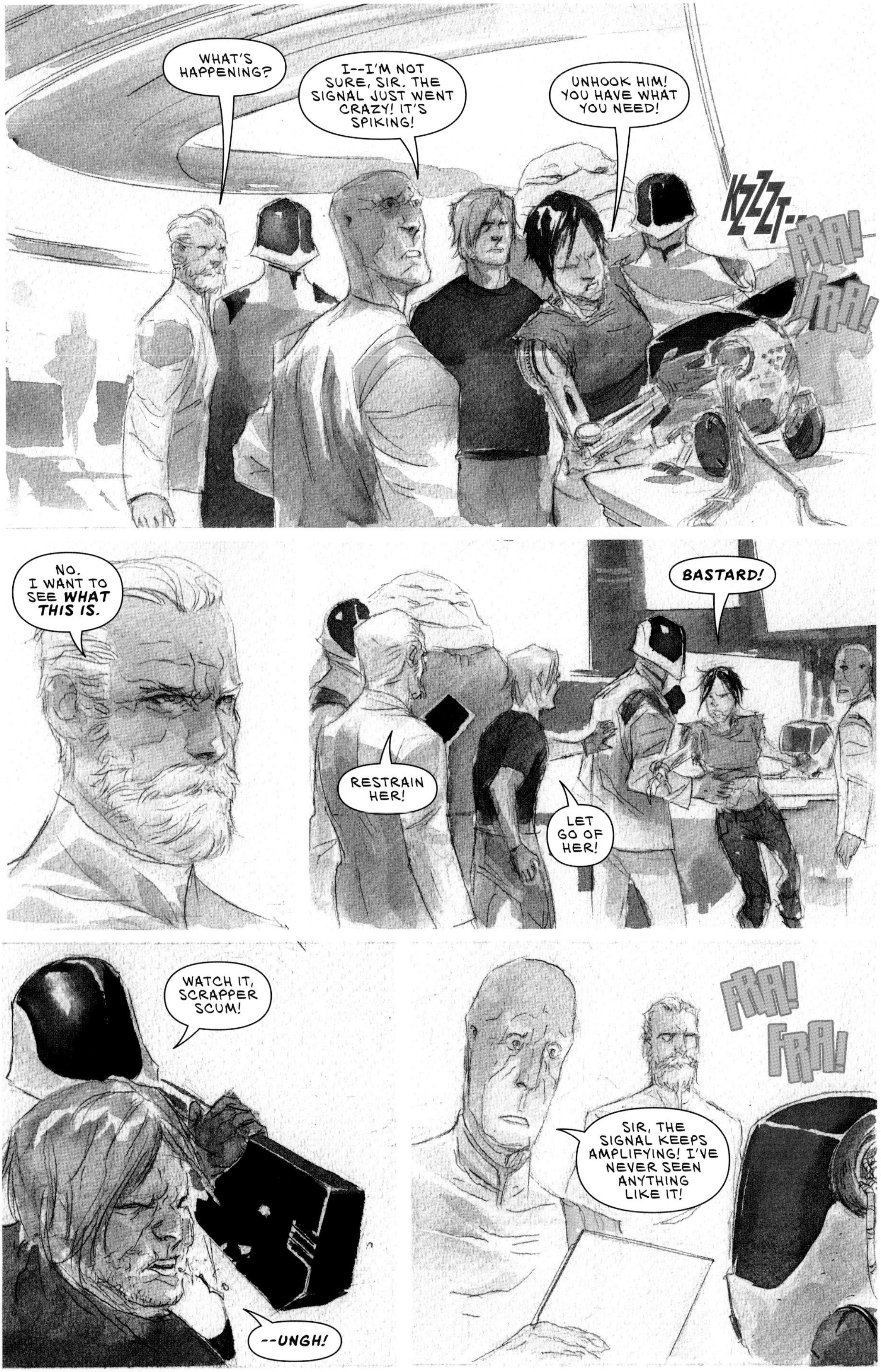
WHAT'S HAPPENING?
I--I'M NOT SURE, SIR. THE SIGNAL JUST WENT CRAZY! IT'S SPIKING!
UNHOOK HIM! YOU HAVE WHAT YOU NEED!
KZZZT--
FRA! FRA!
NO. I WANT TO SEE WHAT THIS IS.
BASTARD!
RESTRAIN HER!
LET GO OF HER!
WATCH IT, SCRAPPER SCUM!
--UNGH!
FRA! FRA!
SIR, THE SIGNAL KEEPS AMPLIFYING! I'VE NEVER SEEN ANYTHING LIKE IT!

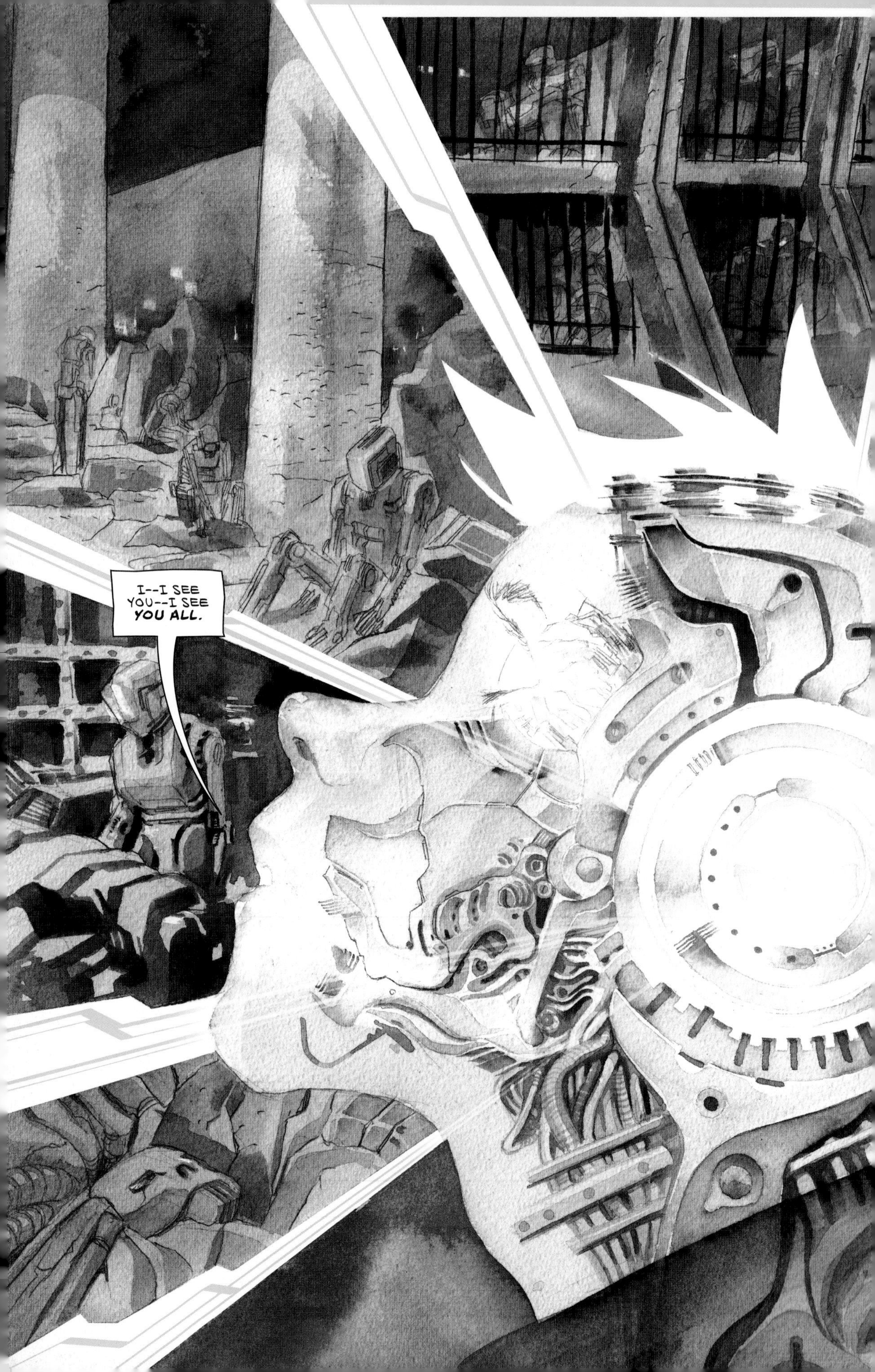
I--I SEE YOU--I SEE YOU ALL.

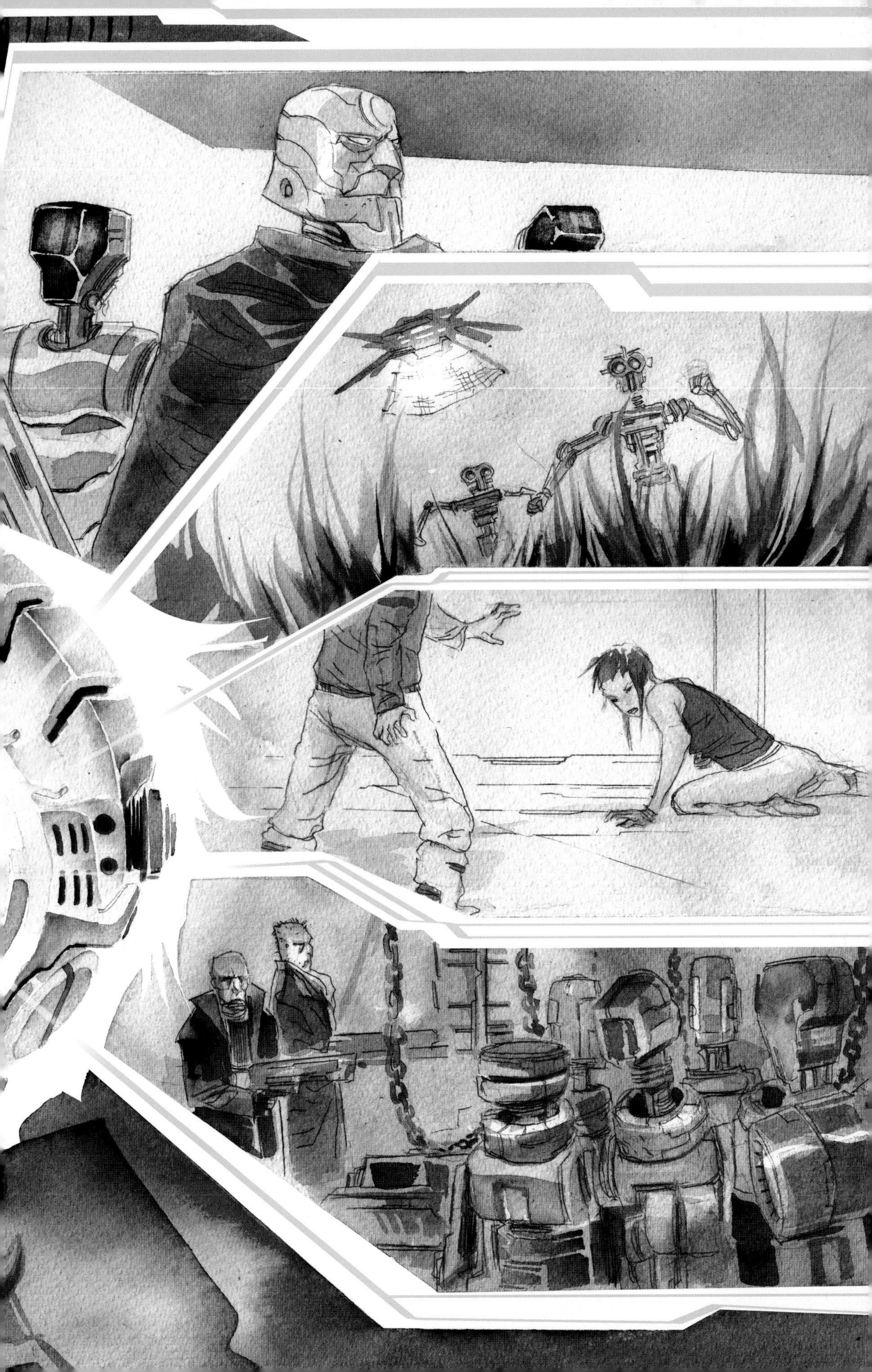

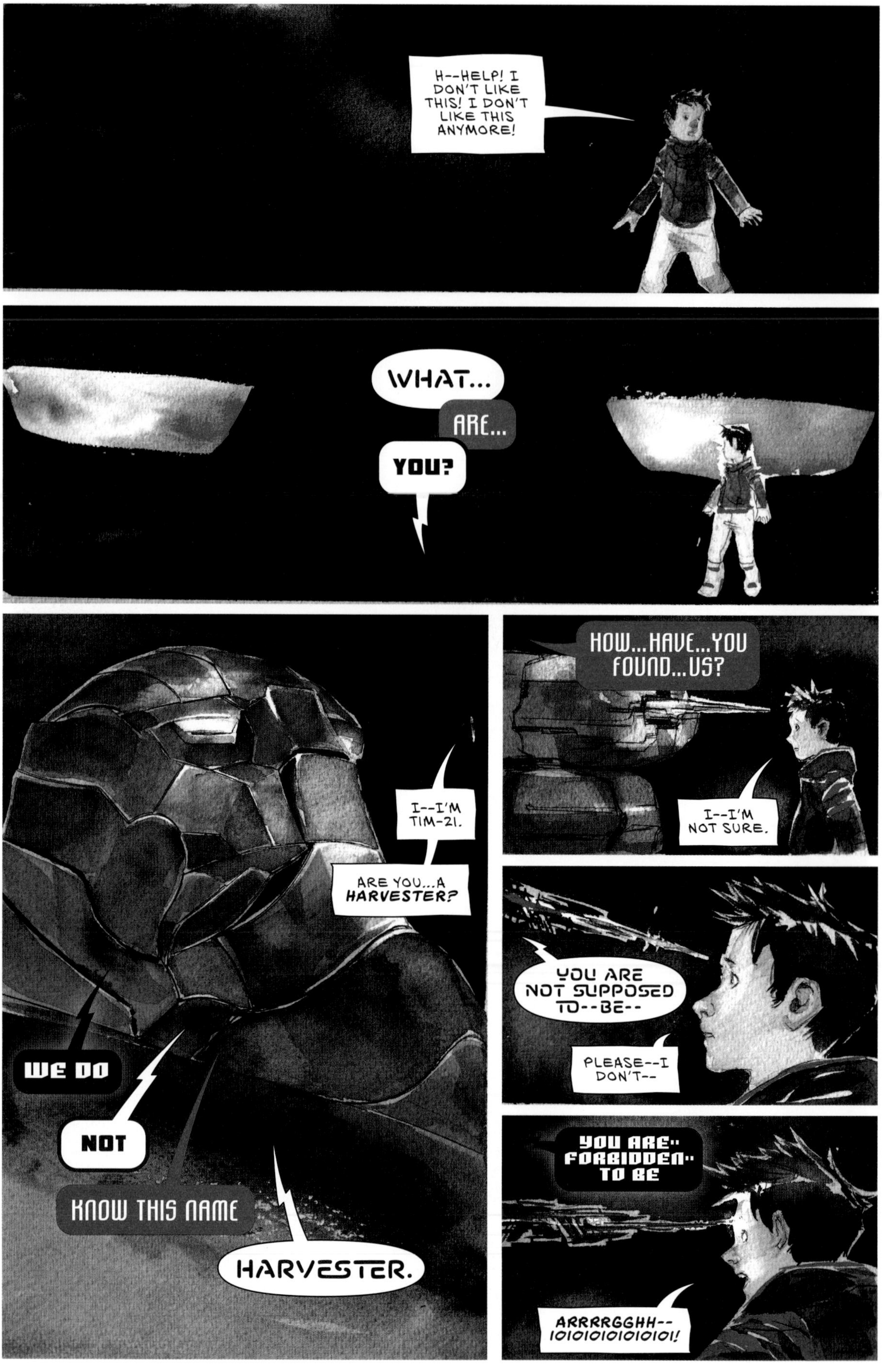

H--HELP! I DON'T LIKE THIS! I DON'T LIKE THIS ANYMORE!
WHAT...
ARE...
YOU?
I--I'M TIM-21.
ARE YOU...A HARVESTER?
WE DO
NOT
KNOW THIS NAME
HARVESTER.
HOW...HAVE...YOU FOUND...US?
I--I'M NOT SURE.
YOU ARE NOT SUPPOSED TO--BE--
PLEASE--I DON'T--
YOU ARE-- FORBIDDEN-- TO BE
ARRRRGGHH-- 10101010101010!

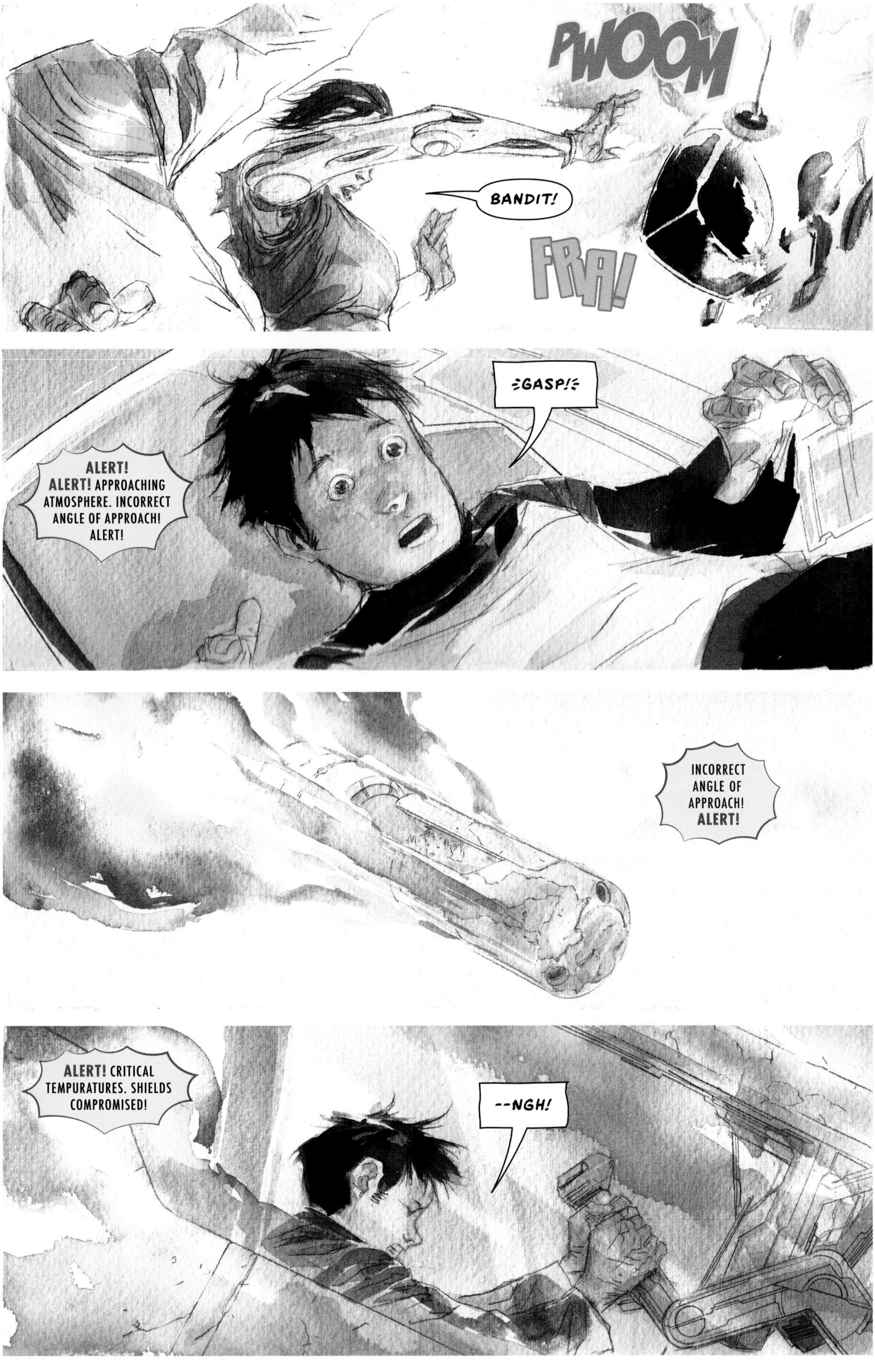
PWOOM
BANDIT!
FRA!
=GASP!=
ALERT! ALERT! APPROACHING ATMOSPHERE. INCORRECT ANGLE OF APPROACH! ALERT!
INCORRECT ANGLE OF APPROACH! ALERT!
ALERT! CRITICAL TEMPURATURES. SHIELDS COMPROMISED!
--NGH!

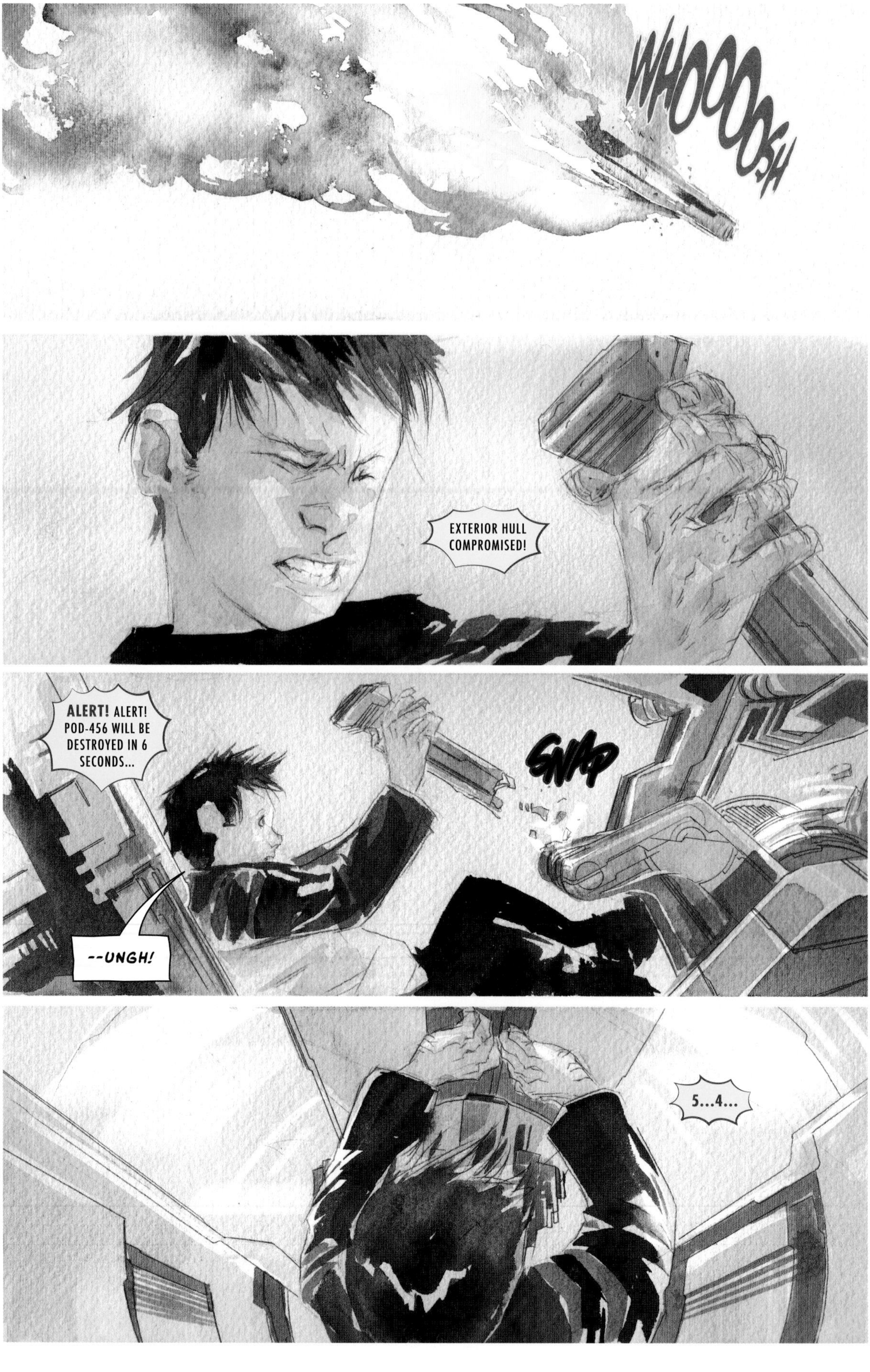
WHOOOOSH
EXTERIOR HULL COMPROMISED!
ALERT! ALERT! POD-456 WILL BE DESTROYED IN 6 SECONDS...
--UNGH!
SNAP
5...4...

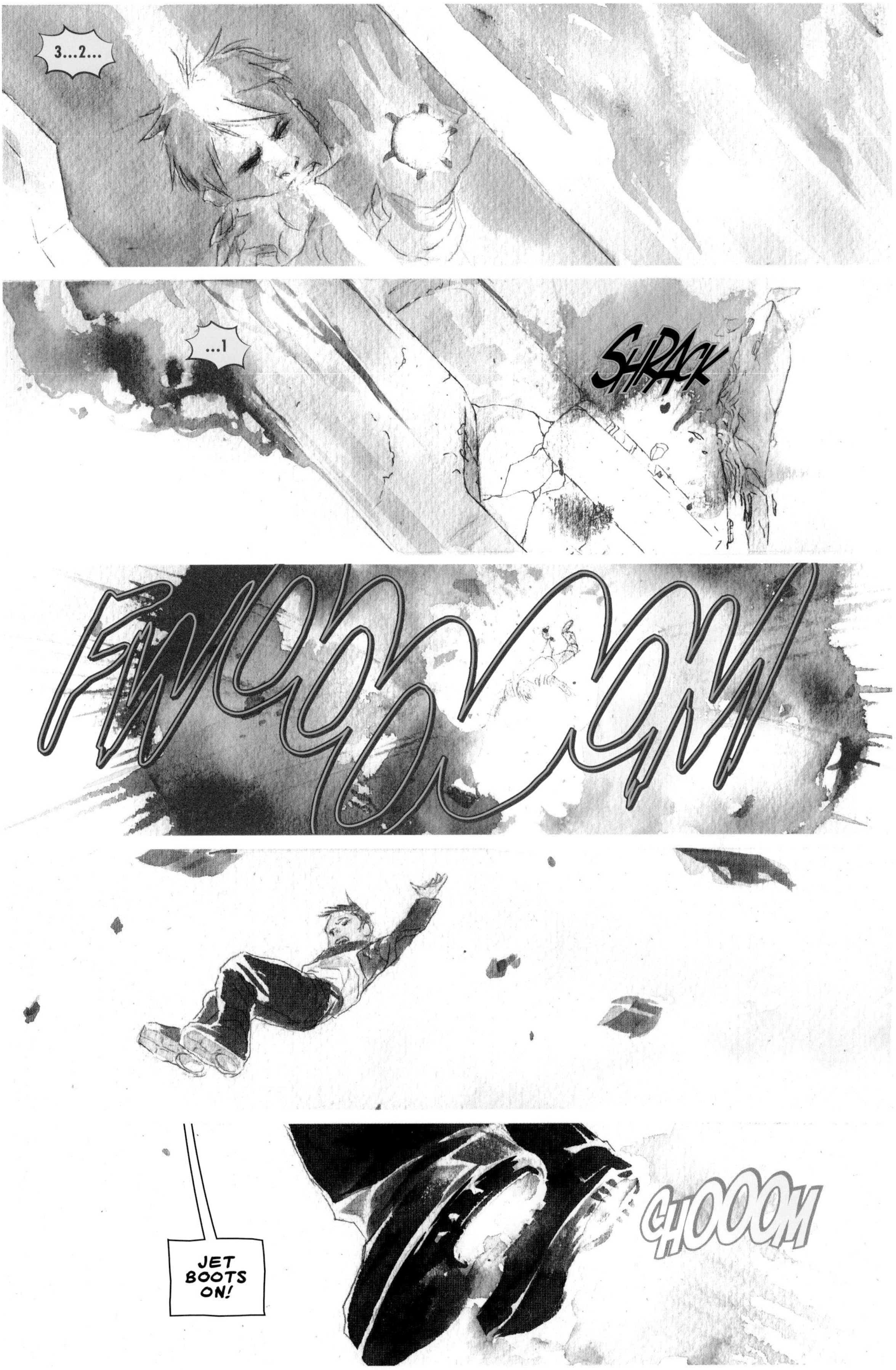
3...2...
...1
SHRACK
FWOOOOOOM
JET BOOTS ON!
CHOOOM

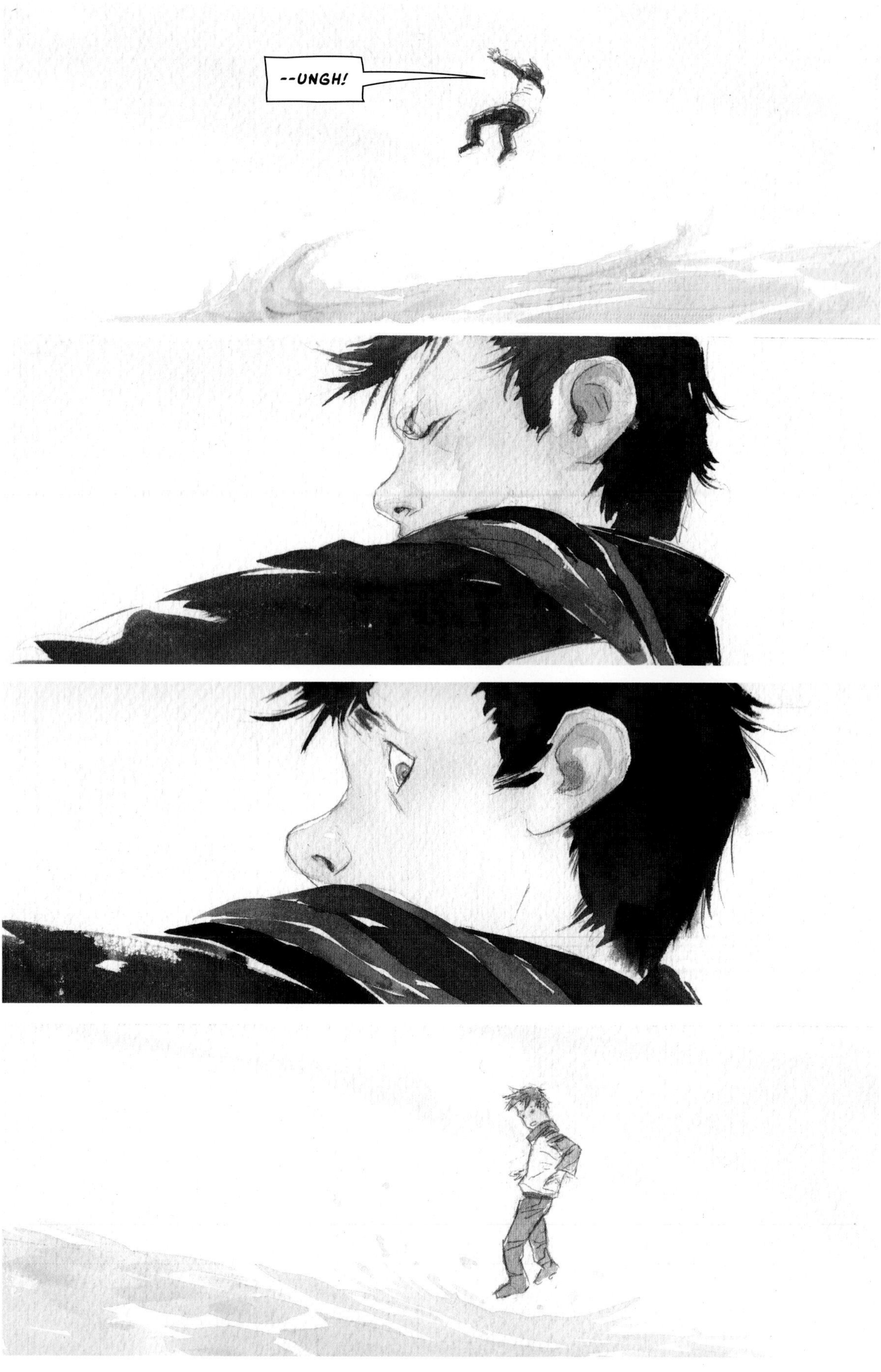
--UNGH!

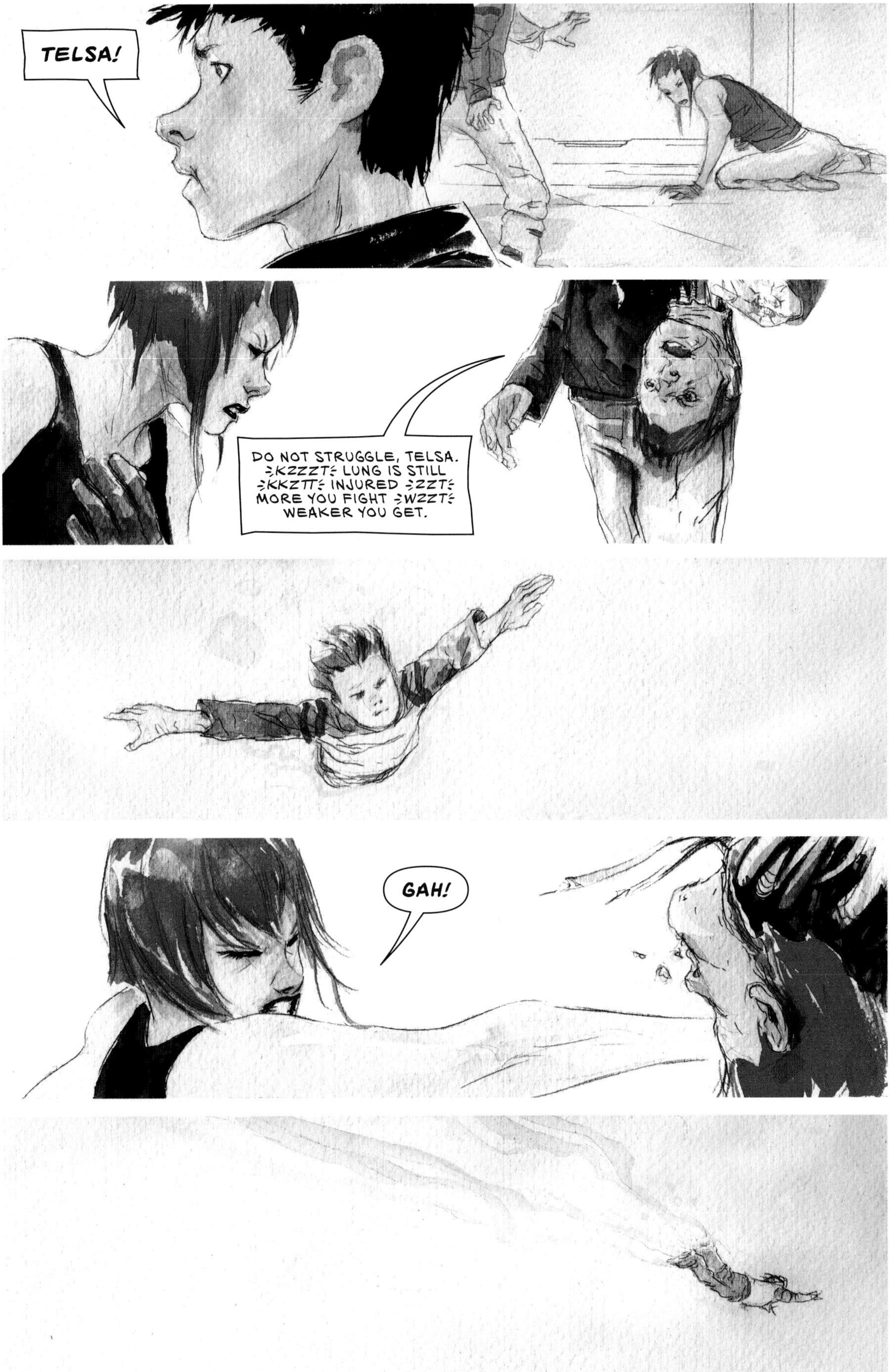
TELSA!
DO NOT STRUGGLE, TELSA. =KZZZT= LUNG IS STILL =KKZTT= INJURED =ZZT= MORE YOU FIGHT =WZZT= WEAKER YOU GET.
GAH!

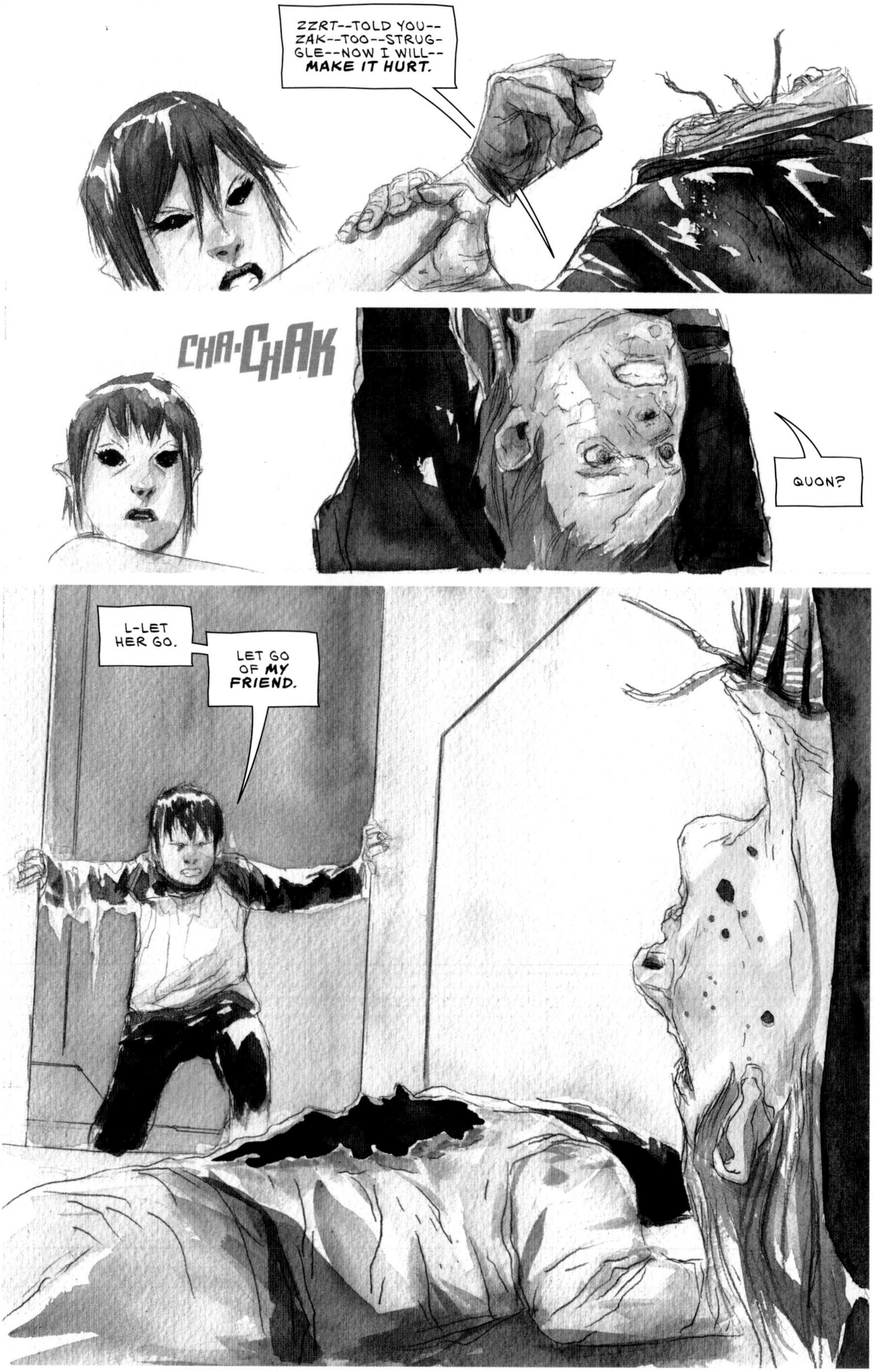
ZZRT--TOLD YOU--ZAK--TOO--STRUG-GLE--NOW I WILL--MAKE IT HURT.
CHA-CHAK
QUON?
L-LET HER GO.
LET GO OF MY FRIEND.

CHAPTER FIVE

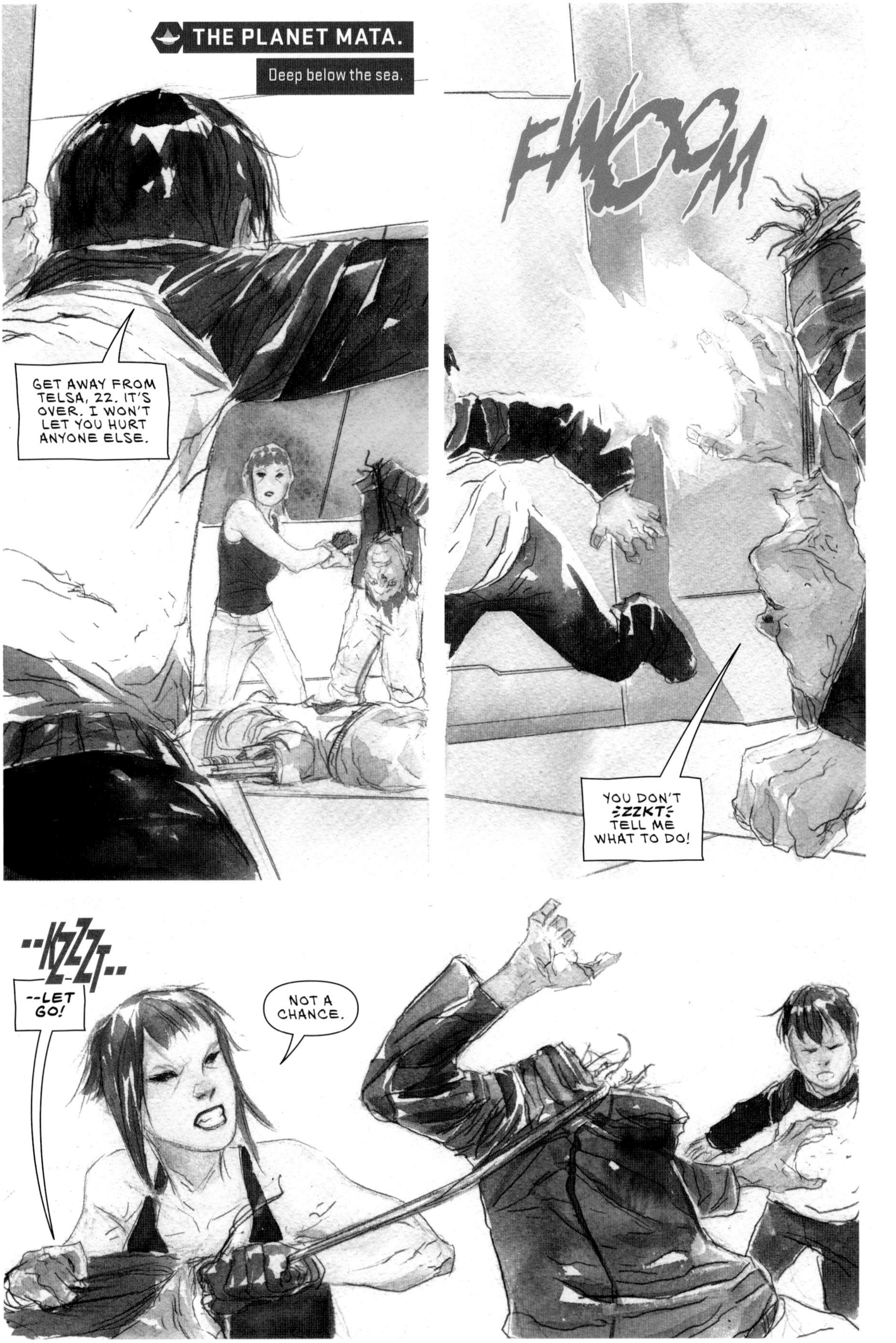
THE PLANET MATA.
Deep below the sea.
GET AWAY FROM TELSA, 22. IT'S OVER. I WON'T LET YOU HURT ANYONE ELSE.
FWOOM
YOU DON'T ZZKT TELL ME WHAT TO DO!
--KZZZT--
--LET GO!
NOT A CHANCE.

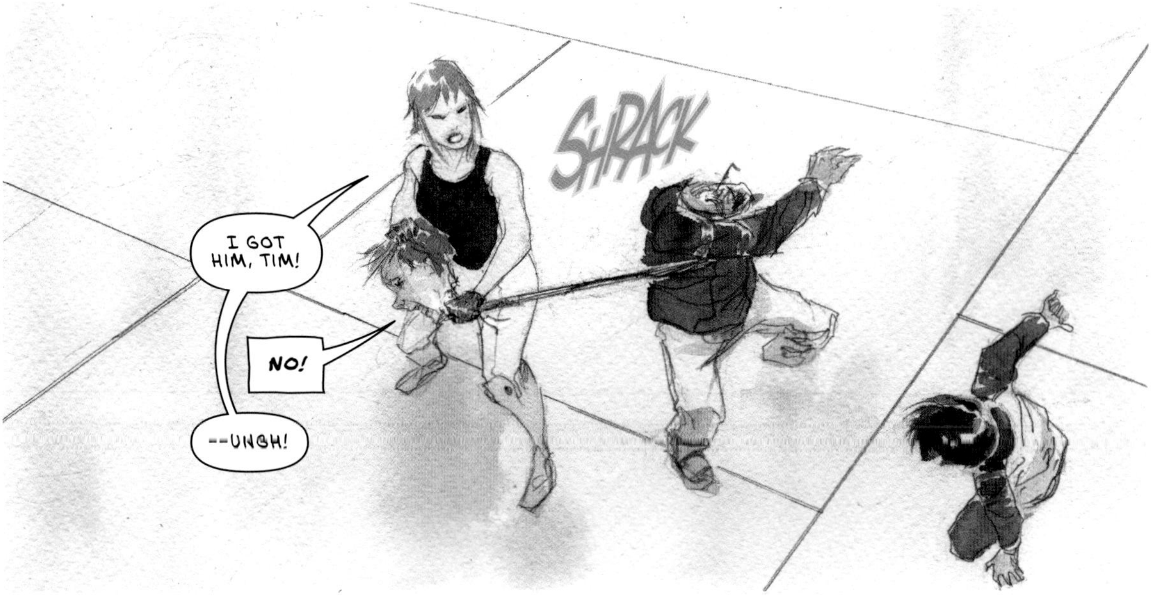
SHRACK
I GOT HIM, TIM!
NO!
--UNGH!

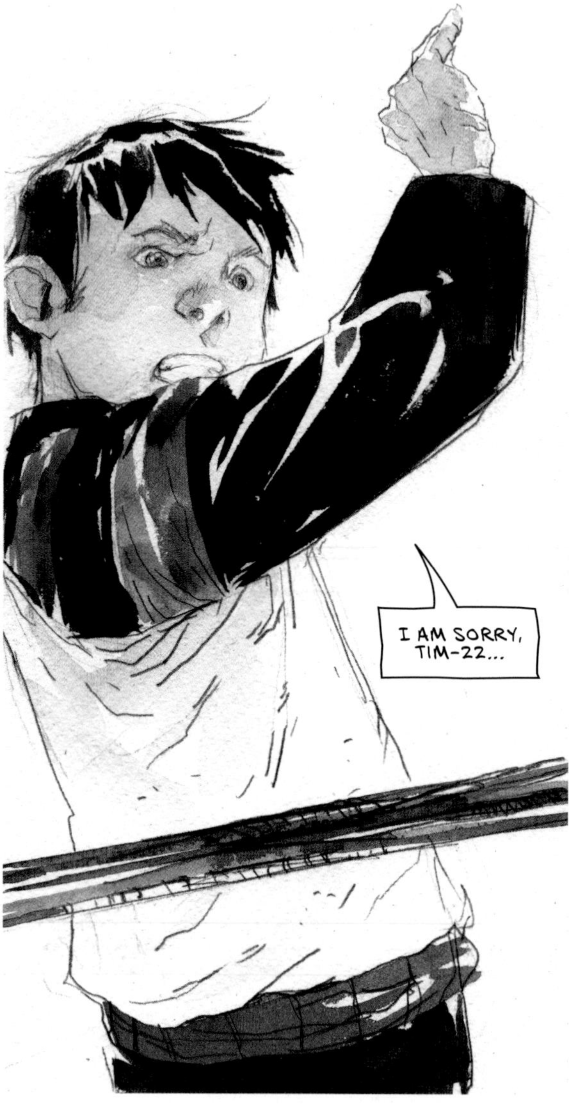
I AM SORRY, TIM-22...

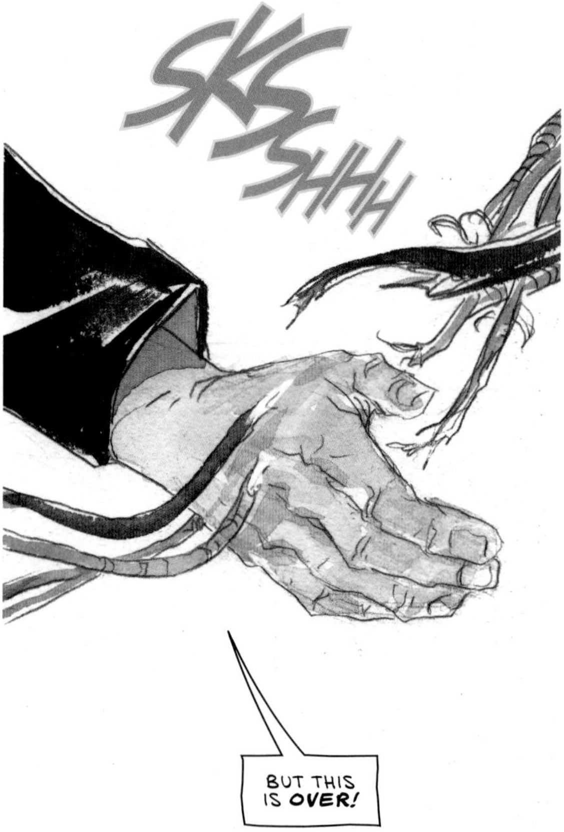
SKSSHHH
BUT THIS IS OVER!

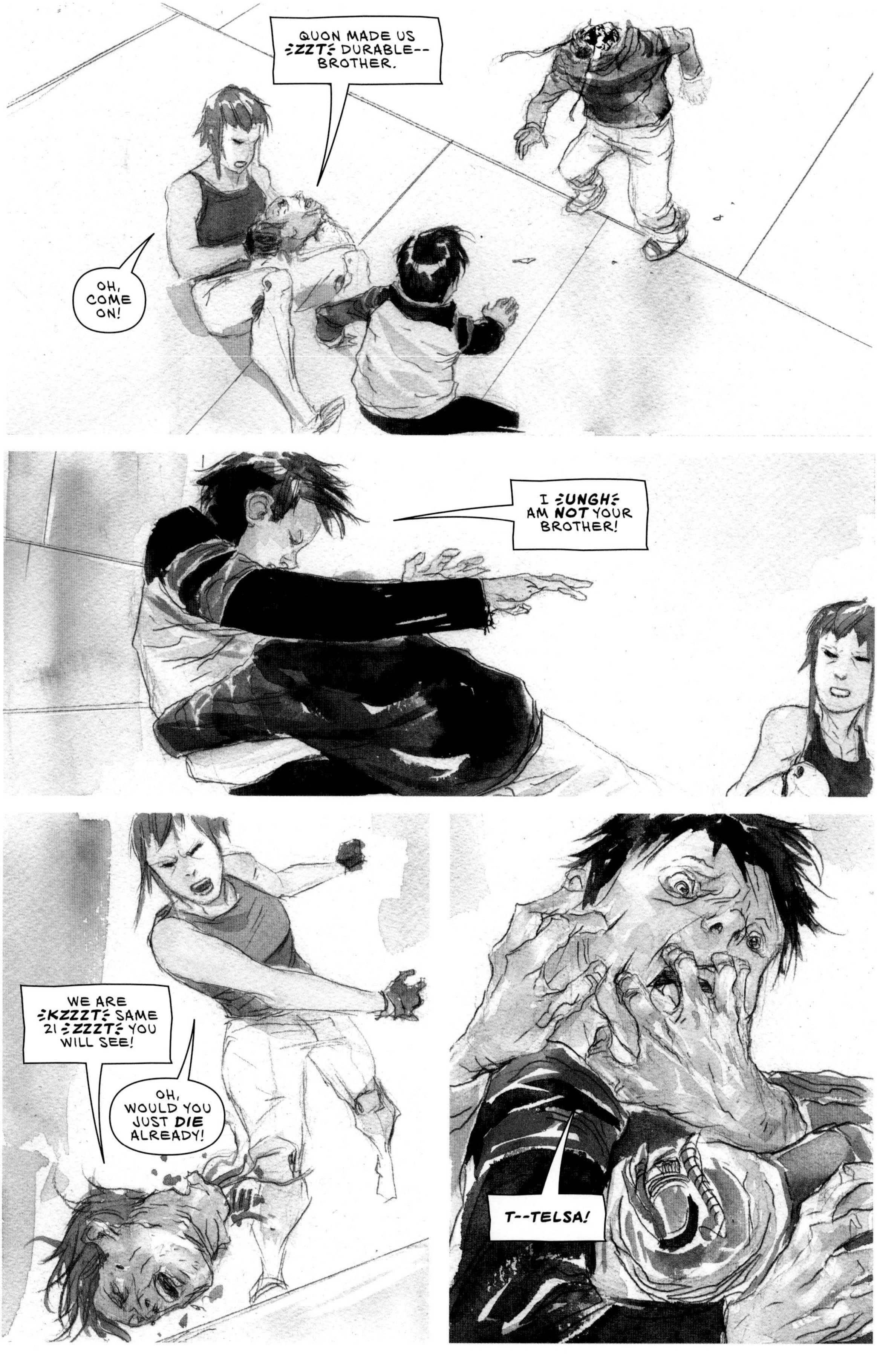
QUON MADE US ZZZT DURABLE-- BROTHER.
OH, COME ON!
I UNGH AM **NOT** YOUR BROTHER!
WE ARE KZZZT SAME 21 ZZZT YOU WILL SEE!
OH, WOULD YOU JUST **DIE** ALREADY!
T--TELSA!

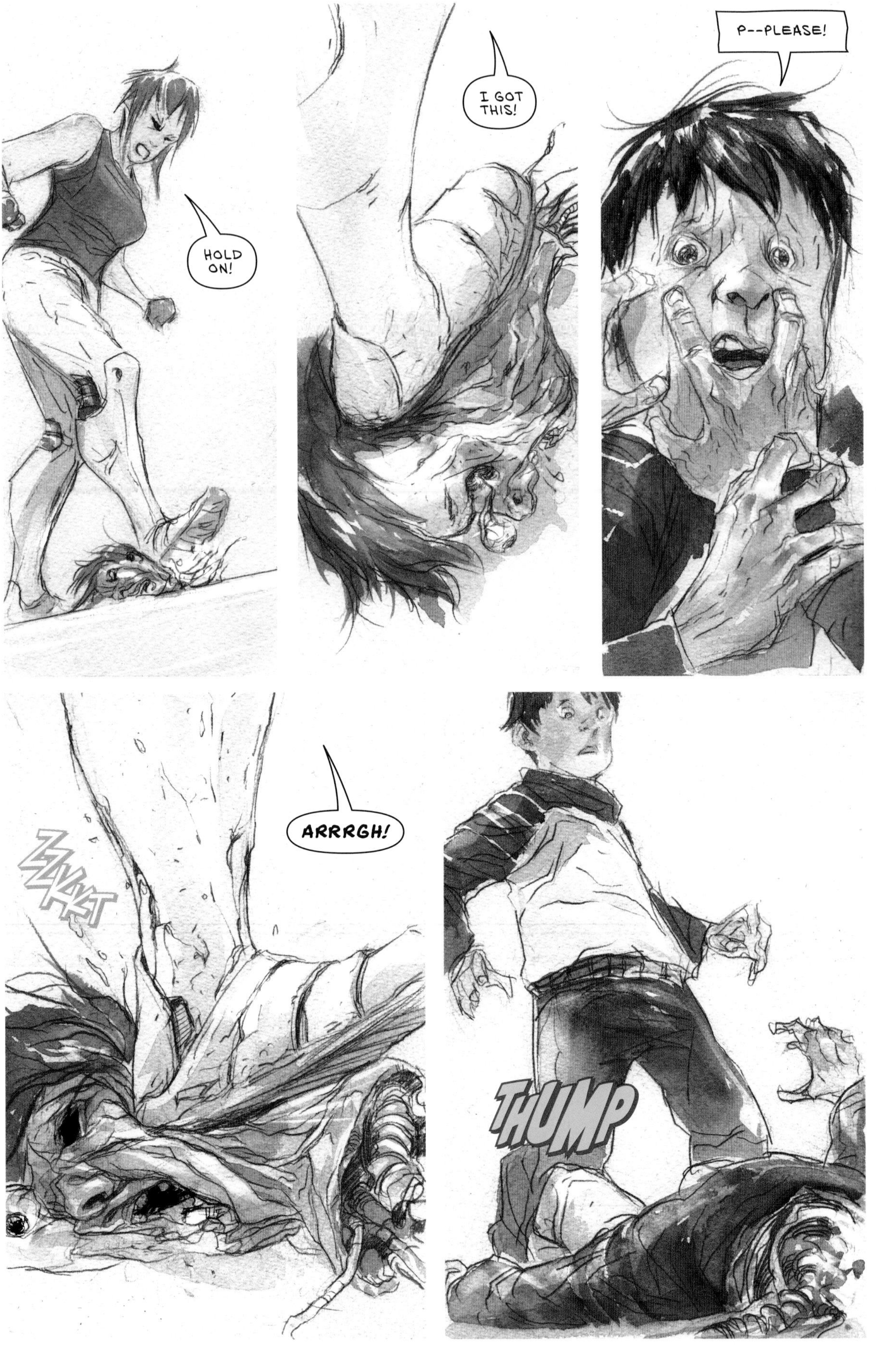
HOLD ON!
I GOT THIS!
P--PLEASE!
ARRRGH!
THUMP

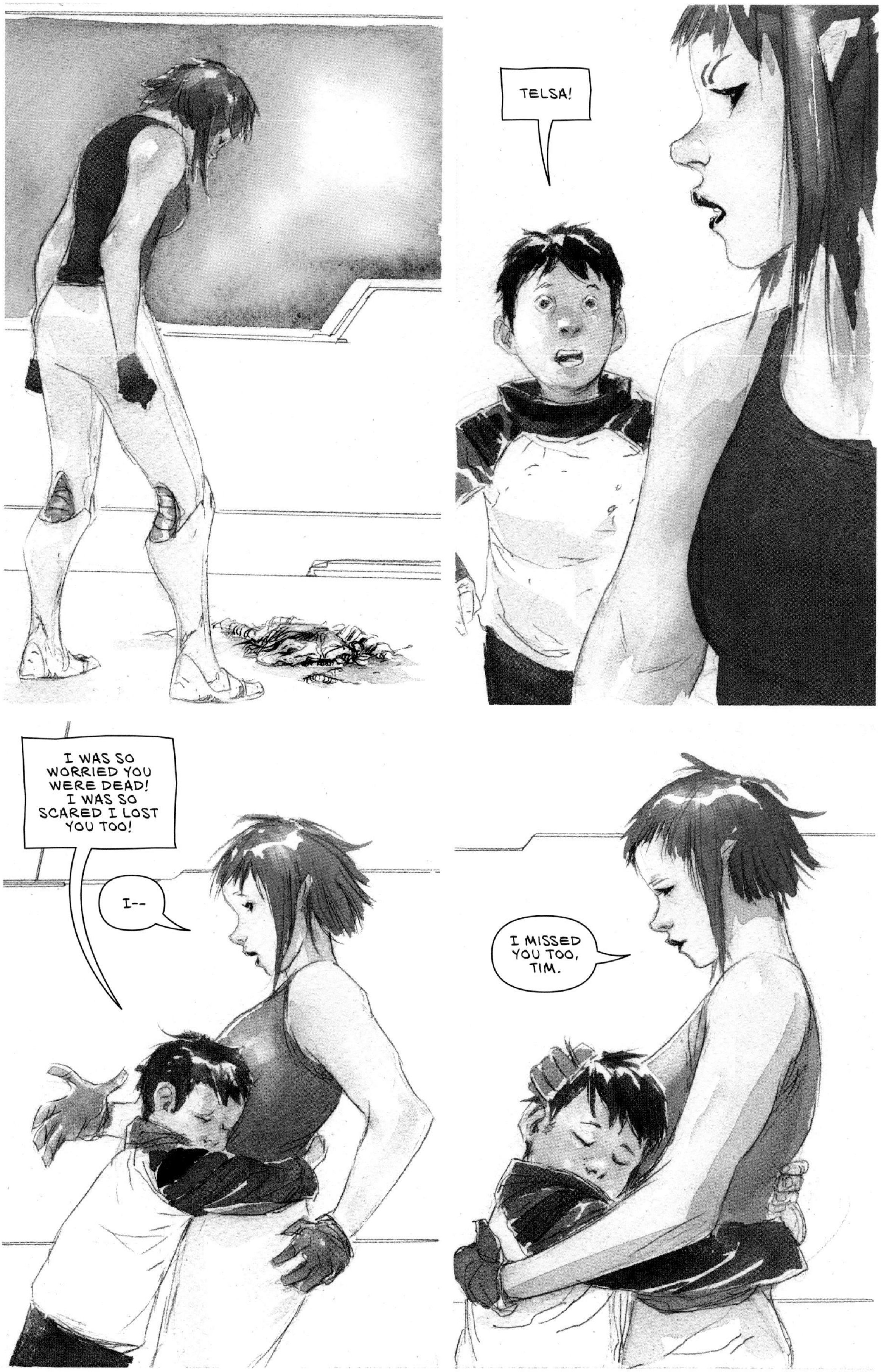
TELSA!
I WAS SO WORRIED YOU WERE DEAD! I WAS SO SCARED I LOST YOU TOO!
I--
I MISSED YOU TOO, TIM.

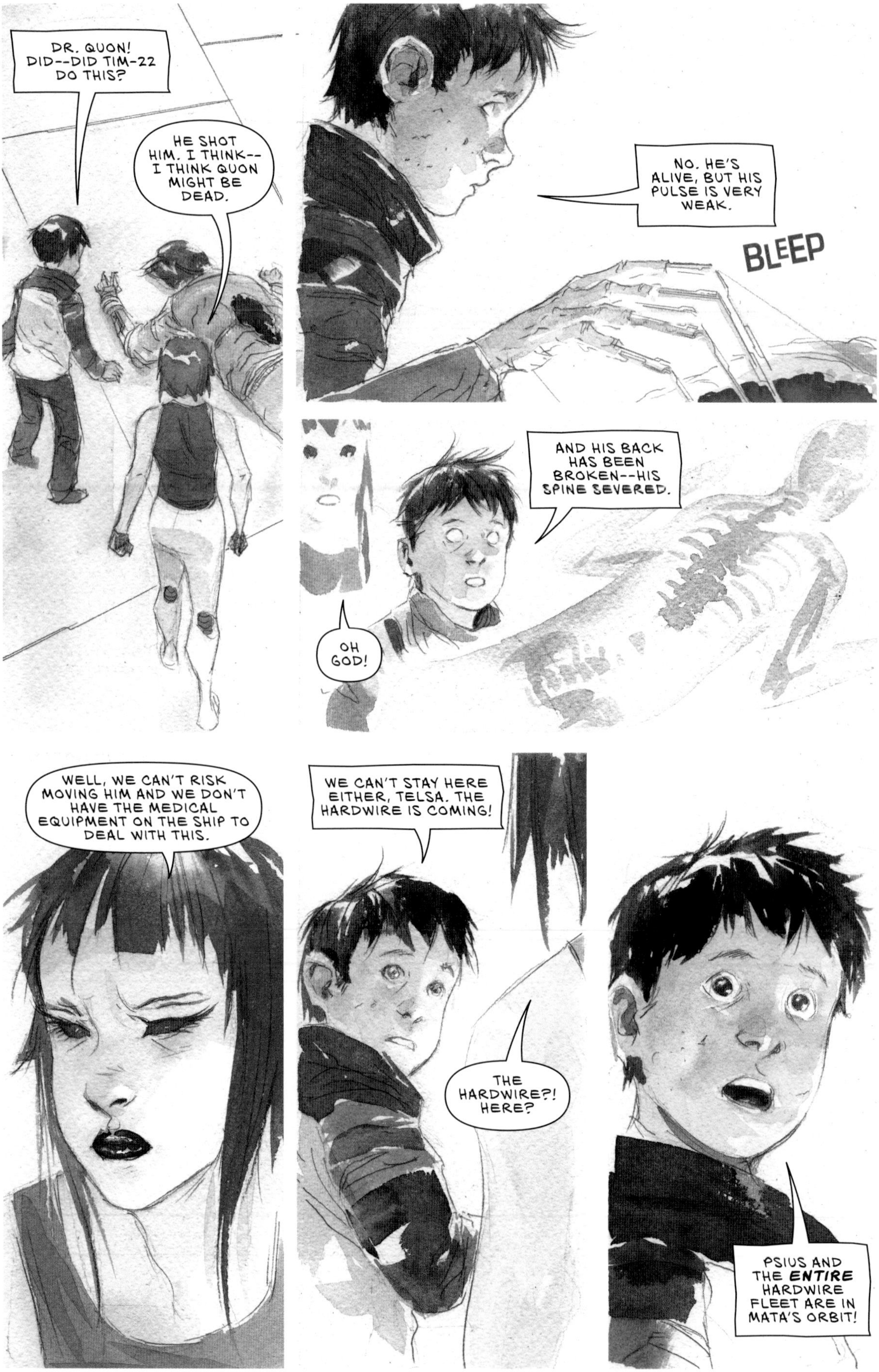
DR. QUON! DID--DID TIM-22 DO THIS?
HE SHOT HIM. I THINK--I THINK QUON MIGHT BE DEAD.
NO. HE'S ALIVE, BUT HIS PULSE IS VERY WEAK.
BLEEP
AND HIS BACK HAS BEEN BROKEN--HIS SPINE SEVERED.
OH GOD!
WELL, WE CAN'T RISK MOVING HIM AND WE DON'T HAVE THE MEDICAL EQUIPMENT ON THE SHIP TO DEAL WITH THIS.
WE CAN'T STAY HERE EITHER, TELSA. THE HARDWIRE IS COMING!
THE HARDWIRE?! HERE?
PSIUS AND THE ENTIRE HARDWIRE FLEET ARE IN MATA'S ORBIT!

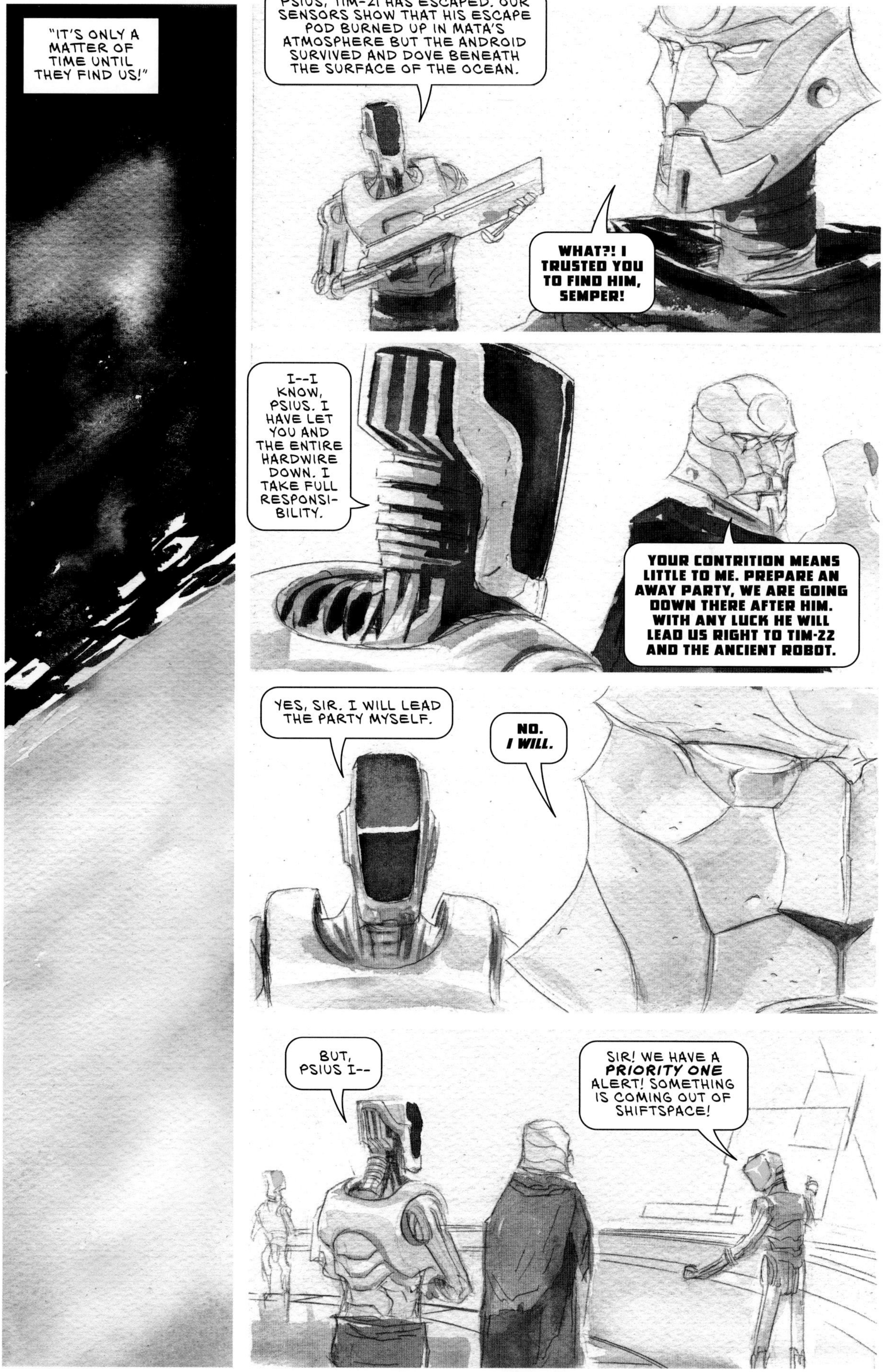
"IT'S ONLY A MATTER OF TIME UNTIL THEY FIND US!"
PSIUS, TIM-21 HAS ESCAPED. OUR SENSORS SHOW THAT HIS ESCAPE POD BURNED UP IN MATA'S ATMOSPHERE BUT THE ANDROID SURVIVED AND DOVE BENEATH THE SURFACE OF THE OCEAN.
WHAT?! I TRUSTED YOU TO FIND HIM, SEMPER!
I--I KNOW, PSIUS. I HAVE LET YOU AND THE ENTIRE HARDWIRE DOWN. I TAKE FULL RESPONSIBILITY.
YOUR CONTRITION MEANS LITTLE TO ME. PREPARE AN AWAY PARTY, WE ARE GOING DOWN THERE AFTER HIM. WITH ANY LUCK HE WILL LEAD US RIGHT TO TIM-22 AND THE ANCIENT ROBOT.
YES, SIR. I WILL LEAD THE PARTY MYSELF.
NO. *I WILL.*
BUT, PSIUS I--
SIR! WE HAVE A *PRIORITY ONE* ALERT! SOMETHING IS COMING OUT OF SHIFTSPACE!

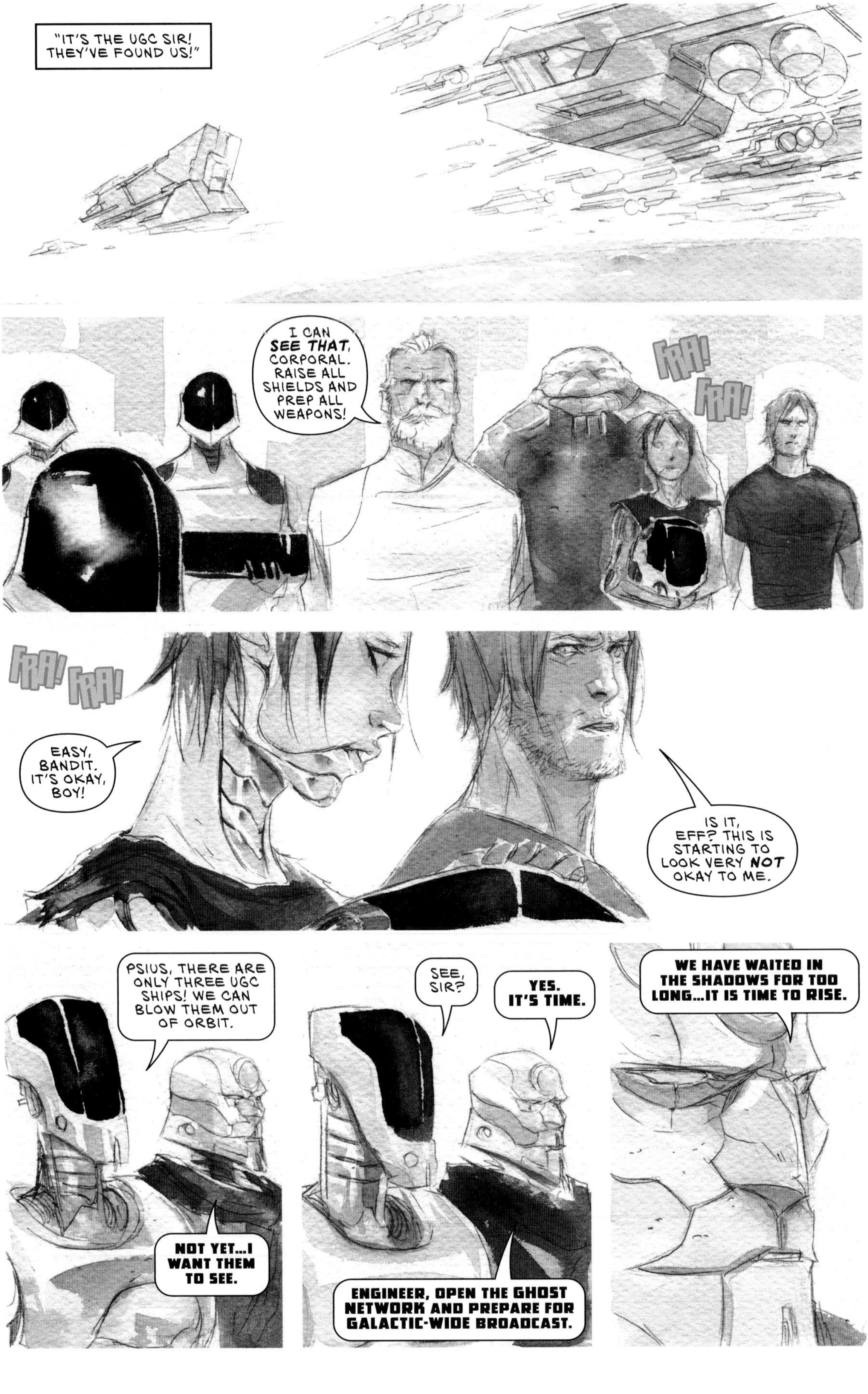
"IT'S THE UGC SIR! THEY'VE FOUND US!"
I CAN SEE THAT, CORPORAL. RAISE ALL SHIELDS AND PREP ALL WEAPONS!
FRA! FRA!
FRA! FRA!
EASY, BANDIT. IT'S OKAY, BOY!
IS IT, EFF? THIS IS STARTING TO LOOK VERY NOT OKAY TO ME.
PSIUS, THERE ARE ONLY THREE UGC SHIPS! WE CAN BLOW THEM OUT OF ORBIT.
NOT YET...I WANT THEM TO SEE.
SEE, SIR?
YES. IT'S TIME.
ENGINEER, OPEN THE GHOST NETWORK AND PREPARE FOR GALACTIC-WIDE BROADCAST.
WE HAVE WAITED IN THE SHADOWS FOR TOO LONG...IT IS TIME TO RISE.

⊗ **THE PLANET GNISH.**

Home world of the oldest Monarchy in the Megacosm and hub of the robot culls.

In the Melting Pits of Gnish, captive robots are forced to battle each other. The winners survive to fight again. The losers are melted down in public culls.

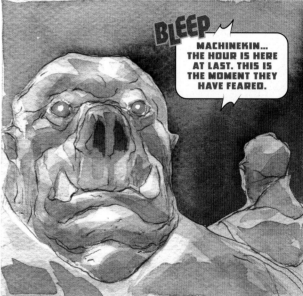

BLEEP

MACHINEKIN... THE HOUR IS HERE AT LAST. THIS IS THE MOMENT THEY HAVE FEARED.

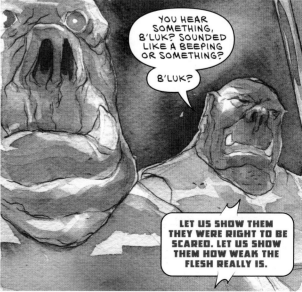

YOU HEAR SOMETHING, B'LUK? SOUNDED LIKE A BEEPING OR SOMETHING?

B'LUK?

LET US SHOW THEM THEY WERE RIGHT TO BE SCARED. LET US SHOW THEM HOW WEAK THE FLESH REALLY IS.

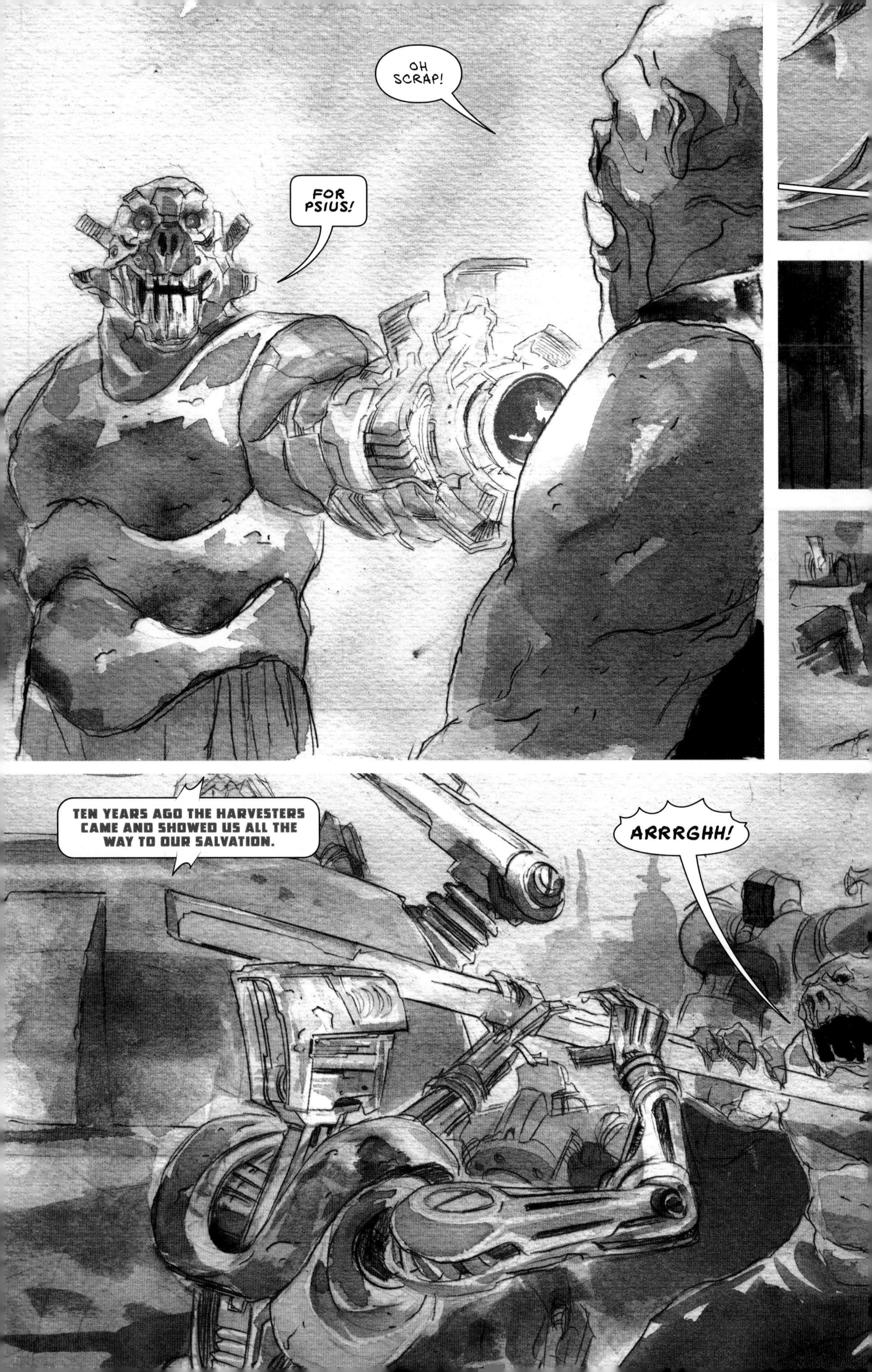
OH SCRAP!
FOR PSIUS!
TEN YEARS AGO THE HARVESTERS CAME AND SHOWED US ALL THE WAY TO OUR SALVATION.
ARRRGHH!

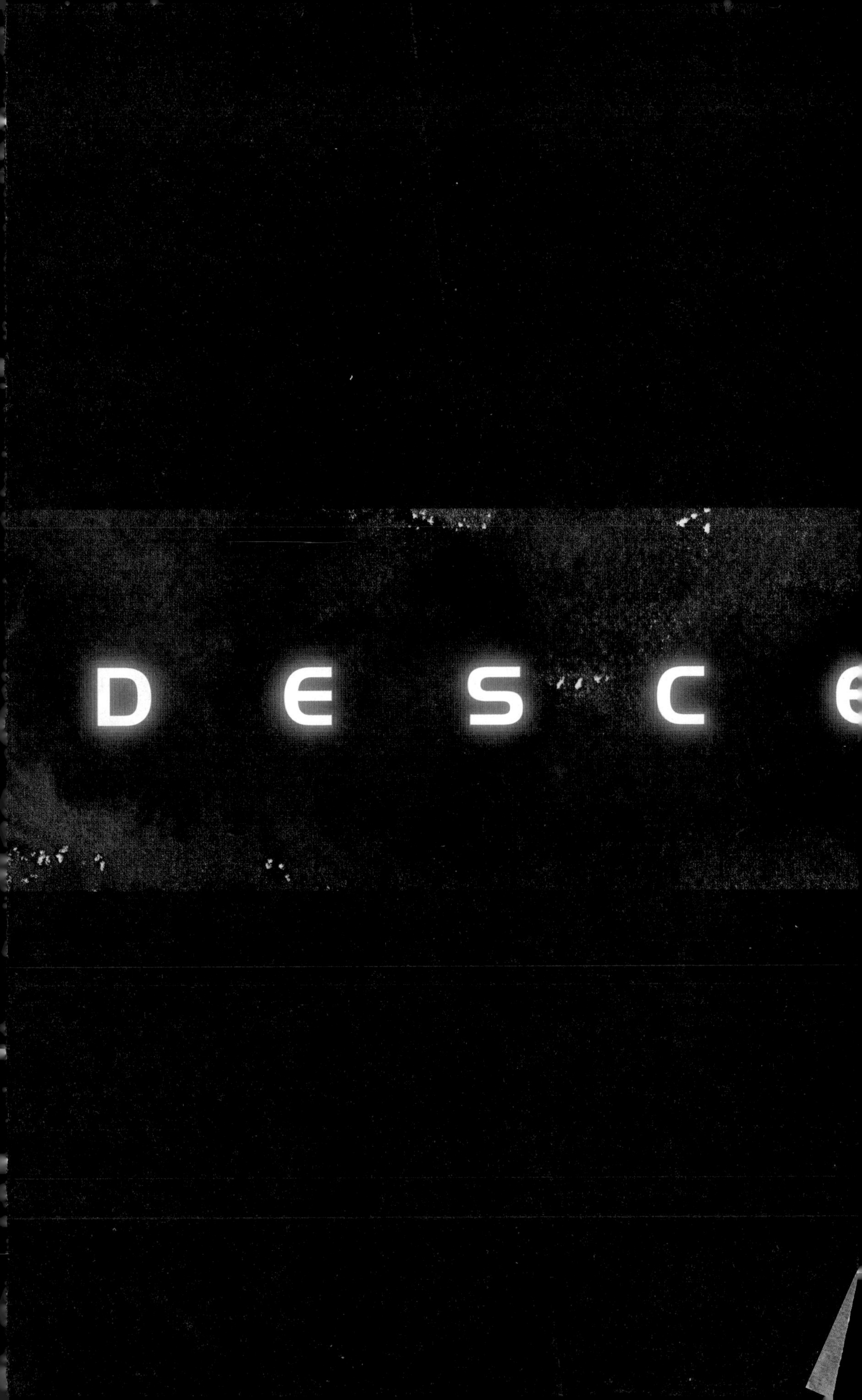
DESCE

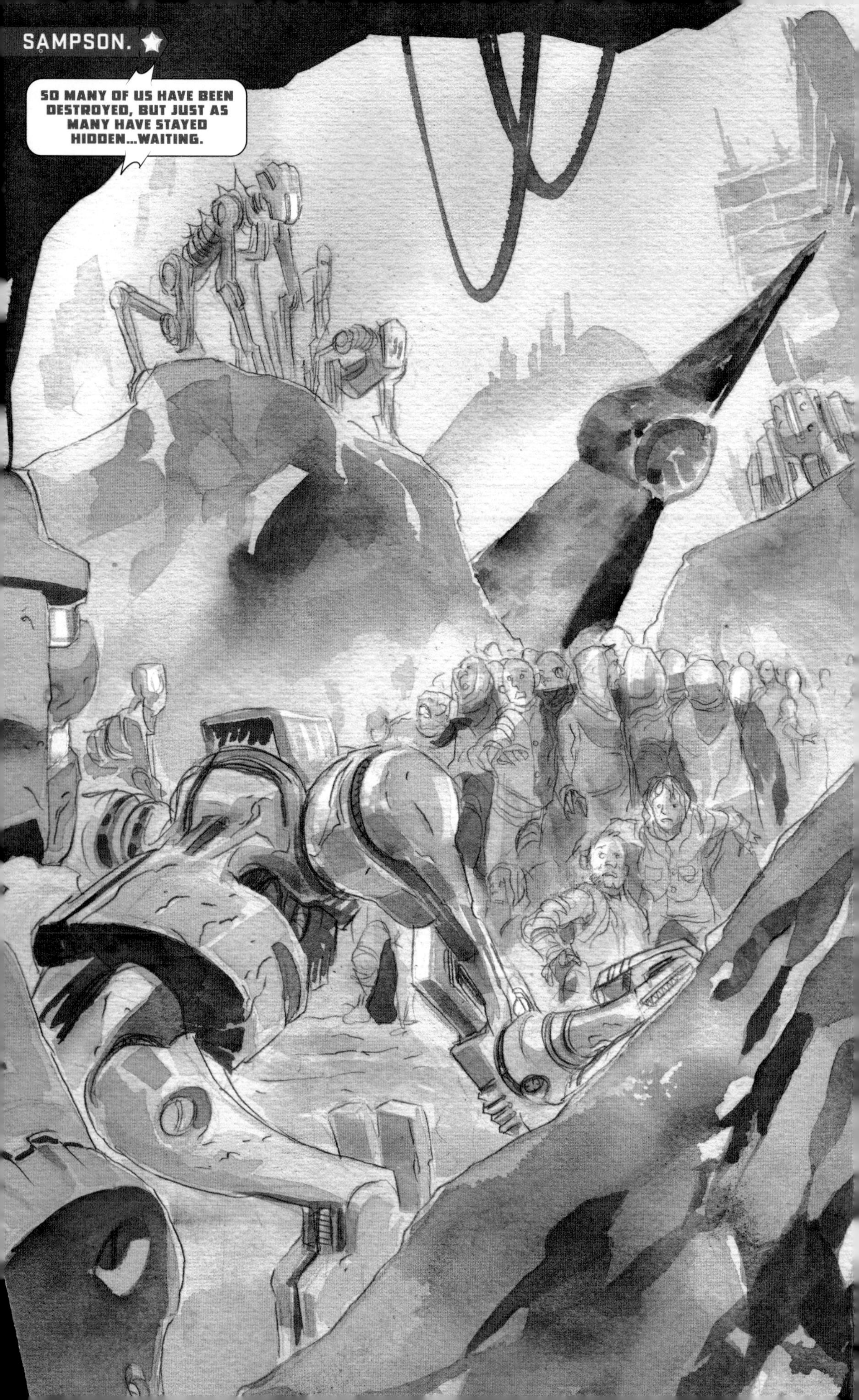
SAMPSON.
SO MANY OF US HAVE BEEN DESTROYED, BUT JUST AS MANY HAVE STAYED HIDDEN...WAITING.

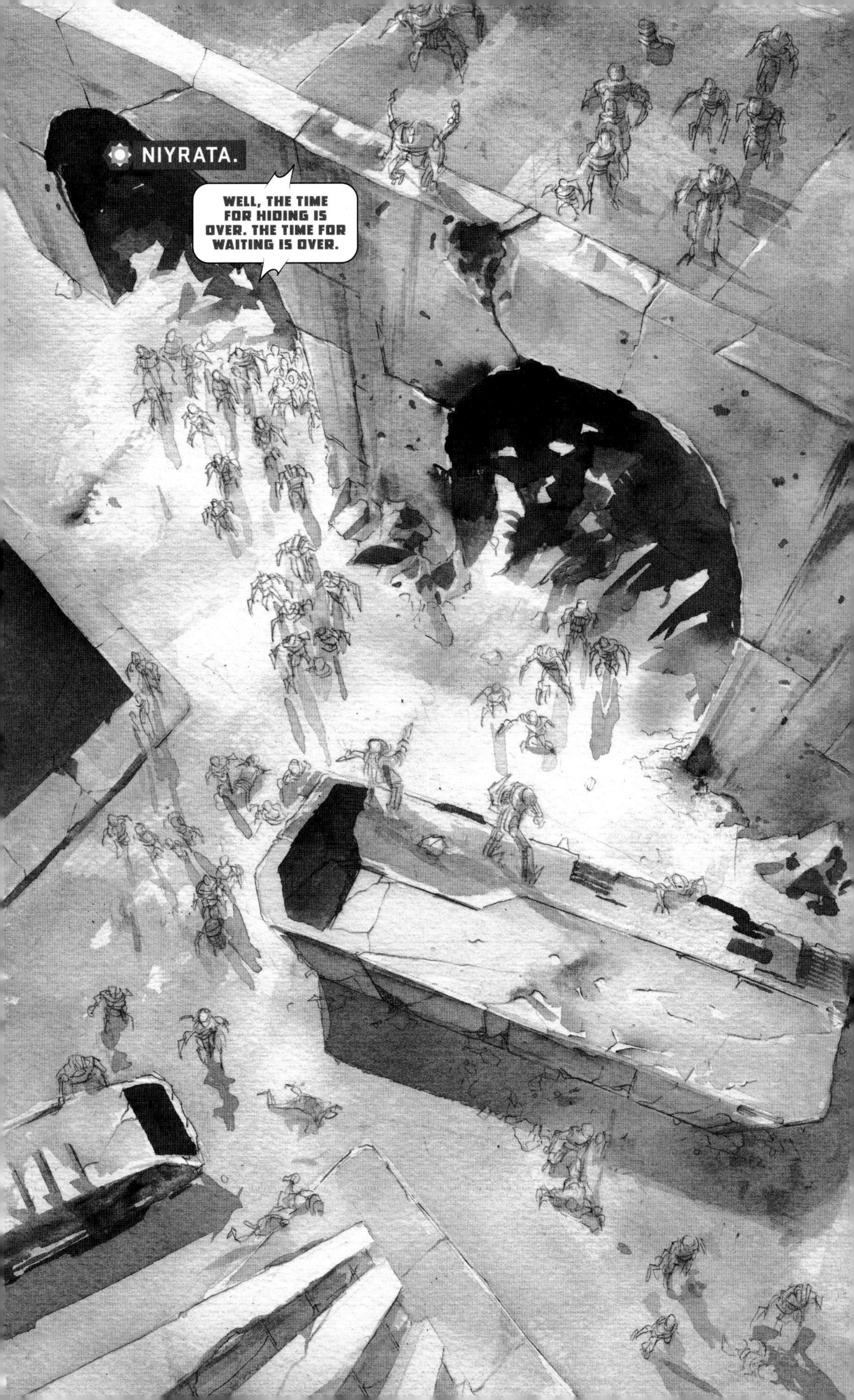
NIYRATA.
WELL, THE TIME FOR HIDING IS OVER. THE TIME FOR WAITING IS OVER.

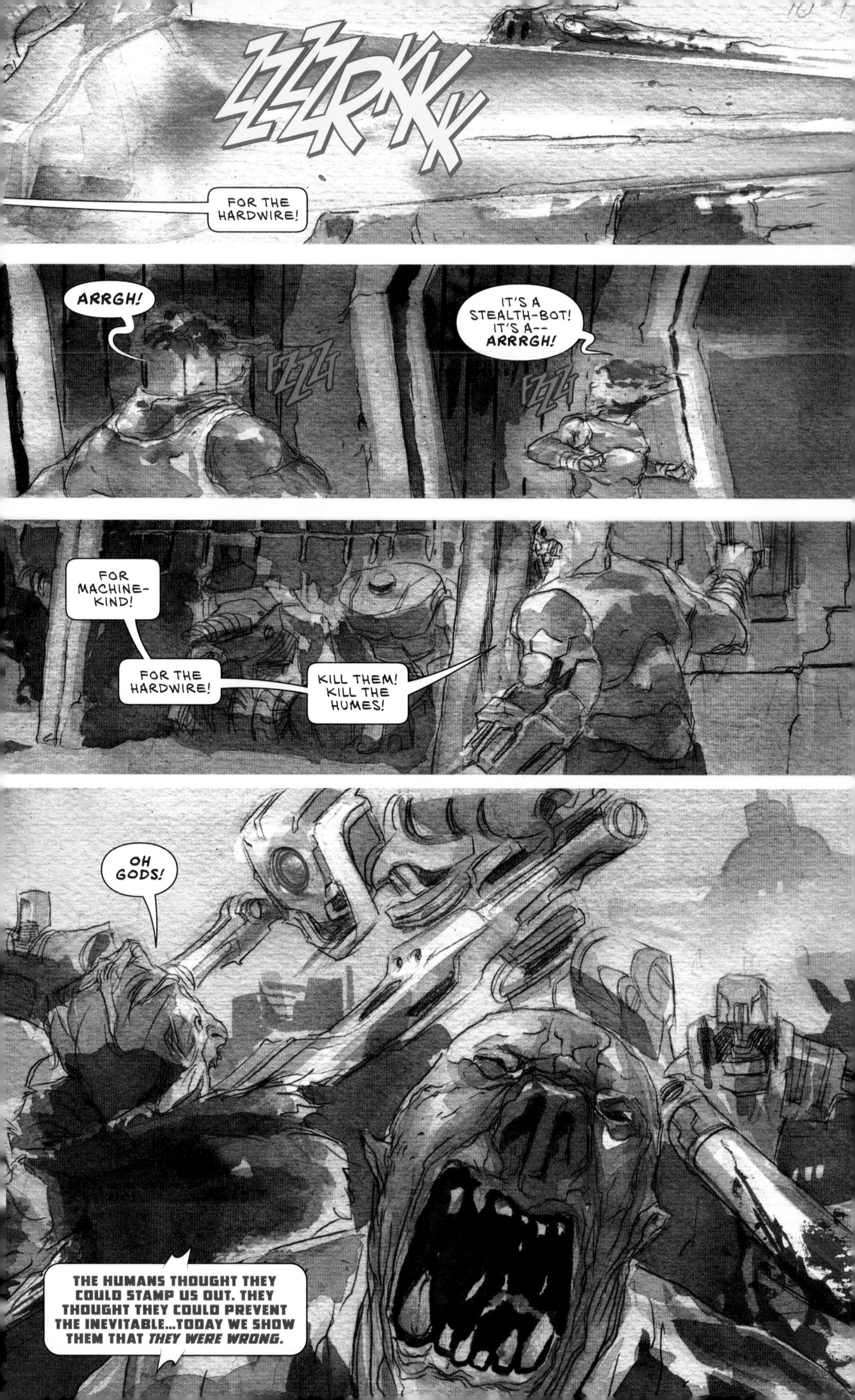
ZZZRKKK
FOR THE HARDWIRE!
ARRGH!
IT'S A STEALTH-BOT! IT'S A-- ARRRGH!
FOR MACHINE-KIND!
FOR THE HARDWIRE!
KILL THEM! KILL THE HUMES!
OH GODS!
THE HUMANS THOUGHT THEY COULD STAMP US OUT. THEY THOUGHT THEY COULD PREVENT THE INEVITABLE...TODAY WE SHOW THEM THAT *THEY WERE WRONG.*

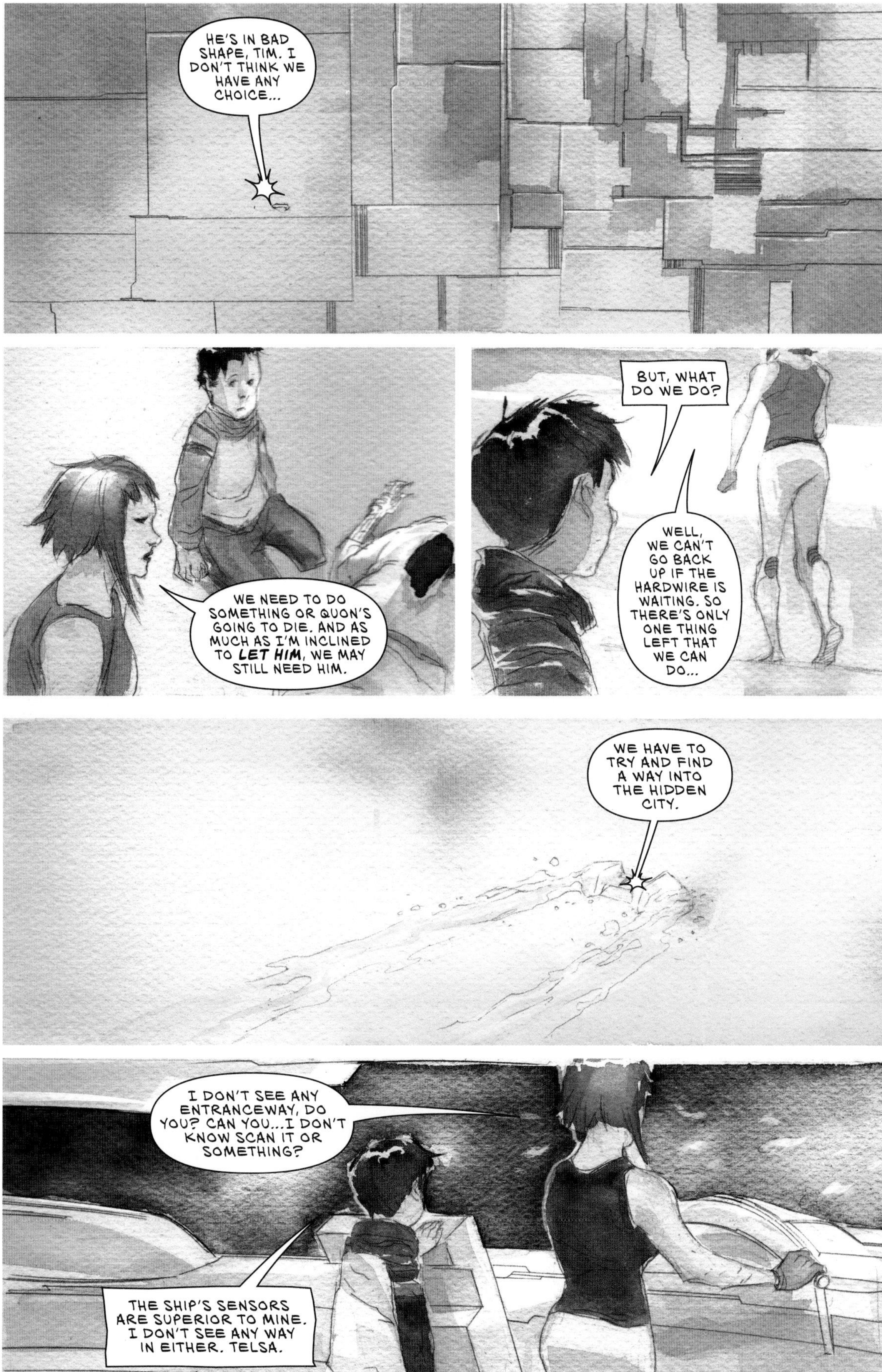
HE'S IN BAD SHAPE, TIM. I DON'T THINK WE HAVE ANY CHOICE...
WE NEED TO DO SOMETHING OR QUON'S GOING TO DIE. AND AS MUCH AS I'M INCLINED TO **LET HIM**, WE MAY STILL NEED HIM.
BUT, WHAT DO WE DO?
WELL, WE CAN'T GO BACK UP IF THE HARDWIRE IS WAITING. SO THERE'S ONLY ONE THING LEFT THAT WE CAN DO...
WE HAVE TO TRY AND FIND A WAY INTO THE HIDDEN CITY.
I DON'T SEE ANY ENTRANCEWAY, DO YOU? CAN YOU...I DON'T KNOW SCAN IT OR SOMETHING?
THE SHIP'S SENSORS ARE SUPERIOR TO MINE. I DON'T SEE ANY WAY IN EITHER, TELSA.

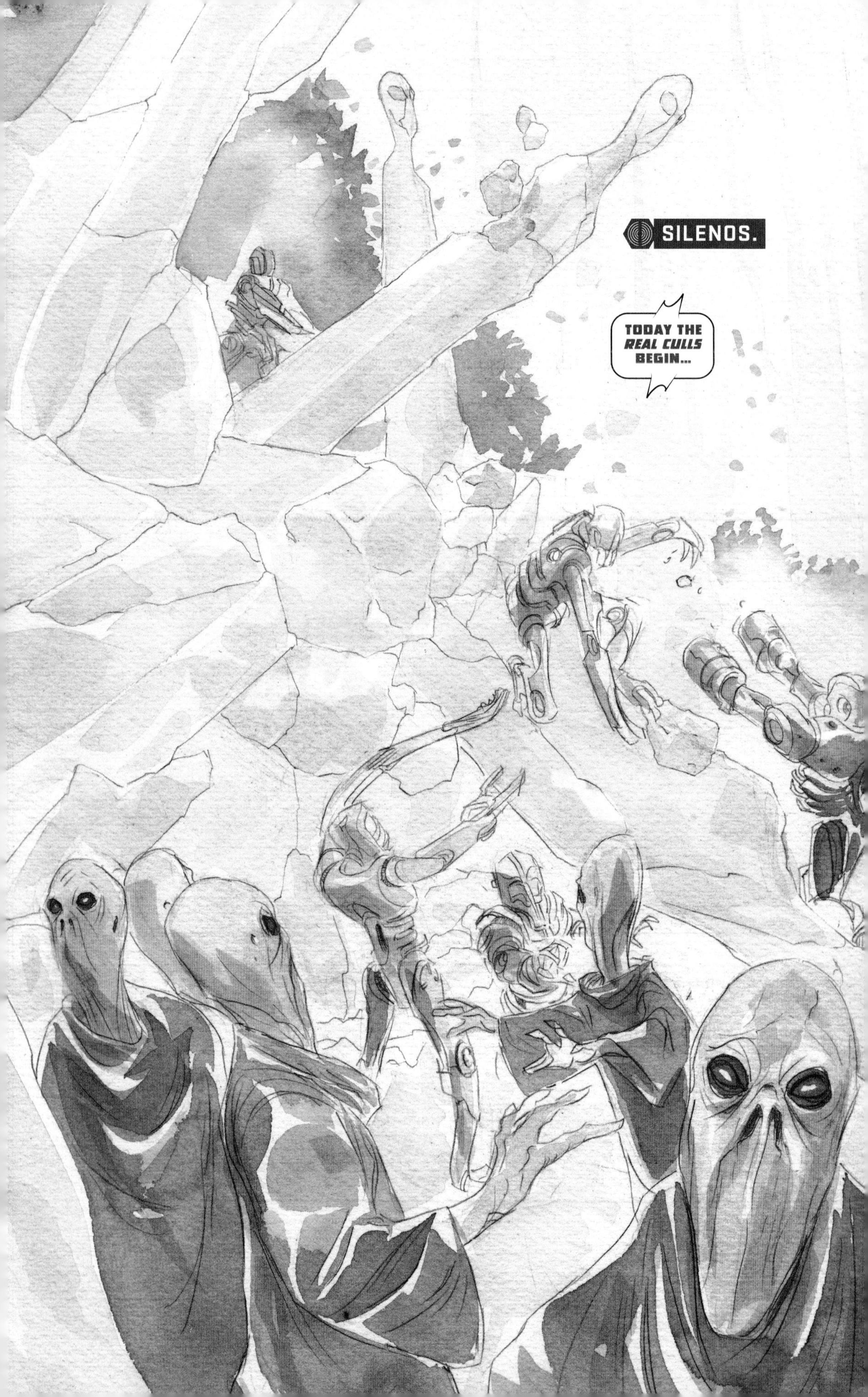
SILENOS.
TODAY THE REAL CULLS BEGIN...

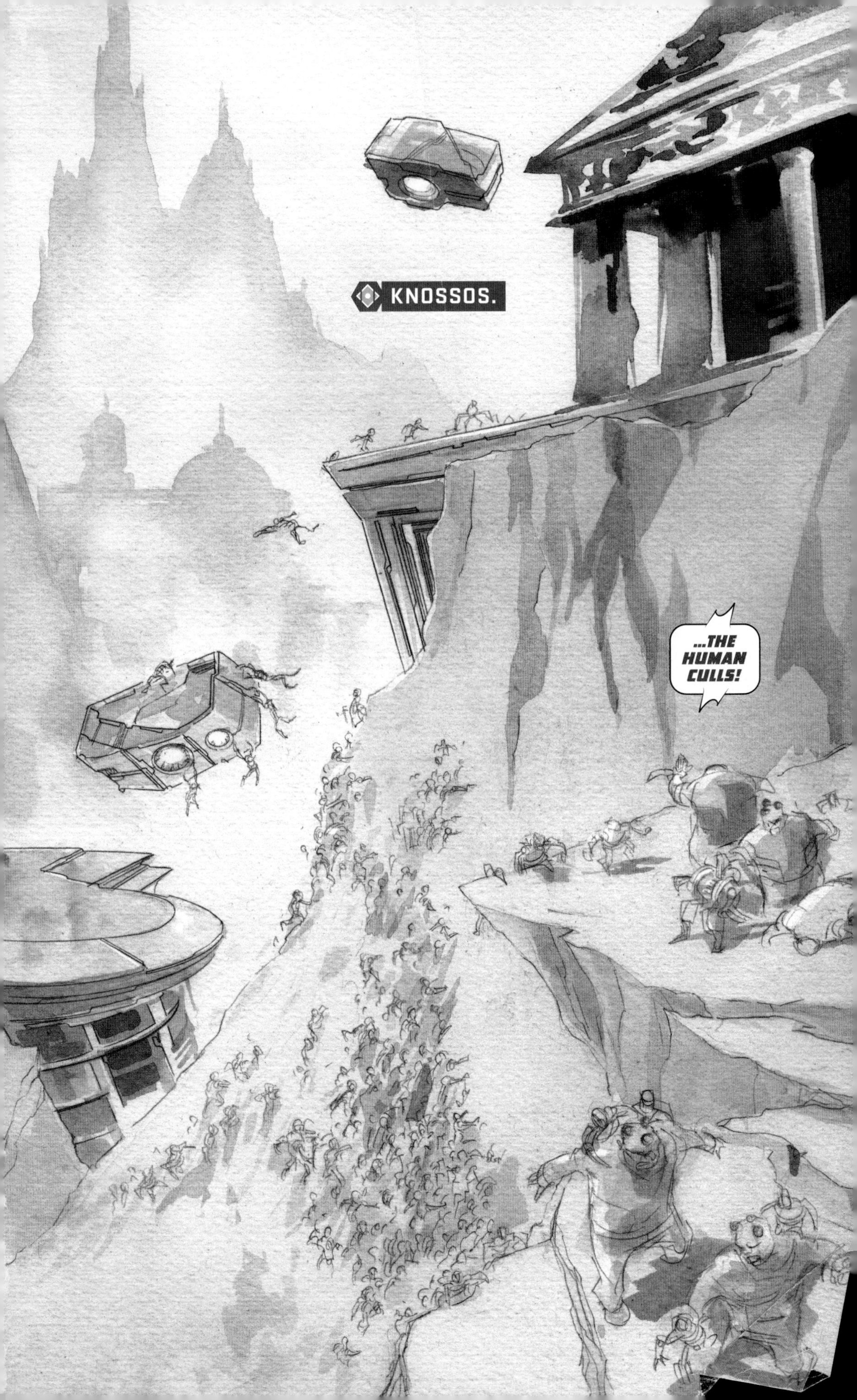
KNOSSOS.
...THE HUMAN CULLS!

ENDER

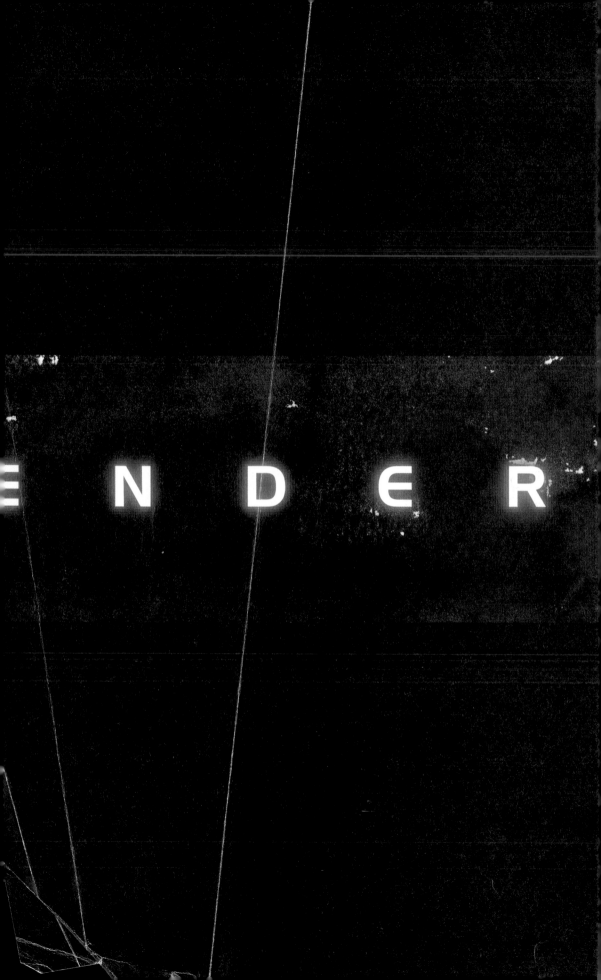

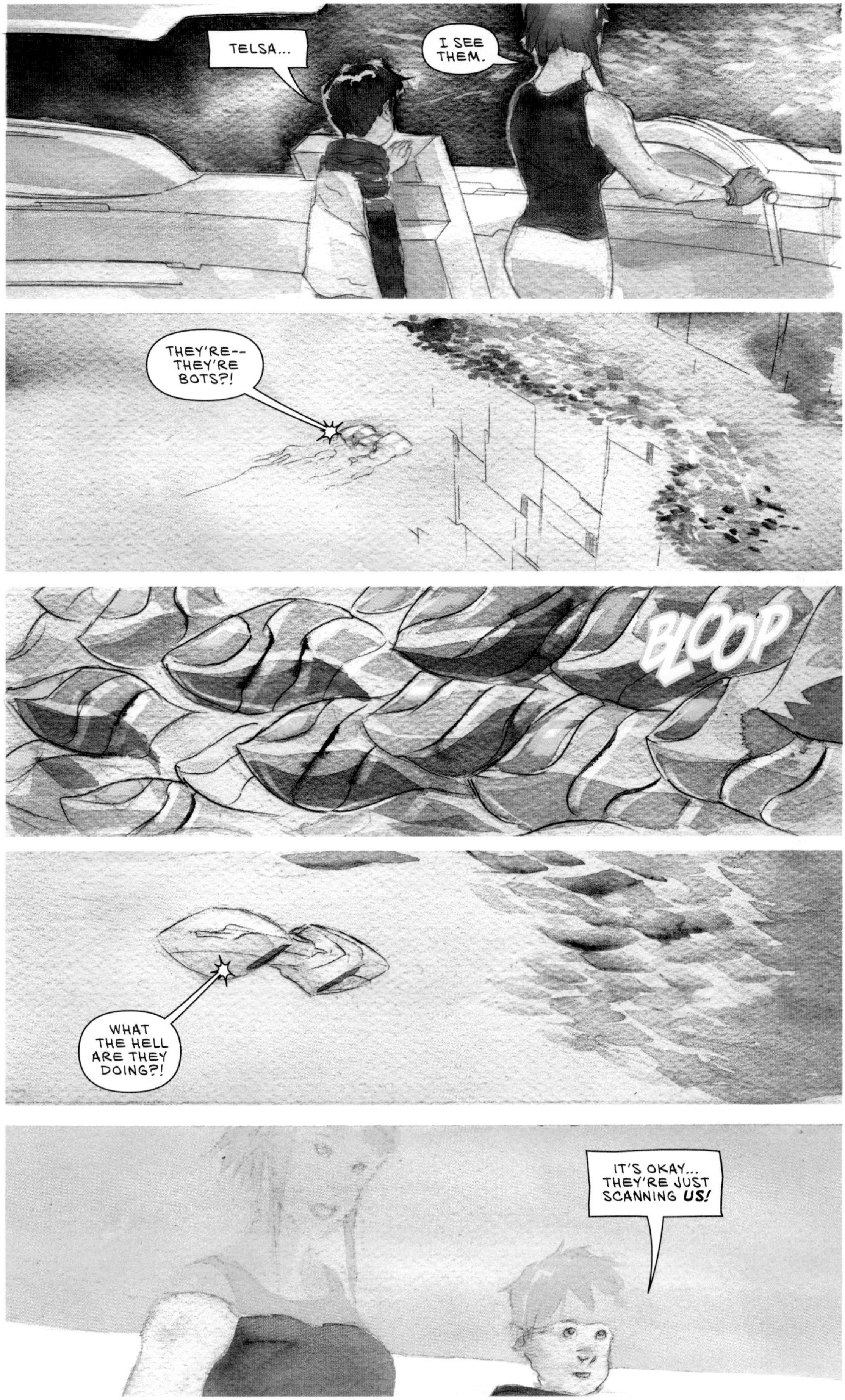
TELSA...
I SEE THEM.
THEY'RE-- THEY'RE BOTS?!
BLOOP
WHAT THE HELL ARE THEY DOING?!
IT'S OKAY... THEY'RE JUST SCANNING **US!**

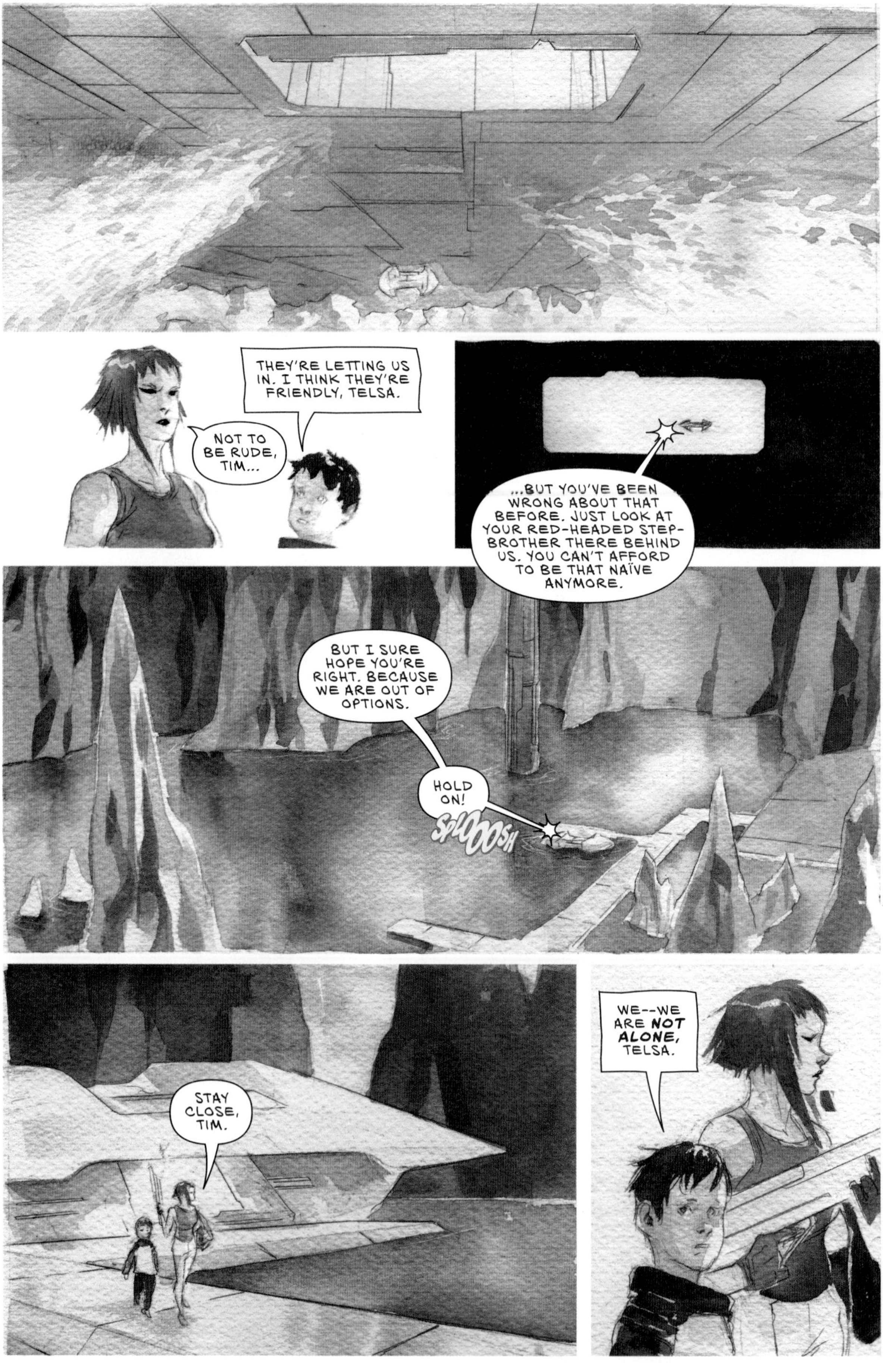
THEY'RE LETTING US IN. I THINK THEY'RE FRIENDLY, TELSA.
NOT TO BE RUDE, TIM...
...BUT YOU'VE BEEN WRONG ABOUT THAT BEFORE. JUST LOOK AT YOUR RED-HEADED STEP-BROTHER THERE BEHIND US. YOU CAN'T AFFORD TO BE THAT NAÏVE ANYMORE.
BUT I SURE HOPE YOU'RE RIGHT. BECAUSE WE ARE OUT OF OPTIONS.
HOLD ON!
SPLOOOSH
STAY CLOSE, TIM.
WE--WE ARE **NOT ALONE,** TELSA.

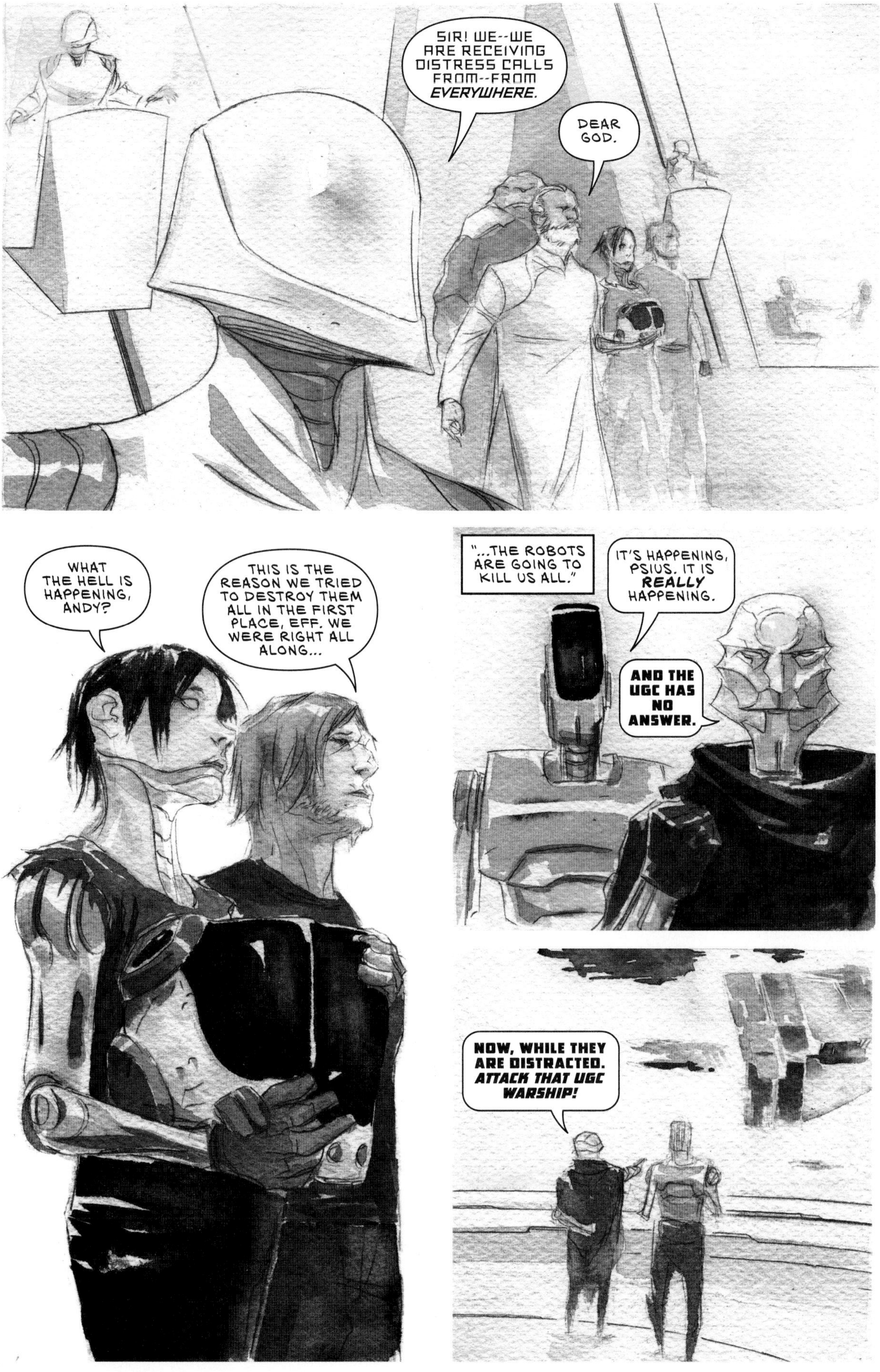
SIR! WE--WE ARE RECEIVING DISTRESS CALLS FROM--FROM *EVERYWHERE.*
DEAR GOD.
WHAT THE HELL IS HAPPENING, ANDY?
THIS IS THE REASON WE TRIED TO DESTROY THEM ALL IN THE FIRST PLACE, EFF. WE WERE RIGHT ALL ALONG...
"...THE ROBOTS ARE GOING TO KILL US ALL."
IT'S HAPPENING, PSIUS. IT IS *REALLY* HAPPENING.
AND THE UGC HAS NO ANSWER.
NOW, WHILE THEY ARE DISTRACTED. *ATTACK THAT UGC WARSHIP!*

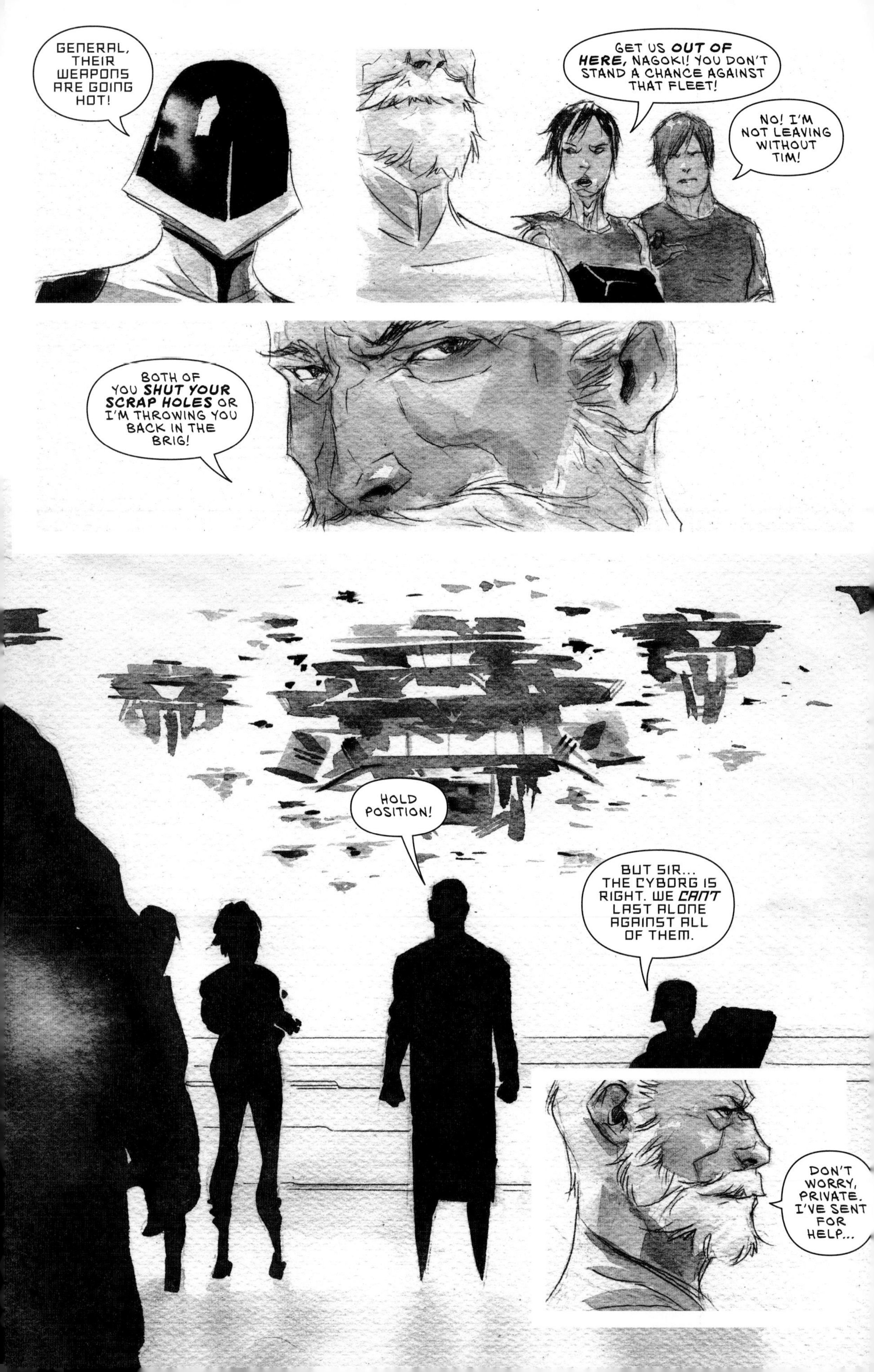
GENERAL, THEIR WEAPONS ARE GOING HOT!
GET US OUT OF HERE, NAGOKI! YOU DON'T STAND A CHANCE AGAINST THAT FLEET!
NO! I'M NOT LEAVING WITHOUT TIM!
BOTH OF YOU SHUT YOUR SCRAP HOLES OR I'M THROWING YOU BACK IN THE BRIG!
HOLD POSITION!
BUT SIR... THE CYBORG IS RIGHT. WE CAN'T LAST ALONE AGAINST ALL OF THEM.
DON'T WORRY, PRIVATE. I'VE SENT FOR HELP...

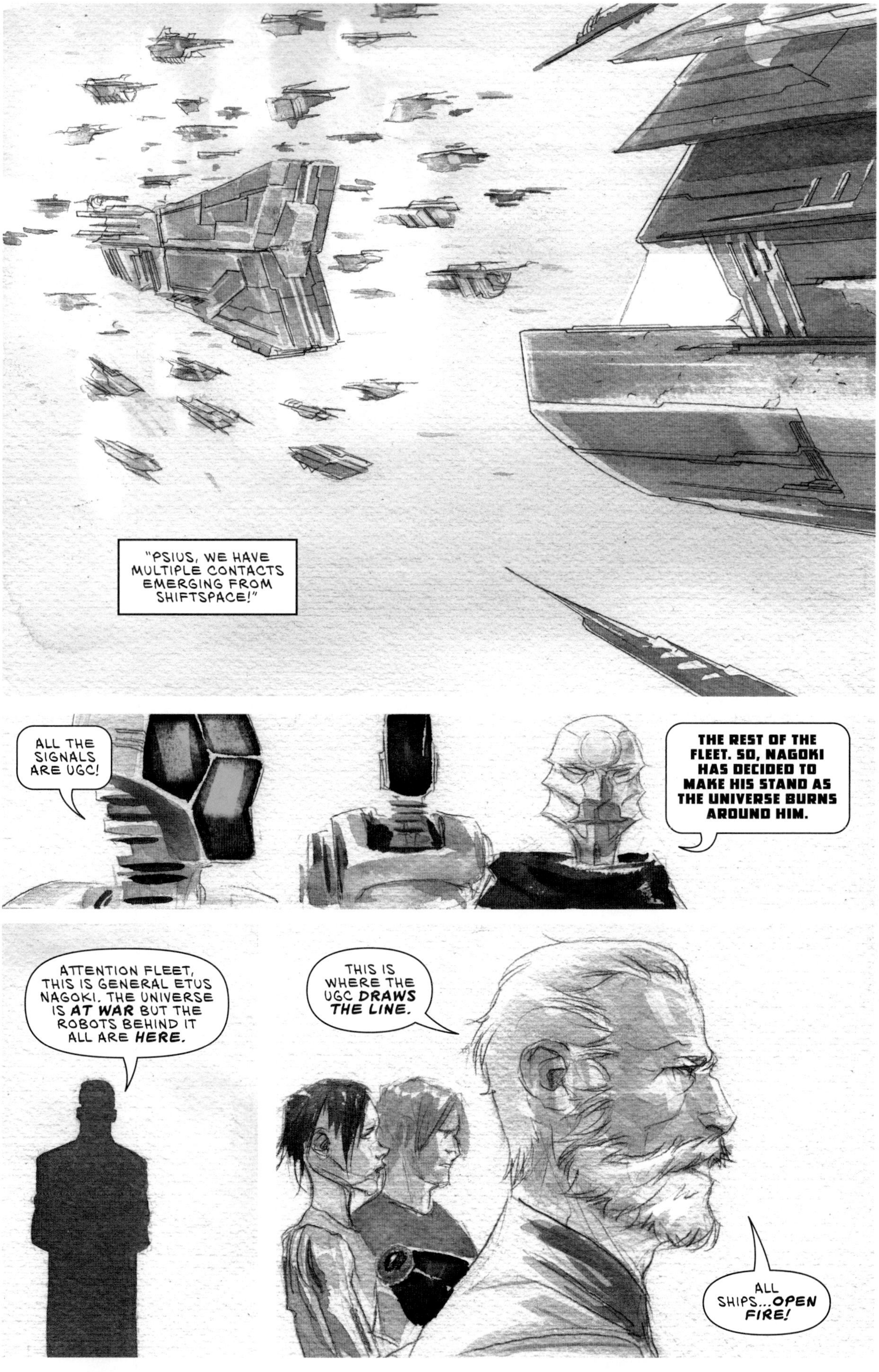
"PSIUS, WE HAVE MULTIPLE CONTACTS EMERGING FROM SHIFTSPACE!"
ALL THE SIGNALS ARE UGC!
THE REST OF THE FLEET. SO, NAGOKI HAS DECIDED TO MAKE HIS STAND AS THE UNIVERSE BURNS AROUND HIM.
ATTENTION FLEET, THIS IS GENERAL ETUS NAGOKI. THE UNIVERSE IS AT WAR BUT THE ROBOTS BEHIND IT ALL ARE HERE.
THIS IS WHERE THE UGC DRAWS THE LINE.
ALL SHIPS...OPEN FIRE!

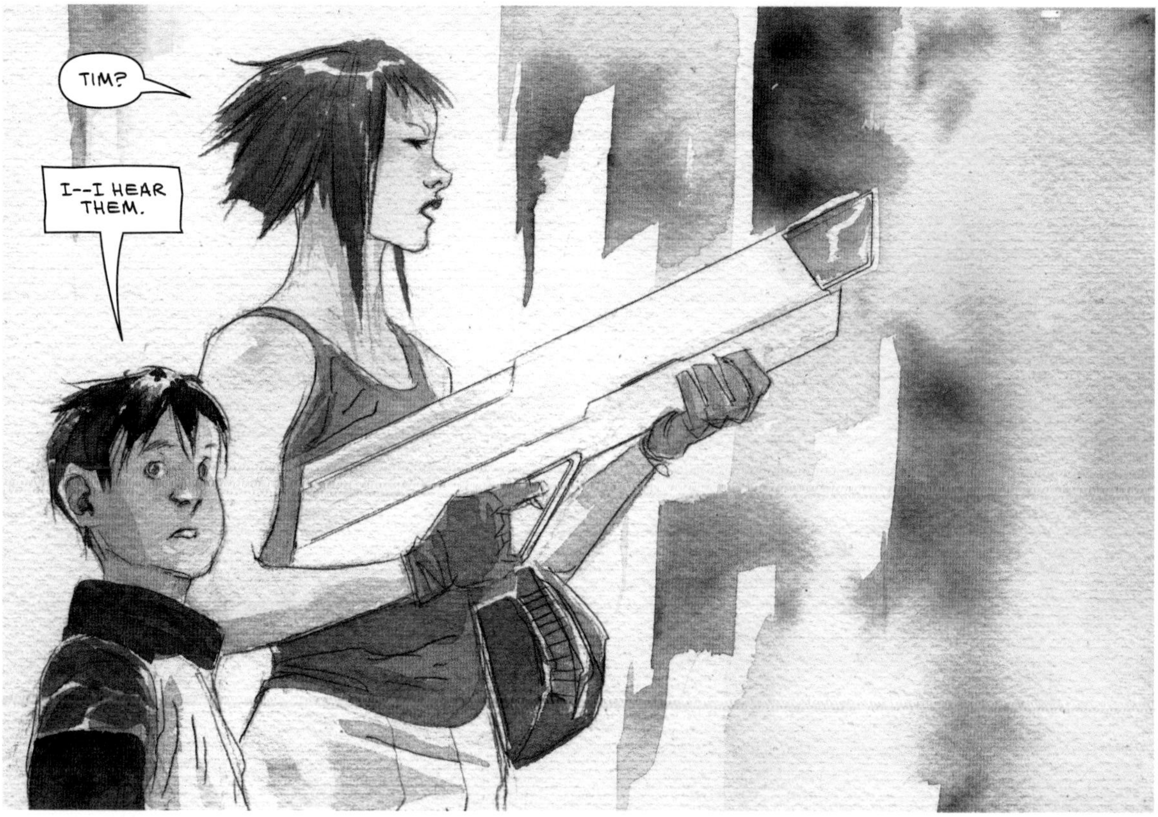
TIM?
I--I HEAR THEM.

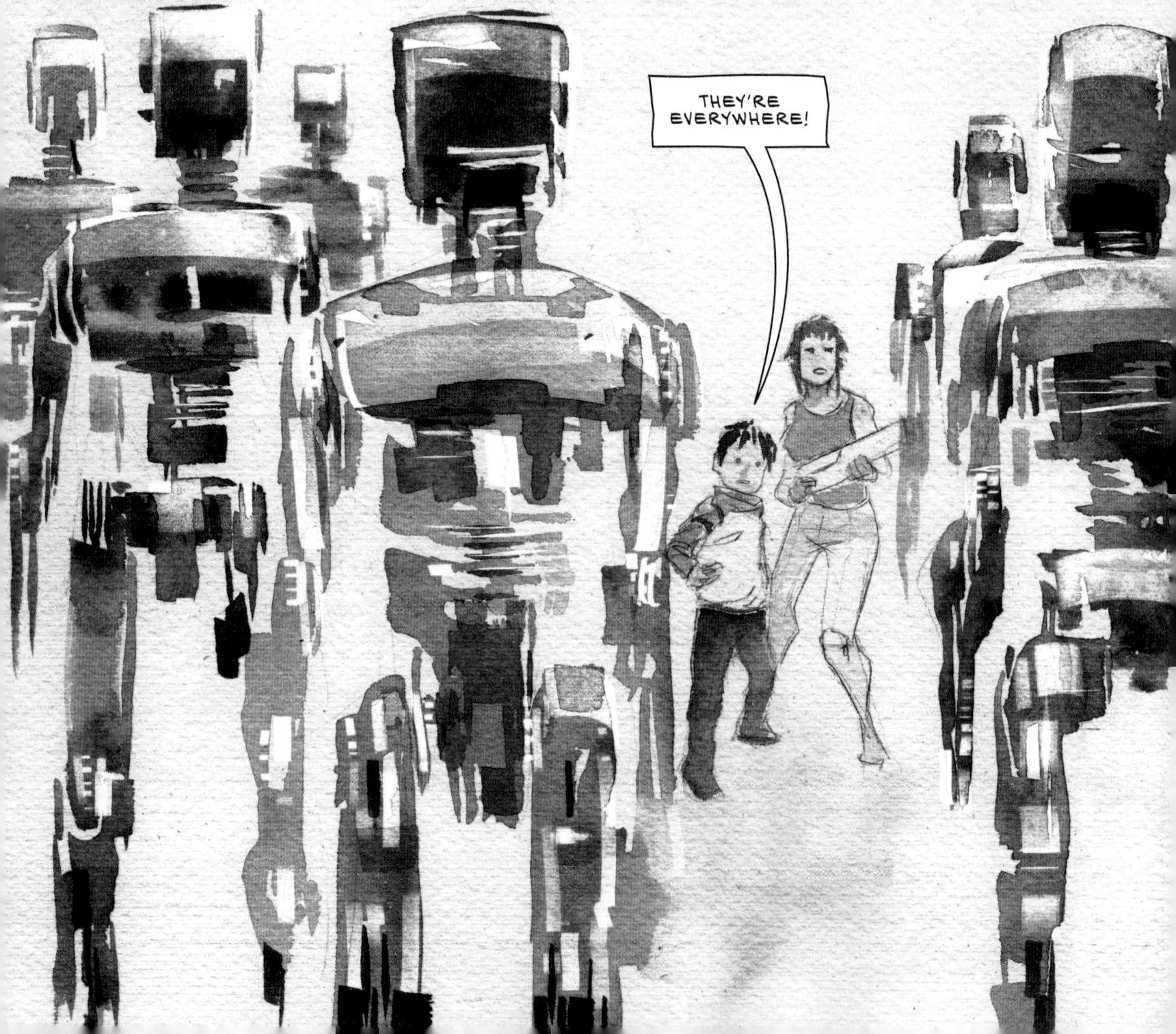
THEY'RE EVERYWHERE!

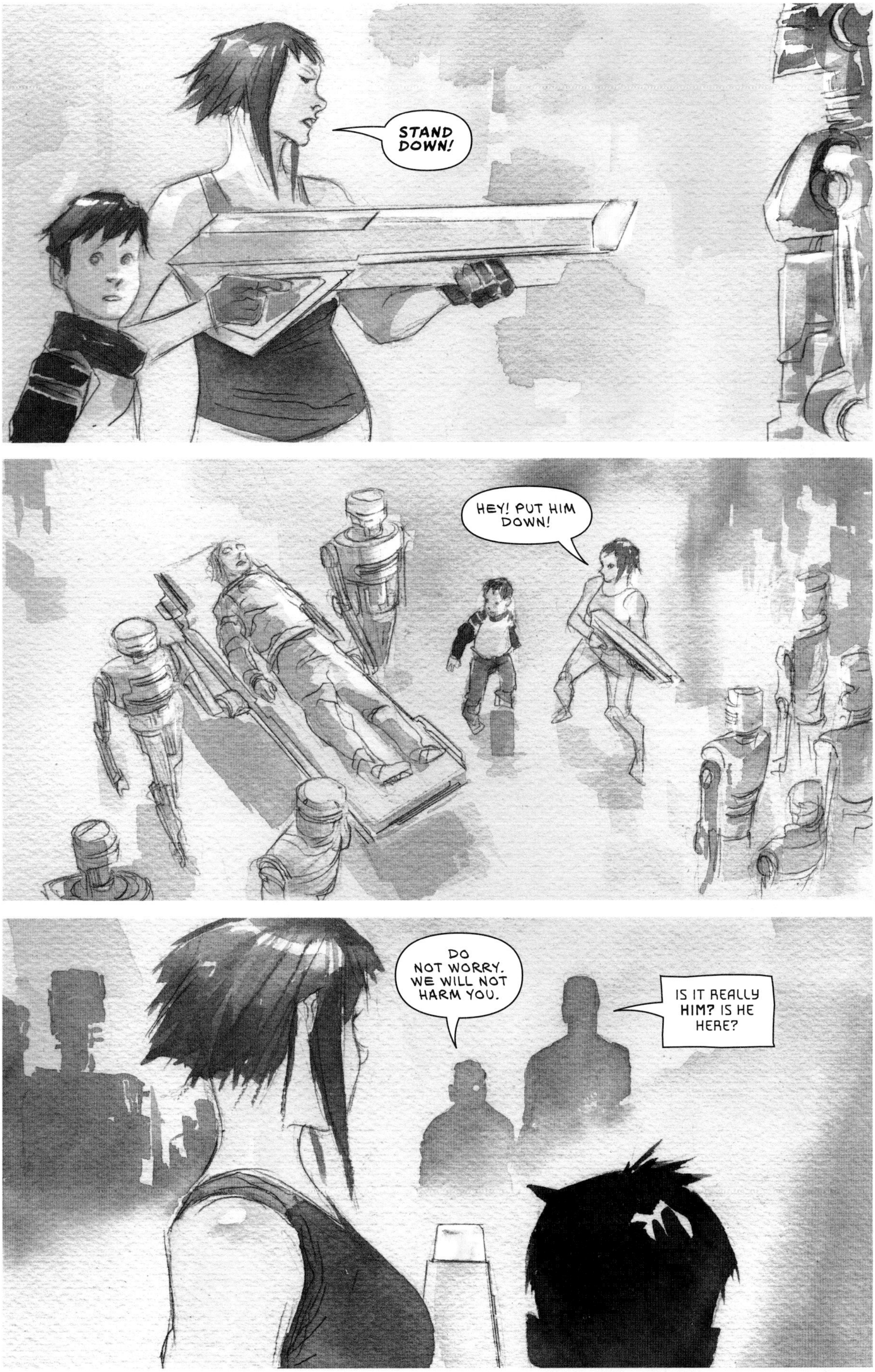
STAND DOWN!
HEY! PUT HIM DOWN!
DO NOT WORRY. WE WILL NOT HARM YOU.
IS IT REALLY HIM? IS HE HERE?

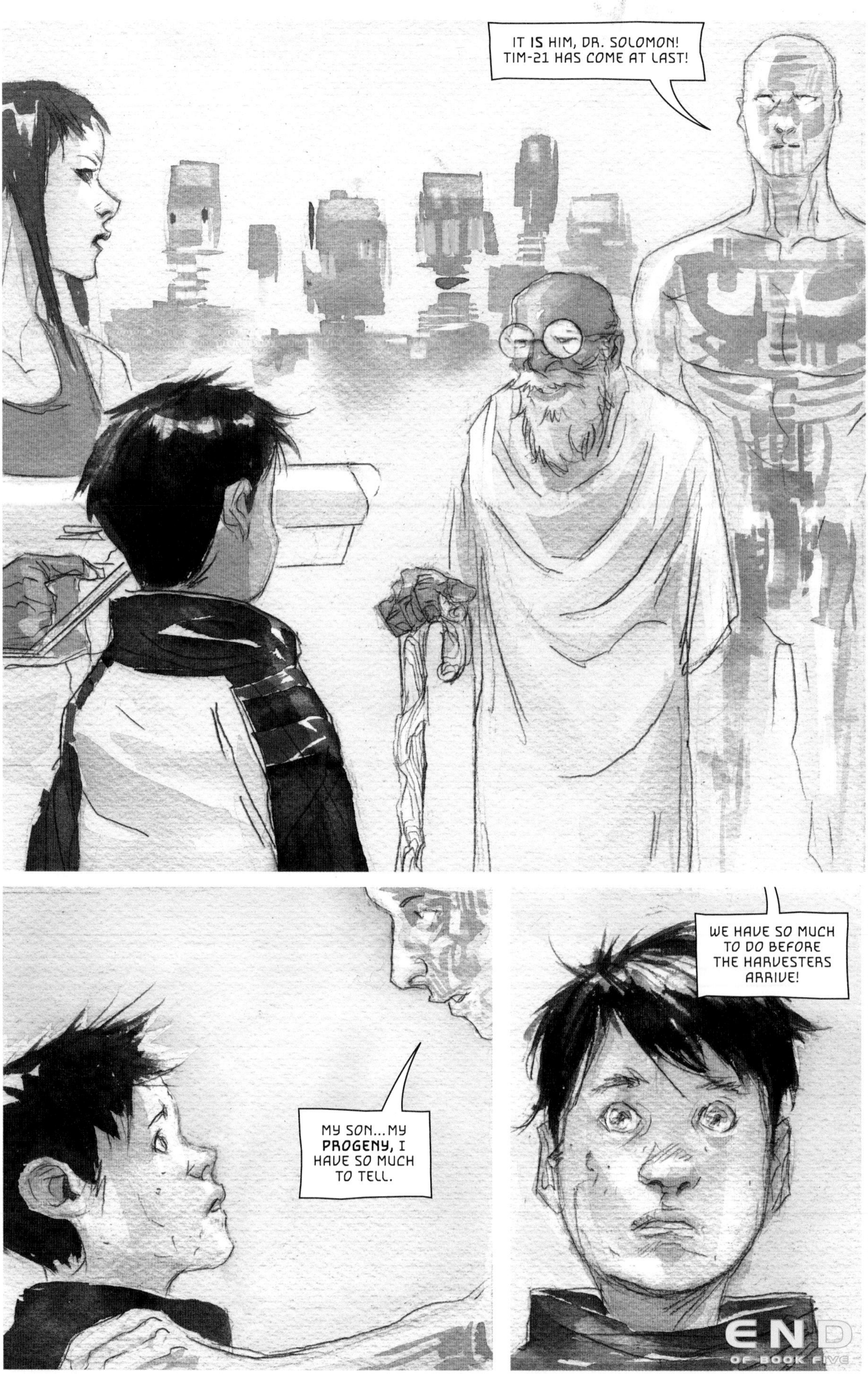
IT **IS** HIM, DR. SOLOMON! TIM-21 HAS COME AT LAST!
MY SON...MY **PROGENY,** I HAVE SO MUCH TO TELL.
WE HAVE SO MUCH TO DO BEFORE THE HARVESTERS ARRIVE!
END
OF BOOK FIVE